Milán

Born in 1888, Milán Füst w... [barcode: CW00551652]
master who was known principally as a scholar and poet in the
earlier part of his writing life. His novel *Advent* (1923) was a
protest against post-war White terror disguised as a story of
seventeenth century England. From 1935 to 1942, as anti-
semitism gained ground, he retreated into a comfortable
Budapest villa and wrote what is considered to be his masterpiece, *The Story of My Wife* (1942). Forsaking the wider can-
vas of Europe's slide into Fascism, he concentrated instead on
the creation of what he called 'pure fiction', in the shape of the
many-sided character of Captain Storr, with his robust humanity and human frailties. In 1967 Milán Füst was considered for
the Nobel Prize for Literature, but died at the age of 79 before
an award could be made.

Milán Füst

THE STORY OF
MY WIFE
The Reminiscences of Captain Störr

translated from the Hungarian by
Ivan Sanders

and with a Preface by
George Konrád

published by Pan Books
in association with Jonathan Cape

First published in Great Britain 1989 by Jonathan Cape Ltd
This Picador edition published 1990 by Pan Books Ltd,
Cavaye Place, London SW10 9PG
in association with Jonathan Cape Ltd
9 8 7 6 5 4 3 2 1
© The successors of Milán Füst 1987
English translation © Ivan Sanders 1987

Originally published in Hungarian under the title
A feleségem története by Magveto Konyvkiado,
© Füst Milánné 1957

ISBN 0 330 30648 0

Printed and bound in Great Britain by
Richard Clay Ltd, Bungay, Suffolk

A Novel of Jealousy

by
George Konrád

THE STORY OF MY WIFE IS ACTUALLY THE HUSBAND'S STORY—
the story of a Dutch sea captain named Störr whose presence in
the novel is substantial indeed: his weight alone is well over 200
pounds. Milán Füst, no weakling himself, was similarly hefty and
broad-shouldered. But his hero is an even more splendid specimen,
and like big men in general, he views other people with good-
natured equanimity, a bit condescendingly perhaps, with childish
wonder at times, but always with some indifference.

Unlike the author, who was compared by friends to Michel-
angelo's painting of the prophet Joel. He flew into wild rages, was
quite the tyrant: a true seer one minute and a great actor playing the
seer the next. Meek like Captain Störr he definitely wasn't. He
wallowed in his mordant humor and could also cry beautifully,
breaking into sobs at the drop of a hat. He was awe-inspiring and
shockingly rude. Anyone uttering the name of Marcel Proust or
Thomas Mann admiringly in his house was promptly shown the
door. You either paid tribute or left. Tolstoy, yes, Shakespeare, too,
a couple of younger friends, perhaps, but no one else. Milán Füst
was not one to squander his encomiums.

In this novel the husband is very masculine and the wife is very feminine. About her we know only as much as he is willing to tell us, and he writes far more copiously about himself than about his wife. This wife, Lizzy, is petite, shapely, a little on the plump side, full of frills and fancies—and utterly unpredictable. She knows something her oaf of a husband does not but is desperate to find out. This blunderhead would have us believe that he is unfeeling and oblivious to everything, yet he is quite perceptive, quite sensitive. The man is full of subtle, narcissistic observations about himself, about his fleeting sensations and moods, and about the most crucial question of all: Is there such a thing as inspiration?

He is also quick to imagine, quick to suspect; from tiny scraps he constructs a whole long narrative which, when all pieced together, seems plausible enough; and its underlying message is clear, too: this dainty and unruly little woman may not just toy with other men, she may also fall for them.

*

On the strength of past experience and his own formidable prowess, Captain Störr tends to make light of other people. So when at a mature age he falls in love, he pays for his nonchalance with the torments of jealousy. The seamier side of love preoccupies him as much as its wonders, and in time it grows into an uncontrollable obsession. In the literature about jealousy, Milán Füst's novel is a basic text.

The inevitable, monumental passion unfolds rather majestically. When a large, bear-like man begins to see ghosts, we are somehow more intrigued than when a puny little chap grapples with phantoms. We might all agree with Füst in saying that to fall in love is to suffer the pangs of jealousy. A lover wants to be all alone with his beloved, though he knows this is impossible, for we all want more, even jealous husbands do.

People tend to like Captain Störr, and when they show it, he feels good about himself. After all, they've invested tender emotions in him, and these investments are bound to pay off. The object of affection inspires affection; whoever is loved by many is wanted by everybody. Captain Störr becomes radiant, he is besieged by women.

There is a prim and proper English miss, and a more sophisticated black enchantress, who happens to be the lover of his friend and employer. The impetuous captain kisses both of them passionately, but we are told that nothing else happens. He nevertheless feels he has cheated on his wife, though for a man smitten with remorse, he holds up rather well.

He would go as far as killing his wife, but doesn't of course. He'd like to get rid of her, actually—to expose her. And after exposing her, either kill her or spare her, but in any case, leave her. The best thing would be to prove that she is a thief, too, or looks like one the moment she is discovered. It would be that much easier to leave her then, to shake off this creature who has so discombobulated the captain, not even his appetite is what it used to be.

The truth of the matter is that this old sea lion is afraid of women. Women to him are sweet, charming, adorable playthings. He himself is a mountain of flesh, so what he would really like is to play house with these little dolls. Of course he loves frisky kittens, too, who try to scratch his hand or bite his neck. Feminists heap terrible abuses on such men and then jump into bed with them . . . Even they like their warmth. But in novels about great love and great jealousy this is the kind of hero we must have.

*

What else could its author, an unemployed Hungarian Jewish school master past his prime, write about—and write with unrelenting diligence, for seven long years, from 1935 to 1942, shutting himself in the study of his pleasant Budapest villa? Füst was known for a long time only as a poet; his writer friends used words like universal and cosmic to describe his single slim volume, and later generations looked upon him as the larger-than-life originator of dramatically innovative poetic forms. This prematurely old master, this genuine professional, who spent twenty years studying Tolstoy's silences and who explored the secrets of prose fiction as intently as painters and composers scrutinize the materials of their own craft, did not set foot outside his house for years on end.

Growing up, Füst was a poor boy; he lived with his mother in a cramped cold-water flat and began writing at the kitchen table. He first came alive in the literary cafés of his youth. After studying law, he became a school teacher and published his books at his own expense. But then he married a wealthy, business-minded former student of his, who was devoted to him, idolized him, and supported him. Their house was furnished with choice antiques, fine paintings hung on the wall—there was no reason to go outside, no need to leave the garden.

He only saw people who came to see him, he chose inner exile—into Flaubertian exactitude and thoroughness. A learned aesthete, a great poet was writing a novel at fifty. Misunderstood, unappreciated, a most unlikely candidate for commercial success, Füst was at leisure to create a masterpiece.

When published, the novel was barely noticed; even discriminating readers were slow to appreciate its unique features. The real breakthrough came only twenty years later when the novel began to appear in foreign translations: first in France, then in Germany, in Italy, and just about everywhere in Central Europe. It is said that in 1967—Füst was seventy-nine at the time—he was nominated for the Nobel Prize in literature; death, however, proved quicker than the Swedish Academy.

*

During the years when he immersed himself in this novel, Füst must have, now and then, skimmed the papers, he must have gotten wind that anti-Jewish laws were being passed, World War II was in the making—the pressure all around kept mounting.

But the solitary giant averted his eyes. He defended himself against the scandal by ignoring it. By creating a world of true feelings in place of the real world. He simply had to protect literature from politics; from the deadly abstractions of both the right and the left. Yet the man who vowed to do this was also the man who in his philosophical-meditative diaries loved to slip into the realm of pure abstractions, wanting desperately to hold on to what was still unsullied, and genuinely human, in this world.

In so doing, Milán Füst, ironically enough, hit upon jealousy, this abstract passion, which has its victim search for tangible evidence but which forces him to chase phantoms in the end, making him anticipate assiduously the expulsion from the Garden.

*

What we are all up against is a state of helplessness: we do not know the person whom, in the Biblical sense, we *have* come to know; so we keep getting reacquainted. But as far as this husband is concerned, his wife is inscrutable, impenetrable. He knows that just as every man must die, love, too, will die. But if it must, then let it die now, let's get it over with. Man yearns for order, for well-rounded stories—he wants to conclude his own, too, give it a proper ending, aesthetic balance, if nothing else.

The more you love, the more you want that love to end. Just so that you won't be so vulnerable. The jealous sea captain suffers from being in love, from being imprisoned. On the high seas, where there are no girlies to bother with, where he must do his job and stay alive—out there is the real world. On land, in Paris and London, in secluded flats, in tiny love nests, there is no reality—there he strays into a world of dubious fantasies; he may be a tough character, but this world will break him for sure, he must pay dearly for all that heavenly bliss.

*

You have a big, foolish man, then, with a good little wife—except he doesn't think she is so good. All this is worked out ever so subtly in the book. It's quite possible that our Lizzy *is* a tiny bit unfaithful, and also that she isn't. Captain Störr, on the other hand, imagines her at times to be scandalously unfaithful. And so cunning that she can gloss over her wildest flings by sitting at home. It all depends on how you look at it. The captain can't help noting that for each viewpoint there is another scenario, and each one is equally valid, and equally deceptive. Such is the master novelist's sense of humor, his amusing and terrifying relativism.

*

Milán Füst didn't know how to deal with the hopeless quagmire that was Hungary in the thirties, he couldn't deal with his own situation in that murky mess. He longed to be in Paris or in London —in a normal, civilized city. London especially seemed attractive to Jews in Hungary at the time. America was too far away, Paris, too close. In the end most of them stayed in Budapest.

When the world around him is about to crumble into dust, a Hungarian Jewish poet decides to create something solid and shapely; he wants to lift his handiwork, his novel, out of the formless, viscous rubble. At least on paper he finds a place where only art matters, where evil fate does not force his hand, where an ideally suitable artistic task presents itself: to develop a grand theme in four movements, with disturbing fluctuations and digressions, naturally.

Milán Füst couldn't think of anything better to do, so he emigrated to his novel. In a filthy age he wanted to write pure fiction. And he succeeded—*The Story of My Wife is* pure, honest fiction. For seven years the author could dwell in this work. But then he had to finish it. Maybe he overdid it a little. He knew so much about the obsessions of an egomaniac, he became suspicious himself —and couldn't wait to be provoked. Like a lion that first gives an angry snort and then waits for his chance to roar and lash out with his lion's paw in earnest.

*

Milán Füst never went to Holland; he was never in Paris or London, either. Yet the hero of his novel is a Dutch seaman, and the action takes place in Paris and London. Then again, we don't find out much about life in Holland, or about Paris and London. What the novel is really concerned with is whether a temporarily unemployed sea captain's wife cheats on her husband or not. The captain is past forty, by no means a virgin, and when he falls in love, he marries the woman on the spot.

What he is is a middle-aged beginner; his knowledge is not deeply ingrained, he is not blasé about the world. On the contrary, he is forever seized with wonder, he delves into things, in his leisurely manner he ponders the mysteries of everyday life. Wild fantasies alternate with sensible admonitions. Does my wife really want to kill me? Nonsense! Hogwash! And on and on in this vein. Füst has a knack for creating uncertainty. He has very little to say about cities and backgrounds; husband and wife have time to observe each other closely; the author places his two characters (actually, one: his fictive self) in a much-reduced, laboratory-like setting.

Let us assume that I am a Dutch sea captain: bigger, stronger, more courageous and overpowering by far than the author who, unlike the captain, is not in the habit of knocking dead, just like that, a miserable little cabdriver when the latter, with pistol in hand, wants to empty his pockets. The captain is out of work just now, so aside from one quite wonderful chapter, we have no time to waste on sea stories, no need to provide social commentary and local color—after all, the captain is a perennial transient, a temporary resident in the great cities of Europe; besides his wife he barely gets to know anyone. Unrelentingly, the novelist focuses on the crucial question: is Lizzy faithful or not? And leaves the reader in doubt until the very end. Our initial hunch that she is indeed faithful may become stronger, we may even shed a tear *à la* Füst for poor, misunderstood Lizzy, yet, ultimately, we can't help sharing Captain Störr's misgivings—maybe Lizzy *is* a flighty and fast woman after all.

It's possible to go on, of course, without ever finding out. What then can we expect from this lengthy book? For one thing, it will make us become Captain Störr; we will partake of his brooding, his naive wonderment, his not always spectacular adventures. His creator truly had no other ambition than to experience first love and its attendant emotions with the heart and mind of a jealous husband.

The novels of old concentrated on the early phases of love affairs, on events that occurred before the lovers went to bed, and they usually ended without proceeding any further. The basic question was always: Will they or won't they be wed? *The Story of My Wife* begins right after this phase. At this point, after the marriage, what other disquieting questions can arise: Should I cheat on her? Does she cheat on me? The trails leading to the conjugal bed may now be pointing to other beds. What latter-day novelists do is follow in the tracks of these wayfarers of love.

In all probability there has never been a man or a woman who did not experience profound uncertainty, who didn't feel that their beloved is not theirs. I could be holding her in my arms and she could still be far, far away. Just look at her: she is daydreaming, about someone else, no doubt. Now she looks sad—she probably doesn't love me any more.

Since I have not yet met anyone who was not susceptible to jealousy, I recommend this novel as a guide not to Paris or London but to one's own marriage, for the true subject of the novel is tense, vibrant uncertainty.

Of course not many husbands have the leisure to play private detective; most have better things to do than snoop after their wives. Captain Störr, however, has been relieved by the author of all other obligations. There is no ship under his command now, his money (whatever's left of it) is still in his pocket. Husband and wife are together the whole day, and yet they are not. The captain can never be entirely sure—and this is both his strength and his weakness. With this burly man as his guide, Milán Füst leads us to raptures and humiliations, to murderous desires and displays of uncommon gentleness.

*

It's gratifying to follow him, for he describes the conditions of his life so very convincingly, and comments on them painstakingly. Whatever is on his mind he rarely blurts out in front of the other characters—he saves it for us.

Füst also keeps shifting our perspective. He makes the long interior monologue more dynamic by switching skillfully to animated dialogue. Our narrator is the kind of person who is forever reminded of other things, he is full of digressions and droll observations—yet, whether the topic at hand is a wild nighttime romp, a murder, or dreamy walks in cemeteries and parks, Füst does what he must.

He develops each sequence masterfully and embellishes them with the most ingenious of devices. The master novelist adheres to his own aesthetic precepts, alternating cleverly and refreshingly between narrative summaries and "evocative delineations," that is, brief surveys of great blocks of time, and focused exposés of shorter stretches.

His somewhat mannered prose has a unique rhythm, a captivating ebb and flow; moreover, the regular alternation of voices and viewpoints suggests the wild contradictions at work in the author himself

—he knows the language of compassion as well as the language of despair; he can be unusually kind and unusually cruel.

Captain Jacob Störr is a man without illusions, but his one passion: his undying wish to know what makes his wife tick makes him so alert, so eager, so tormented, we can't help liking him. I wouldn't mind joining the captain for a good stiff drink in a bar. Even if I didn't see him again, I'd remember him. If you, too, want to remember this decent seaman, who, though not at all stupid, is still a big fool for bungling life's greatest gift simply because he's too worried about it not being really his—if you want to listen to a commonplace story as told by an irresistible narrator, then do read Captain Störr's reminiscences about his wife.

THE STORY OF MY WIFE

Te vocamus, quod sic plasmavisti hominem et hominem itidem vocamus, qui tamen debet praestare seipsum . . . percipe hanc altercationem in corde nostro diabolicam, Domine! Et oculos sanctos Tuos in inopiam nostram conjicere non gravator, sed conspice portentum clam nobis abditum, in extis . . . accedit, quod allectationes nutriunt ipsum velut alece. Et ne nos inducas in tentationem, supplicamus ad versprum, peccatum tamen ostium pulsat intratque domum et intrat prorsus ad mensam. Amove ergo sartaginem igneam, qua caro siccatur, nam animal in me debile crebro.

(From a medieval devotions)

One

MY WIFE'S BEEN UNFAITHFUL, THIS MUCH I HAVE LONG suspected. But that she should take up with a man like that . . . I stand over six feet tall, weigh 210 pounds, am a veritable giant, in short, the sort of person who—as they say— only has to spit on someone and the man is finished.

That's what I first thought I would do to Monsieur Dedin . . . Ah, but this is not where I should begin . . . It's no use; I still get worked up when I think of him.

The truth of the matter is that getting married was a mistake— all the more since up until then I had very little to do with women, I was cold by nature. I look back on my early youth and find that the only story of an erotic nature worth recollecting is the following: I could not have been more than thirteen. The place was a park in the Dutch city of Sneek, in Friesland, where we then lived. A governess sat in the park with a small child, whom she kept admonishing:

"*Veux-tu obéir, veux-tu obéir?*"

I loved the sound of the words. She also said to the child:

"*Vite, vite, dépêche-toi donc.*"

And I liked that too. It's quite possible I decided right then and there that I would marry a French woman. At any rate, I enjoyed

5

listening to that sweet melody. Then, as though by divine inspiration, I walked to the edge of the park, tore out a page from my exercise-book, and wrote two words on it, in Dutch (for I could not yet then write in French, nor did I speak the language, though I did understand it when others spoke it).

"*Greppel, greppel*," I wrote, that is, let's lie in the ditch a little. There was indeed a rather deep, grassy ditch nearby. With the piece of paper I walked back to the governess and stood meekly before her, looking at her sweetly, the way I did when as a little boy I was sent with a list to the corner grocer. Then I held up the little piece of paper in front of her.

Naturally, the governess thought I was crazy.

She understood the word but not the thing I was getting at. True, I was a good-sized lad and could have been taken for a boy of eighteen, but I did wear short pants and knee socks; what is more I had on a nice blue sailor suit top, with a bow my mother herself tied that morning. I still had rosy cheeks then, though I admit my ears were also red, and large-sized ears they were, too. But my teeth were white and my eyes fearless—I was a boy with earnest eyes. And I was not yet corrupted, honestly I wasn't. Just how I got the courage to put those words down I still can't say.

The governess simply stared at me, she nearly swallowed me with her eyes.

"*Que c'est que tu veux?*" she asked finally.

But I was not embarrassed even then. I stood there graciously, then ran away. I did the same the following day and the day after.

The governess, as soon as she saw me coming, would start laughing—she laughed so hard she nearly fell over. Arms akimbo, she continued laughing, and the child with her laughed too. But I stood my ground, my gaze remained steadfast; I did not budge.

"*Mon pauvre garçon*," she intoned sympathetically, laughing still, though also blushing hotly. "*Eh bien, tu ne sais pas ce qu'il te faut.*" A woman of the world, I thought. "My poor boy," she repeated; "you have no idea what's bothering you, do you?" And she stared into my eyes, wonderstruck, like the hot sun, and even pinched my face. Whereupon I ran away.

Finally, though, she caught on. Why not? she must have asked herself. At least this sort of thing can't lead to scandal or other problems. The thought of the ditch appealed to her too. There was also a little bridge there with overgrown bushes underneath. After discovering that the park-keeper passed by only twice a day (because of the summer heat, the place was deserted most of the time), she met me by that bridge early in the morning, bringing with her a basket of food or a jug of milk. She was uncombed, sleepy—oh, I was crazy about her. For it should be understood: I was a young lad and I could still feel the warmth of her bed on her.

At home I accounted for my early departure with some lie or other; I tried to avoid my mother anyway and walked about all day in the sunshine as if in a dream. . . . This lasted the entire summer. Then I lost all interest in women.

A year later, one of my uncles, my favorite, my thoroughly depraved uncle, whom I happened to be visiting then, set out a hooked ladder for me so I could climb up to the upper floor of a neighboring house; each night I observed a beautiful lady taking a bath. It was summertime then, too, and in the sweltering heat she kept the windows of her apartment open. One day, while hovering between the ground and the sky, I decided to land on her window sill. So as not to scare her, I whispered to her:

"A little boy is here."

Rather than getting scared, she turned very somber in her bath. Actually, she knew me already by sight. Then, without saying a word, she motioned me to come closer. I stepped down from the ledge, and she with a hazy look in her eyes embraced me.

These were the only two amorous adventures of my early youth, which, though awkward, both of them, are worth mentioning. The others are negligible. I had to laugh at men who were panting after them. . . . I was full of unattractive thoughts about women. How haughtily they sat in restaurants, holding their heads oh so high. But I knew things about them that would have made them less haughty, surely. I conceived of man's business with them as being fairly straightforward. In this I was not unlike many a young man. One must deal with them quite simply, I thought.

Instead, I became more and more interested in good eating, especially after being exposed to new worlds during the course of my travels. An acquaintance of mine, General Piet Mens, once made the observation in my presence that man is worse than the filthiest hog because he tastes everything. Well, I disagree. It's by leaving nothing untouched that we discover the tastes, the uses, of this world. And besides, I am convinced that anyone who wants to delve into the souls of nations must eat their foods.

That is what I have done. I can't think of a single dish, not even overspiced dried mutton that burns like the sand of the Sahara, that I wouldn't eat. I walked through Eastern bazaars where meats sizzle on open, communal fireplaces. I watched dough rise on a pastry chef's stand in Persia. The Mohammedans do make wonderful pastries, and prepare them tastefully and cleanly too, in spotless aprons, and serve them in hot bronze dishes. You get sated with the fragrance, it stays with you for months. When I had no pressing business, I would sit for days on end in those bazaars and *souks*—it was my way of relaxing. I couldn't imagine anything more fascinating than the ceaseless bustle, the stream of alien color, the strange tongues, the laughter. If after a time all this did get to be a little too much, I ordered one of their dishes and continued daydreaming.

My friends thought I was a savage, mainly because I ate everything, though for other reasons as well. No job was too hard for me; I tackled everything. I would think nothing of sweating and slaving for three months straight. Needless to say, the shipowners knew this about me, too.

"You buffalo, you," said one of my mates, a kid named Eberstma-Leiningen. I had to laugh at his squeamishness—I always found work, whereas he didn't. I am a buffalo, eh? So be it. The buffalo's a very useful beast. And anyway, I can do something a buffalo can't, which is going without eating or sleeping. To repeat, nothing was too much for me when it came to enduring hardship. But then, nothing was good enough when I felt like letting go. If there were limits to pass, I passed them, and not only in attacking a job but also in seeking out pleasure . . . But gone are those heroic days. I listen to myself tell my tale and it's as though I am talking about somebody else. I listen with some sadness, I do admit.

About my soul I used to think: a painful frill. And that's exactly what it was.

Then again, I became a shipmaster rather early on. While still a smooth-faced youth, I was entrusted with all sorts of fine wares, precious cargo worth fortunes. Now and then I struck my own deals, private deals, on the side. There are ways. I began to prosper, and before I reached thirty I had accumulated a handsome fortune.

But then something happened, a minor accident. Not even so minor, actually. The nemesis of seafaring men. Stomach trouble. It felt as if an armored plate was pressing on my belly . . . I couldn't eat. Here is how it happened.

We were laid up in Naples, and I bought some things in a delicatessen shop. I like to shop in Italy: the merchants are high-spirited and their stores well-stocked. In this shop, too, there were first-class foodstuffs: smoke-cured ham, poultry, even game, from woodlarks and thrushes and tiny quails to good-sized ducks, some already roasted, others uncooked and therefore pleasantly yellow, with their heads tucked under their wings, looking as though they were made to rest plumply on a marble slab. I could watch them for hours, as well as the appetizing breadstuff, the nuts, the clusters of grapes, the pyramids of apples and chestnuts, even the golden-yellow dessert wines which remind one—who knows why?—of cheerful old women.

I ended up with quite a selection; and as I fingered my crisp banknotes I anticipated the swishing sound the little packets would make. (I walk down the street and they begin their little chatter. I like that sort of thing.) But then I thought: Why carry all those packages? They can be delivered. I had to stay in town to attend to a few things and thought of inviting a few people to my boat.

"*Ah, ah, Jacopo, carissimo amico mio.*" My Italian acquaintances greeted me with noisy effusiveness; they even flung out their arms. The Italians love this sort of self-generated conviviality, everybody knows that. What my friends also knew was that if I invited them for supper, they wouldn't regret it.

On my way home I had another idea.

Why not have a bite before dinner? I was in the vicinity of Posilippo, so I stopped in at a place near there. Right by the water, on the pier in fact, there was a pleasant little tavern, pretty much deserted at this time of the day; the area around it was quiet too, all of which made the place kind of inviting. A hearty snack with a couple of the local boys would be just right. They were having ordinary shellfish with white bread and wine. I joined them straightaway, and we had a pleasant chat. The shells sloshed in the buckets as we rinsed them one by one. Everything around was spotless: the pier on which we sat, the sea, life itself, it seemed, including the hearts of those sitting around the table. And to top it off, the sun setting across the bay was a glorious red.

This isn't half bad, I said to myself; rather nice, in fact. And as I had always been fond of a little make-believe, a little pretending, I imagined for a while that I wasn't me but a languid world traveler on a rest cure. I paid for the boys' drinks, whereupon they stood up and bowed. (Italians are fond of such ceremony.)

But I did suspect that the shellfish I ate there was the cause of my undoing. To this day I think of that little snack as the beginning of my troubles. That night nothing tasted good, the excellent supper was wasted on me. There was a coldness in my stomach from all that wretched seafood.

Not even the preparations gave me any pleasure, though ordinarily that's the part I like most. First I check if they sent home everything, making sure nothing got switched. As a rule I buy the finest cooking oil, as yellow as the warm light of a lamp. The one I had just bought was naturally of this kind. I held it up to the light; it was flawless, perfect. Normally, the mere sight of such a fine product gives me a little thrill of pleasure. Now, too, I stood in the kitchen, waiting for the snails to cook, telling myself: You have to learn to anticipate those little pleasures. But I *had* learned it, I knew how to live. I watched the kitchen boy drying the plates and stuffing and twisting the dishcloth in the glasses, and holding them up to the light to see if their sparkle was brilliant enough. An even tempo can be so soothing. I like quiet, measured movements; I also like quiet brilliance. So I usually prepare for these dinners with great inner calm. I tried now too, but it was no use; my insides were going haywire. Watching my friends didn't help any; they were noisily devouring everything in sight, while I hardly touched a thing. They sang boisterously, while I remained silent. Years ago, in happier times, I bought rich, heavy tobacco in the Levant. In some ports the fast-talking merchants would lug on board vast quantities of the slender leaves, as golden yellow as the hair of virgin girls. I brought out a few sheaves of the stuff and tossed them in front of my guests. Later I also tried smoking one cigarette after another, but it just didn't taste the same, nothing did—life itself appeared futile. Until then I was never sick, never had a stomach upset; but now I felt this was it: an evil fate. I was desperate.

Meanwhile the gramophone was playing.

"*Niente, niente*," I told them; "*sono un poco amolato cosi*." I pretended to be drunk from the resin-colored wine.

But they had a fine time without me.

"*Vieni, vieni*," they told my boy. "Eat this, for your master." They fed him all the delicacies, though eating on duty was never allowed on my ships. But now even this didn't bother me.

I was angry enough, however, to toss the leftovers into the sea.

This painful interlude, I am now convinced, led me to my marriage. In a way I began to hate people that night. And no wonder. They gorged themselves and ignored me completely.

It happens often that for all our experience and wisdom we get deeply offended when people, seeing we are in trouble, pass us by like a speeding car, without so much as looking back. These rejections hurt, as can disappointments suffered at the dinner table. Indeed, some people take these even more to heart, and not just youngsters, as prigs and pedants might think, who belittle such grievances. For instance I had a crony, a captain by the name of Gerard Bist, who lapsed into melancholy every time his cook spoiled his dinner.

"What's the use of living?" he'd say to me. "You're stuck on that bloody boat for months on end like a goddamn prisoner; and then you can't even have the satisfaction of eating a decent meal." He was right. Me, I was doubly offended, as can be imagined. For if I can't enjoy good food, what is there left for me? I who had always been intemperate should now start being careful, stick to diets, visit hospitals, medicine women? Well, I did; I even tried acupuncture, and counting therapy, for God's sake, in Japan! There isn't a cure under the sun I didn't try, but nothing helped. Finally, I was directed to a so-called psychoanalyst, and for all I know this man may have been responsible for my even greater misfortune.

"Women," the psychoanalyst said to me. "Women." And he looked into my eyes significantly.

Women? So be it. Let's look around. But I didn't even have to do that, for it was just then that I met my future wife.

She was a French girl, very much a flirt and very ticklish. She laughed all the time, mostly at me, and always so hard as if someone was tickling her. She called me Oncle Douc Douc and Dodo and Cric Crac and Croc Croc because of the way I laughed, which she said sounded like an explosion. And she called me Papa Bear, too, because it was so funny to see the points of my napkin stick out behind my ears. She rolled in delight like a little pig. I do happen to tie my napkin in the back of my neck—who knows why, an old habit, I suppose.

"Your big ears," she cried, "and those two points . . . it's too precious." And she kept clapping her tiny hands.

"Sloppy again," she'd yell at me from her window when she saw me trudging up the steps behind the church (her house was rather high up, on a hill behind the church), and I had the feeling already then, I am not even sure why, that God alone knew how many men—and what sort of men!—she must have greeted like that, leaning out of the upper story window, a fragrant French rose. She was a sinful creature, she had to be; I sensed it immediately. But it didn't much matter then, I had a grand time with her. I asked her to repeat the words "*Veux-tu obéir? Veux-tu obéir?*" and she repeated them diligently, greeting me with the phrase after a time. In other words, she was quite smart, and quick too, because she learned in no time how to handle me, always letting me have my way, saying mine was the correct way, urging me to do as I please. From all this I could have surmised a certain degree of expertise, but I didn't want to. I refused to consider the evidence.

I thought to myself: If I like her, I'll marry her, so why fret? Seafaring men get nowhere as anxious about these things as landlocked folk do. I say this because I've seen enough of them ponder the matter endlessly before finally making up their minds. But us?

My life is always in danger, was then too, and not only on the high seas. I was consorting with some pretty dangerous Levantine gentlemen at that time. Why then should I have been bothered by such minor worries? Will my wife love me? Will she be faithful while I am gone? Women are never faithful, especially sea captains' wives—it comes with the territory.

So I bought her a bunch of bracelets and necklaces and married her. We sailors don't like long courtships. I had a mate who ingratiated himself with the ladies by saying *"Andiamo a letto"* after his first evening walk with them. And with some, this abruptness worked wonders. If not right away then two weeks later. It's no good being shocked by these things—they happen. It may not be very nice of me to bring this up just here, but why pretend? That's just how I felt. Matrimony to me was not any more sacred than, say, a carrot stick. I was beyond all sacredness, or so I thought. (I was wrong; just how wrong is what I intend to relate here.)

Anyway, I married her. I think she had a little affair right away, soon after the wedding, that is—at least that is what all the signs seemed to point to. I will not say I cared very much for her speed, but I tried to get over it. Told myself not to be petty. After all, I wasn't used to having a woman who was only mine. Was I to follow her now, spy on her, gather evidence? What the hell for? If she didn't do it then, she'll do it later. How could she not be unfaithful? I was away for months at a time, often as long as a half a year at a stretch. Can one expect superhuman behavior from a mere human? Or should she pine away, for years, all alone? Were she really to do that, she probably couldn't say *"Veux-tu-obéir?"* in such a beautiful sing-song. And then she'd no longer give me pleasure. I said I didn't make much of the affair, still I want to put down everything about that first night. Not because there was anything extraordinary about it, but because I do believe that every "first" has some significance. But I also have another purpose, and that is to give some idea of the circumstances and conditions under which my wife lived—to demonstrate, in short, what an utter fool I would have been if in full knowledge of those circumstances. I still had anxieties about her fidelity.

Motley groups of people inhabited the island of Menorca at the time: displaced Italians, Slav émigrés, and a whole band of Swedes who hadn't made it in South America. The story was that they were twice sentenced to death but escaped both times, and trudged on buffaloes across the continent, from the Atlantic to the Pacific. There were also German Communists and Polish insurrectionists on the island, and others who could easily be taken for spies. I am thinking of one group in particular, an ignorant bunch that never-theless managed fairly well—just how they did it, nobody seemed to know. One of them was forever performing, wretchedly, needless to say. My wife had lived among these people, which in itself was not objectionable to me. At least she had a chance to learn what life was really like, and not just on the surface but way below, in the depths. She could learn about things I saw around me all the time, in port and elsewhere . . . Why, the life story of someone like me must be like a compressed version of mankind's history. And what sort of history is that? Once I thought this through: if some day, after the earth had cooled off, someone were to read this history, he would have to come to the conclusion that only rogues, rapists, murderers, monsters inhabited this earth, and the only way to survive here was to kill. . . . Take my profession; in this line of work you can go for years without meeting a decent human being. Since my wife had also seen some rough things in her time, I didn't have to worry that one day she'd give herself airs and become sensitive, and say things like "oh my" and "dear oh dear" and tell me I didn't express myself properly—all of which would drive me straight up the wall. In this respect she seemed like a suitable mate for me. But let me continue where I left off, with a description of living conditions among those gentlefolk on the island of Menorca. This is how my landlord there, a certain Don Juan, described one well-mixed group—the one that had been my wife's home base. I'll try to quote the Don himself:

"I have to start with the first, now divorced, wife of Koch, a writer from Berlin. This woman lived, harmoniously, I would say, with an Italian automobile dealer by the name of Samuele Annibale Ridolfi. Signor Ridolfi was a rather amiable chap with nice white teeth; I knew him well. This, then, was the first couple: Madame Koch and Ridolfi. Their house was on the beach. On New Year's Eve that year a Scandinavian couple (Norwegian? Swedish?) visited them. These two, though they knew each other from childhood and married for love just a year before, were not very happy. While here, the Scandinavian woman came down with acute appendicitis, on New Year's Eve, mind you, and had to be taken to the hospital. When it was all over she returned to her friends' house on the seashore, to Madame Koch Number One, that is. Are you with me so far, sir?" asked my landlord, a gossipy old gentleman.

"Why of course I am; what a question? But why do you refer to her as Madame Koch Number One?"

"You'll find out in a minute, dear sir. Let me just take a piece of paper; I shall draw a picture of three *inammorati*, so as not to mix up the order. Oh yes, there is a fourth, I just remembered. I will moisten my pencil like so, and make a mark next to her, and this will represent Uriel, a clever youngster who I myself am quite fond of."

"Uriel? Who is Uriel? And why moisten the poor dear?"

"In a minute, sir," my landlord said and smiled profusely. "Here is where it gets complicated. The Nordic woman—Gerda was her name—was rather pale to begin with, and during her recuperation she acquired the complexion of an unripened tomato, so it was natural that she should capture the heart of the amiable Annibale—the passionate Italian fell madly in love with her. Consequently, the first (now divorced) wife of Herr Koch was obliged to leave the waterfront house. But she didn't leave alone, she had someone with her . . . You guessed it: little Uriel, why of course . . .

"Now I'll just moisten my pencil once more (the old man relished the sarcasm), for I must tell you finally who Uriel is. Our friend, the multifarious Koch, got married a second time, and this nimble-witted boy was the product of that union. But he divorced his second wife, too (which, I am sure, couldn't be helped either, that's just the kind of person Herr Koch was). At any rate, the child didn't stay with his mother—how could he when he lived with her predecessor, Madame Koch Number One? And what that meant was that the boy, too, had to leave the beachfront house.

"I think I am doing quite well," Don Juan now said, puffing contentedly on his cigarette. "By God, sir, show me another man on this cursed island, *en esta maldita isla*, who could recite all of this so well. But to continue: this little boy, Uriel, had a beautiful mother, a delicate little Jewess with a neck as white as an Andalusian mare's. Hanna was her name, and being involved in an affair herself, she did not appear to be interested in a child. She lived with her lover, a German aviator, on the island of Foradade, and theirs too was said to be a harmonious relationship. He operated a hydroplane and frequently took off from the sea. But Koch himself had recently written a letter to Ridolfi in which he complained that things weren't going well for him in Berlin. Consequently, Madame Koch Number One contacted Madame Koch Number

Two who, as you know, was the mother of the child, lover of the aviator, living on the island of Foradade. Anyway, Madame Koch Number One suggested that they find a place on the island where Koch could join them, and they could all live together ... Wouldn't it be wonderful?" My landlord guffawed happily as he said this, and to show just how pleased he was, he even put on his red skullcap.

"But now comes the final balancing act, the dénouement, when complications lose heart and wither away. As you may or may not have guessed, this household did come into being, exactly as planned, and in total harmony, too. Five people were now living under the same roof: the Mesdames Koch, Number Two's lover, the child, and Koch from Berlin. And in this salad bowl they all seemed quite happy."

But this was merely the exposition. Only from this point on did my wife-to-be begin to play an active role in the story. As related by my old landlord and others in this gossip-ridden island, she hadn't until then paid much attention to the amiable Signor Ridolfi. At the time there was only one man whom she considered worthy of her affections, and that was Eugene Hornmann, the young flier. I was given to understand that as soon as the couple arrived, my wife lost her little composure. The aviator, it seems, made quite an impression on her. And why not? A young little thing, a language teacher, among all those strangers ... It is only natural that she should be happy to hear someone speak real French. And this Hornmann fellow spoke a number of languages well, though it was rumored that he used his knowledge of languages, his impeccable French pronounciation, and even his skills as an aviator, to carry out delicate, dubious missions—not spy missions exactly, but missions nevertheless, in the service of his native Germany. And though my future wife was not happy to hear these tales, she didn't stop liking him. And right she was: one can't be too finicky, or else one can't make it in this world. It's no good attaching great importance to things that are in fact unimportant. Take me for example: when I was still healthy, I would eat a piece of buttered muffin even if it fell on the floor before my nose. Let's just imagine the situation: I am standing on the upper deck, the sun is beating down on me, and cook has just surprised me with a fresh-baked muffin. I swallow in anticipation. And then, right in front of me, he drops it. So I simply pick it up [and] eat it. Why? Because if I have him bring me another, it's not as good. I want that first, irreplaceable piece. And so it is with everything; I've learned that lesson many times over. Let the know-it-alls say what they will. All you can do with that second muffin is kick it in the sea.

I saw all this quite clearly then; only later did I begin to change in this respect, as I will reveal in these notes. But let's proceed. Where was I? Ah yes, my future wife, who wasn't much disturbed by what she heard, and loved Hornmann despite her misgivings about his activities. She couldn't very well blame this man for loving his fatherland—she herself felt the same way about her own native France. And the fact that this Hornmann chap belonged to someone else, another woman, why, that didn't bother her too much, either. My sardonic landlord told me that to avoid the jealous Hanna they used to meet in public squares and cemeteries and on the ramparts, in the early afternoon sunshine, when the whole town was indoors resting . . . Much later I heard an amusing little story about them. It seems that one day Hanna followed them in the sun, and on a hillside terrace saw a lady's hat being blown by the wind. She picked up the hat, recognized it, and struck it with her parasol, but then let it go, let the wind have it. She confined herself to exclaiming, in Spanish, for all the world to hear:

"Oh, the hypocrite, the deceitful hypocrite." Then she went home.

I didn't make a fuss, not even then, though my good friend Don Juan was becoming more sarcastic than ever. And it wasn't because I myself became cynical; I just liked to look at things objectively—then I still could. I never thought, for example, that the universe came into being with me or for me. Or that a woman couldn't have a life of her own before she met me.

When discussing our impending marriage, I told her: "The time has come for you to choose, for a while anyway, between me and your friends; because I surely don't want us to move in to Herr Koch's place as the sixth and seventh guests. I am clearly not as gay and bohemian as these people, but you will admit you can't live that way for very long. One must have some semblance of order, wouldn't you agree?"

...ully agree. She said one did indeed need order in
...st definitely. What is more, she herself came to me
...we leave this crazy island. For just then a storm was
...pt, which threatened to destroy the entire Koch
...hat happened was that Madame Koch Number One
(the one ... n spectacles) began to realize what a fool she had been
for letting herself be evicted from her lovely seaside home, all on
account of a silly appendicitis attack; and she made such a row, the
whole island heard it. She'll show them, they'll be sorry, and all
the rest. She threatened to move to London. To hell with these
patriarchal arrangements, she said. This would have meant trouble indeed, because she at least had some money stashed away, and
what's a commune without money?

But let's leave the poor woman (the further details of the affair
are in any case unimportant). The main thing was that my wife
now expressed a desire to go to Paris with me, even though up
until then she wouldn't hear of moving there. Frankly, I got the
feeling she didn't care all that much for her native land. But now
she couldn't wait to go. "I feel we should leave right away," she
said. "Very well," I answered. And in less than a week she wound
up her affairs, got her things together and said good-bye to the
island. We were in a hurry because she insisted on holding the
wedding not in Menorca but in Paris.

In other words, in those days we still agreed on some things,
even if not for long. I was inclined to look at this as agreement
based on a temporary overlapping of interests. My wife, however,
didn't see it that way, and wouldn't hold herself even to this
modest accommodation.

What actually happened was that shortly after we left the
island, the amiable Annibale Ridolfi, the one who banished
Madame Koch Number One from the seashore, turned up in
Paris. And it was no coincidence either, I know that for a fact. I
heard his name mentioned, and in connection with my wife, too,
at a Paris police station (I'll recount the details presently); I was
also told, much later, that he had complained to a friend of his that
he allowed a sweet little quail (my wife, that is) to slip away in the
rye (the rye being me, I suppose). He was sorry, in other words,

that he didn't taste the joys of love with this lighthearted French woman. . . .

As I said, I learned about this complaint years later, and quite by accident, and by then I no longer cared. Back in Paris, though, the following surprising thing happened early one morning.

We hadn't been there for more than a few months (I was just opening some newly arrived packages in the hallway), when the bell rang and I was handed a police summons made out to my wife. I found it somewhat strange. What business could my wife have with the police? I looked at the note: it said she was to appear in a few days.

"Look what came for you just now," I said to her and handed her the piece of paper. To repeat: it didn't mention what it was in reference to—*pour l'affaire vous concernant* was all it said. She too perused the note, and then burst out laughing.

"What is this all about?" I asked.

"Must you know everything, *Jacopo mio*," she said, still laughing. And though her laughter wasn't exactly offensive, there was something impertinent about it. Why shouldn't I find out if she got into some sort of trouble? But I kept my mouth shut.

We were still living in town then, on the Place Saint Sulpice, thrown together with all sorts of people, hawkers of religious articles and such. In her most voluble manner she now replied that a few days ago, on her way home, while she cut across the square in front of the church, someone snatched her purse. But until now she was too scared to tell me about it.

"Now I don't have a purse," she said, laughing, and opened her wardrobe door wide. "No purse, it's gone, see?" she repeated sweetly, like a child. This was too much: lying to my face like that was simply too much. I decided to go to the police myself.

And I did, that very morning.

But you have to know about the French. Not only are they tough, they are not easily fooled, either. I was lucky, though, because I wound up with a dullard of a clerk. On his door the sign said: "Motor Vehicles Bureau. Traffic Violations Unit." What traffic? What violation?

"Fenders broken, two injuries, two pre-trial interrogations," the clerk recited.

"You don't say," I said quietly.

"And I can also tell you why. You were parked illegally, on the wrong side of the street."

"*I* was?" I said and smiled in his face, which may have been a little disingenuous. The man became suspicious.

"Who are you, may I ask? A lawyer perhaps?" He looked in the file, searched the text and stopped his finger on a line. I took a peek and was able to fish out three characters from a sea of letters: RID. Who was Rid? I didn't have to wonder long. "Do you happen to be Monsieur Ridolfi?" asked this blockhead. Needless to say, I was stunned. I didn't expect to hear about, or meet, this man ever again, let alone in this place. But then I became talkative and felt a strange and sad melody spring up in my heart.

"I am no lawyer, and neither am I Monsieur Ridolfi, my dear sir. I am just a foolish sailor; an inquirer." The only thing I forgot to tell him was that I was my wife's husband.

"You are not a lawyer, then?"

"No, I am not."

"And you have no power of attorney? Then I have nothing further to discuss with you. (He was shouting by now.) I provide information to interested parties only. Good-bye and good luck."

But why was he so angry? I wondered. Unless it dawned on him that he did a stupid thing by letting the name of that man slip out. I was clumsy too, of course, though it hardly matters now. I could have hired a lawyer, I suppose, even then, but what for? Didn't this incident say enough? A young woman, married only a few months, goes out for a ride with a stranger, and they have a little accident because he stopped in the wrong place. But why did he stop, why did they go out, what did this strange man have to do with her anyway? All this did give me a bit of a jolt. And then that clerk: why did he get so scared? On account of a twisted fender? Not very likely. But then . . . Perhaps there were other things in that file which I should have tried to pry out of him.

Oh and finally: what could a young woman hope to achieve with her phony story? Attacked and robbed on the street, indeed. I thought it odd even then, and more so later on. But she stuck to her story, and a few days later even produced some sort of official paper which mentioned stolen pocketbooks, though as everyone knows, such papers could be easily gotten. But that's not even the point; what *is* noteworthy is that a similar thing, an adventure with robbers, did happen again. I will have more to say about it in due course.

Couldn't this easily become a hopeless morass? I was confronted with that question already then.

But I brushed it aside, and did so again and again. And this is what I don't understand, it has preyed on my mind on many a sleepless night since then. Why was I so lax? Was it lethargy, melancholy? What? Did my senses fail me? It did seem very strange that I should let something slip away, something I already had in my hand: to watch the little bird take wing, as if I was a sluggard, a man without mettle, without character.

But I could also be a tough customer, if need be, let's not forget that, either. If something starts gnawing at my inside, not even God himself can put a stop to it. I know myself. Life had just begun for me, was it to end so soon, in misery? I asked myself: Don't you like this woman? Don't you enjoy being with her? And hasn't your health improved, too? This last was the decisive argument, I think. After all, it's not a minor consideration for someone who is not well. And let's remember, I'd been feeling poorly for years; I couldn't enjoy life, nor food either, I grew quite weak. And then after my marriage everything came back. (In this respect the psychoanalyst may have been right.) My appetite returned, too, I felt like singing at every meal—and I hadn't even given it free rein yet. But after the incident at the police station, I no longer felt like holding it back. I walked into a fine restaurant and had myself such a feast, I was red in the face by the time I was through, but more from the eating than from the drinks. I guess at my age that's the way it is. And I had to pay a visit to another place as well, I just had to indulge myself . . . as a consolation. It wasn't like in the old days, of course, still, it was something.

That evening I said to my wife: "I went to the police station, my dearest." She just smiled. And I could have composed an epic about that smile, it expressed so much. I suddenly remembered how her little feet trembled when she saw me pick up the summons and leave. Oh, how she must have just sat there afterwards, numb with loneliness, maybe even self-contempt.

All that was expressed in that smile.

"So?" she responded gently. I looked at her and was overcome with pity. Here she was, a young married woman who waited all her life to become just that: married. And now that she was, she still did such crazy things. An irresponsible brat is what she was, who chased after her pleasures like a child after a butterfly. Her face was darkened by shadows, which were really furrows of contentment, of bliss.

"Naughty child . . ." I said, caressing her gently, brushing the hair from her forehead, and taking a good look at her face. It was the face of a pug-nosed rascal, impudent, and somehow also innocent-looking and appealing, as though she couldn't add up two and two, the poor dear. In reality, she was used to playing hide and seek; and when caught, she didn't give up, she played along slyly, like a kid.

"They couldn't locate the files," I said quietly.

You had to see her at this moment. She didn't let her relief show right away, lest she betray herself. She held in her joy, the way you'd hold back a wild colt. Still, she wasn't that clever. I wouldn't have believed her even if her expression stayed gloomy for half an hour. But as it was, she started singing, and before the half hour was up she was dancing. What's more, she began calling me Oncle Douc Douc and Monsieur Houine, which she did only on special occasions. I didn't want to be angry at her, so I cranked up my silver gramophone and with a smile asked her to dance with me. And we were quite polite and gracious with each other, I must say. I bowed, she squeezed my hand, as though we were only secretly engaged. And at that moment I think she liked me a little.

"Our friend, Annibale . . . does he own an automobile?" I asked her one day casually, seemingly with little interest, as though we had been talking about him just before. And as if I didn't know he had a car.

Naturally, I was still irked by the whole thing.

She put up her guard of course, got herself ready like a bird of prey, you could tell, though controlling herself all the same.

"I saw him just now, near the Etoile, driving a beautiful car."

"Annibale, Annibale," she mumbled to herself. But then she exclaimed with great interest (the most practical thing she could do under the circumstances):

"Ah, Annibale Ridolfi. You saw Ridolfi?"

"Yes, I did."

"In Paris?"

"Yes. We even said hello." All of which was untrue, of course, except for the fact that he was in Paris; that much I knew.

"But why didn't you stop him?" my wife asked. And she was ablaze by now. "Such a pleasant fellow, so entertaining, it would have been so nice to spend some time with him." In short, she started singing his praises, and all the while I was watching her face, curious to see just how far she will dare to go. Daredeviltry was in her blood, after all, impudence flowed in her veins. She was telling me in so many words that she didn't get scared, even if I did find out a thing or two.

"Yeah, I saw that shithead all right." And must have sounded like a raging bull. But all she could ask was:

"Feel like getting together with him?"

"No, I do not," I replied with all the forcefulness of a simple denial. And looked away.

Maybe if she had a child she would be different, I thought at times. But she wouldn't hear of a child.

Life, though, did have a way of taking my mind off this matter, and off my other private misfortunes as well. Things got tough, you see, what with the slump in business, the world-wide depression, which the shipping companies are always the first to feel. But I always managed to stay afloat, miraculously at times, it seemed, though always through tremendous effort. Once again I spent most of my time down in the Levant, and it happened that I wouldn't see my wife for months. One time I remember traveling sixty hours, via Constantinople, just to be with her a few days. And another time I brought myself to boarding an airplane in Port Said (flying was still a big deal in those days), because I was tormented by premonitions. I got restless and shaky in my work (I even fell ill on the plane; flying isn't for me). But I longed to see her, why deny it?

Actually, it did me a lot of good to spend a little time at home. After all that hustle and bustle, on both land and sea, it felt nice and quiet. With the blinds drawn, the sun shut out, it was as if peace had finally touched my heart. And she did furnish our place rather pleasantly, I must grant her that. (Why shouldn't I be grateful to her at least in these reminiscences? So I will note that

those brief periods were nice enough.) And she herself was kind
and quite beautiful. To come home, therefore, was the greatest joy
imaginable. Was it any wonder, then, that while away at sea, I
thought not of Signor Ridolfi but of her—not of dubious affairs
but of her eyes that lit up the starless nights for me. And then
there were the memories of what I left behind. Sometimes I
smiled at night when I thought of her powder puffs and talcum, of
how awkward a woman really looks when she's getting dressed,
what with her corset showing, her bodice sagging . . . how very
sloppy all that is and still how enchanting. I kept thinking of one
scene in particular.

She shook me out of my sleep. I must have been having night-
mares, she said, because I was moaning. And she suggested we go
out and have a night on the town—she also felt kind of closed-in.

"It's so stuffy in here, I can hardly breathe," she said, and
leaning closer she added: "I'll be very pretty, you'll see."

She was out of bed already, and bubbling over as usual.

"How about going to a very fancy restaurant?" It was early in
the morning.

"At least you won't spend your money on others."

"I won't?"

"Only joking," she said somewhat absently. But her eyes were
burning. Something had to fuel all that excitement.

And she was at it already, pulling things out of her wardrobe. I
had no idea she had so much stuff: furs and silks and lacy things
with little velvet roses, all of it ready to take off and fly. It was a
strange night. Everything around us lay dormant, and we were
getting ready to go out, in the dead of night, to have supper. There
she sat in front of her vanity, dolling herself up shamelessly, like a
putain. We even laughed about that. Considering I'd just had a
nightmare, I was in a pretty good mood. She pulled down her
lashes and painted them black, then gray, then purple.

"To make you want me more," she said.

Next to her mirror was a pair of shoes which were so tiny they
wouldn't fit a fawn, and an equally tiny pair of gloves, a handkerchief, a scarf, a pin, all thrown together in glorious disarray. What
was her secret? I wondered. Yes, what *is* their secret?

The room was filled with all the scents one keeps remembering
when alone: the smell of her hair, her perfume, and all those

powders: rice powder, talcum, and the kind you blow into gloves.
. . . I just stood there in my dress shirt and watched . . . watched
the whole colorful spectacle.

Should I then have bothered to figure out how much all these
frills: the brushes, the lotions, the fineries were costing me?
Should I deprive her of these little pleasures? I wouldn't do it, by
God, come what may. She was still a young woman, she was
entitled to this much, and besides, seeing her in them gave me
pleasure—I even enjoyed the thought that while I broke my back
on those bloody boats, all my labors, all my sweat were turned
(dear God) into laces and tulles.

The thing was that I did have a little nest egg put away at that
time, but I knew that using it up would spell disaster; the slide
downward would be inevitable. And what then? I'd be at anyone's
mercy, would have to take any job that came along, provided there
were any to be had. The economic situation kept getting worse;
and in the shipping business things were downright catastrophic.
For instance, this is what happened to me in Southampton one
day. I was sitting in a restaurant, a mediocre one, at that, and I
noticed that the waiter was staring at me. I suddenly let out a cry:
"What on earth are you doing here?" "What am I doing here?
Wake up, man, don't you know what's going on out there?" Of
course I knew, I heard enough about it. Skippers with fine reputa-
tions signing up in British ports as ordinary seamen. Expert
engineers happy to be taken on as stokers. . . . I heard all about it,
but who believed it? Now, however, I saw it with my own eyes: an
officer with excellent credentials working as a waiter in a restaurant. This scared me.

So I was soon on my way to the Levant again; the thought of
something like this happening to me was incentive enough. But I
went there for nothing. Purses were sealed tight, as were people's
hearts. As is my wont, I made them irresistible offers—to ship
Bohemian glass, fine textiles, porcelain, and who knows what else,
for nothing, for a song, but even so there were no takers.

"Wet your money with a little spit and stuff it in your pocket,"
advised a shipowner, a very shrewd old woman, from Sebenico. I
was shocked; I never heard her talk like this. She weathered every
storm until now, nothing could faze her, she was shrewd, persis-
tent, insidious. If she wasn't let in through the door, she'd climb in

through the window. We were like small-time grocers, we dealt in tiny quantities of goods and chartered our boats when business was bad. Or we'd buy a rusty old ship, run it to the ground, and try to sell it at a tiny profit. We'd sit up nights, she smoking a pipe, I puffing on a cigar, trying to come up with a workable idea.

But now there was nothing. I went home. As it was, my wife had been pestering me for some time to quit those tar-paper boxes (that's how she referred to the ships I'd commanded then), and was after me to try to get a better position somewhere (she obviously would have liked her husband to be a more respectable sea captain). So I wrote to an old friend of mine in London, a Greek shipowner named Alexander Kodor, who also knew how to pinch pennies, though when I met him his star had already risen—he became a very wealthy man. The second time I met him, in Italy, he was swelling with pride as he embraced me. "I am the king of the seas," he said and gave me a very significant look.

He exaggerated, of course; he was no king of the seas, only the principal shareholder of a maritime insurance company. Which is enough if you also happen to be a speculator and wheeler-dealer of the first order, which he was. He could easily help me, in other words, if he wanted to. And he did help, this time he really did, he spared no effort. Later that year I became the captain of a lovely little boat, a truly wonderful vessel . . . oh she was dainty and delicate like a young miss—a birthday cake if I ever saw one. Not a scratch on it anywhere, though it had been in service for eight years. Five thousand tons but very fast and geared for Mediterranean travel. Daphne was her name, and they made good use of her, I must say. After the war an international group took it over, who were small on capital but big on ideas. They fitted it out as a kind of excursion boat for inexpensive runs between Europe and the Near East. Such cruises were a novelty then, though the need was there, for never was there such a longing to visit the Holy Land as in those postwar years. And even people of modest means began to feel like traveling. So the company's gamble paid off. They refurbished the boat in a hurry, at the height of the depression (before it was used to freight tropical fruit and wine), and sparing no expense, they advertised heavily. We got all kinds of people—devout pilgrims, pleasure-seekers, tourists from America, in short, an interesting and mixed crowd, and my cargo also consisted of a better grade of goods (we still carried some, the Daphne wasn't exclusively a passenger ship). And as far as the route was concerned, I could pilot a boat in those waters in my sleep, that's how well I knew the region—the sea, the coast, the offshore conditions, etc. Everything, then, was fine, the pay decent—need I say more? I could find nothing wrong with the arrangements, really, still I felt pretty miserable. Indeed, I thought my luck had run out when I had to switch from heavy freighters to this powder puff. There were signs of trouble on the Daphne's first voyage, but I discounted them. The second trip, however, was calamitous. One night, less than a hundred miles off Alexandria, fire broke out in the ship's interior.

But let me describe the incident in a little more detail, partially to unburden myself. For as far as I am concerned, this is still unfinished business and will remain that, I fear, to the end of my days. I feel the accident also explains a lot of things. After it I was like a man who lost his footing. But let's not rush ahead.

I will start by saying that I've always been a sound sleeper and what's rather unusual, I rarely dream. (As a matter of fact, I didn't quite know what to say to that certain psychoanalyst. Do I dream? No, I don't.) However, on this new boat I couldn't sleep very well, was restless—I worried too much about the boat, I think. At the same time I was also absent-minded, though it's all the same now. Suffice it to say that that night I sweated a lot and felt a kind of pressure on my chest. I may have been asleep, for all I know, but didn't feel good about it. I was glad when I was awakened. For a moment I thought it was my turn on the bridge. I always liked night duty, especially when it was pitch dark and you did nothing but work, steadily like a machine, and had nothing else on your mind.

At any rate, one of my officers knocked on my door and reported:

"Captain, we are on fire."

"What are you saying?"

But he didn't have to repeat it. I knew right away what was up, at such moments I always do. It's scary how fast I can act in a crisis.

"Let her heat up, let her sweat," I gave the order quickly. I knew from experience that cotton and wool and other such material will turn white-hot, like charcoal, before starting to burn, they absorb their own heat. If we can only trap that heat, we've gained precious time.

"And don't wake up the men if you can help it," I called after him, and also reached for my robe—it was a cold night.

Try as I might, I don't think I could really describe that night. The little motor pump was hissing away, otherwise there was eerie silence; only occasional footfalls could be heard on deck. And there was this great brightness, as if all the lights had been turned on for some non-existent guests. For ghosts.

Slowly, quite peacefully, the bow of the boat began to smoke; it gently curled through the cracks at first, then rose swiftly, as we were still going full steam.

It wasn't the first time I found myself in such a fix; it happened twice before, in fact. Once, on a short run between China and Japan—the boat was a Dutch three-master, as I recall—we ran aground. The vessel was loaded with rice. For two days straight we kept dumping the world's finest rice into the ocean, still we couldn't break loose, though after a time we were so light, we nearly tipped over—we were hit broadside, to boot. . . . I had contended with fire too, just outside Trieste. But we managed to steam into harbor in the nick of time. It was so hot on board, our bones were about to melt. In short, I'd been in sticky situations before and sweated out each one, but nothing like this night.

I was helpless, especially at first—that was the main problem. As though my ill fortune had made me lose my senses, preventing me from thinking straight. I just didn't know what to do. Went up on the bridge, raced down to the fire, issued the most contradictory orders. Told them, for instance, to let out the throttle, increase speed, and immediately thereafter demanded to know why they hadn't flooded the hold with steam. I ranted and raved, though I knew full well, as does everyone, that if I wanted to pick up speed, I needed engines operating at full blast. Still, I was half-insane with rage and about to attack the engineer. My first officer just stood there, staring.

And that irritated me, too, his look did. So I vented my anger on him as well, blaming him, absurdly, for everything.

Luckily, we had no trouble with the passengers, not with those in steerage, that is (we had plenty of them aboard, we were that kind of ship). With their sorry belongings, they proceeded to the upper decks, pale and frightened, like so many prisoners, but in perfect order and without a murmur. Yes, *they* could do it. I must say that this orderliness—the solemn composure of the poor—moved me. They've grown accustomed to misery, and danger, the things other people consider indignities not meant for them. I do like the poor so much better . . . But let's not get into that just now.

I had some of the clogged-up vents cleared, in the hope that something would flare up and we could locate the source of the fire. But all we got was more billowing smoke, it assailed us like some dark beast. You couldn't see a thing: below deck all the lights went out, and even lanterns were useless. But my men grimly stood their ground, exerting themselves to the breaking point. Only when overcome by the smoke did they wheeze and cough and grope for fresh air. Out in the open things were dripping wet; down below the fire raged on.

All I wanted to do was quickly get to the storage area and close off the entrance. Whatever lay in the way had to be tossed overboard. I always know exactly what kind of cargo I am carrying, even its shape, its size, the way it's placed in the hold, since my main concern is keeping the proper balance and making sure nothing slides or tilts—that's why I never skimp on rope and packing material. . . . So I did make myself useful, after all. What is more, my head began to clear up by then. What else? Soon, more steam than smoke was coming from below, and that, too, was something to be cheerful about.

But by then some of the first-class passengers began to appear.

"What is it, captain, what happened? Why is it so hot?" Such questions they put to me. As if they'd gone batty and couldn't see what was happening.

"There is a fire, damn it," someone in the foredeck yelled, and even gave a jerk on the bell.

By then I was myself again: I rounded up these gentlemen and hustled them into the first-class lounge. Even turned on the gramophone for them, let them enjoy themselves. And I ordered a few sailors to stand at the door and not allow anyone to leave that room.

I had a schoolmate at the Academy, a boy from Friesland by the name of Ebertsman-Leiningen, who once invited me to his house for winter recess. He'd checked with his parents first, but curiously enough, when we arrived no one was there except the gardener. The master and missus had gone off to the Riviera, we were told.

My friend was furious. "But I told them I'd be bringing a friend," he said indignantly. "But wait . . ." and there was a mischievous glint in his eyes.

Sure enough, when it got dark he broke open the larder. Of course I helped him too, gladly. We set a splendid table; the damast tablecloth gleamed like a field of ice under the bright chandelier. And our raid yielded the very best: beautiful pieces of ham, mouth-watering sausages—we created regular still-lives with the red and brown meats. Later, though, things soured. For one thing, we broke open a cupboard—my friend wanted to get his hand on some money, too. And then, another unpleasant memory: we were trying to distill brandy on the kitchen table when a young girl walked in, a maid apparently . . . When it was all over, she started crying, and kept it up, there was no consoling her.

Adolescents are awful creatures. The beast in them has not yet been tamed. We didn't make much of the incident with the girl, though the next morning we couldn't look each other in the face, my friend and I. He wrote a brief note to his mother, thanking her for their hospitality, put it on her desk, and we left.

But I couldn't get the crying girl out of my mind. For a long time afterwards I kept hearing her sobs, even her quickening heartbeat, as if she was secretly taking me to task, making me pay.

And now this boat.

Again I felt like a wastrel, a scapegrace, who's got corruption in his blood, who is sure to come to a bad end.

And then the tormenting questions, the self-reproaches. How could I let this happen? How will it all end? Why was I entrusted with this beauty. . . ? Because it *was* a splendid boat. And so well maintained. We were encouraged to be on the lookout even for minor defects. At home port the inspector came around regularly, and we had to report the slightest damage, even scratches on the woodwork. And now all that painted and varnished woodwork was sizzling, the whole goddamn handcrafted frame.

Well, Kodor, you picked out a winner, I said to myself. (He was the one who recommended me to the post. Why on earth did he do it?) The boat began to smell like burning wooden play dishes, freshly painted toys, Christmas boxes—a sickeningly sweetish smell, it almost made me sick. To this day I get nauseous when I see such wooden dishes. But that's the way we old-timers are; we get very attached to the boat we serve on. Keeping things intact somehow means more to us. A broken cup, a lost key causes us grief, let alone something as big as this. Ah, it's a terrible heartache, enough to drive you mad.

"And the passengers' lives meant nothing to you?" someone asked me after the accident. Sure they did. Even my life is worth *something*. So at half past three I decided to give the distress signal. But let's face it, this was a mistake, too. I did it late, much too late. What was this with me: just a lapse, a sudden paralysis, temporary insanity? God only knows. It must have been around one thirty when my navigator first came over and saluting me stiffly, asked:

"Hadn't we better signal for help?" Just at that moment I was staring at the barometer and then at the sky.

"Let's wait; I have a feeling it's going to rain."

"If we delay, the entire deck is going to burn through."

"It will not. In any case, it's the captain of the ship who must take the responsibility, not the officers. In case you didn't know."

He withdrew.

But half hour later he came up to me again.

"Do I have your permission?"

"No."

I have some explaining to do. Again. Where do I start? For one thing, I was always taught to be ambitious and self-reliant, which gave rise to such an inflated sense of responsibility, such vanity . . . It was madness, I know. The man was right. And still. There's always that urge to prove you can do it, on your own, without help. Just then we were getting close to the seat of the fire. I was there, I saw it—deep inside, a gentle little flame, a mere flicker, hardly more than the light of a candle. Could that be all?

Well, God be praised, I said to myself, like a man obsessed.

The sky was overcast, there was a sluggish breeze, the barometer kept falling, and I felt like saying, hold on, hold on, it'll soon rain, very soon, in a few minutes, I'd stake my life on it. And I left it at that, I wouldn't budge.

There *is* something strange about me in this respect. I can never really believe in danger, that something can be final, fatal.

So there we were; at 2:30 p.m. the upper deck did give way, and we began burning in earnest. Imagine our little ship, if you will, as it kept burning and still pushing ahead in the pitch-black night. And the engine still working, doggedly, faithfully, like the heart of a dying man, holding out to the bitter end. Ah, what a splendid little engine it was, what a fine boat. . . . I thought I should cry or try saving it with my bare hand, or plunge into the flames and howl and rave until it's over.

"Now he can tap away," I heard the first officer say to someone, after I finally relented and relayed a series of distress signals, and gave orders to sound the alarm.

He wasn't a disrespectful chap, my officer, but he was tired— the poor man staggered about like a drunkard. I myself was hardly conscious of fatigue, though God knows, I must have been tired, too—as tired as if I had caroused for three days nonstop. But as I say, I didn't feel it, only my eyes burned and my throat filled up with bitter smoke. I drank glass after glass of lemon squash in my cabin where I escaped, to do some desperate figuring. According to my calculations, if we held out for four more hours, or even three, I could sail into a harbor safely, as I had into Trieste years ago, aboard the Guidetta.

We are sixty miles off the Alexandria coast, I kept fretting, there have to be boats around. But no, there was nothing. Just before it got dark, we did spot a Czech steamer heading in the same direction we were, but then we lost her. . . . There we were, close to the desolate coast, with no island, no rescue station, nothing to pin our hopes on.

At that moment I swore on the Virgin Mary that I would never again take charge of a fancy ship like this (provided we come out of it alive). It just wasn't for me. I'll go back to my old ships, my old routes—to hell with what my wife will say.

Oh, how I hated her then . . .

At 3:00 a.m. a morbid-looking Spanish passenger, a certain Don Pepe, shot himself in his cabin. Luckily, no one besides me found out. His younger brother, Don Julio, a freeloader, if there ever was one, came over and asked me to support his claim that as next of kin he was entitled to all his brother's worldly possessions. Sure, I said; why not?

And that's when treacherous gusts began to rock the boat. I was desperate again. Should I stop the engines? I knew full well that only speed could save us. I walked into the lounge and told the passengers to start boarding the lifeboats. I didn't get very far. They were ready to tear me to pieces.

"What kind of ship is this? What kind of captain?" I heard from all sides. "Why didn't you radio for help earlier?" a hulking, wild-eyed young man demanded. Clutching a pale-faced wisp of a girl under his arm like a pitiful bundle, he came menacingly close. "We can all croak for all you care," he barked, his lips quivering with rage.

I had no choice; I took out my pistol.

And immediately had second thoughts. They quieted down all right, but remained hostile, ready to pounce. I took advantage of the tension, and for once seized the right psychological moment. I threw away the pistol and addressed the crowd:

"Listen, everyone: A trap door just cut my arm, I am covered with blood. My jacket burned through and with it pieces of my flesh. So you can see, I am doing my best. But you must help, too. If you go haywire, you put *me* in a foul mood, and that won't do you any good, believe me. Without me you don't have a ghost of a chance. But if you stick by me, I will save you even if it kills me. . . . Look at me, people: Do I look like the kind of man who doesn't keep his word?" And more of the same. I am too embarrassed to repeat all of it, it was such rubbish. But the effect was stunning. The mood changed; it swung to the other extreme. People began pleading, imploring; someone picked up the revolver I flung away, and the way he handed it back, I felt he was offering up his heart. After a while this, too, became insufferable.

Some Armenian pilgrims began to torment me with their love; they caressed my coat, and droned on and on, obsequiously but unintelligibly. They spoke very little French; five of them tried putting together one decent sentence but couldn't—it was horrible. And just then their priest held his cross over me and amidst much wailing and moaning held an impromptu mass. The resulting commotion got to be too much; so as not to make a further spectacle of myself, and fools of them, I got up and left. But a young English girl threw herself at my feet and wouldn't let me go through the door.

"I adore you, can't you see?" she cried, and smiled at me with a strange, seductive smile. She then hugged me and tried to clasp my neck. She was a beautiful girl, actually, but right now she was too busy shrieking: "Don't go away, pleeease . . ." And then: "I had my eyes on you the whole way, you didn't notice. . . ? It's all right, it's all right, I can say it," she explained to everyone around. "He is my true love, my ideal." Her mind apparently became unhinged in the crisis. Her parents, a tiny old couple with idiotic smiles of their own, just stood there, seemingly in total sympathy with their raving daughter, though their eyes were imploring me to save their child, for God's sake.

After a time I was able to extricate myself from her embrace. I caressed her hair and—inappropriately enough—began to think how nice it would be to make love to this girl. In no time a fever of desire coursed through my veins . . .

There is madness in all of us, I concluded, and its source is deeper down than we care to reach.

There wasn't much left for me to do. I had the ship's foremast sawn off, lest that, too, come crashing down, and issued a few more orders in anticipation of a final catastrophe. The engine began emitting furious hissing sounds. Ominous grinding noises were coming from the direction of the propeller. And what did I do? I had a sailor arrested for trying to jump ship. I gave one more command, told them to release the steam, to avoid an explosion, after which I headed for my cabin. Once inside, I bolted the door. I was all set to do what that Don Pepe fellow had done just before: move on to the next location, as it were. I was just waiting for the lights to go out. Responsibility be hanged—let them manage as best they can. The first officer was a capable enough man.

I can't even say I was depressed. All I kept mumbling to myself was: enough. Enough! You blew it, you are worthless, so why go on? Not that chucking everything is so commendable—ach, it's awful, despicable, today the mere thought of it makes me shudder with horror and shame. But then I was so utterly broken in spirit, I longed for death, thirsted for it.

Strangely enough, I didn't think of my wife, and even if I had, it wouldn't have been enough to stop me. In any case, I decided she no longer loved me, and therefore dismissed all hope, turned away from a life gone awry. I knew strange things were beginning to happen back home, but I no longer cared to investigate. I was much too tired.

I had to stuff cotton in my ears because the noises from outside—the stamping and crashing and screeching—were becoming fearsome, apocalyptic. All I wanted at the moment was some peace and quiet, a little time to sort things out. But what? Everything I believed in—life, ambition and the rest—seemed like so much foolishness and vanity. The scales fell off my eyes, yes. What was the good of all the drudgery and pain? I may just as well have spent my years whistling on streetcorners—it would have amounted to the same thing. No, I was not sorry to leave anything behind.

But I did wash up, I washed my head and neck in cold water. Why did I do that? Not to clean up for the hereafter, I assure you. I once saw an old man suffering excruciatingly, his eyes ablaze with pain. He was ready to end it all and was just waiting for his deathly sick boy to expire in the next room. But even that boy, in the final minutes of his life, asked for—of all things—two soft-boiled eggs. Why? Because he was hungry. And that's just the point: life goes on till the last breath . . .

My washing up, then, ought to be seen in this light.

In the meantime, there were rumblings outside, followed by loud cries; I didn't even bother to look.

A sailor knows more about chance than anyone else; his whole life, after all, consists of nothing but chance. First I thought we were in for a big storm, and that was actually one of the reasons I locked myself in my cabin. I figured the coming storm would seal our fate—we would all perish.

All the signs were there: strong gusts, a rough sea—it seemed as if some awful underwater demon was churning up the sea. Northeast of us I saw lightning, even rain, but where we were, not a drop. The wind blew the clouds our way but then drove them on; they passed rapidly overhead. And though the barometer kept falling, the chances for rain, precisely because of the wind's velocity, seemed nil. If anything, it seemed to be clearing up, though I was no longer interested. I even drew the curtain over the porthole.

And as I sat there, immersed in thought and pipe smoke, a kind of blessed tranquility came over me, the like of which I had never before experienced. It had to be serenity of a celestial sort, for all my bitterness vanished, I felt light, and my thoughts, too, seemed weightless, evanescent . . .

Is this what death is like? I wondered. But just then I sensed a change, something must have happened out there. But what? It got awfully quiet; I began to listen.

The wind . . . has it stopped? I jumped up, but somebody was already knocking on my door.

"I felt a drop," he said jauntily, and moved on. "Sure looks like rain," said another. I was so shaken by that word, so devastated, I froze. Ah, those fine boys. I had abandoned them, let them down most shamelessly, but they wouldn't dream of doing the same. All night long I'd been a frantic beast, still, they didn't forget me. But that's the way they are. A little blessing from the sky and they think all their troubles are gone.

The wind changed direction, the storm grew more intense; it felt almost like a hurricane. And moments later: a thunderclap and then a downpour—we were in the eye of a life-saving electrical storm. While lightning flashed all around us, our boat began hissing and steaming.

By then, naturally, I was up on deck somewhere, cautious like a convalescent, though by no means happy. Still cold, I wrapped my coat tightly around me. It felt good to shiver, though to be alive did not. And oh yes: I saw the little miss again, if only for an instant. She looked fine to me, quite normal, and not one bit embarrassed.

"Oh Captain," she cooed, and blushed just a little as she fixed her tear-stained eyes on me. Caressing her face ever so gently, I took another good look—she *was* beautiful.

A day and a half later, we limped into Alexandria.

"Fire and water are bad masters," my officer said the following day, somewhat meekly, as if trying to defuse something in me.

"And we're not even liable for damages," I quipped as we

looked over our still steaming boat. We kept dousing the old girl generously, inside she was still hot as hell.

It was around this time that my wife fell in love with one Paul de Grévy, a man of noble birth, related to counts supposedly, a descendant of the Latour de Pin clan, a "historical" family. The young man's friends called him Dedin, and now in company that's how my wife began to call him.

That she adored him I knew from the start. For one thing her whole being seemed thoroughly worked over; she was soft now, receptive, eager. She didn't look at him all that much, but when she did, her look conveyed blissful fellow feeling, transcendent loyalty. When she introduced him to me, she said:

"This is my *dearest* friend . . . after you, of course." Why did she have to add that? Better yet, why did she have to be so honest?

I was on to her, naturally. Her openness was meant to allay my fears. If she tells me what's in her heart, I can't possibly think of the worst. But I did. She could say what she liked, a woman in love has a certain glow, a halo almost—and she had it.

This wasn't anything like the silly Ridolfi affair, oh this was far more serious. This time she was in love. Very well, I decided, we'll keep an unobtrusive eye on them, and just bide our time. For the young man didn't seem to be in love, not just yet.

With his sporty mustache and casual airs, he looked like a self-assured chap. His mouth had a sweet and sensuous curve, but his face also expressed boredom—this man was not at all anxious to please. And his attire complemented that look: a sloppy but expensive jacket, extremely baggy trousers, a tiny, silly-looking hat, and what I took to be mountain-climbing boots—I swear he looked like he was going off on a hunt. And his arms flopped about, as though enervated by his own boredom.

Must be his aristocratic origin, I thought. That sort of thing does count for something.

Still, there was a glint in his eyes, an impudent glow, everytime he saw me. As though he were letting me know:

Your face may launch ships, but in my eyes you are still an ox.

Come to think of it, he called me a sea dog the first time he saw me. "You old sea dog," he said. To which I replied:

"I am no more a sea dog, sir, than you a landlocked rat." Or

some such thing. And gave him a friendly smile. I smiled at him
constantly after that, curious to see how he'd respond. Will he
notice that I detest him? (If only because he insisted on trying out
his maritime expressions on me.) He did know something about
ships and sailing, hence his insufferable expressions. And oh yes:
when I first met him, I immediately thought of Don Julio carrying
off his dead brother's things that dreadful night on the Daphne.
He definitely reminded me of that Spaniard, not only his off-hand
dignity but also his mustache that looked as if he waxed it with
honey—that's how soft and shiny it was. With red, fleshy lips to
match.

I thought of asking my wife when we were alone:

"What does this man do for a living?"

"Oh, he is a writer."

"A writer?"

"He also has a rich uncle," she said demurely.

"A parasite, in other words." I never did like beating around the
bush.

She got very frightened. A sight to behold.

"You mean you don't like him?" she purred. "Not at all? Not
even a little?" This was one of those rare moments when I truly
detested her. For being so dense. What was there to like, for God's
sake? And for her to beg so? . . . What was I, a kindly old uncle
who was going to protect her lovers? What did she want, some
friendly advice, a monthly allowance perhaps?

"Please, please, Jacques," she pleaded, "do love him, I beg of
you; he is so very nice to me." This was strange, passing strange.
Until then we rarely talked about things like marital fidelity; I just
don't care to discuss such topics. But now I asked her:

"You'd have me love your boyfriend, Lizzy?" And burst out
laughing. My wife, on the other hand, blushed.

"How can you be so vulgar, Jacques" she said indignantly,
contemptuously. "He is not my boyfriend, he is not, how will I
make you understand?" She was up in arms, a regular rebel; she
even hit the table with her fist. "He is not a boyfriend, all right?
He is a dear old friend whom I've known a long time and whom I
now met quite by accident. You, Jacques, must be completely out of
your mind."

I am out of my mind—that's rich.

"You can't decieve my eyes," I shot back, and quickly thought of a comparison. "Why, you are like a hen about to hatch an egg." I laughed again and just kept on laughing.

"Look at you, you're all hot and bothered . . . Do you know what I once saw in a village? A farmer's wife who didn't want her hens to hatch their eggs simply dunked them in a bucket of cold water. That's what I'd like to do with you right now."

She gave me a dumbfounded look. "You are comparing me to a hen?"

"Yes, I am. For now only to a hen, and you had better appreciate that."

"For now?"

"Yes, for now."

"Are you threatening me?"

"You've guessed it." And with that I got up and went into the other room. I was gasping for air, I noticed.

But she came after me and touching my arm with her finger, said:

"How you've changed . . . How nasty you've become." That's all she said and left the room.

Have I really become nasty? Could be. Irritable? Entirely possible. I was even willing to concede that my wife was innocent. (She did have such an innocent and offended air about her.) It was all in my mind, right? Women are such romantics—he was just an admirer. But what did that make me?

Actually, she had no idea what's been going on. She didn't read about my misfortune on the high seas, she missed it, and by the time people showed her the newspapers, it was all over, everyone was fine, nothing more to worry about.

"You had a fire?" she squealed when she found out. "Oh no! Was it dangerous?" Like that she started carrying on. What was I going to say? Start in, like her? Pant and hang out my tongue and show how my insides were ready to come out?

I did nothing of the sort. Even her voice annoyed me.

"Yes, I had a fire." And that was it. I really didn't need anyone to sympathize with me, or relive my troubles, which is impossible anyway. I don't expect any appreciation, either, it means nothing to me. Whatever happened happened, case closed.

I was somewhat agitated, I said before. She did have a way of stirring me up. And when in company, I felt even more of a stranger. What they found amusing, I found pointless; even their calm irritated me. I almost attacked a waiter once because he wasn't polite enough with my wife. And had a run-in with an old woman who . . . But what's the use? The truth is a sailor always feels edgy and offended on land. On sea I am somebody, if only a seaman. Here I am nothing, I turn into nothing. And contend with the filth and smut of the big city. It can be dirty aboard a ship also, but there I can have the crew clean up, can have their souls scrubbed down, if need be, until everything sparkles in the bright sun. Here what am I going to scrub down, the air? Might as well: it's pretty dirty. And people look pallid and sickly in the city, as if shut up in old mildewy attics, especially on winter mornings when they are still sleepy, and wheeze and hawk on crowded streetcars.

I am saying all this to demonstrate once again that for men like us it's no good being out of our element. We lose our aim, we stagnate, I especially, after what I've been through. Buried deep inside an endless, horrible night, unable to break loose. I often felt I was still on that lovely, graceful boat as it kept plowing the waves, all ablaze, its engines rattling and whining, struggling as if alive, refusing to yield. That whole night was like a huge void, a vast, dark expanse, and in that vastness, the flaming ship was . . . I don't know how else to say this . . . my own living soul. For a long time I'd wake up in the middle of the night, screaming, drenched.

And all my wife could say even then is: "What's wrong? What's wrong?" And sit up in her bed and fret. But I'd say nothing to her; I would rather talk to myself. On the street or in a train, I would launch into endless monologues.

Here is a sample: She may be lovesick but I am not.

Or: I won't ever set foot on land again. If it means anything to you, follow me, come aboard my ship, for that's where I belong. Other times I said just the opposite: I'll never go out to sea again; it's a good life but no longer for me. In short, I, too, experienced that wretched state when you no longer know what to think and the opposite seems just as reasonable. . . . I was almost sorry I didn't shoot myself that night.

Mind you, I was still sound as a bell, nothing was wrong with me, as of yet. All the same, I was like a watch that kept perfect

·time but with a funny, hollow tick, as if something had already snapped inside.

But it so happened that Monsieur Dedin, his mere existence, gave me strength to go on, if only because I began to take him seriously now, and noted other things as well, which I will relate presently.

One day we were sitting in the Café de Saint Luc, which was owned by an old friend of mine, a sea captain from Normandy. And of course Dedin was with us, too, which was now the case almost all the time. Don't ask me how I could stand it. Or how *he* could do it.

When does this writer write? I often wondered. I was inclined to believe he did absolutely nothing, let alone write. Maybe he carried his rich uncle's chamber pot around. And then put on his little hunter's hat and headed for a wild night on the town. The man, as you can see, irritated me to no end.

Nevertheless, I told my wife one day:

"That Dedin seems like a decent fellow."

Well, she lit up like a lightbulb.

"You see, you see; I told you." And she beamed.

That's how far this thing has gone, that's how open she was about it, damn it.

Why, then, did I make that appreciative remark? For two reasons: First of all, I was pleasantly surprised. He didn't steal, though he had the opportunity. He returned my wallet which I left on a table in a bistro; he didn't pocket it but brought it back. A promising beginning, surely.

The other reason was that I could no longer put up with my wife's suffering demeanor. Ever since that time when I was a little rough on her, she'd been giving me dirty looks. As though I'd killed her papa. But now that we made up, she showed no mercy. We had to be together all the time. I called him a decent fellow, didn't I? She tried so hard to bring us closer, to match us up. This is how a typical conversation was conducted:

She'd be walking in the middle, between Dedin and me, and turn from side to side as she talked.

"Dedin says you can get finer cigars than these." "My husband says it's time we went to a different cinema." Like that. Dedin would sometimes send me messages, too, but I never sent him any.

All I kept thinking about was how to get rid of this guy. For no matter how I looked at it, this arrangement was not very good. Even under the best of circumstances, he'd remain the ideal friend who brought her books and things, and kept feeding her stories about how she could make a pretty good movie actress. (With this sort of claptrap, I noticed, every woman can be swept off her feet, even the very best.) He'd still be the cultivator of her soul, and I, the uncouth husband, the breadwinner, the workhorse.

The truth is I was dimwitted enough to fill the role.

At my friend's place, on the other hand, I felt more comfortable. He was a man after my own heart. To him I didn't have to explain what it was like to have things like "What kind of captain are you? Where is your sense of duty?" thrown at your face.

"Tell me the truth," my friend now said to me, "do you really like the blasted sea all that much? (And the question, needless to say, could not have come at a better time.)

"I myself love it," he went on with a grin, "always have, especially from afar. Come on, man, be honest: aren't you glad when you leave those rotten tubs, those floating prisons, when your foot hits dry land? Especially after that accident of yours?"

"God only knows," I sighed.

But he persisted: "Can you eat anything this good on a boat?" (He was serving us some chewy meat cooked with a kind of polenta, a regional specialty, apparently, prepared in my honor, expected to be praised.)

"But let's chat about something good . . . It just occurred to me: Why don't you and me open a nice little inn. . . ? What do you say? It's no life being away at sea all the time?"

"You know, you are on to something," I said. "But that inn . . . it better be classy. My wife likes only the very best. . . ." I glanced at my wife. My friend laughed. But she calmly continued her needlework, as though she didn't hear a word I said. The little woman was embroidering a pair of slippers, with very fine, brightly colored threads.

"Well?" I inquired, pressing the point, "what would you two say if I decided to stay home?" But Monsieur Dedin didn't budge either; he kept smoking his cigarette furiously, immersing himself in a magazine.

"Good meat," I said. And it was, its texture anyway—nice and firm. And I always liked to chew my food properly, I had damn good teeth.

"And the sauce?"

"That's good, too."

"We'll have to make this in our new hotel," he said.

"Oh yes, definitely." And to myself I thought: Damn that woman. What's with the embroidering all of a sudden? She never used to embroider. And the silence between us, this incredible silence. As if she were saying: Go on, talk to your friend, talk all you like.

I don't know if others are familiar with the feeling: the intimacy of those long silences between lovers. Picture it, if you will: she peacefully stitching away, he turning the pages of his magazine, but with an air of confidence that said: I know you love me and you know that I love you, and that's all the two of us need to know. Just to illustrate how this silence affected me: Years and years later, in South America I believe it was, I thought about that evening once and promptly flew into a rage. Even then I did, I saw red even then. My wife appeared before my mind's eye just as she stopped sewing for a minute. Like someone emerging from a dream, she lifted her pretty head, to cast a glance at her friend, not even at his face, only at his checkered jacket, his hand, even that was enough. And as if drawing strength from that mere glance, she bit off the end of the thread and continued working.

This scene, as I say, had such a powerful hold over me, I was ready to explode even years later. But that's the way I often am. Implacable. And then not even rivers of spilled blood can appease me. But let's go on; maybe this book will vindicate me.

"Who are you making those charming slippers for?" I asked her finally, when I thought I could no longer contain myself. Ah, but these two would not admit a stranger into their own little world. "For Monsieur Lagrange," my wife said. "A surprise." Just like that. Case dismissed. (Madame Lagrange, by the way, was a friend of hers.)

"You know something," I turned to my friend from Normandy, "we will buy ourselves a little hotel and fill it with little mam-

'selles." I just had to say something. Actually, I wanted to use another word, but they all knew what I meant. In fact, my wife was already gathering up her slippers—she got offended.

"Let's go home," she said abruptly. "I don't feel well."

Let's go then. By all means.

She did look rather pale. We left the café and Dedin of course came with us, he sat in the cab and said he'll see us home. Ah, the faithful friend . . . I was trembling already. And at the door, as though I didn't even exist, he took his time saying good-bye, making it sound like a confession. He clasped her hand, gazed intently at her. And all that before my very eyes. But then I had a fiendish thought.

"You will go to bed, won't you?" he asked very solicitously. Asked *her.* Asked *my* wife. "Promise me you'll go to bed right away." This was altogether too much, this tender loving care was too much, when I happened to be right there. I thought I'd give the young man a little scare.

"Why don't you come up, too, for a drink?" For a moment I had this mad idea that as soon as we got upstairs, I'd seize him, drag him to the window and push him out. We lived on the sixth floor and had a nice view of the park, and the apartment itself was roomy and almost completely empty.

What the hell makes these two so dreamy? I wondered. They must be over it by now; they had this whole place to themselves, they could do whatever they wished. That this was no casual friendship I could no longer doubt. That interlude in the café convinced me, though there were other signs as well. For example, my wife said to him: "Give me a match, will you?"

Just like that. Real intimate. But how does one preserve such evidence? How does one prove after the fact that it was no mistake, this is precisely what happened? Sooner or later you forget yourself. Night comes and you forget. For the words, ah, the words, disappear.

Once we were upstairs, I put my wife to bed. Her teeth did chatter and she did shiver a little, and though I thought I knew why (obviously because I was still there), I said to myself: Never mind. I'll stay no matter what. As long as I must. As a matter of fact, I felt like making love to her right then and there.

But she started crying, the woman actually started crying. And when I see that, I simply melt and am no longer responsible for my acts.

"What's the matter, my precious?" But she just went on crying, inconsolably, like a child. And me, I was trying to pull down her stockings.

"Don't cry, my sweet," I said, my voice hoarse with desire. (Man *is* a strange beast, I tell you.) Why not have a beautiful moment, I thought, while our young friend is waiting in the other room? I was giddy with lust by now.

But she resisted me, which was only natural, turning blood-red as she did. "Let me be, let me be," she hissed. But that aroused me even further. The more she fought, the more I wanted her. Each touch was like a burn, I felt her tears on my face. She tried with all her strength to push me away but of course couldn't.

"Now, now, you know I won't let you go if I don't want to." And I grabbed her and lifted her, blanket and all. But then she struck me. I stopped.

I could have broken every bone in her body, of course. And then take a shoetree maybe or a clothes hanger and beat the young man's head until there was a breath of life in him. But flareups like these have a strange effect on me. If a woman goes as far as she did just now, I let her go, I lose all interest. I put her down and started walking toward the door.

But she began to cry even more desperately, it made no sense to leave; I would have heard her sobs even in the other room.

So I stayed and began pacing the floor.

What's making her cry so much, I wondered. What's got into her? Or is that what it is? I happened to glance in the mirror. My eye was bloodshot, she scratched it, the little bitch.

And there was her blouse, too, a beautiful Chinese silk blouse I brought back from one of my trips, in shreds, completely torn.

Maybe this is why she is crying, I thought, and smiled. Or was it the hotel business that got her so scared? That they'd be stuck with me for good in this empty, silent apartment?

"What a horrid man you are," she sobbed. "You take me to that boorish friend of yours and all you do is insult me. And now I am to become an innkeeper's wife."

I had to laugh.

"Is that what's eating you?"

"Oh no."

"What then?" But she didn't answer.

It was just as well. What else *could* have bothered her but the thing I'd already mentioned—the fear that she'd be stuck with me. I knew as much. Saying it would not have made any difference.

So I continued walking up and down, with a wet handkerchief over my eye, mulling over decisions that seemed pretty final.

"Tell Dedin I am feeling better and send him home," I heard her say after a while.

"Yes, *ma'm*," I replied and bowing slightly, left the room.

This won't work, I decided. When you are patient and understanding, people take advantage of you. It was a mistake to allow things to go this far. I should have thrown the bum out long ago. I walked into the other room, handkerchief still in place, which he didn't seem to notice. He was reading again.

"You must be a well-read man. How old are you, anyway?"

"Thirty."

"I am forty-two but I bet I could still knock you down with one finger . . . what do you say to that?" He laughed. And he was right. What sort of talk was this? Like that kid at the academy.

"It's quite possible," he replied with a broad smile.

"And if I did, I don't think you could get up again. What is it you do for a living?"

"I was a sublieutenant attached to the medical corps," he answered and straightened out a little.

"I am not interest in what you *were*, my good man; what are you now, What is your livelihood? I can also say that I am a master violinist just because I once owned a violin. What I am asking you is what you are right now." Monsieur Dedin cast curious glances all around.

"I am not much of anything," he said with an enigmatic smile.

"Now that's more like it . . . you are nothing, that I can understand. What do you live on, then?"

"That *is* rather a mystery," he replied and cracked a sugar cube in his mouth. Our gallant was invulnerable, I realized, he was totally impervious. The sugar was left on the table after tea, and he was sucking on them now quite peacefully. He really didn't feel like answering my questions and would have liked nothing better than to walk away. But he couldn't—not just yet.

"A mystery, eh?" I said. "Might you have a rich uncle supporting you?"

"An uncle?"

"A rich uncle. No need to get embarrassed, young man. Someone generous enough to help you." He turned a deep red. I thought this is it: something is going to happen, at last. (Ah, how I wished it, with all my heart.) But no: the young man kept smiling.

"What uncle?" he repeated, still quite cheerful. "I have no uncle."

I almost fell over. It so happened I believed my wife when she told me the business about the rich uncle. Usually I don't believe a word she says. But this I believed. Maybe because it confirmed my suspicion that the guy was a parasite.

That was the first shock. The other came when he appealed to me heartrendingly not to be overhasty in my business affairs. I was in a bad frame of mind right now, he said, and it was important not to act rashly.

Amazing. What's my frame of mind got to do with him?

I should avoid getting involved in a business venture right now, he said, especially something I knew very little about. And certainly not with that fellow from Normandy.

(Aha, he's talking about the hotel.)

"And why not, may I ask?"

"Because he is a scoundrel. He'll trick you, he'll fleece you. Trusting soul that you are." (Is that what I am, a trusting soul?) And he kept harping on my troubled state of mind, my low spirits, my anxieties.

"My anxieties?"

"It's perfectly understandable. Someone who suffered as much, put up with as much as you have these past few months."

"Why, what have I put with? How would you know about that? And what's more to the point, what's it got to do with you?" (But as I said, the man was impervious; that was the secret of his being.)

"Oh let's not make light of it, captain," he said, with some feeling now. "Let's not." He knew exactly what happened on the high seas, how heroically I piloted that boat; he was well-informed on the subject. He even knew I made sure no fee would be paid to any of the rescue services. . . .

This interested me somewhat because it happened to be true—not having to pay special fees, that is. I was rather proud of it, actually. But how on earth did he know about all that? I discussed it with no one; nor do I intend to.

But that's man for you. I felt myself getting warmer. He went on to name the person who had related all this to him, a well-known authority, a maritime specialist, for whom I myself had the highest regard . . . And he said I acted heroically.

That *is* man all over. You start praising him and before long you can slip a ring through his nose. And I am no exception. Especially when it comes to the accident which was still a sore point and will remain that to the end of my days.

"Won't you sit down?" I now said to the young man. I was that interested in finding out if I was a hero or some odious wretch. Alas, you can never be sure. But I have often told myself to let things take their course, not say anything—I might just be vindicated in the end. Maybe they are right; maybe I did do a good job navigating that ship.

"Do sit down, my friend," I said to the bastard. And remembered that I promised him a glass of brandy when I invited him up.

"How about a drink?" I asked, rather embarrassed now.

"Oh yes, please," he said, his face all bright and animated. He was smiling at *me* of course. And I knew why. He got the better of me, he outsmarted me. His intentions? Simple. To get himself out of a tight spot, to take the wind out of my sail. He saw I was a wild animal and treated me as such. He was nobody's fool.

To this day I am ashamed of myself for being so gullible. Then again, I am no different today . . . But we'll leave that for now.

Anyway, he pulled a fast one on me. And there was nothing surprising in this, come to think of it. Doesn't it often happen that elaborate arguments keep running through your mind? The same old story, actually: that maybe I *was* wrong and he *was* a decent fellow, a dear, selfless friend looking after my thoroughly honest wife. It is possible. Such things do happen. Let's remember how unconcealed his admiration was for her, and how very open hers for his. Even that speaks well of the man, damn it, plus the fact that he so graciously returned my wallet. . . . I once saw a statue, in Italy, of a young hero. With a menacing lion wrapped around his chest, he looked straight ahead, stout, courageous. Believe it or not, I kept thinking of this statue now, for that's how honest and upright this youth seemed to me. What is more, he took a lively interest in my financial affairs. At the moment he was suggesting ways of making money I had never even heard of. Ingenious possibilities, which he was sharing with me. With *me*.

"Why, that's a capital idea," I said. "How did you come upon such a capital idea?"

And already we were drawing closer.

"How did I come upon it? I hear things. And I would bet any amount of money that it would be just the thing for you. Made to order. Not that silly hotel venture but this."

Everything he said sounded so bright. I was astonished. An outsider giving advice to an expert, and in shipping matters, to boot—I have never seen anything like it. He was talking about the rescue service. Brought up the accident again. Mentioned my courageous stand and all that.

"Why don't you try to get into one of those companies, the rescue companies?" he suddenly asked. "I can't think of a more suitable place for you." He was right. It *was* a capital idea.

I ought to tell you, I suppose, just what sort of companies these are.

It's simple. They send their ships into dangerous areas and help boats in distress, for a proper fee, of course, for such things are not cheap. On the other hand, they pay their employees handsomely. The work is not easy, but what would suit me better than hard work? As I said, it surprised me to no end that such a simple solution should come from somebody else.

"But how does one join such an operation?"

"Well," he said warmly, "how about moving on to London?"

"To London?"

He explained: Didn't I know people there? (I did mention this before, *en passant*.) Things were picking up in London, you kept hearing about it. Business was definitely on the upswing. He happened to be right about that.

"But to move there for good?"

"Why not?" asked this kind-hearted young man.

Why not indeed. A short trip wouldn't make much sense, would it?

"You know, you are absolutely right. Why shouldn't I go to London? What a first-rate idea. What's keeping me here anyway?" And with that I got up and went to my desk for a pencil.

"I'll make a note of it right now. I'll write to a friend of mine in London first thing tomorrow morning."

And this was the moment when something did finally happen in that room.

Nobody should take me for a fool, for I am not. My instincts are as keen as can be—they haven't failed me yet. So if I say that something stirred in that room that moment, you must believe me. What I said to him while casting about for my engagement calendar was this:

"It's really decent of you to be so concerned about my affairs. Frankly, I had no idea you had such a feeling for business.

"Only other people's business," Monsieur Dedin replied. "When it comes to my own affairs, I am not very clever, as you yourself were good enough to point out."

In other words, he paid me back. For my churlishness first of all. And how artfully, with eyes all agleam.

"Now if you permit me, captain," he went on, "I will also make a note to myself." And he smiled at me shamelessly.

This was the moment when I came to my senses. I shall never forget it. As surely as I am alive, he wrote down something about me.

Oh, how many times I thought of that scene; how many nights I spent agonizing over it. I would give a lot even today if I could put my hands on that notebook of his.

For there was this strange gleam in his eyes, as I said. Who he reminded me of, which one of the many scoundrels I came across in my life, I can't say. What did flash through my mind was that this man got tired of my poor wife. He was urging us to go to London because he wanted to get rid of her. Why, of course, of course . . . how stupid of me.

That's what the note must have been about: that he succeeded royally in playing me for a fool. One does like to take note of somebody else's stupidity, I've noticed that. . . . A lot I cared about the quarrel, or my eye injury at that point.

"You see," I would have liked to say to my wife. And already felt a strange pang around my heart. "You see . . . the scoundrel."

Ah, the thought, the very idea that this lovely creature, my bright little star could be that blackguard's slut . . .

To be perfectly frank, I had no idea what to do next.

For life, alas, is adhering to norms. It would have made no sense at all to start raging again, or act indignant, not after you had been kind of chummy with the fellow.

And still. I didn't want to make a fuss. I walked over to him, and putting my hand under his chin, lifted his head, as you would a little girl's, to make her look at you. He turned pale straightaway.

"Enjoy your notation, my friend," I said to him gently. "It's sure to be instructive," I added, just as gently. "But now, go." This was a little more abrupt.

"You mean you are throwing me out?" And he even tried to laugh a little. He couldn't say very much because I was still propping up his chin.

"Yes, I am. You gave me good advice, I think I will take it, but now it's getting late." Though what my eyes were expressing in the meantime was probably this:

I'll let you go this time, but if I get my hands on you again, watch out.

And with that we shook hands. Which was kind of funny. Laughable. And we did laugh a little, believe it or not.

When he finally left, I just stood there, unable to move, weighed down by one thought: So that's what I am up against. But then other thoughts took over: It can't be that bad. I'll write to Kodor in London. Why not? Why shouldn't I go there? Because he suggested it? That shouldn't bother me in the least.

I gave the matter quite a bit of thought after that; I tried to reason it out. If I worked four or five years for one of those outfits, we'd be all right. I would be forty-seven then, which, granted, is not that young, but not terribly old either. We could still have a life. . . . I could start a business of my own, or invest my money. Yes, with a little nest egg I could do it. I'd come back here and settle down with her . . . put an end to this gypsy life. That, at least, is what I kept turning over in my mind.

And one more thing: thirty-one and five make thirty-six—she wouldn't be that young by then, either; women do calm down at that age, hopefully. In any case, I decided I would definitely try to join one of those firms, if only for the money.

That note Dedin made in his book did have an effect on me, indeed such an effect, that I went out and bought myself a little notebook, too, in which I jotted down my thoughts and plans, including the one just mentioned. Although now I can only find this one brief note pertaining to it:

"Five years forced labor. Only way to look at it." As brief as that.

About Dedin, nothing. And no wonder: he disappeared. See how fast he ran? I would have liked to say to my wife. See how scared he got? For obviously, a little gloating is on order at such times. Now at least you see the young man for what he is, I would have liked to say to her.

I have to admit, though, that the girl got sick over the affair. It was plain to see: she was wilting right before my eyes, this business was making her pine away with grief. And all out in the open, too. After taking to her bed that time, she didn't feel like getting up again. Her voice grew weak and thin, like children's voices after they've had the whooping cough. And her face got all puffy, as though she had a terrible case of the flu, or as though she'd been crying on the sly.

Now she's really learned to hate me, I thought. And getting ready perhaps to do something about it. For this wasn't the first time I scared off such questionable gentlemen. There was a young whippersnapper right after the fire, a drawing teacher with ambitions of becoming a movie director. But he was an easy target. All I had to do then was show him how I could rip apart fifty-two playing cards with a flick of my wrist, or how to break a horseshoe in half without even propping up my elbow, and the next day he was gone. And there was a doctor, a specialist in heat cures. With him it was enough to display my bulging biceps and dare him to put his scalpel to it, and then see it bounce off my skin. (And it did bounce, by God, at that time it really did.) True, as a send-off, I also told him how a mulatto sailor broke his jaw when my hand happened to land on his face once. The fools . . . As though weakness could not be as deadly as brute strength. But these chaps, as soon as they smell danger, get cold feet and run.

I must say, though, that my wife was not overly upset about them. But now she was, this time she was crushed. And I could feel her hatred for me: it was smoldering in her eyes, in her flushed face, in every move she made. She loved this fop, what more proof did I need?

But why, why must a wonderful girl love a heel? The thought tormented me night after night. I realize it's ridiculous for a man to be choosy about his wife's paramours, but that's the human heart for you. Sad. And no amount of sorrowing, or wisdom, can change it. We all know that perfectly reasonable men can go crazy over mere hussies—waitresses, ballet students and such. Still, you say to yourself: If only she fell in love with a man of distinction, a professor . . . That would be pretty awful, too, but I could understand it at least. But what did she see in this good-for-nothing croupier? (For I looked into it: Monsieur Dedin had even worked as a croupier in his time, and in a very questionable club, at that.)

Still and all, I felt sorry for the woman. And why shouldn't one feel sorry for a love-sick person, especially one so frail, who could hardly stand on her feet. Indeed, my wife appeared to grow younger, more timid and childlike with each passing day. It broke my heart to know that she wasn't as brazen as before. I may have mentioned already that we lived near a large square. My wife always liked the open sky, the broad view from the window. She would quietly concentrate on her reading during the day, but at sunset, she'd rise and gaze at the world below. And at such moments she did look like a flower, a rose perhaps, still in bloom but already touched by blight. And what if it's true, I thought to myself sadly; what if that blight was really me?

But that's when my time came, my "moment of enchantment" as I would later call it, when I'd invoke the power of imagination. I would walk over to her, help her out of bed and into her robe, take her by the hand, and walk up and down, pretending it was spring and we were strolling in the garden. (It was nice and warm in the flat, and outside spring *was* in the air.)

"Just look at those gorgeous birds on the lawn, at that shimmering lake, oh look at the clouds." In short, I began to lull her unquiet soul, naturally with things out of reach. For I know, how well I know, that they always work better than reality.

"Now look at the moon, it's moving with you." Such fanciful things I said to her. (Actually, there was an antique clock in the living room with a large round face—that's what glimmered over us in the growing darkness.) At last she gave me a tired, wistful smile: "Is that the moon?" To which I said: "Didn't you know?" And even embraced her a little. She looked at me, kind of surprised, and began to cry.

It seems I did love her, after all.

Four years of servitude, maybe five, I thought, and then we'll quiet down. Peace, at last. It will come, it must . . .

I sat down and wrote a long letter to Kodor, again to him, this time not even trying to make excuses for the accident. I realized I had to share my pain with someone. I didn't call myself a hero, but I did try to fake a litte self-esteem. I put down that saving the ship was an achievement, that I was proud of it—a few empty phrases, in other words. But the upshot was the same. I was again without a job.

(Kodor didn't care for humanity as such, hated family ties, despised procreation and didn't take kindly to marriage, either. "The very idea of being shut in with another person . . ." he used to say. "I'd rather have all my teeth pulled out.")

This is what I wrote to him, then: "Alexander, I didn't take your advice at the time and got married. Now I see you were right. To take such a step was to tempt the gods. (This much sincerity I allowed myself; I had to, I felt a great need to open up.) I am in a difficult situation right now, for as you know, a single man can live on practically nothing, is free to take up anything he likes, but I am tied down." In short, I asked him to do all he could to get me a position with one of those previously mentioned firms. And if he thought it was a good idea and would help matters along, I would travel to London myself. I then wrote another letter to Marseille, to a certain M. Saviro, who was also a patron of mine, and a well-to-do gent himself.

I wrote these letters in our living room one Sunday afternoon, sitting at my wife's small writing desk. When I was all through writing and thinking, I picked up a book lying on her desk and leafed through it. I confess I cannot much read anymore. I'd skim a few passages in the middle, restlessly, absently, skip to another sentence, and if I liked that, maybe I'd go back to the beginning.

This is just what happened now. I still remember the title of the book: *The Story of A Quiet Man*—a promising title indeed. It happened to be about a wonderful old bird-catcher, a shy meticulous old codger, and I got pretty interested. (As a schoolboy I used to catch birds, too.) It seemed like a funny book and also cruel; before I knew it I was immersed in it.

All of a sudden, I heard someone moaning behind my back. My wife was standing at the door, coughing, wheezing, her face flaming red, and her bathrobe unbuttoned, as though she'd just stepped out of the bathtub.

"For God's sake, what's the matter with you?" She was in tears, disheveled, dazed.

"I am dying, I am dying," she muttered, and threw herself in my arm. Her body felt so hot, I decided she must be delirious. So after that I didn't press her, didn't ask any more questions, for I knew well what tricks the mind can play on you. One question kept occurring to me throughout all this: Is having to live with me really causing her so much anguish?

I should point out, by the way, that my wife was on the short side, she was a petite woman, and I kind of liked this about her. At times I caught myself thinking about how small she was, even while on duty, and having a chuckle over it. I could have her do a dance on my palm.

I often think of a scene in this connection, not a scene really, just a remark passed by an Andalusian clod.

It happened in Spain, at the beginning of our marriage; we were traveling south, by coach (I had put in at a Spanish port and she came down to meet me). We were detained because there was a religious procession in the city, complete with flags, flowers, incense. This chap in a black hat and embroidered vest stood near the coach and kept ogling us; he wouldn't take his eyes off my wife and me.

"What does a big hulk like that do with such a tiny woman? he asked his friends. "Break her into little pieces?" The rascal asked just that, and then laughed, too, in the midst of the holy procession.

The comment sure made my wife come alive, though.

"Did you hear what that fellow just said? What nerve . . ." She got all fired up, and her eyes, even her eyes spoke of a knowledge that only she possessed.

"What nerve, really." And she pressed her flushed face against my hand. Then, still blushing, she said: "Nobody but nobody knows what you're really like. Except me."

And this is just what I am getting at—that she wasn't at all indifferent then. And it is precisely that scene, that sudden flare-up, that I kept going back to when I felt she might not have *any* feelings left for me.

Once again I thought of it. And it is the reason why—miserable as she was when she came after me in her robe—I didn't say anything. I didn't ask, didn't look into her eyes, didn't try to puzzle out her secret. I wouldn't have, under any circumstances. I never did like showdowns and final pronouncements.

"If you like, I can even be more frank," a hot-blooded classmate of mine once told me at the academy. And my response even then was: "Don't bother. Let's not be that frank with each other." And I hold to this even today. For where does all that frankness get us? One never really knows what to make of another's version of the truth; each one of us sticks to his own story, and we proceed alongside of each other, toward a dead end.

Which wouldn't be half so bad. But certain words may be uttered, fatal words, which may not even be true, or not completely. As soon as she blurts out things like: I don't love you, I can no longer live with you, the damage is done—she can't really take it back the next day, can she? It's those damn conventions again. I hate you, she says. There can be some truth in that. But if those nights we spent in Granada were any indication, the matter was not so simple. And for that reason, it was still better to be cautious.

In any case, where *are* the people who are perfectly suited for each other? Who will show me these blessed ones? Life, alas, is one long test of endurance.

So I chose to keep quiet, and made sure she wouldn't have to say anything, either. After all, I was trying to calm her down, not unsettle her more. The seat of unhappiness is in the neck, the old sailors used to say; and if one of them went crackers, they'd start working on his neck muscles. And that's exactly what I did now. Sometimes it's those clever tricks and concoctions that bring relief to an aching soul, by relaxing and then toning up the muscles. And the neck muscles are crucial, those old seamen knew what they were talking about.

Sure enough, she began to cry. And smile, too. We all know how lovely a young woman can be when she smiles through her tears. Sunlight piercing through the rain clouds, and all that. I myself was almost happy. Life does have a way of fooling us.

Pretend she ran to you in her hour of need, I told myself.

This happened on a Sunday, when the maid was out. I was happy about that too, happy to while away hours, outside of time. I made a nice fire and got some food in the larder. Because she was hungry by now. And we simply stretched out on the carpet and nibbled, as if on a picnic. I didn't even turn on the light, I just let the darkness close in on us.

And then I began to talk, too. Told her about . . . well, what? My travel experiences, mostly. About the urge that's in every young man to find out if there is happines anywhere in this world. For what else is a young man interested in but to learn what goes on in those dimly-lit huts after the hypnotic din of a sun-drenched day subsides? When light fades from the walls and he stands alone in the cold tropical night. Who are those shriekers and clamorers, he wonders, who during the day simply gobble up the sun. What goes through their minds when night comes and the moon shines into their shabby little rooms?

"This was when I wound up in Selangor," I said to my wife, "on my way to even remoter parts of Malaya. I can't tell you what fascination life there had for me. I had seen indolence before but never such voluptuous idleness . . . The way these people could stretch out and lounge about and chew tobacco in the shade, their eyes forever bright, as though they were always drunk, always burning. They kept sipping life as if it were some delicate wine. I, harried and overworked as always, thought I had finally reached the happy isles.

"Until, of course, I found out a thing or two about the place. 'You can't measure happiness,' a member of one of their ruling families told me once. (He, of course, studied in Paris and London and naturally spoke Dutch, too.) 'Take a look at them when they are raving mad,' said this pale-faced descendant of a long line of sultans, 'when they seethe and whip out their knives.'

"'Life is a but a struggle,' this oriental aristocrat informed me. And laughed rather coldly. And to illustrate, he told me little stories about these people, to help me understand what this serene-seeming island paradise was really like. He mentioned unusual goings-on under the surface, disappearances, strange pilgrimages—God knows what else. But mainly he told me about the grandmothers and their sorceries. He asked me to consider just that: a world ruled by women who were tiny, by the way, the older ones smaller still, and all shriveled, though tough and immovable, like a mountain. It's easy to imagine, how all this can lead to ruin, how it can devastate the young especially, who become generally apathetic, oblivious, interested in only one thing; the Dutch guilder. And when the scramble for those guilders gets to be too hectic, the women just chuck everything, very proudly put on their chadoors and journey to Mecca to kiss a stone.

"And I say the same to you now," I continued, turning to matters closer at hand. "Life is indeed a struggle, as you can see, that's what it is all about. It's no use looking for happy people."

I tried hard to make her see my point. There are people, I know, who think only they are unhappy. The whole world writhes in ecstasy, only their skies are overcast.

"Take my life, for instance," I said to her and smiled. "After all, I am human, too, and believed with all the rest of them that I was entitled to a little happiness."

And strangely enough, I began to talk about my own life, something I hardly ever did.

I talked about my struggles, my work, about the odd and baffling world I sprang from—my family, in short, whose members in a way also put on a chadoor and disappeared when they felt too stifled, or simply fed up with those around them. They were also forever preoccupied, oblivious, never paying the slightest attention. Our mother only liked to cook and play the piano, these were her two passions. Father, on the other hand, had not much use for fancy feelings and moods—one night he took a pitcher of water and dumped it into the piano. All he wanted to do was think, to figure things out. What was it he kept turning over in his head?

Not much, I suspect—a new type of camera maybe, an old hunt he'd gone on once, or whether the czars of Russia were right about anything. And if we add to this an extraordinary brother who cared about nothing in the world except his own little pleasures, whose pocket always jangled with money of mysterious origin, and whose head too was full of mysterious schemes—well, if she were to imagine all that, then she would surely see why I left that world behind, and why I didn't care to waste another thought on them.

I brought all this up because I figured: Why shouldn't she know? It might just make her realize that she *could* do things if she wanted to. But when I got this far I suddenly stopped and said to her:

"Now why don't you tell me something?"

"Me? I don't really have anything to tell."

"You don't? All right, then. But then what are we to do. . .? What *is* it with you, anyway?" I suddenly asked, and already felt my blood pressure rise. Here I was talking to her, putting my soul on display, and she won't even respond.

She did make a move finally; she got out of bed and groped about for something in the darkened room.

"I was going to swallow this," she said casually, with a laugh.

"What is it?"

"A drink," she said, lighthearted still. And lay down again.

I tasted it: a bitter, vile potion, I disposed of it quickly. So she wanted to poison herself. While in the bath, she wanted to poison herself but couldn't go through with it.

"Why did you want to poison yourself?" Dead silence.

"Strange, this silence of yours. But it's all right. Don't speak if you don't want, I will not make you. But I will get to the bottom of this vast silence, I assure you." And put this critical question to her: "Why can't you live with me?"

I swallowed hard. For this was the touchy area about which I spoke earlier: the area that had been out of bounds for me for so long. But no more rational arguments. I must get through to her somehow.

"I will not dissuade you from doing anything," I began. "At the same time, there are limits, you can't expect me to condone everything. To live here and at the same time to be thinking of someone else, that's something I can't put up with."

There, I said it; no more roundabout phrases, no more gentle hints. Why not talk plainly for a change, the way God intended for us to talk?

"But if you are after the impossible I will give you the impossible. I'll support both of you—you and your lover, how is that? And you won't even have to live in this house. Well, are you willing to go that far?"

Utter silence.

"I know, I know, we can entertain wonderful thoughts about the subject. Why shouldn't a woman feel or think as she pleases, right? Especially if she is no ordinary woman? What business is it of another man, of her husband even? Just because I work for you and support you? A contemptible argument, I am sure you will agree.

"But we can even go further, if you wish. You can't love on demand, that's quite clear. Even I can appreciate that. Either it's there or it isn't—no philosophy can change that. However, if you don't find it in your heart to show some interest, then say so. Because in that case, I will let you go. (I even said that, come what may. I had to know where I stood, once and for all.)

"Or I shall go away. I can, you know, just as I did years ago, when I left my parents' house."

She sat there in the dark, perfectly still.

"And as far as the young man is concerned, he's a first class scoundrel, believe me. (I got to this point perfectly composed. I was proud of myself.) He invited us to go to London, you know. (I told her that too. And that he's had it with her, wanted to get rid of her. I told her everything, in other words, the whole pitiful story.)

"But only because I want you to see it for yourself," I said. "You are nothing to him, you understand. No, don't even answer, I know, I am convinced it is so.

"Wouldn't it be better for you to stay with someone who does love you? Think about it. Or does that really make you want to die? Is it such a big crime to love you?"

And then once more, the same question: "Why shouldn't you want to live with me?" And after that, nothing.

"Shouldn't we turn on the light? I asked her a little later.

"Oh no, please," she said, terrified.

This wasn't so bad, I thought. And tried to convince myself that I was still quite calm. No damage done. I kept whistling loudly.

Besides, I tried to approach this thing from another angle. It occurred to me that she might be involved in some other mysterious and messy business. Maybe she gambled or played cards —hence her nervous condition. She could be in debt up to her ears and afraid to tell me about it. Could I have misread her signals?

She did sometimes tell me she had no money left. And I could see there was more on her mind.

Also, right around that time she again informed me that 3000 francs were stolen out of her pocket. Once again: a mystery story. Money lost or stolen, probably the latter, she thought. She was ready with a couple of versions. She took off her gloves and suspected that while she did . . . A familiar story. And obviously phony from beginning to end. Let's look into it then.

Not because of the money involved. I wanted to know what she spent it on. Because she went through an awful lot of money, an unheard-of sum, considering my circumstances.

She once started telling me about some sort of time payments but I only half listened. It had to do with door-to-door salesmen and how she always fell for their pitch. She'd be standing in the kitchen, over the stove, and they'd be pestering her, she couldn't get rid of them. I also remember her telling me about bills she got from booksellers.

Her books . . . there's another story. We should talk about that, too. My wife, you see, was a rather cultured woman, a high-minded person, really, who loved literature, philosophy, and, in a light-hearted sort of way, even the occult—she didn't believe in it or anything, she just wanted to get a taste of that, too. At one time she bought all kinds of books, rare old editions, journals, too. I don't really know what the hell for. As though there weren't such things as lending libraries. But she never liked things that passed through other hands, she was finicky that way. I let her be, though, I didn't interfere.

Needless to say, I didn't join her in her pursuits—how could I?

Reading requires your heart to be in it, and who had time for that? At most I'd glance at the titles.

"What sort of books are these?" I would sometimes ask her, sounding sarcastic, the way unschooled people do when they want to appear superior about the very things that are beyond their comprehension. Among her books were such titles as *On Human Emotions, The History of Philosophy*. She was especially interested in psychology.

"Yes, what sort of books are these?" I'd ask her casually, pretending to be even more ignorant than I was.

"Tell me the truth, are you really interested in this stuff?"

"Why, of course. I am interested in all that's odd in nature." So there.

What could I do with this woman? I put down the books and didn't discuss them any further. When I asked her the next time what she was reading, she just said:

"Serious literature."

"What for?" I'd ask.

"Because I have a feeling for such things," she would answer.

"And what else do you have a feeling for, you strange creature?"

"I am not about to tell you. Must you know everything? You know too much already." In other words I couldn't delve into her affairs, the better part of her world remained shrouded in mystery.

All this, however, is besides the point. The only reason I mentioned it was to raise a question: How does one reconcile these "finer things" with her lies? The edifying tracts with titles such as "Educating Your Soul" or "Know Your Conscience" with murky uncertainty and the shady affairs involving three thousand francs which, supposedly, was stolen while she took off her gloves. . . . She lied through her teeth, that woman, she lied shamelessly, all the time.

If she said she was going one place, she'd be sure to go to another; if she said she had no cigarettes with her, she did. It was all so baffling. Why should she go through contortions even over such petty things? She even went so far as intimating that she may be the daughter of a Turkish major—she actually made a statement to that effect one day.

"What was that? What are you saying?" I mean, this was too much. She was lying on the sofa, staring into the air. Daydreaming with her eyes open. And this is precisely what was—and is, even today—so alien to me. But I guess it was in her blood, all this romantic nonsense. Or should I call it plain childishness?

I realize now that I should have spoken about this earlier. It is strange, after all, that she never answered my questions. All those searching questions about the meaning of life and never an answer. And I just let it go. But why did I? Because I wouldn't have believed her anyway. With her I could never escape the feeling that it was all play-acting, all make-believe, and it was her wild fantasies that did it. After a while I couldn't even believe what I saw with my own eyes. For all I knew, her wanting to drink poison may also have been mere play and illusion. And when she sank into silence, perhaps all she wanted to do was torment me, to pretend she no longer loved me but loved someone else, and couldn't care less about my probing questions.

Come to think of it, it took some daring to dish up the story about being robbed—twice. It took impudence, come to think of it, and skill. She'd have me believe that if the same happened to her again, it must have happened the first time, too.

But it didn't, not the first time and not later. And now I was determined to get to the bottom of it, at least of the three thousand. Was it cards, after all? Or the races? I even thought of drugs. I went through her books again, the latest shipment, and her clothes, too, to see if she didn't have a fur coat or an evening gown stashed away someplace—anything that might suggest extravagance. But I found nothing. And as far as cards were concerned, she didn't know the first thing about them; I discovered that several times. Just then I began to teach her *trente-et-quarante* and another game, *meine-deine*, favored by sailors.

"Take it, it's your winnings," I reminded her during a game— she obviously wasn't paying attention.

"Yes, yes," she said, and yawned. A blind alley, clearly. I had to find a different lead. One day I went into the kitchen where our maid, Äubchen Marie, a good-natured, obese old woman, was doing her chores. (We called her Äubchen Marie because whenever she saw a child, she called it Äubchen, or little bonnet—who knows where she may have picked up that German word..) I put a practical question to her, though using a approach that was the opposite of my usual strategy.

"Last winter we spent altogether too much money on electricity, isn't it so Marie? I am about to pay the bill and I want to know how come?"

"Madame spends the whole night reading, that must use up a lot of electricity."

"All she does is read?"

"All the time."

"She's always home then . . . But do you let her? She is supposed to be in your care. At the rate she is going, she'll ruin her health, she'll just waste away." (I scolded her, just to be on the safe side.) But Marie's smile was guileless, genuine.

"She doesn't go out much," she now said, and turned a little sad. "She is rarely in the mood."

"Not much, you say, that's all right. But where does she go when she does go out? Among interesting, entertaining people, I hope."

Marie gave her finger a lick and tested the iron she was about to use.

"Where?" she reflected. "To see silly women, I would say. She always lets me know exactly where she will be. She'd say to me: 'I'll be at Madame Lagrange's' or 'I am going to Mrs. Pigal's.' Aren't they kind of silly? Next to madame, I mean? They are not good enough for her," said our very own dairymaid, and lapsing into blessed docility, she continued ironing.

"Of course they are not good enough for her," I said. "That's just it. But what about her? Does anyone ever come here? Women I mean, friends . . . you know . . . Does she ever have parties here?"

"Not really, *mon colonel*," she answered (as a rule she called me colonel, though I explained to her more than once that I wasn't one). "These are the people who come to the house: Madame Casa, but she comes seldom. (This was a Dutch lady who married rich but then went broke.) Madame Lagrange (a very religious lady against whom I had no objections . . . then.) And sometimes Mademoiselle Sanchi." I had to agree with Marie; they were all rather stupid females.

"All right. And what about men?"

Marie immediately became defensive.

"What do you mean men?" she said, no longer very docile. Even her cheeks turned red, like a shiny apple, and her eyes clouded over. I was quite surprised. But wasn't it amazing? That she mesmerized everybody, even this love-starved old spinster to whom jealousy came naturally? That even *she* was willing to back her up? And now got all worked up because I dared to utter the word men in connection with my wife?

Should I insist then that I was a crazy fool?

Because to top it off, she didn't have one real friend, which was odd, to say the least. So she was cooped up in these rooms for months by herself, reading up on the role of the inner voice, the conscience. Isn't it quite understandable that such a woman would one day find herself desperately in love with the very first man to come along?

If there was no one around her except the likes of a Dedin?

There couldn't be any other explanation. I had to assume that most of my money, not just the three thousand but much more, ended up in his pocket. There was no uncle, that's for sure—my wife must have invented him on the spur of the moment, in desperation. Come to think of it, the poor woman must have invented quite a few things—an uncle here, a pickpocket there. Childish nonsense, all of it.

She was neither shrewd nor sneaky, but quite, quite gullible, an easy prey, I tell you, an easy prey, for all her machinations. Just imagine, then: if such a muddle-headed little romantic, at Madame Pigal's or some other place, where the common bond, supposedly, was a belief in some highfalutin brand of mysticism—if in such an environment, under such circumstances, she met a languid-eyed hunter who gave her fancy books to read, filled her head with claptrap, and even had her believe she could be an actress one day, wouldn't it be fair to surmise that the young man's plaid suits and ample overcoats and smart hats were bought with money he got from this poor creature?

But then, all these thoughts vanished, the clouds lifted from my heart. My wife recovered. One morning she woke up in good spirits, her gloom had vanished, she knew how to laugh again. Did she really get over that love of hers? Did she finally realize that the man simply walked out on her? Which he did, of course, vanishing without a trace.

You see, I would have liked to say to her: Who is it but I who sticks by you no matter what? (I deluded myself with the hope that she would realize this herself.) That no one was as concerned about you as I. That I devoted my whole life to you, neglecting practically everything else. . . .

What followed were happy, peaceful days—days that were like the fading sun: weak but still warm. This was our real honeymoon, happier even than the time we spent in Granada. We roamed the city and did quite a bit of shopping. I knew how much she loved to shop, so I let her splurge. Ah, the excitement, the anticipation of it . . . she was beside herself with joy. May she have that, too? Really? Maybe she shouldn't. She realized we couldn't spend so much, but still. We happened to be discussing a snakeskin portfolio. She was dying to get it.

"It is a handsome portfolio," I said.

"You like it too?"

"I do, very much. I've been meaning to get one for myself," I added slyly.

"This, then, is for you, all right?" She was trying a new tack.

"Very good." And I won't deny it, my heart was glad. After all, she was once a poor girl. To this day I don't know how she, a peasant's daughter, made it as a school teacher. She never had a thing, this girl. Why even now, when she saw ordinary candy, her eyes lit up. So I bought it by the bagful, and always those brightly colored ones, fiery reds, deep greens.

"Look at the little devil's eyes," I said to her. She may be a grown woman, she still looked in the bag. And her smile retained some of that childish wonder. And why not? I knew myself what childhood memories were like. Why shouldn't she crave for pretty things?

"Isn't it beautiful, though?" she exclaimed ecstatically when we got home. "Isn't it?" (She meant the portfolio.)

"It is, it is," I said and then added: "It's funny when you think about it. You first say to someone: you are beautiful; and then you say: I love you." She knew right away what I was getting at.

"A man doesn't have to look beautiful," she said, crestfallen.

"Oh yes," I said and gently caressed her face.

I had to teach her how to eat again. We munched hot donuts in department store snack bars, and feasted on tiny crabs in crowded diners. I dragged her to bakeries for a whiff of fresh-baked bread, and even to make-shift barbecues. I like places like that. "It's no good being so particular," I explained to her, "for who can tell in advance when or where you will have the time of his life?"

"Go on, take a look over there," I yelled to her on one occasion, "look at the size of that dumpling the man is trying to bite into." I was pointing to the signboard of a surburban dining place, at a huge blue figure who stared open-mouthed at a dumpling in front of him, which will remain that way, dangling, tantalizing, to the very end of time.

"The poor devil. It's right under his nose, but he will never sink his teeth into it."

"Too bad," she concurred, shaking her head. "It's terrible being a signboard," she sighed. . . . "Come on, let's go inside, I suddenly feel ravenous." And she pulled me in.

The place seemed like a hangout for foreign workers. We had tripe sprinkled with lemon juice, and oh yes, dumplings too, the very best, and plenty of it. And to wash it down, some robust red wine, which made her eyes throw off sparks.

"See, isn't this wonderful?" I said. "Food to warm the heart and all for less than ten francs."

All that wholesome food did enliven her spirits. She got drunk but was still sweet; actually, she could be captivating in such a state. She nestled her little head in the palm of my hand and left it there. She lay like that in my hand, giddy, her eyes all aglow, winking, and at one point even kissing the palm of my hand.

It's also true that as the wine got the better of her, she could no longer resist and exchanged glances, discreetly but undeniably, with a tall, lean workman who just then got up to stretch. In this regard she was in no need of instruction; when it came to life's gifts she was receptive and open-minded. What could I do? Absolutely nothing.

And after that her darkening eyes had an even fiercer glow.

And so it went. We toured the countryside, wandered about a little, got off the train at unfamiliar stations. It began to feel more and more like spring, and when spring comes, both France and my wife are lovely. She looked as if the sunlight had settled on her eyes. She would stand in some arbor in her pert little hat, her light parasol, her frilly dress covered with rings of sunlight, and she would laugh away, at me, mostly.

"How clumsy you are, how very clumsy," she said to me when I presented her with a bunch of baby roses.

"How can you hold flowers like that?" And she embraced them as if they were her children.

"It's easy for you to talk. Is it my fault that I am such an oaf? You're right, flowers don't look good in my hand, nor anything else that's pretty or refined. A piece of red onion or a cow's leg would be more like it"—I tried to think of things that would make her laugh again, but she didn't she just looked at me timidly, like somebody who wants to please, may even know how, but is afraid to try. Finally she spoke up:

"Is it my fault that I am so bad for you," she said gently, with tears in her eyes.

I am not one to cry; I wasn't brought up that way. (What evil spirit was it, I wonder, that forbade me to cry?) But when I heard her say this, something gripped me, a sudden seizure, I dare say. I am embarrassed to say it but I broke into tears.

There was a wooden fence, and behind it a farmhouse with animals; I remember hearing pigs grunt. The louder they grunted, the more desperately I sobbed. It was on a narrow, grassy path where the unfortunate accident occured. My wife just stood there and didn't say a word. I think she was whimpering herself, she had to be, because when I regained my composure, I saw that her bouquet lay in the grass and her handkerchief was all wet. Even so, she kept squeezing and pressing it to her silent lips.

"Don't cry, Jacques," she said at last, still sniffling. At last she wasn't laughing at me, and that, to me, made all the difference.

I was still in this mellow, vulnerable state when one evening, to my great surprise, I met up with Miss Borton. (Let's just call her by that name; it wouldn't be fair to divulge her real identity.) She was the young lady from the ship, who on the night of the fire, in the most desperate moment, embraced me and said she adored me. We were just coming out of the Opera (we had been looking at the program; why not go there once, I said to myself), and she was walking up the steps, bathed in light. I must say she was beautiful; I recognized her immediately. . . . Indeed, I had once seen an old, old painting of the Virgin Mary, a very childlike virgin, ascending the steps of a church with great aplomb and charm—and the young miss now reminded me of that lovely picture. She was youth herself, light as a cloud. She wore a lacy green dress, with a star over her bosom, and a wide, floppy hat with ribbons that fluttered with every step she took, revealing something of her roving spirit, or maybe the devil-may-care solitude of her being. When she saw me she was so stunned, she could hardly speak.

"Captain," she said finally, but as if still sunk in some gorgeous reverie. "Captain, you, here?"

I also had difficulty answering. I certainly would not have expected her to accost me and strike up a conversation, after what happened between us.

· "How are you?" I said, quite embarrassed. "Have you, er, quite recovered?" Like that. One inane question after another.

But she got over her embarrassment in a jiffy. In fact, she made the best of the situation. How could she not be well, she said, especially now that she had seen us. No, she was not going to the Opera, she wanted to get tickets for tomorrow, but it can wait. In short, she unloosed her tongue pretty quickly. I almost forgot to introduce her to my wife. But Miss Borton stepped up to her, with great self-assurance turned her sparkling eyes on the little woman, and said:

"The captain's wife, I presume." And in French, too.

She was so beautiful that Lizzy, a great admirer of beauty, forgot to take her eyes off her. She again had flowers in her hand, roses again, and without hesitation gave her the whole bunch.

"Here you are, you lovely, lovely creature."

They hit it off well, I must say. They even kissed each other (which, what with Miss Borton being English and all, I found rather odd). Then, arm in arm, they started walking toward the Avenue de l'Opéra. I trailed after them, quite pleased.

"Ah, Jacques, Jacques," my wife cried out. "Where are you, love? Why, Miss Borton is mad about you." And she was positively beaming.

"What are you saying, Lizzy?" The young lady blushed.

"I am proud of you, I really am," my wife went on, undeterred.

I tried to laugh off the compliment as best I could.

Miss Borton decided not to protest: "Why shouldn't she say it?" she declared. "It's true." And laughing to herself, she embraced my wife again.

"Isn't she sweet?" my wife trilled.

"Oh yes, adorable," I answered.

In other words I got into an absurd situation. What was I to do with this new-won glory? My wife was still beaming at me with puckish delight.

"Miss Borton really envies me," she whispered when we got into a car, intending to spend the evening together. Did it seem so strange to her that I was capable of making a conquest? Or did she really like the idea? Who cared? At least she found out it was possible. Yes, let her hear somebody sing my praises, and not just anybody, but this lovely Irish rose.

I should mention that I did not tell her about my encounter with Miss Borton; her surprise, therefore, must have been all the greater. It seems the young lady told her everything, not only about the big fire, but about the other, smaller ones as well, and with an air of abandon peculiar to sarcastic natures. They kept up their tête-à-tête even after dinner, while I was discussing business with two government officials I chanced to run into at the restaurant where we were dining.

The encounter with Miss Borton had quite an effect on my wife. I saw evidence of that already at dinner. But when we got home, in a strange sort of way, it became even clearer.

She sat up with me for a long time that night listening to me speculate on business matters. I began explaining to her the present state of my affairs, my discussions with the two officials, not leaving out the possibility of my joining a rescue service. Leaning her frizzy head on her tiny fists, she wrinkled her forehead in concentration. And although she kept repeating: yes, yes, she was extremely interested, her thoughts, her soul, were elsewhere. Then, all of a sudden, she surfaced from the deep and her face brightened, as though she'd made a realization.

"Forgive me, Jacques, I just thought of something and I must tell you about it."

I smiled a little: Could she be actually thinking of my business ventures?

"But I'll be honest with you," she continued, "as well I should, as you always are. For as shrewd a man as you are, you are also open-hearted."

Again I smiled. If she keeps this up, she'll get to know me yet. But let's hear what she has to say.

"Well . . ."

"Go on, don't be bashful."

"Do I make you happy?" she asked and looked sadly into my eyes.

"You do in a lot of ways," I quickly answered. And to myself I said: Miss Borton is responsible for this, her sudden appearance.

"I am getting old," she said and her eyes filled with tears. And then the words came pouring out: "What good am I to you? And this girl is so beautiful. Why don't you marry her?" I was still smiling, and tried to make light of it.

"And you? Am I not still married to you?"

"Me? I might as well be dead."

But all this was nothing. I might have expected as much after what happened. I was happy even that she reacted this way. For if a wife gets so upset over the unexpected appearance of a younger woman, one can only rejoice.

So I didn't try very hard to calm her and perhaps that was a mistake. I was too relaxed, not convincing enough. I left her with her doubts.

"Come, come," I said to her in my best off-hand manner. "She's a mere child. How foolish can you be? Silly little girls never interested me." (How untrue.) But all along what I really wanted to do was put my arms around her. But I couldn't. She wouldn't let me.

"No, don't even touch me," she said bitterly, turning crimson. "Or kiss me, either. I don't want you to, not now or ever."

"What are you talking about?" I said, somewhat startled. "Listen, Lizzy, don't be a fool; I have nothing to do with that girl."

"Nothing to do with her? Oh God. You think I am jealous, don't you? Well, I am not." She was shrieking by now, and her eyes turned ugly. I had never seen her like that. It was as if she was unleashing anger that had been building up in her heart for years.

"What's the matter with you?" I asked her again.

"Nothing, nothing at all. It's just that I find all this . . . oh life itself, so very strange." Her words almost sounded like a song now. And what followed then were such tense moments that I tremble even now as I try to describe them. The realization suddenly hit me that this was nothing short of rebellion. But still I tried to smile; I still did.

"You are convinced I don't love you, and still you want to stay with me. How come? Oh, I just don't understand it. But help me, I beg of you. . . . To be so unconcerned . . . are you that timid or that cruel? It should make your blood boil. What kind of blood do you have?"

This made me perk up. Damn it, she must misunderstand my silence. Should I really show her what kind of blood is in me?

I began to talk, too, and God only knows what came pouring out of me. Such things you cannot reconstruct.

"Why do I stay with you, you ask. For that there's no explanation. (This was still said on the quiet side.) I can neither understand nor explain. I don't know myself why I am still here, and even if I were to crack open this blasted skull of mine . . ."

"Don't squeeze my hand so hard," my wife cried. That's when I realized I had grabbed her hand and began gasping for air myself.

"There is no adequate explanation for suffering, for self-degradation, none whatsoever. Anyway, you should feel flattered that there is a girl who loves me."

"But that's just what I am trying to say . . ."

"Don't talk, don't breathe a word," I panted, and began hitting the back of a chair. "You don't suppose that all this time I hadn't thought of leaving you."

"So you see," she said, although much quieter. I seems she did get scared a little bit.

"Once in a while a thought does turn up in my thick skull. Give me some credit."

She turned pale and her hands began to shake. She picked up a cup, then put it down. It seemed the look in my eyes had quite an effect on her. But no matter, I thought; I'll giver her a little whirl while I am at it. I won't let her off that easy. We'll just face up to things.

"You know what? If you want a divorce, I won't say no. (At this point I stopped pacing, though my heart was still pounding.) I have no intention of keeping you in bondage, no intention of shackling your soul. (I sat down beside her.) But give the matter some thought, that's my advice to you. Because I can't predict all the consequences. Even if we do get a divorce, you understand. . . . But just listen to this story . . . I once had a scalemaster, a decent, clever chap who also used to hire longshoremen for me, steve-dores, the English call them. As my trusted friend, he boarded my ship often and traveled with me from port to port. Well, this man one day was cruelly cheated by his wife, or rather he found out that she had cheated on him . . . So much for the exposition. (Here I paused and rolled myself a cigarette.)

"How my scalemaster held up after that I don't know, suffice it to say that one day he divorced his wife, broke with her com-pletely. But it didn't help. He was a fidgety man—there is no help, alas, for the unhappy sort—and he got even more excitable. Until one day he decided to return home after all. And though at first he sat down and even took a cup of tea from her, right afterwards, he strangled her." I paused again.

"Why are you telling me all this?" she asked quietly. "Is it some sort of parable?"

"What if it is? Make of it what you will."

Oh but I was so far gone by then, I thought my heart would burst. I no longer cared about anything. My mind darkened, my temples were throbbing, but all the while I could see that her eyes were fixed on me. She watched my every move, and it was a good thing she did.

An ill-timed word out of her, and I could easily imagine myself destroying the whole apartment, and her and myself with it. That's why I must never reach my breaking point, must never utter final words. I know my own true nature.

"It might just be a parable," I repeated hoarsely. "Interpret it as you wish. One thing is certain: acts such as these don't make one bit of sense. Why should one choke a woman to death? She, too, is a human being, you say to yourself—she needs air. Yet people do it, even if it means interfering grossly with the natural order of things. But we know all that, he knew it too, and yet he did it. And what did he gain by it? He kept on suffering and pining for the woman just the same. 'You were one big fool, Peter Kilian,' I said to him in the end." (That was the man's name.)

He was over it by then, I think. He was no longer a scalemaster, of course, but helped out on the docks, where they don't ask too many questions. But what he said to me was this:

"The days I spent in jail, they were God's own days, captain. But I'd do it again, I tell you. And he laughed. There are times, you see, when nothing helps. You may be a smart man, captain, but only if you tried it, could you understand how it feels. Finally, he leaned over and whispered in my ear: 'I was a fool for divorcing her . . . If you really want to know, that's what started it.'"

"You see," I said to the poor devil.

My story ended here. But I swear my heart almost gave way, I really thought I was going to fall dead on the floor. That my wife really loved me I could no longer doubt. . . . And this wife of mine was sitting just a few feet away, trembling. And already my heart ached for her; I could cry. But all I did was pace a little more.

It says here in my journal that I did the right thing. I did indeed. It was time I shook her up a little, brought her to her senses . . . It was all rubbish, though. As if it were possible to do the right thing.

There are even threats in that journal. That I was fed up with my chivalrous attitude, the cup ran over, etc. When she was ill, that was one thing. But she had no business being sick, I noted, love-sick, that is, over someone else, in my home. Because if that's the case I throw her out. If she feels like being in love, I feel like throwing her out.

I still remember how furious I was, how humiliated I felt—I kept making entries in my notebook all night long.

It's easy not to be jealous, I wrote, easy to dismiss the Ridolfis of this world, when you don't really care. But now it was different—I did care. About her. So she had to decide what she really wanted. After our last conversation our future was placed in her hands. It was she who had to speak.

For it was much too comfortable for her until now. All she did was criticize and make faces. If she was that unhappy with her lot, let her do something about it.

Let it be on her head now.

I jotted this down too.

And in the morning I left the house, and stayed away the whole day. But then, a surprise: though I got home quite late, she very humbly waited with supper, she even toasted my bread herself, which was quite extraordinary—never before was I treated this royally. And after supper she came over to me.

"Please, Oncle Croć Croc". . . And then: "Listen to me, Monsieur Houine." (She called me by two names now, which was also peculiar.) "Can I say something?" she asked meekly.

"Yes, do."

"I will then: You are one big fool . . . But it's all right . . . And don't you be angry with me." And she touched my vest with her finger, as was her custom. It *is* all right, I thought, everything is.

People say that we Dutch make good planners, good builders. But when it comes to sorting out our own lives, heaven help us— we are as inept as can be. Yet, we stick to conventions and forms, I could never understand why. Take a clean-cut young man, for example; how come he knows how to sit at the table and hold his tongue, and lower his head when the host wishes to drink, and lift his beer glass skyward just at the right moment. . . ? But that's us, all over.

God, are we a strange lot. Naturally, we have our difficulties with the sanctity of family life, with the virginity of our buxom daughters . . . But laughter is somehow beyond us, and that's the main problem. The French are of course different; they can laugh, though their laugh is like a cold stream hit by sunlight—happy and cruel.

And that's just the point I want to make.

That we are a joyless people, drab and without spirit. Well-intentioned but hard. Unhappy, in short. Can people bound to duty and reason have any flair? People who try to understand the world—this impenetrable tangle—with their heads?

Those who want to be consistent *all* the time?

"Why shouldn't I be open to the Holy Spirit?" she asked me not long ago, and I couldn't figure out why she'd want to go to church all of sudden. It happened to be a holiday, but still. She of all people, who was not the least bit religious, who treated devout people with haughty disdain. (A pious friend of hers, a certain Madame Lagrange, for instance.)

"Come now, why are you so surprised?" she said then. "How stupid those people are who decide never to humble themselves."

But this is just what I am getting at. The woman was devoted, on that I am willing to stake my life. At times it seemed her heart was filled with nothing but devotion. She was also a cheat. There are people, alas, who, try as they might to change their true nature, are forever tempted, charmed by it. By their own falseness and duplicity. It's enough to drive a man to distraction.

From such a creature I expected constancy? When the very thing I admired in her, and hated and envied, was her playfulness, yes, the teasing, dubious games she played with everyone . . . And of course her laughter.

How that woman could laugh! And at the littlest things, at everything, really. She fairly swam in it, splashed about like a child in the bathtub.

And I can't even laugh any more, I noted at the time. Is it any wonder, then, that in spite all my bitterness, in spite of the promptings of my soul, I said to myself at times: Maybe she is right. Maybe that's how one ought to live, that's what life really demands. It's there in my notebook, summed up in a single phrase. No one reading it would know what's behind that simple, lonely phrase: "Maybe she's right."

But I do; it cost me, but now I really do.

And with that a chapter in my life came close, and a new one began, a whole new period that was suspect from the start, if only because it was so sweet, so disconcertingly, tantalizingly sweet. . . .

What my wife may have been up to remained a mystery. I stopped searching for clues, I was just too tired. A case in point: Why was my soup lovingly stirred and cooled now? For it was. And why were my slippers placed exactly where they belonged, whereas before they weren't? And in general, why was everybody so goddamn solicitous of me in my own house? Why all this mockery? But let's take an example.

It's early in the morning; from somewhere in the house I hear her voice: "Sloppy again; definitely sloppy." And before I know it, she is standing next to me in the bathroom, watching me shave, straightening my robe; she even gets up on a stepstool and starts brushing my hair.

"Don't make me look ridiculous," I tell her gently.

No, no, she'll have none of that: "This is a married man's

privilege. Especially after he has returned to home and hearth," she adds with a chuckle.

"To hearth, in spring?"

"A cool hearth, then," she says.

"A cold one, you mean."

"Go on, you know you're not cut out for love. What's all this fuss?" And she starts tapping my nose with her finger. And I let her.

"And why am I not cut out for love?" I insisted. But there was no answer. Instead, she began to knot my necktie, nice and slow, as one would a young boy's. In the old days the mere thought of somebody pawing my neck would have sent me into a rage. But now I said nothing. I had the feeling I was getting fat. So help me, I suddenly experienced the uncomfortable sensation of being overweight.

"Now you are all right, you look handsome," she declared, turning my face this way and that, to get a good look. "Yes, quite handsome."

"I handsome?"

"Yes, you; look in the mirror."

"No I won't. Why am I not cut out for love?"

"Well . . ."

"Come on, out with it."

"Well, is this what lovebirds supposed to look like?" And she asked this the way a schoolmistress might quiz her unruly class, or the way boarding school girls toss out naughty riddles, at night, after the lights have been turned off in their bedrooms.

"My, you're being mysterious. What *is* a lovebird like?"

"Brazen," she said without hesitation.

"And what am I?"

"Honest."

"You don't say. . . (As though she read what I jotted down the other time.) In other words, I shouldn't be honest? I ought to be a scoundrel, I suppose."

Then, changing tack, I said:

"You know something, I am not even that honest. But let's hear more about this pigeon of yours."

She started hedging again: "Well . . ."

"Come now, don't be shy."

"It's mischievous, it bites, it's not nearly as gentle as you may think . . . You don't have to be that manly, you know." Or that tough. *Mon capitain*. (She always liked to poke fun at my profession.)

"I shouldn't be manly, you say. Fine. How would you like me to be then? Tell me."

"How should I know that? Be impudent, I don't know. Be a scoundrel, like you said, just make it look good . . . Women are gullible, you know. They're like hungry calves, you can feed them anything, just make sure your teeth are bright and your smile is rougish. Pretend you've ruined all the virgins around and you'll be all right . . . Now you understand? Do you?"

She said all this with such passion, I began to wonder. But there was one more reminder:

"Don't expect life to cater to your whims. For if you do, it will play you for a fool."

That's just what my wife gave me to understand. That life will play me for a fool. A curious warning. Or her way of letting me know what sort of man was her ideal? Perhaps.

"There now," she concluded, "you've been properly instructed. Now go and play the ladies' man for a while."

"For a while?"

"Yes," she said firmly.

And that's what our life was like in those days. As I said, it was an unnerving, crazy period, dreamlike almost. And in this dream my wife was as mysterious as ever, and I as apprehensive.

I knew, however, that there are always two possibilities. You can either give up a race or go for that last push, hopeless though it may seem. I for one gave up, threw away the oars. Does she love me? Doesn't she? I no longer asked. Dedin didn't trouble my thoughts, either. I simply forgot about him.

But this was only part of the story. The other part was that I became quite interested in that little Irish girl. For she was still here. She came over from London for what was to be a short excursion but didn't feel like going home. And she told me she was in love with me. She said it in jest but really meant it, I could tell. And that's what made it so strange. . . .

At any rate, the young lady gave me to understand the following: that I was just like Micislav Mickievic. We were sitting in the garden terrace of a hotel; my wife left to try on some hats. She wanted the kind our Irish ladyfriend was wearing: a floppy one with ribbons that fluttered when she walked.

"But who is Micislav Mickievic?" I asked the little miss.

She dreamed about him, she said. Somebody approached her in a dream and said: "My dear young lady, I'd like to present Mr. Micislav Mickievic." And this dream vision of a man was very much to her liking . . .

Her nose quivered with excitement as she said this, her eyes gleamed—this young thing was teasing and mocking me with all her being.

And then she had the cheek to ask: "You don't believe me?" Sounding just like my wife did when she was this young and wanted me to swallow some big lie.

But she breezed on. She's been looking for this man ever since, she said, he became her ideal. And now at last she found him, in me. I had to laugh.

"And you never met him before, this Micislav fellow?"

"No, but I found him now."

"Listen dearie, that's not very nice of you," I tried to tease her back. As much as I could, that is. For my voice was getting a little shaky. In short, I was smitten, and drawn into this game fast. What did it, I wonder. Her wonderful smell perhaps, that virgin smell, the smell of dolls still unwrapped . . . But I kept up the banter:

"It's just not nice of you," I said again. "You are a heartless young lady, it seems, making fun of a poor old Dutchman. I weigh well over two hundred pounds, in case you didn't notice; how can you compare me to an apparition, a dream. . . ?" Then, I thought about it, and declared, quite simply:

"I love you." And took her hand.

And choked up as I did. And no wonder. Rarely in my life had I come out with such a statement, and never so abruptly. I felt as if I was on fire. And the same with her: her eyes were aflame.

"I love you too," she said, all flushed, but remaining still.

I upped the ante: "I adore you." And felt the blood rushing through my veins. I switched to French, for that seemed more intimate:

"What if I followed you to London?" This was sheer madness, of course, but I loved it.

We were soon at the point where you lose your voice, your throat goes dry, your eyes pop out, and you want to smile but can't. As I always said, such is the power of the spoken word, the peril of outer limits, which dare you to decide how far you will go. As soon as she uttered the words "I love you too," I could almost see the blood engulfing her heart. We were excited all right. Terribly excited. Like wild children. But then we had to come down, for it was impossible to go any higher.

"Look at that horse and buggy," I said, just to distract her.

"Oh, yes, yes," she mumbled, dewy-eyed, as though she had just tumbled down from the sky.

Well, that's how it all started. And an adventure-loving, funny kid she turned out to be. But the thing to remember is that I really meant what I said about leaving my wife and going after her—I meant all that giddy nonsense.

This girl was even younger . . . Oh God . . . And wouldn't it be wonderful to be free of . . . well, what? Of all the perplexities, the questions, the doubts—to be free of my wife, in short. . . . Yes, let's come out with it; it's the truth. Ah, but to live this way from now on, to be able to say things like "love" and "adore" . . .

It would be like sailing out to the open sea, where it's all stillness and light . . . And that is just how I felt then. My eyes, my heart, were filled with that light. This must surely be a highpoint, I said to myself on that garden terrace.

And it looked as though fate itself approved, because the next day I got a letter and a telegram from London, both concerning the same thing. The letter came from a large agency informing me that there would be a vacancy next winter, and exactly where I wanted it: at one of those rescue companies. Wasn't that fate pointing a finger? An offer just then? And from London, to boot. They also wrote that it might be useful to appear in person. And why not do them this courtesy, or anything else they may require? Good God, I'd have stripped to the waist, if that's what they wanted. The telegram was from Alexander Kondor who also asked me to come as soon as possible. "Where there is a will, there are beans to spill," wrote my always jolly, madcap friend, for that was his style. He never wrote letters, only lengthy telegrams full of popular sayings he made up himself. But most important, he wasn't angry about anything, must have forgotten about my accident at sea. . . . Weren't things working out just fine?

And to top it all off, music by Pergolese was coming from some window, a piece I first heard as a child when my lottery number was picked. At that time I thought I'd be fortune's pet and have a charmed life.

And here was Pergolese again. Maybe it could still come true. Oh God . . . the thought alone gave me goosebumps. Wouldn't it be something, dear God, if once, just once in my life, you treated me differently. If everyone would love me from now on, and in London, too? My wife *and* this pretty young woman? It could happen, couldn't it. . . ? I kept gushing and raving like this on a street corner. I couldn't walk on, I had to take another look at the letter and the telegram. And kept shaking with senseless joy.

The decision was made right there: I would move to London for good. That's right, for good, taking everything with me, including my wife. Yes, it has to be done that way, if only because she had been keeping an eye on things, knew all there was to know.

In fact she, too, was quite happy about the telegram.

"Bravo, Jacob," she exclaimed after reading it. "This is really something, this makes me *very* happy."

Why is she so happy, I wondered. Could it be that she herself was trying to escape? Get away from Dedin at last? That would really be a laugh. I felt like a man who had just wrung his chief enemy's neck. How sweet that was.

But why go into details? There comes a time in a man's life when he is prone to illusions, beguiling suggestions. That's what must have happened to me. Otherwise I could not easily explain how a man as cautious and circumspect as I could decide to just chuck everything, dispose of his house, sell his furniture, all because of a telegram he received from a friend. Some people, it seems, enjoy throwing away a life's work.

But word was out: we were moving to London. I began seeing the move as my salvation, the key to my future happiness; the image persisted until I began to float about listlessly, laughing vacantly, like a man without a soul.

"We're moving to London," I told my young friend, and for good measure waved the telegram before her eyes. She was somewhat taken aback.

"Really? You are coming?" Actually, she was quite crest-fallen, the poor thing.

But only for a moment.

"That's just great," she then said. She was happy for us, of course. But will I still keep my promise and take her to see one of Paris's *beautiful* cemeteries? I *had* promised her I would.

"Why of course I will," I said, feeling at that moment as generous, as exalted, as a true knight.

"Lizzy, you'll come too, won't you?" she said to my wife, ever so demurely, casting down her eyes, wanting to say of course: You're not coming, are you?

But my wife was too smart for her.

"Oh no, my dear," she said with a laugh. "I hate cemeteries. You go ahead. And have a grand time without me."

The young lady looked around hesitantly.

"Why wouldn't you go?" Lizzy went on, still smiling. "What could possibly happen if you went?" And her eyes, like two bright planets, turned on me with a knowing, appealing look.

It was no use. I was simply unable in those days to make any sense of my life. In those days, did I say? I am not much better at it today. . . .

Two

BECAUSE OF A FEW MINOR DETAILS WE COULDN'T LEAVE FOR London till early fall. I had made a couple of investments in Paris which had to be liquidated, our furniture had to be stored someplace (as it turned out, my wife couldn't part with them), she still wanted to order a new wardrobe, and so on. Time passed without our noticing it.

But finally we arrived. For the time being we didn't take a flat but moved into a fairly decent boarding house near Charing Cross. It wasn't that decent, actually; in fact it was pretty awful, and our landlord was a sanctimonious old scoundrel, but more about him later. To get to the heart of the matter, though: what was planted in Paris bore fruit in London. The sun came to shine upon me on two sides, or however that's put. When I met Alexander Kodor he sized me up and said:

"Jacob, you look dumber than when I last saw you. You used to be a pretty smart fellow, what happened? On my word, I see an idiotic expression," he added with some sympathy. Then he made me sit down and offered me an "extraordinary" cigar. "You haven't smoked such a fine cigar since Maurokordatos."

I didn't know who Maurokordatos was and didn't bother to ask. As I said, Kodor loved to make up such nonsense. I lit up and

83

began to look around in his office. How very fancy, I thought to myself. Brocades and marble all over. This chap's got it made, damn it . . .

But what about me?

A good question. I was sitting in that posh office and realized that I *was* kind of slow on the uptake. My fine friend was right, in other words: I did become dull. For would a man who was on the make act this way? Sit around meekly? So as far as that was concerned, Kodor was right. I grew lax . . . that's it: lax and sluggish. Absent. Before this I was the kind of person who said: either or. I lashed out, I pounced, I struck. Now all I could come up with was a maybe. I floundered in empty space. Kodor couldn't get over his surprise.

"Something's happened to you, Jacob," he said, quite worried, and twice passed his hand over his bald spot. "What is it, old chap? Have you become an illusionist or something?" By which he meant an idealist. And he happened to be right—I did become an idealist. I began to despise these people in London. Traders, hucksters, I called them. Stop your jabbering, I felt like saying to Kodor but thought better of it.

So he carried on and on, wanting to know why I had arrived now, three months late, and why I had to bring all my stuff with me when he cabled me to come at once. Things here changed by the minute.

"Now they don't want foreigners any more," he declared. "Still, why did you talk to those agents like some marquis of the sea?"

The truth is that I did act like a marquis of the sea with them. "Thank you ever so much," I said as I rose from my chair in the office of one of the rescue companies, adding with great dignity: "Another time perhaps."

By the way, I didn't believe a word he said about having arrived too late. They sent me on a wild goose chase, that was all. I knew what kind of people I was dealing with. What was it to them to summon me here? It was the least they could do for a man like Kodor, if that was his wish. And when I got here they couldn't care less. "At the moment there are no openings," they said obligingly. It was obvious that they were not the least bit serious about the offer. That's why I behaved like a marquis.

That the whole bloody business did not bother me much is

another matter. The best position, the best prospects couldn't get a rise out of me. I got involved with sentiments instead.

But how was I to explain this to that jackass Kodor, whose ideas about women were what mine used to be before all this happened—namely, that they were not worth discussing. That it was all right to please them when it came to bonbons and burlesque shows, but much better to get over them. But with the passage of time I've changed somewhat in this regard, and my new outlook was enough to make me see him as a stranger.

"Why show up at those agencies by yourself when I was the one who called you over?" Kodor started in again. "And most of all, why are you so damn complacent. . . ? Listen to me, Jacob, if you'll start acting like office girls, you are sunk, take my word for it. This is not Italy; this place is full of nasty people." (Apparently, he only liked nasty people.) "Be straight with me: what the hell is the matter? You've got no money? Is that what it is?"

"It's women, old chap, women," I said jokingly, smiling my stupidest smile. Even my voice surprised me, even that made me feel ridiculous.

"Women *are* a problem, wouldn't you agree?" I said hesitantly, realizing with alarm that if need be, I could be much more forthcoming on the subject.

What I really wanted to ask him was to get me a good job right here so that I wouldn't have to go out to sea again. I wanted to tell him everything, in other words, but luckily something held me back.

I should point out that I used to treat this swarthy little man with nothing but disdain. I'd get tired of his stupid conceit in no time. "I've had enough of you for a while, good-bye," I would say to him when I thought he was getting too big for his breeches. But now I had the feeling he was getting fed up with me. I just stood there, unable to move, ready to yield to some great emptiness. For a long time I stood there, like an oaf, in my neatly knotted necktie, placid, inert. . . . Good God, where was this going to end.

But when Kodor heard I had trouble with women, he eased up a bit and became quite understanding.

"So that's what it is," he said somberly. "That little minx . . . I see. But don't you worry. There are always complications . . . We'll think of something . . . But now run along, I still have work to do." It was the first time *he* dismissed me and not the other way around, but that too I swallowed. I staggered down the stairs and thought to myself: This is it, I am finished. I felt so wretched, I could hardly breathe. That I should become a love-sick old fool, that sweet nothings should be my undoing . . . this I never would have believed. No, not at my age.

Outside it was a glorious autumn day, brilliant sunshine after a quick shower, and the familiar, bustling traffic. I stopped now and then, gazed about, then stumbled on. I moved slowly and when jostled by the crowd, I got so angry, I thought I'd grab a passer-by by the neck and fling him on the pavement.

"Hey there, whoa," a policeman shouted at an intersection. "Are you deaf, man? Out of your mind?" And he angrily motioned the cars to proceed. That's right, I was almost run over. But not because of the state of mind I was in; that obliviousness had more to do with my refusal to believe in danger. The very idea that I could be run down by anything seemed . . . But let's not go into that just now.

"I am not from these parts," I said to the policeman, trying to pacify him. He was unmoved, though; a choleric sort, I decided.

After that I went into a barber shop and then did some shopping; bought myself a handsome wristwatch, twelve English handkerchiefs, real fine ones, and other assorted trifles. But then an inner voice asked: Where is the money for all this coming from? What's going to happen if you and your wife go on spending money this way? (For my wife also went on a shopping spree, in Paris, just before we left.) But I brushed aside these thoughts. It doesn't matter, nothing matters, I said, and began whistling a little tune in that crowded city. That's how *she* is all the time, I kept saying to myself. Lolling about, with not a care in the world. Her life was one long, sweet song.

Whatever was colorful now caught my eye; bright things made me take a second look. When I saw a pretty woman I had to turn around. The truth is, women began to have a maddening effect on me, in my old age. I realized, for instance, that my wife may not be as pretty as I had thought. Take her nose: it was a little too turned up, and such things do restrain the imagination. But that's man for you. If her nose were one millimeter longer, I could say I was perfectly happy. (It was rubbish of this kind, I am afraid, that I kept mulling over.)

I can still remember one young woman, in uniform, who stopped me. (She was in a procession, a member of the Salvation Army or some such group.) And I felt I could follow that woman to the end of the world. From behind a blue veil her eyes were laughing at me; and did those eyes ever sparkle . . . You could fish gold nuggets out of those eyes, I thought sadly.

"*Au revoir*, my sweet," I waved after her. In fine, I went completely dotty. "I need a change, a change," I kept yammering, like some nervous little bird.

Speaking of nerves, one hears more and more about such ailments nowadays, and how widespread they've become, though I have never given much thought to their cause. Now I have a rough idea. It may just be due to men having to dance circles around their women. I for one have always wanted to see and know everything about them, all at once, and then see everything all over again. But these mysterious creatures, dolled up like painted dummies, make you doubt your senses. Are they living beings? Are there petticoats under their frilly dresses? Can they speak, or do they just sigh and bob their heads and flutter their lashes?

"Nothing's ugly," I cried out, as happy as if the world itself was my creation. Everything is beautiful. Even old crones, even policemen . . . And the wind, too, can drive you wild, by turning things topsy-turvy; and even the freshly-sprinkled pavement can be like a streak of light . . . Oh yes, the world *is* beautiful, it *wants* to shine, its women especially. And they were everywhere, in a thousand shapes and sizes, forever on display, forever beckoning. There were those who tripped along with their tidy packages like Christmas angels, lighter, airier than any human being had a right to be. And then there were huge black women who swayed dreamily toward the City like large, lit-up barges (London *was* the world's Babylon, after all). And here and there slender, panther-like figures flitted through the crowd, in whose exotic eyes smouldered the dark Orient. And there were gentle little mothers carrying babes in their arms, tiny snowmen swaddled in thick pure white; and they would stop now and then, these lovely madonnas, to whisper mighty secrets in those tiny ears . . .

Dear God, I thought; I'll be lost if I stay on land too long. Let's just go home. Inside a cab, I closed my eyes to escape the darkness within. For I began to sense a strange and profound weariness, which no amount of exertion could produce. But we all know: sweetness devours the soul. Where do I go now? Why home, home, I realized with sudden alarm. And what's waiting for me there? More of the same . . . Puzzles and mysteries, which I will never ever get to solve.

But let me relate anyway what I found at home. A warm room decorated with flowers, which, however, was quite empty. So I knocked on the door of our other room. "Come in," I heard, as always, for entry there was never denied. Once inside, I felt myself surrounded by quiet serenity, the kind you feel in Moorish bathhouses where all you hear is the quiet purl of the spouts. (Here that gurgling was my wife's laughter greeting me.) But that quiet . . . it is so basic to life, so much in the world depends on it. A Dutch poet once wrote:

> Flowers are for loving
> Men for forgetting.
>
> In raiment of white
> An island I sight.
>
> I fly there with books . . . etc., etc.

That's how my wife was then. She read even more than before, reclining as a rule on the sofabed. It was as if she really did live on an island, far away from people, in a state of complete repose. And she always had lots of flowers and potted plants about, which made the air somewhat misty; the smell of soil also lingered in the room. If I close my eyes I can still recall this smell, which usually mingled with other, delicately feminine scents and light, fragrant cigarette smoke. All together it used to make me quite heady. It was also dim in that room most of the time—we got little sun, and only in the morning.

"What did you bring me, Papa Bear?" she would ask whenever I got back from town. "A little present maybe? A little something?" And I made believe I didn't bring her anything.

"I have no money," I said despondently. "What could I buy you? We are poor."

"Oh no, what a shame," she replied, "I am sadder than I can say." But her lament sounded so frivolous, a stranger would surely have thought it odd. There was no content to it—almost like the mock cry of a hysteric.

But we kept it up:

"It is a shame, isn't it," I sighed.

"Ah, life is not worth living," she moaned.

We both gave way to grief, and were quite, quite miserable. I sat on the trunk and grieved there, while my wife, bent on hiding her tears, turned to the wall and covered her eyes. But only one of them, with the other she peeked and laughed. . . . My pockets of course were filled with presents, and she knew this, and was dying to find out what they were. For that's what that woman lived for in those days, those little pleasures and surprises. But right now she restrained herself.

"Your pocket is torn, let me see it," she said at last, but by now she trembled with curiosity, with desire.

"You'll mend it some other time, leave it, my sweet."

Thus we tormented each other thus, with all manner of sweetness, until we could stand it no longer. I should also mention that we didn't even use intelligible language, as would be expected of grownup people. We gave words our own meaning. My wife would say, "Give me a kiwi fruit," and I was supposed to know that she wanted to be kissed. She called her slippers dunderheads, and me she called Captain Liverpool for some reason. I remember we had an argument over this. "I know perfectly well what you're hinting at," I said to her, cool and collected, though I knew perfectly well she wasn't hinting at anything. This went on for a while: I was reasonable, she was uppity; I was earnest, she was sarcastic. At one point, though, I lost my composure.

"I will not stand for such insinuations," I said furiously, and brought down my fist on the table, which promptly cracked.

God Almighty, if Alexander Kodor would have seen me now. Me, a seasoned, tempest-tossed veteran. These are your great feats, he would have said most certainly. A sea captain reduced to breaking table tops.

One day I was making coffee. Enveloped by the silence of late afternoon, I felt pleasant vibrations all around, and then the even richer emanations of the aromatic espresso. Such moments almost put you in a poetic frame of mind. But then she came through the door in her rain coat.

"There is a storm out there," she said, quite indignant.

"You don't say. My goodness."

"And my heart, my heart is aching, too."

"Come then, we'll take care of it."

"You will, really? But my hair hurts, too," she said gently.

"Oh no, that too. My poor darling, my sad little pet." And I embraced her.

"Tell me more, what else is the matter?"

"You know what?" she whispered. "Growl a little."

"Again?"

"Yes, I want you to growl." Just to please her, I set about growling and since I was an old hand at it, I growled ever more raucously, like a wild beast gargling. Then she said:

"Oh Mr. Lion, how do you do?" and she curtsied sweetly. But she turned pale too; I think I scared her a little.

"This is such a dreadful city," she said all of a sudden.

"Why is that?"

"I am just afraid I will die here."

Why should she be afraid of dying in London? It wouldn't hurt to look into that . . .

One day I came home and found her sleeping. She woke up with these words: "I slept under a cloud." That told me a lot. She was feeling low from time to time, apparently. But why, over what? I didn't ask; I didn't pry.

Why should I have? Why brood and worry when the games we were playing were so intriguing, so delicious?

For instance I would wrap a scarf around my head like a turban—I was sent to the corner just then as a Persian soldier. And I had to sit there with my legs crossed, and not budge, for I was the guard. Imagine now the total silence. "Where is my mirror? Where is my apron?" she'd ask, but there would be no answer. Then, wearing nothing but black silken knickers, she would start preening and strutting, displaying herself like some oriental courtesan. I once saw two women who, not knowing they were being watched, bared themselves to each other. That's how she was now, putting a hood over her head, shrouding herself, then stripping before her mirror, as if she had the room all to herself. Then she called out: "Mazud, oh Mazud," and clapped her hands. That was me. But I was supposed to sit absolutely still and ask: "Is your husband at home?" And ogle her shamelessly.

"No, he is not," she crooned.

"We are all alone then?"

Whereupon she lit into me: "You stay where you are. What got into you anyway? Listen, you disgusting creature, I will not cheat on my husband . . . on such a fine, decent man . . . You pudgy servant, you . . ." And she was quite outraged.

Pudgy eh? I'd had enough. Leaping to my feet I yelled "Mutiny!" And then, darkly: "Enough of this comedy."

Ah, but what all this led to . . . What voluptuous pleasures, what renewals; and more than once, what unsurpassable raptures. By the time darkness descended, we didn't dare look at each other; huddling in our corners, we wrapped ourselves in blankets and fell asleep, distant, forlorn, like two black heaps on a field of ice.

At other times the first light of dawn found her by the foot of my bed, with her hand on her side, shaking with laughter.

"Please don't make me laugh," she begged. I had been telling her risqué little anecdotes about men who were hopelessly clumsy in lovemaking.

"Somebody ought to write a Casanova story in reverse," I said.

Not that that was what I was doing. I was talking about myself, of course, twisting things a little, to make me look even more ridiculous. Let the precious woman have some fun. Let her remember what an oaf her husband used to be . . . How many times it happend that women kept caressing my foot under the table, and I still thought it was an accident . . . Now I was telling her about the peasant woman who asked me to pull out my rabbit.

"What did she want to see?"

"My rabbit. Of course I didn't know what she meant. Where was I going to get her a rabbit?"

"Don't go on, please," purred my wife. But I couldn't be stopped. I told her now about the time, long long ago, when I gave violin lessons. (Yes, yes, I even did that.) I wasn't very good at the violin, but where we lived in the provinces it didn't much matter. My student's mother happened to be a splendid woman, grand in spirit, and in body too. Whereas I was young and unusually skinny. I was too scared to even look at her, though she did tickle my fancy, as can be imagined. One day she sent word that she wished to discuss her son's progress with me.

Well, I was open to discussion. It was early spring, I remember; the apartment was flooded with light. I pulled on my necktie several times before opening her door. Once inside, however, I was shocked beyond words. For my student's high-minded mother received me in bed, submerged in downy softness.

"What are you doing to me?" squealed my wife once again, in vain, for I went on, undettered.

"I sat down in a chair, though just barely (you always leave a little space behind you at such times, just in case). I was going to regale her with everything I knew, and even what I didn't, about education and childrearing and such, and thought of including my thoughts on metempsychosis, too, when I noticed that this beautiful lady pulled her leg, nice and easy, from under the fluffy featherbed. What could this mean? I wondered. And even thought of the French Revolution—maybe she was a freethinker or something. She stuck out her leg *all* the way, you see, not just halfway, and her leg was stunningly white . . ."

"Oh, look, for heaven's sake, it's getting light," my wife said in a plaintive voice, and pointed toward the silent windows. The sun was indeed coming up, emerging gold and bright from the mist . . . And a beautiful sight it was . . .

But let's stop here for a moment. I was so overwhelmed by what happened that night, I thought I was ready to face the music. We had raged all night long like jungle beasts, ravished each other with out teeth . . . And then that bewitching laugh, and the dawn that followed . . . Can one take more? You have quite a lover, I said to myself; won't she do? And this night, wasn't it enough? But what I really would have liked to do was whisper in her ear:

I have another lover, you know. Yes, for once I have one too, and even more beautiful than you. And do you know who my other lover is. . . ?

Ah, what a thrill it would have been to tell her.

* * *

She wasn't even my lover.

It's true, we kissed now and then, in cemeteries, on country roads . . . just like in Paris that first night, in the famous Montmartre cemetery.

"No, you mustn't, Micislav, you mustn't, for pity's sake," she said every time, with an imploring look in her eyes. But I didn't care; all I ever wanted to do now is kiss. Another time she said:

"Oh, what am I doing here, Micislav? I must be mad." To which I replied:

"It's an irresistible force, my dear." (She herself told me one time: "Love, Micislav, is an irresistible force.")

"But is that what it is to you?" she now asked. "Tell me. Look into my eyes. Do you love me at all. . . ? No, you don't," she said abruptly and walked away. I ran after her and gave her a song and dance about how much I adored her . . .

I didn't, of course. I loved no one. No one. And I reached this conclusion with a light heart, I was proud of myself, in fact.

Actually, I discovered a wonderful way out: it's what people call sensuality. . . . Why take these women seriously? For, instance: does she love me, does my little sweetheart really love me? Then why does she call me Micislav? Whenever I thought about it, I had to laugh. It was all a game. The young lady was having fun at my expense. In the meantime, though, kissing her was very nice.

One day I decided I was going to divorce my wife and marry the other one. It all came about so fast, I was quite surprised myself. Here's how it happened:

I had a date with her and was late (not the first time, either). When I arrived she came running toward me.

"Are you all right, are you all right?" she sobbed, and in front of all the passers-by threw herself into my arms. Actually, though there was quite a crowd (we were in a suburban railroad station), the people didn't really notice us. They seemed preoccupied with their own concerns and appeared quite sullen. There was one old lady, however, who seemed to approve. She kept staring at us, and while her demeanor was grave, too, she twice nodded her head, apparently thinking we were husband and wife and very much in love. . . . Not knowing what to make of the whole thing, I was somewhat embarrassed.

But not ashamed. If anything, I was proud of this "wife," this slender young thing with airy footsteps ... Who would have believed that such a girl would reward me with her love—*me*, who was way past his prime. Up until that moment I couldn't imagine such a thing. But when I heard her say, "Are you all right?" and felt her quickening heartbeat, something stirred in my heart, too.

But back to the incident. She had all kinds of premonitions that day, she told me. The night before she had a dream in which she was leaning out of a window and crying. That was the extent of it, but she was terrified all the same, because it was me she was crying over. In the morning she was in a great hurry to see me, fearing all the while that she might be too late. Just as she got to the railroad station, she saw a crowd of people; they were taking a man away. Something had fallen on him from a scaffolding and he died. They had shouted after him not to go that way, but apparently he didn't hear, he was absorbed in his thoughts ...

"And you are the same way," she scolded me. "You never listen, you're never careful. And trouble can strike so fast ... It doesn't take much."

Of course she tried to find out right away who the victim was. Somebody from Copenhagen, they told her: a Dane. In other words, her suspicions were confirmed. For in her confusion she thought I was from Copenhagen. She may have acted very silly, but she *was* terrified. And no wonder: She even asked if the victim was a large man, and they said he was. She just stood there on the sidewalk, weeping. At worst, I'll die, too, she decided.

"You see, you see," she now said to me. "I love you so much and you treat me horribly."

I cannot begin to describe what gladness, what calm filled my heart at this moment. She was a good girl after all, despite her odd ways. And I suddenly remembered other little incidents which at the time I hardly paid attention to. Like when she brought me some pills for my headache; or the time she berated me for not buying a wintercoat, and other such trifles. Who in my life had ever shown such concern, who ever cared about me so much? And such a young girl, who was not mature enough to be this considerate. I said to her now:

"I did treat you badly, I know; and it pains me, too. But what am I to do if my fate turned me into such a heartless man. With a life such as mine it was inevitable ... I want to talk to you openly."

And I was ready to tell her everything, above all, that I hated my wife; and that only now that I was with her did I realize how much I hated her—I didn't even feel like going home.

I also meant to explain to her that my life was not yet over, and implore her to save me, save my wretched life—she was the only one who could . . .

"I wasn't always like this," I said to her, and already felt myself getting a little warm. "But do you know what it's like to be tormented? Tormented until you are ravaged, your mind, your heart, until you are turned into a thoroughly despicable man. . . ?

At this point I suddenly fell silent.

How was I going to tell her the rest? The most important part. About my wife and me, how we lived even now. For even if I had just thought of our fun and games . . . But no way did I want to think of that when I was with her. I was ashamed of my life, realized how loathsome it really was. Being with her was like stepping out of some dive into the fresh air and seeing peaceful, beautiful country all around.

How very different this girl is, I thought wistfully as I glanced at her. How sweet and pure; and how beautiful.

But why did she lower her head?

And why didn't she answer? Or did she find everything I said— my whole miserable story—so self-evident that she wasn't even surprised? Maybe she knew about it all. That's what her demeanor seemed to suggest.

And not just now. I had long suspected that she knew more than she let on. But if she did, how did she? This puzzled and intrigued me more than ever.

I thought the best thing would be simply to ask her. Actually, something happened at home just then that I mustn't leave out.

It was nothing much, really, though the consequences were momentous. I found a couple of withered violets on the top of the cupboard, amid a dusting of green moss. This in itself was nothing unusual, of course, except that it followed another discovery. A few weeks earlier I had found a handsome little box in the wastebasket and that also had a sprinkling of the green stuff. It appeared that someone had sent my wife flowers in that box. I've seen it before: when flowers are sent in a box, they are packed in ice and placed in a bed of moss. They can be exquisite, these arrangements, and that is probably why she didn't have the heart to throw it all out.

But even if it wasn't so, even if it was a mistake . . . Should I make myself crazy again, start all over, wonder if Ridolfi, or somebody else, followed her here?

No, no, I've had enough.

I decided to be quite frank with the girl. I asked her quite plainly:

"Why did you become so quiet last time when I started talking about my wife? Do you know something? Are you angry with her for some reason?"

By now I had no doubt in my mind that I was right in surmising that the two had a falling out, possibly while we were still in Paris. That they must have quarreled seemed pretty obvious, but could things really be that bad between them? Apparently, because here in London they no longer wanted to have anything to do with each other.

Whenever I mentioned our English friend to my wife, she'd say with utter disdain, "Oh, that silly goose." In other words she made no secret of her feelings.

"What makes you think she's a silly goose?" I'd inquire, trying to get her to tell me more. And thinking to myself: In Paris you didn't think so. In Paris you fell all over her. And now all of a sudden she is a goose. Another time I said to her quite casually: "Yesterday I visited that Irish family." Like hell I did, but let her think I frequented their house. But she said nothing, I simply couldn't draw out her anger.

Her eyes, on the other hand, told a different story. They seemed to be saying: I know exactly what you're up to, I know your every move, so spare me your explanations. I did, as a matter of fact . . . We were both kind of sly, actually. On days when I had a date with my little miss, I began sighing and scratching early in the morning: "I should really get some exercise," Or: "I should go and see that blasted Kodor again." Or, fretfully: "Another damn business appointment."

My wife, who was a smart woman, kindly endorsed everything. "You should get a little more exercise," she said. Or: "You mustn't neglect your business affairs." In short, she was encouraging me, if not as openly as in Paris in the old days, but still. And truth to tell, I didn't need that much prodding. I just ignored the flash in her eyes.

"I won't go out today; not today," I'd say in the morning, and by early afternoon I was on my way.

But let me expand a little on that famous falling-out. I already mentioned that my wife and the little miss were all lovey-dovey when they first met in Paris. But shortly before Miss Borton left, it was all over. That in itself is not so unusual; after all, such friendships can never last. But that it should end so abruptly, from one day to the next . . . One minute they were fine, and then suddenly things turned sour, as if they had both drunk vinegar or something . . . I was there, I saw it with my own eyes. My wife wanted to appear very grand, which made me immediately suspicious, for that sort of thing doesn't become her, she is anything but grand. The girl noticed it too, and even said: "Lizzy, stop putting on airs." That's what did it, I think. My wife gave her a smile, a tight little one, a smile of hers I knew only too well. You and I are through, my friend, is what that smile said.

But what did happen between those two? For that whole business remains a puzzle, for a number of reasons. Miss Borton was, after all, a smart young lady; how was it possible that somebody like her would stand by me and get seriously involved? What happened in Paris could be seen as a lark of sorts, a jest. (English ladies on holiday do get strange ideas, everyone knows that.) But this was London. Strangely enough, she never mentioned my wife, took no notice of her, pretended she didn't exist. In short, she became callous.

But why did she? Why? Did she find out something about her? Or did Lizzy herself say anything? About her gentleman friends perhaps? I wouldn't put it past her, she did have a loose tongue, she was famous for it—something like that could very easily have slipped out. It's these questions I wanted answered when I asked why she was sore at my wife. I just wanted to get the story straight. It was high time.

"Did anything happen between you two?" I kept pressing her, turning her head toward me. "Be honest with me."

"I don't want to talk about it," she retorted. Then, with sudden passion: "I don't even want to think about her. I . . . I don't like Lizzy any more."

(She *was* a different sort, I knew it. An honest kid. Sincere.)

"Really? And why don't you like her? I don't quite understand; couldn't you tell me a little more about it? It's very important to me, even if it's just one word . . . Did you confide in her at all?"

"Yes, I did."

"I thought so. And I think I also know what happened. She must have purposely, spitefully told you something that isn't true." (I realized I was changing the subject. But why did I try to defend her? To get the girl to reveal her secret? Or was it just a natural reaction?) "That's how she is, you know. She just wanted to annoy you probably, she never misses an opportunity to do that, to provoke a young girl like you—that's Lizzy for you. But you know, she is not as spiteful and mean as she makes herself out to be."

"Is that so?" she said ominously. "Then I must have misunderstood you last time . . . But maybe she isn't," she corrected herself. "Maybe you're right . . . I don't know her all that well. So you see, I couldn't really tell you anything special, it wouldn't even be fair; she *was* nice to me. She even gave me something—look, here it is, this is what she gave me." And she pulled a ring off her finger, a narrow little band, quite lovely actually, studded with tiny garnets.

"But now I am going to get rid of it," she said suddenly, and actually flung the ring on the floor and crushed it with her foot; you could hear the little gems cracking. (We were sitting in a small restaurant near Haymarket.)

"You just go on loving your wonderful wife then," she said, "I will not stand in your way . . ." I was right in other words: she *was* nursing a grudge. But never mind, I said to myself, I have time, I'll get it out of her yet; and she won't even know it.

"Oh that Lizzy," she continued, with a great deal of emotion, "she told me the only reason I loved you was because you were the captain of that ship. Isn't that ridiculous? Does she really think I am that stupid?"

"And is that the reason why you are so angry with her?"

"No, it's not, not really. But the real reason I shall never tell you."

"Look here, Mrs. Murray," she said irritably to her milliner, "it's no good sleeping all the time; what will you do at night?" She was angry because we had to knock on her door for a long time before she opened up. Then in a different, even sterner voice, she said:

"We just want to sit in your parlor for a while, like last time."

We *had* been there before. These visits were a new development. Miss Borton, you see, didn't like to sit in restaurants, she liked to walk. But she had to realize that we couldn't go on doing that forever, either, mainly because all those walks were driving me crazy, but also because we were plagued by bad weather; it was constantly raining. And as soon as she felt raindrops, she insisted on going home. After a while I didn't let her, I simply refused to let her go home. With the result that she caught a chill and started sniffling. Which made her very angry.

"You'll be the death of me yet," she said to me, quite annoyed. But then she came up with this solution, telling her milliner that she'd like to use her room now and then for a little chat. Of course we were terribly well-behaved while there; the lady was sawing hats in the next room.

But on this particular day she had to leave, which may have been a mistake. She stuck her head in through the door and said:

"I am going to the green grocer."

So we stayed alone in a flat that smelled of green apples.

Miss Borton was a little taken aback; we were never alone before.

I began stroking her hair.

"Don't be afraid of me," I said, and looked into her eyes. Whereupon she broke into tears.

"Oh, you do really love me then," she said, flaring up with passion.

I then told her what my plans were, or rather, all I said was:

"Will you be good?" And miraculously enough, she knew right away what I was hinting at.

"You want to marry me then? But how can that be? You'll never do it, you are like me. You could never banish her from your heart."

I looked at her in amazement. There was something about this girl, something so unusual, it baffles me still. On the one hand she was immature, child-like almost, but sometimes, out of the blue, in a deep sleep, as it were, she said something which made you sit up and take notice. She had a way—I don't know—of stumbling upon your most secret feelings. Could it be that she knew me better than I thought, better than I knew myself?

"That *would* be a shame, wouldn't it," I said at first, "if it were true, I mean." Obviously, it wasn't so pleasant hearing such a thing from somebody else. But then I tried to make light of it:

"Don't frighten me so, little girl. Is that the kind of man you think I am? A sad sack who's too scared to make a move, too scared to touch anything new. . . ?"

And already I was getting hot under the collar.

For if this was really so . . .

I tried to change tack: "Look, what can I tell you about all this? Where should I begin? Should I tell you my whole life story? You ought to be smart enough to get my drift. If I told you I wouldn't want to go on living if my life stayed the same, you should know exactly what I have in mind."

I shocked myself in a way. As soon as I said these words, it was as though somebody touched my arm and said: That's enough. I realized just then why I fell silent the other time, why I needed to defend my wife in front of Miss Borton. It seems I had not known the meaning of the word shame till then. The very idea that I should make confessions, to anyone, about my life, what it had been like before, seemed absurd, impossible . . . Tempting but impossible. No way was I going to own up. No, not to anyone, let alone to this girl.

So I started berating her, for that's something altogether different. It makes dealing with serious matters so much simpler.

Did she think I was a fraud and a cheat? A prattler who abused her confidence? What else would explain why she never believed me, why she kept asking me if I really loved her?

"I am here, aren't I?" I said to her. "Or is it only words that you need? You, too, like all the rest? A man, in the flesh, is not enough? I by myself am not proof enough? Or should I start proving to you now that my feelings are genuine? Whatever I said or did up to now doesn't count? Don't you *feel* right now what my life is all about? Can't you see that for me being with you is better than anything else in the world?"

The funny thing was that all this time I was suffused with such warmth, such tenderness . . . There she stood before me, her mouth moist and half open, but also determined and defiant, like a sulking child. With all her little might, it seemed, she wanted to think this through. So I took her hand and would have looked into her eyes, but she turned away.

"Could this be true?" was all she said, but so gloomily, as if she didn't dare think on the matter any more.

This felt even better, even more titillating. Here at long last was someone who was all mine; I could tell her anything I wished, anything at all, and she remained unflinchingly loyal. At this point I tried, like a strict uncle at a family council, to advise her against me:

"Now the only question remaining is whether you love me," I said, half in jest. "No, no, just a minute; let's be rational about this. It won't hurt you to think it over, young lady, to look into your heart one more time. To make sure it's not a mere infatuation. For here we have a young girl who's decided to marry a sailor. Now we know all about sailors, and also about young girls' dreams. Life is hard as it is (and here I raised my voice) but with men like these . . ." And I began to list the faults of seafaring men: we were uncouth, unreliable, tyrannical—not too many women would be willing to put up with us . . .

"I would," she said, and so eagerly, too.

"I am not so young any more, you know," I added. The girl shook her head.

"And I am not a rich man, let's not forget that either. You couldn't live the way you have until now. Do you have any idea what it's like to take a two-penny notebook, rule it carefully, and enter every single expense? Would you really like to live that way?"

"Why," she whispered, "what is your income?" And at that even my heart began to beam, so sweet that word "income" was, coming from her lips. And her eyes became dewy, her brow glistened. I gently swept back her hair, and explained to her that I had no fixed income—sometimes it was more, sometimes less. In such circumstances one had to learn to economize. Did she have any idea what that meant?

"Oh, you don't know me then," she said. "I have lots of experience. You just have to be thrifty, that's all. Suppose you have an income of six hundred a year. That's not very much, is it? But it's enough for me."

She figured it all out, she said, and it was enough. She even began to learn to cook, in secret.

Here I had to stop. What absolutely captivated me was the idea of her cooking for me. Which was a proposition not without its danger, as I was a man with a sensitive stomach. But that this angel should want to do it still, with her lovely, fragile hands . . . It was sheer enchantment.

I began to tell her about my mother, herself a wonderful cook, to encourage her perhaps to go ahead and learn as much as she can. Ah, those cakes of hers . . . Our mother did her baking in a huge, wood-burning oven and used a long baker's peel. What fantastic fires we saw through the curtained glass door when the oven was opened (mother usually baked at night), and how those breads purred and seethed . . . as if they were having a hell of a good time in there. And how exciting it all was for us children; we got out of bed even in winter, just so we wouldn't miss any of that music. *De wafels*, I said to myself and smiled. Yes, de wafels, the waffles, and all the rest . . . I was touched.

Wasn't it strange, though? Decades had passed and I never thought of any of this. I realized now what power my own words have over me.

But what is it with me? I wondered. Am I such an eloquent speaker, such a clever conjurer? Though what I spoke of did seem beautiful, to me at least. I could almost see the golden-brown loaves being removed from the fiery oven, I could almost touch them with my hand.

Ah well . . . In South America I once tasted a curious sort of berry—or was it a fruit?—that the Indians enjoyed on their feast days. Well, those things induced an intoxication a hundred times more powerful than wine. I can still remember seeing mounds of berries shimmering, and feel the whole world rising in a crescendo of motion. It was the same now. And what followed was pure enchantment—visions out of a dream.

I told her I would work very hard again, but this time it would be worth it. Until now I was chasing after an impossible dream, but now I realized these dreams were life's own gifts to me. . . . It was with such high-flown phrases that I tried to impress her, though I knew that much of it was vapid nonsense. And I realized, too, that I wasn't exactly in a rapturous state, I wasn't a lanky young man confessing his feelings to his beloved for the first time, touching her knees with his under the table and leaning close to hear her say, breathlessly: "This was a magical afternoon."

"Oh my heaven, you can touch fire," she suddenly said, and her eyes lit up in amazement. Yes, a bit of glowing tobacco fell out of my pipe and I swept it off with my hand. Only what's so amazing about that?

But that's enchantment for you.

Outside it was raining quietly. I touched her hand, and felt for the first time that afternoon that this was an ineffable moment. Her hand was burning, and that made me shiver. This whole exchange, I realized, was more significant than I could ever imagine; the significance amounted to . . . well, love. Which *is* an extraordinary thing, after all; we all thirst for it, like dry soil for rain. It cannot be helped.

Still, I didn't kiss her, not just then. It would be all wrong, I decided. Now she trusted me, I ought to be virtuous.

It may have been a mistake, though. But then, who can ever be sure what another person wants? How do I know if she'll take it as a sign of cowardice or as evidence of sublime virtue? Actually, she may have wanted to be kissed now, because she was still in a daze, walking in a dream. . . . I asked her to bring me a glass of water, and she went to get it. But I couldn't sit still, I ran after her . . . There she stood by the sink, letting the water run, not knowing what to do next. Her hands shaking, she looked at me, her eyes wide open.

"Marry me," she said quietly. "Please?" But as if in a dream. Then almost pleading:

"I will be very good, you'll see." She leaned back her head on my shoulder, and her mouth was like a flower offering itself to the spring sun . . . And with that the enchantment was over. For as soon as she said these words, as if caught by a flame, she fled to the other room.

She sat in the middle of the room, sulking. "What's the matter, why are you angry now?" I asked.

No, no, she said, she wasn't angry.

"Why do you say you aren't when you are?" And I tried to kiss her hand. But that's just what she wasn't going to let me do; it was definitely too late for that. I turned on the light, but that was even worse; she prefered the dark.

"Come now, don't be cross," I said and leaned over closer.

"Ah, let me be, for Christ's sake," she exclaimed. And went on, telling me not to torture her, she wasn't the type of person who got angry. But then she got so flustered, she almost broke into tears.

"You don't know us Irish," she said, flushing crimson. "Just don't forget who you are dealing with; I am not one of your French chippies."

What was that supposed to mean? The Irish never lost their temper, was that it? I tried the lighter approach:

"Do you really hate French girls that much?" But there was no answer. "Look here, you are angry with me now because of my wife; but that's not quite fair. Besides, what have you got to do with her? I already told you that I will be divorcing her shortly."

"Oh, stop it," she cut in, "you will never marry me and you know it." And she said this with such finality, such bitterness, I didn't quite know what to answer.

"What must I do to make you believe me?"

But she turned away, still angry. And no wonder: I no longer sounded that convincing, my words just didn't have the same force as before, when it was dark in the room.

"But you mustn't be quite so impatient," I said, trying again to bring her around. "You must realize that getting a divorce is never easy, especially in a case like mine.

Actually, I had no idea what I should be telling her.

But then, a sudden inspiration: "There is the other party to consider. I don't even know if she is willing to divorce me. So you see, it's not as simple as all that. I have every hope that we'll be able to go through with it, but what if I can't get her to agree, if she says she won't do it, what then?"

"Then kill her," she blurted angrily.

I had to laugh at that, though at least it was a practical idea.

I didn't bother to ask why she felt I should kill my wife. I was getting ideas myself.

* * *

One of which was that my wife may have been thinking of the same thing herself—that it wouldn't be a bad idea to get rid of me. I surmised this from the following tell-tale signs:

She began to show a lively interest in stories of this kind, in crimes reported in the newspapers, for instance. She began to follow these conspicuously, provocatively even, now that I think of it. Some of them she even read to me. There was an interesting one just the other day. It seems there were two women, two cousins, who lived together somewhere in the Highlands, one of them still young, the other quite a bit older. The young one was getting awfully tired of her old cousin who gave her no peace. She was also in love, so she didn't waste much time and killed the old hag; and she did it cleverly, too, with nicotine. No one would have found out if she didn't give it away herself; for after the murder she stopped being so clever. . . . My wife wanted to know what I thought about the story.

What could I say?

"Is it so easy to kill somebody with nicotine?" she inquired.

"How should I know? Why don't you try it?"

At first I didn't pay much attention to the whole thing. But then, what I heard began to sound more interesting.

"Poor woman," sighed my wife. I though she meant the older one, of course, the one who got killed. But no, she felt sorry for the young one for giving herself away. She even defended her, and proceeded to give me a little lecture about people who become unneeded, superfluous. About those insolent and aggressive powers, as she put it, who are no longer useful but who nevertheless linger on, for the sole purpose, it seems, of torturing those around them.

"You know something?" she continued. "I not only sympathize with that woman, I think she was right for doing what she did. Whoever becomes a burden to others should learn to be modest and get out of the way. That's exactly what I will tell myself if I should find myself in that situation. If you're no longer capable of making anything of your life, at least let others live. That's precisely what I will say to myself."

Was I one of those superfluous powers? No, she couldn't possibly mean me, I wasn't that old yet. So I even smiled at her words, and couldn't get over how forthright and incisive her train of thought was . . . No wonder she liked to read philosophy. She was at once impartial and passionately involved, as though it was her personal concern. With such conviction she spoke, such empathy . . . What an odd creature . . .

"Fine," I said, "with yourself you *can* do as you please. But with others? Your are not trying to suggest, I hope, that you can always tell who is superfluous and who is not."

"Oh please," she said with a dismissive wave, "of course you can."

I took her word for it; she may have been right, for all I knew. I am uncertain about so many things, and have been all along. So like often before, I told myself: This is her great advantage over me, her instincts. That's what gives her such confidence; and that's why she is so original and so vigorous mentally. She is not overburdened, as I'd always been, with the clutters of an anti-quated and self-absorbed world.

I couldn't even decide which was the greater act of folly: not to take what she said personally, or to start believing, as I did the following day, that she did in fact had me in mind. Perhaps there was no way of knowing. One thing is certain, though: the more troubled your conscience, the more menacing your imagination becomes. And as a matter of fact, I was pretty guilt-ridden at that time; I thought of many of these things when I was with Miss Borton, and even afterwards, while walking home alone.

"Superfluous power?" I'd mumble to myself on these solitary walks, and my words seemed to lighten the black pavement.

I ought to be more modest, then. That's what my lady wants. Because I am in the way. Because I no longer count. What could be clearer than this?

And didn't she do a fine job explaining to me what I had never understood before: that we were two people thrown together by chance, who were now mired in cloying sensuality? Ach, it turned my stomach just to think about it. . . .

But why does she want to get rid of me? I tried arguing with myself. And why now, when she seemed perfectly happy lolling about the house all day. It didn't make sense. Or maybe it did. She was in love, or would have liked to be. With whom? Somebody. Anybody. But so soon after the bitter Paris disappointment?

Why not? When it comes to love, everyone is in a hurry, trying to get a little more, a little faster. Am I not the same way? Didn't I once threaten to turn my scalesman loose on her, if she was going to leave me? Now she was threatening me, daring me to get out of her way. Why, of course. . . .

Now no one should misunderstand me, and imagine that I am a hotheaded fool who trembles for his life and is beset by terrifying visions. That's not the case at all, we seamen are made of sterner stuff. And while we are at it, let me say something about this grand subject: Life and Death. Let me explain how our kind of people feel about it.

We don't easily get scared, and don't much bother about death, if only because we don't put such a high value on life. For example, this is what my dear papa said a half hour before his death:

"I am so very tired of all this," and he put down his newspaper. But then he corrected himself: "I am tired of all of *you*." And shortly thereafter he gracefully expired.

But that's how we all are. We are not crazy about life; we are pessimists, yes, let me emphasize that (though I am not using the word pessimist the way the philosophers do, but in a simpler sense).

"Have you ever seen a little pig?" my father once asked me. "It's a soft little thing, isn't it? People hold it in their hand, but when they want to kill it, of course it squeals. Well, that's your lot in life, son—to squeal," instructed my old man in his calmest, friendliest manner.

Yes, that is my lot, my soul's burden. That man is not happy here I never doubted. This is not just an opinion I hold—the feeling is part of me. The hole world is a desperate joke, and to be human is an outrage. The soul man is endowed with is most cruelly abused; he is deceived, led on with untold promises. He carries within him—how is it usually said?—the momentousness of his existence, a longing for eternity. And what is his fate? Fear and flight; mortal danger from first to last. That tiny, borrowed fire is forever threatened with extinction.

And what about all the rest? Like a charging battery, I absorb memories, but even so, much of it dissipates, or is altered, transformed, by time and distance—no one can find out about them. . . . So that is my life story, a story nobody else knows, a story I myself do not believe in the end. And yet, all this is not proof enough, because in the end you still want more and more. . . . your're insatiable, like a man who drinks too much water and, though ready to pass out, is still thirsty. In fine, this world is unfathomable for the human soul, this is not its real home, it longs for something else. But if it is an alien place for man, who is it for. . . ?

Oh, but why go on about this? Some superior intellect may find it diverting, pleasurable even, to assay the futile struggles of my life. But I am no philosopher, and may not even be expressing myself properly. Yet, I must let my feelings be known somehow.

To sum up, then: I never feared for my own life. If I have to go, I'll go. I will even do it as a favor to someone, if they should insist on it. So that wasn't what scared me, it was something else—the mere thought of having to continue living with my wife. For now I felt I could really tear myself away.

And that's why Miss Borton saying I will never ever leave my wife had such a terrifying effect on me. My believing her is what scared me. It was as if she held a mirror to my face, in which I saw a terrified face—a distraught and terrified face.

In the end, though, I calmed down; my girl was so sweet, we made up. She said, "Micislav, I am not angry with you, I'll be patient." And she even took me into her confidence, lessoning me, chiding me. She'd give me an apple and ask if I was hungry. Or she would want to know if I had a toothache, or if liked beer, and if I didn't, why not?—she liked it a lot. By now, you see, she let me in on her secrets.

"I just love a mug of dark ale," she'd say demurely, like a little angel, casting down her celestially chaste eyes. And I could just see her dashing off in her flounced green dress, a pale pink rose on her bosom, holding a giant keg of beer, and even licking the foam off her lips like a kitten. However, that's not the only thing she loved; everything that's of this world was to her liking. Like money, for instance, which she loved not only in the abstract, like good people generally do—she simply adored coins, especially if they were shiny new. I took her some, in modest amounts at first: a few sparkling half-crown pieces, newly-minted Maria Theresa thalers, even commemorative gold coins. And how she agonized over accepting them:

"Oh, but this is gold," she squealed, all flushed and moist, struggling still. But how quickly that little piece of gold disappeared once she has brought herself to accepting it.

"Oh, dear . . . thanks so very much, really," she said somewhat guiltily, "I might as well take it then." Her pocketbook clicked and the gold piece vanished.

All right, this can't be called greed yet; this may still be a childish fascination, an old, old obsession. But she did make sure she got what was coming to her; and she haggled if necessary.

"Do you think I am made of money," she'd say to merchants indignantly. And to me, too, she once said:

"You are altogether too wasteful, Micislav. You work too hard for your money; don't squander it." And to the owner of the restaurant where we happened to be then:

"I get better service for my money elsewhere. So there!" And with that she got up; we had to leave.

She gave me the following explanation for her behavior: "There are people, you know, who have to work very hard for every penny they own." She too had a difficult time selling some baskets she had weaved herself, put a lot of effort into them, still, some went to waste. Or you are in a store, she said, and they give you the wrong change, or you buy a dozen eggs and three of them are rotten. . . . Wasn't all of that quite annoying?

She went on and on about this, teaching me, giving me pointers on how to live more frugally. We were out taking a walk. We still did a lot of that, an awful lot; she must have had a great inner need for these walks.

Once, however, she caught quite a chill. We were out again, quite a distance from London, and it suddenly got very cold. We had spent some time at a quarry, walked about, stopped on a bridge to stare at some old-fashioned wagons.

"My feet are ice-cold," she announced. "I think I got frost-bite, just now, I actually felt it happening."

I suggested we run a little, that ought to help it; there may be a pub nearby. So we began to run in the dark, in the blowing wind, through open woodland, toward the nearest village.

"Feeling better?" I asked while she was trying to catch her breath.

"I am dying," she replied briefly. So I picked her up in my arms and continued running. At last I smelled beer.

"Good, here is a tavern; I am going to put you down."

"Don't," she said gently. "My feet feel like wood." At that point I kissed her; and she kissed me back. There we stood, kissing passionately, until we almost tumbled over. Finally a shaft of light fell before my feet; someone was leaving the inn. (For that's what the place was.) So I walked in, with the girl in my arms. The people inside thought I was bringing in a corpse, they raised their hands. But when they saw this beautiful creature, they smiled.

"I need a room, quickly," I said, "my wife is ill." Luckily, they had one, which they kept warm for a veterinarian who visited there every Friday. I took her upstairs immediately.

And now let me relate an incident which I myself witnessed in the city of Hamburg. A man sat in the middle of the street in a puddle; it was raining hard and he was moaning loudly, for he couldn't manage to stand up. Mainly because as soon as he made a move, his mate pushed him back. "*Ich bin der Herrgott*," he told him, and just wouldn't let him get up. "*Was machst du mit mir*," whimpered the other one, but his friend showed no mercy. "*Ich bin der Herrgott*," he was told from above.

It was the same with me. And here is why:

"The young lady should be put to bed right away," suggested the innkeeper's wife. "And let's get something to warm her feet."

While she went to get the legwarmer, I did as she said and put her to bed. But first, I had to undress her. And that was something else. . . . I removed her blouse and skirt, and she let me do it. But when it came to her garter belt, I got so entangled in the pink and blue straps, I almost broke out in a sweat. "If I knew it was this hard, I wouldn't have begun," I grumbled to myself.

I did feel kind of odd, as can be imagined. For even though there was a tiny pendant in her neck, to protect her from all the calamities of this world, and though her shoulders and arms were oh so delicate, undressing her was like peeling away a tiny bud or unwrapping a dainty box with luscious fruit in it. . . . No wonder I was all discombobulated. After I put her down and covered her up,

I even straightened out her clothes (I was truly crazy by then); laid out her little skirt nice and tidy on a chair, her little blouse on another one, so it shouldn't get wrinkled; her shoes I put under the chair, though by now I thought I was going to hit the ceiling.

Finally I said to her: "Now it's time for a good-night kiss. I earned it." I tried to be matter of fact about it, thinking to myself, if I don't kiss her now, I'll be declared a certified idiot for sure. And anyhow, didn't she get sore at me last time, because I didn't ask for a kiss?

"One little kiss," I said, and tried to look at her amorously—as amorously as a man like me *can* look. But she didn't answer, or at least not right away, and when she did, she yawned: "I am sleepy," and blinked her eyes lazily, like a cat.

"Just one kiss, come on, before you fall asleep."

Whereupon she stretched out her hand. That's what I kissed first, and then, without much delay, her mouth. Or rather, her arm, her hair, too—for all I know I may have devoured the pillow as well. I wouldn't be surprised because in kissing back she almost broke my teeth. Nobody ever kissed me like that before; I never knew such passion existed, and surely never thought that a skinny kid like her could have so much fire.

And here I must pause and expound on a troubling thought. It has to do with how very predictable men are. For when I think about it, what have I done all my life? Whatever anyone else would have, in my place. Let's be frank. Whenever I had the chance, I kissed, without fail, without much ado, like a machine. That's how life pressures us and drives us on. For what would have happened if the girl had really fallen asleep, with me at her side? Yes, let's entertain that unlikely possibility. Two lovers who, for once, for a change, do not jump on each other, but fall asleep in a sweet, infinitely trustful, unearthly embrace. However odd the thought may seem to others, that is really what I would wish for today. And not because at this point I am beyond carnal passions—the truth of the matter is that this is what I wanted even then. No, my memory is not impaired: I am convinced it's trust that I sought all along. . . . But let's not pursue this just now; I have no desire to become sentimental. Suffice it to say that everything in my life happened differently from the way I intended it.

But let's continue where I left off. I confess that nowadays I consider what happened—and what didn't happen—that night rather fortunate, however despondent I may have felt at the time.

It began when she heard noises and placed her hand on my face. I immediately jumped up and rushed to the door. The innkeeper's wife was puffing and blowing outside; she had a pile of bricks in her hands and couldn't open the door.

First I didn't understand. What did I need bricks for? I wasn't about to build a house, for God's sake.

They were the hot bricks for her feet, why of course. I took them from her and put them down someplace. What followed, however, was a little more complicatd. After the woman left, I naturally locked the door. The result was a terrified scream, but so terrified, as though someone were holding a knife to the young lady's neck. I am still surprised the help at the inn didn't come rushing in.

"What are you doing there?" she asked, aghast. "Are you locking the door? Are you trying to seduce me?"

I got so flustered, I almost started laughing. Oh, the terror that got hold of her. . . . She sat on her bed like a disheveled little angel, her eyes filled with bewilderment. As though she had just realized where she was and what could happen to her. She mussed up her hair, like frustrated children do; her bodice slid down, her breasts were half bare. . . . So it goes, I guess. We men cannot begin to fathom what these things mean to them. Virginity. Seducer. He is more terrible than a killer.

"Go away," she began pleading all of a sudden. Her reason? I am ashamed even to write it down. She didn't want me to ruin her life. She was begging me on bended knees, she said; if I loved her just a little, I should get out of her life for good. Or else, she'll be destroyed, she can't go on living this way.

And for good measure, she started crying, quietly and sadly.

She used to love her father so very much, she said; but now she couldn't look him in the eye.

"I've gone so far downhill," she lamented, "I am like those awful, awful creatures."

And in her agitation she began beating her blanket, and then kicked it off. I dutifully picked it up and tried very hard to calm her down. What else can a man do at a time like this? Especially if he himself feels terribly ashamed. . . .

No matter how I look at it, I must conclude that what happened to me there that night was typical. I am not saying something could have come of it, though I can never be sure—people have it in them to do all sorts of things, I have seen much of it myself in my time. And I for one did have the feeling that I was never closer to changing my life as I was that night, while standing in the dark in front of that tavern. It *was* one of those rare moments—All my doubts were gone, and the only question I asked myself was: What makes you run? Doesn't your entire life right now consist of dreaming about this child . . . ? But it wasn't to be. I couldn't even dream. As soon as I began hoping for something better, a greater force shoved me back, right in the middle of the puddle, mercilessly.

The matter is worth pondering. For I wasn't *such* a weakling, after all. If I mustered all my strength, no power on earth, no *Herrgott*, could stop me. Yet, let us not forget that the whining man in Hamburg was drunk, and so was I, and just how drunk, I am only beginning to realize. Every drop of my blood was full of the poison I then called my wife. . . .

This is why I brought up the story of those two wretched Hamburgers.

It is why I, too, was unable to climb out of the puddle.

"Why do you send me away when I love you so much?" I said to the girl.

"I don't need your love."

"And you love me too, that's what you said."

"I don't want to love you ever again," she sobbed. "I don't want to see you." and she sobbed some more. I tried to embrace her.

"No, don't," she screamed, absolutely horrified. "I hate you, I never loved you; all you wanted to do was seduce me."

I was deeply wounded. And why, of all things, over this? The case of the two men in Hamburg should make that clear.

So I took my coat and headed for the door, without saying a word, making it clear to her that I wasn't going to dignify that charge with an answer.

Then she spoke again in that silence. An ethereal, angelic sound, the tinkling of glass bells:

"Farewell."

I had to stop, my heart ached for her so. "Should I wait for you outside?"

But she hid her face from me.

I continued walking. Outside, in the dark, I stopped once more. I had to. I kept stumbling.

And what about the turmoil inside, in my heart? Well, in my heart there was dull silence. But in my ears I heard jabbering, music even. As if they were ringing bells; I had to listen. "Are you leaving, sir?" someone seemed to ask. "So soon? What did you do up there, kill the young lady?" Such things were buzzing in my ear. And there was more: "What *did* you do up there? Undress her? Bravo. Had yourself a little fling, I bet."

I should have started running, to cool my blood, to ease my shame, but I couldn't.

"Am I nailed to this God damned spot or what?" I said to myself and began cursing.

I also thought of going back upstairs and breaking down the door. How dare she send me away when she let me undress her? What nerve. Am I an animal, a pet she can just toss out? And I almost keeled over, I was so hot. That's when I really felt it. For I saw the slivers of light again, dancing around her lips, and felt the fragrances that permeated the room, as if someone knocked over a bucket of honey up there.

It even crossed my mind that she didn't really want me to go. Can one ever know for sure what these creatures want? I was ready to rush back upstairs, for, you see, I also heard my wife's laughter chiming in, that outrageous laughter of hers, with which she used to mock my bumbling ways with women—my own invented stories, which, lo and behold, came true. Is that what you are? her laughter seemed to ask. A bumbler, an oaf? There is a pretty young lady upstairs in bed.

But suddenly I got very tired. And after that it wasn't hard. Clip-clop. I kept listening to my own footsteps. There: all you have to do is begin. By now I was anxious to get back to London; I began to hurry, as though I had urgent business to attend to.

But what was I to do now in London? Go home? No, that was out of the question.

So I went to see Kodor who this time made a big fuss over me. There were two reasons for the ovation.

First, he wanted me to go at once to Bruges; exciting things were happening there, prospects were excellent, not in the rescue service line, to be sure, but he'd just been discussing some very attractive leasing arrangements . . . And the main thing was they paid their men very well. I should therefore be on my way to Bruges as soon as possible. But not just yet, I should wait, he'll tell me when. In other words, I was not to go to Bruges. That was the first urgent matter.

Secondly, I should go with him right now to a "charming little get-together" which otherwise would bore him to tears, since the people who will be there were all bearded sourpusses, and he never knows what to do with such people.

"Come on, Jacob, entertain those bearded fogies for me . . . Besides, a few new contacts cannot hurt you. And who knows, somebody there may quickly fall in love with you." Kodor said all this in Italian; when in expansive mood he always used that language.

Meanwhile I almost had a fit straining to pay attention, and pretending to be overwhelmed by all these offers and the man making them. But I had to pretend. I thought to myself: Come what may, I'll keep pressing him until I squeeze something out. I had no intention of continuing my walking tours of London. I had enough.

"Wait a minute," Kodor said, "first we'll have a little taste of this milk." (Milk stood for wine in his vocabulary.) He spun around and moments later was filling my glass with something dark.

"Well, what is it?" he asked, beaming, and stuck the bottle under his arm. "Go on, tell me if you can . . . Don't keep on smelling it. . . . Ah, you know nothing about these things." He was running me down, as usual, and shaking with laughter as he did.

I didn't have to taste it. It smelled of resin and smoke. That was enough.

"It's from Samos," I said, like a judge.

"My birthplace," he whispered excitedly. "But the deal, old chap, the deal is marvelous, too." He was on another subject now, and became even more ecstatic.

It seems two Greek companies went brankrupt, and he bought

up all their assets. "And there are British interests, too," he enthused. He just went wild over those British interests.

"I am a brilliant man, don't you know?" he roared. "A regular genius." To make certain I did know, he proceeded to tell me just how brilliant he was. These people thought he was doing *them* a favor (who they were I had no idea); what's more, it was going to ruin a Greek named Nikander, which was the nicest part of the venture—he loathed this man.

"A little subtraction, a little addition, and I end up with a tidy profit," he explained triumphantly. "By Jupiter . . . or by Jove, I should say." For he now switched to English. Still, I didn't know what the hell he was talking about. To this day I can not understand why people do this. Say a young man wants to learn a trade. Why can't he be taught everything from the beginning? For that's not how it's done, oh no. He is thrust in the middle, and left to figure out the beginning by himself. And that's how these geniuses operate, too. They wouldn't dream of starting at the beginning and allowing people to catch their meaning.

I did finally gather from all the mish-mash that the deal involved oil, vast quantities of cooking oil, enough oil to make the entire United Kingdom sizzle. And top quality oil, too! When you looked through it, it sparkled like crystal, its lovely amber captured the sun.

"Show me a sample of that precious oil," I said.

But he didn't have an ounce to show me. That's how these people are. They do big business, but the stuff they buy and sell is never seen. There are transactions but no tangible commodities. I never did conduct business on such a grand scale. When I struck my deals, I sat on those barrels and crates myself, by God . . . But why go into that. . . ?

Anyway, the upshot was the following: he formed a veritable oil ring, bought up everything "for a tune," (he meant a song). In a month or two the oil would start pouring into London. (What for? I would have liked to ask but didn't. Let it pour.) For the time being the oil was stored in one of his native country's "great" ports, which one he was not in a position to tell me. (To this day I don't know any more about the whole arrangement.)

"And that's why we're meeting tonight," Kodor informed me. "To celebrate. With the major stockholders, I mean. I'll let you in on it, too, don't worry. Do you think I'd pass over an imposing man like you?"

Well, my befuddlement at all this was total. I still don't know what happened to me, Did I fall into a deep sleep? Did my senses grow numb? I felt as if I was in some brown fog. I sat there nodding, pretending to be intensely interested in these wonderful developments, until I realized I wasn't even listening.

I watched Kodor open a cabinet door, and saw him walk right in. The cabinet, I discovered with some amazement, led to a whole other wing, complete with dressing room, washroom, etc. How odd it all was, like everything else around Kodor. He undressed, changed into fresh clothes, and all the while kept on talking. At one point I interrupted him:

"Listen, Kodor, could you get me some coins from your bank? Brand new ones, of course."

"What's that?" he inquired cheerfully. Only then did I come to my senses. (Actually, I thought of getting hold of a few coins and sending it to the girl, without any letter or anything, simply a terse note—"In rememberance, from Captain J. S.")

"I am working on a coin-tester," I told Kodor very quickly. "A little device that would identify counterfeit coins used in vending machines. That's what I need brand new coins for." I couldn't come up with anything better on the spur of the moment.

"You don't say." Kodor eyed me suspiciously. "I had no idea you were so clever." But he looked at me as though he wanted to say: You are a shrewd one. Hope you are not trying to trick me.

In a red, silk-lined private room of the Hotel Brighton, I took out my fountain pen and wrote the following letter to my wife:

"Tiny *tresor*, I am with Kodor and will have to stay with him tonight. Business. Then I am off to the home of the wild pigeons: Brazil, possibly for as long as six months. (I underlined the word six.) But before that, next week, that is, I must go to Bruges. But right now I have to get drunk—good manners demand it. And so does life. I must spur this rascal into action, for everything now depends on him, alas. Things may still turn out all right if he is on our side. One more thing: try not to read all night tonight; I don't want you to be in bad spirits when I walk in, bringing you the rays of the morning sun . . . Your Apollo."

When I was finished I turned to Kodor:

"Do you want to send greetings to my wife?"

"I sure do," he said, and on the back of the paper he wrote: "I am busy inciting your dear husband against women. An old devil: Sir Alexander Kodor." "Sir?" I asked, horrified, "Didn't you know? As of last week."

The lucky bastard.

So I sent the letter, along with a bouquet of roses which I bought in the hotel lobby. Then I sat down and gave myself over to pure pleasure.

"Meat, bread and wine, I am content with these three," I informed the guests at the party. I can tell you, it's not hard to win people over, especially if you have some feeling for it. It doesn't take much. Just being fat may do the trick. Or if you knew, say, how to neigh, if you could imitate animal sounds. Now Kodor was famous for his roguish smile but also for a crinkle around his eyes that gave him a sweet, raisiny look, a look that promised profits galore; they all fell for it.

I decided I was going to turn on the charm, too. And why not? There were two little angels among the invited guests. So I showed them how much I could eat and drink. Sure enough, Kodor introduced me by saying:

"A well-known devourer of oysters." And to others he said:

"This, ladies and gentlemen, is Morbidani, the courageous sea captain." Everyone laughed. There was a morose old codger there, even he laughed. (He was some sort of doctor, actually, a retired physician, as I later found out.)

What was more important, however, was that these two sweethearts for some reason took a liking to me and urged me to eat. They put the mustard, the dressings and other necessary items in front of me and were shaking with laughter. It seems they were in a mischievous mood, or had been waiting for just such an opportunity. They marveled at my appetite and were outdoing each other in trying to pamper me and mock me. In minutes the party was in full swing, and this made Kodor beam even more.

"A wonderful fellow," he said, pointing to me. "Now I see at last what he does to bowl over women."

"Does he bowl them over, really?" asked one of the little darlings.

"Does he ever? They just have to spot him and they're ready to jump off trains. He is some charmer," concluded my friend.

The two ladies laughed even harder.

"And what a giant," one of them said with a shudder, though not of course without interest. I didn't even raise my head, I just cast a few intimidating sidelong glances in her direction, and continued eating.

"He is an enchanter, I tell you," Kodor went on, "a real spell-binder." "What are some of your feats again?" he asked. "To begin with, his net weight is around three hundred pounds. Honest. And he can polish off four geese and twenty knockwursts in one sitting, isn't that right?" I nodded gravely.

"A monster, in other words," said one of the ladies. I don't mind such comments, really. It gives them a little thrill, and that's all right. So they were having fun at my expense, so what? Why make a fuss? The world is a patchwork, just a flimsy patchwork, it doesn't pay to get touchy. For how is one ever to get satisfaction?

I looked around the room. Actually, a rather interesting group of investors had gathered together: six men including us two, and the two women. Needless to say, nobody had a beard. What's more, you could tell they had very little to do with one another; they were all after big profits, that's about the only thing they had in common—that and the fact that they seemed to know very little about business (the other four, I mean), especially the doctor, the old man with the disagreeable look, whom I already mentioned. And what can I say about the stocking and undershirt merchant, who already had a play of his produced in Vienna? He didn't seem to have a nose for big business, either. And the two others: a shipowner and a major stockholder in a glass factory were likewise small potatoes compared to Kodor. In my younger days I would not have believed that one could encounter such naiveté in the heart of London. But for all their childish notions, they seemed to be doing all right. It was quite odd, I must say, yet where but in England should one find such eccentrics. And Kodor treated them accordingly—gently, that is, like a mother. But that he was out to bamboozle them, I had no doubt whatsoever. What's more, I was sure that the reason I was there, and the two lovely chippies, was to provide the entertainment. Large sums of money must have been at stake, or else that charlatan would not have invited all these people to a plush hotel room.

But a lot I cared. I was eating leg of veal, an excellent cut, and quite a chunk, too. ("Make it at least two pounds," I had told the waiter, knowing well that veal was best when roasted in one piece and served piping hot; it's tender and light then, like a pale pink cloud.) I could shout for joy, I was so pleased. No one can imagine what goes on inside me when my juices start flowing.

"My stomach is quite healthy." I said quietly. "Ladies and gentlemen, I am in fine health. Why should I bother my head about all these complications?" But it made no sense trying to explain. Those who were never afflicted with stomach ailment cannot imagine the joy good eating can bring.

"And now I will bust the old gut," I said to myself playfully, and kept pouring all that fine wine down my throat. Kodor didn't miss a chance to make a big production of this, too.

"Just look at him," he cried. "He is not even gulping it, he is pouring it down, as if his belly was a big tub."

"I want to see, I want to see," clamored my nosy fans. So I demonstrated again how to do this, how to lap up a quartful without gulping.

"Could it be that he doesn't have an Adam's apple?" asked one of the little darlings.

"Maybe he has no soul," said the other.

There is a smart girl, I thought. No, I don't, I felt like answering her.

"As far as the inner self is concerned," I said, out loud this time, "let's hold off mentioning it, for at least five minutes, in deference to the soul of the calf whose meat I am eating. What would *it* say, I wonder. First we eat it and then put on our usual lofty airs."

Now it was the lady's turn to look away and reflect on what I'd just said.

But the time has come for me to describe the two sweethearts in a little more detail. They *were* sweet, and enchanting, and black, both of them, like two graceful, shimmering leopards—yes, they were delicate *and* vamp-like. To begin with, their eyes were black, yet their blackness was not of the same kind: one was a soft black, soft and dreamy, while the other's was a fierce smouldering black . . . And their dresses were all dark too, as well as their hair, and their teeth were sharp and pointed. I almost felt like asking them to please bite into my ear.

Actually, I could understand anyone who did not take my words at face value, who doubted my assertions about feminine wiles. The truth is that at the time just about any young woman appealed to me. All the same, I'd like to assure everyone that these were capital specimens. Yes, but how do I prove my assertion? If I said that even the grave-looking old physician was off in a dream, and in his glum way casting sidelong glances at the girls, it wouldn't be much of an evidence. The undershirt merchant didn't count, either. It may be more convincing to reiterate that Kodor had good reason to bring them there. They were supposed to captivate our hearts. Besides, one of them, who had a black lace butterfly over her chest, had to be Kodor's mistress. A chance remark brought this to light.

"Why are you staring at me, Sir Alexander?" she asked. "I take pleasure in looking at your beautiful head-dress," replied my friend. "And even greater pleasure in looking at the rest of you," he added impudently.

From that you could tell that he got her that bejeweled head-dress—hence the overriding pleasure.

Music was playing in the next room, to the accompaniment of exotic, gamelan-like percussions and mean little shrieks, while in here the ladies were nibbling on grapes and cake and sipping champagne. They even clinked their glasses, like sailors in a pub, and said things like: "A thousand a year," and "chin-chin." And they wouldn't stop laughing. Evidently, the two sweethearts got drunk on a few drops of champagne. At midnight, Kodor's girl, the one with the butterfly, whose black silk was so slippery, the light just kept sliding and gliding on her curves—well, this beauty turned to me and said:

"I decided to sweep you off your feet. But how do I do it?"

Well, Jacob boy, I tried goading myself on, now's the time to show what kind of friend you are. The situation got to be some-what confusing, and not only on account of all the drinks I put away—I was full of apprehension.

For this lovely creature did take a liking to me, I can state that without boasting. But the other one did, too, both of them did, that's where the thing got complicated.

You can't pursue two loves at the same time. Or can you? Try it, Jacob, try it, I encouraged myself. But I really couldn't. Kodor's dame was impetuous, slender, slithery, and very quick. It was clear from the beginning that she wanted to have me all for herself. The other, however, was a more gentle, sweeter soul, and easily frightened. The onslaught tired her out, she immediately re-treated, and became as forlorn as a drooping leaf. I had to grasp her hand under the table.

The question remained: which one should I make love to? Frankly, I liked the softer one better. Or was I simply scared of Kodor's girl? Could be. One does owe some loyalty to one's friend, after all . . .

Ah, never mind, I thought, the thing will straighten itself out somehow. Tomorrow I'll send her a beautiful bouquet with a note that I had to leave suddenly.

But I do, I do have to leave, I reminded myself. We just talked about it, Kodor told me this very day. Why couldn't I leave tomorrow or the day after? I am going to Bruges, by God. And my heart leaped with joy. How wonderful! How convenient! I am going to Bruges and the complications are put off.

In the meantime, Kodor was addressing the gentlemen present:

"Since our gathering was such a success, and there is agreement on all the main items of our agenda, let's adjourn to the corner pub where the waiter's face is pockmarked but the fish is first rate."

It was a mistake to say this, a definite mistake, as the grave doctor's face happened to be pockmarked; indeed, he perked up when he heard it, and said something to the effect that perhaps they didn't quite agree on everything. (Let's remember this little interlude, for we'll have occasion to return to it.)

But it made Kodor brighten up, oh and how. He, too, noticed the mistake, how could he not, cunning man that he was.

"Of course we agreed, how can you say we didn't, my dear doctor?" he replied, smiling his sweetest smile, smoothing the man's ruffled feathers like a tender mother patting her baby's bottom. And all the while he was glancing at me, the scoundrel.

After all that it was only natural that I walked home singing. And the song that sprang up in my heart that glorious morning was a song of victory:

I could take on the whole world now if I so desired. I've become a conqueror of hearts now, in spite of myself . . . Ah, I was triumphant, and in my rapture, I began caressing my winter coat.

"You see, my little pussy cat, women really like me. (I talked to my winter coat as if it was Miss Borton or my wife.) How they coddled me, how they *loved* me . . . Why, they ate me up, those two . . ." And the thought alone made me chuckle.

Oh, I tried to feel sorry for my friend, tried telling myself it wasn't fair, it wasn't decent . . . I went as far as to sit on a stoop in front of a tobacco shop and squeeze out a little remorse. The tobacconist wasn't there yet, so I kept muttering: "You've really turned into a heel, Jacob, you really have. What did you do to your dearest friend? To his dearest mistress? Didn't you smother her with kisses in the hallway of that awful pub? What a terrible thing to do, Jacob; what a rotten, terrible thing to do.

I tried shocking myself, as I say, but it was no use. Nothing could induce me to feel sadness or guilt. On the contrary, I couldn't stop laughing.

All along I kept thinking how funny it was when I suddenly caught a glance of myself in a mirror in that hallway (yes, they even had a mirror). I saw then how cross-eyed one can look when all steamed up with passion. Which *is* kind of ridiculous, when you think about it.

The other darling, the tender one, breathed the words "*Du und du*" in my ear. (She was fluent in German, the only one there who was, so she had the courage to utter the lovely word twice in front of her friend.)

It makes no difference, I told myself sternly and got up from that stoop. It makes no difference whatever, I am leaving. I must get away from this . . . this field of conquest. If I don't, the family will go hungry. (But as I uttered these sacred words, I was rolling again.) Of course I will leave, I chastised myself. But really, what was I to do, go on panting after them? And what if tomorrow one of them will again say: "I demand your love?" Should I start panting all over again, and whisper in her ear: "I love you, I adore you. . . ?"

All in all, I was in a blissful mood.

And as if all this wasn't enough, after I finally made it home, in some broken-down cab, my famous landlord came up to me. He was the sort of man to whom I gave all kinds of nicknames: old capon was my favorite. He was that, and more: a mealy-mouthed blockhead, a two-bit prophet, a pea-brained, salad-munching mystic, who rose each morning with the birds. This was the man I had to face on the stairs that morning.

Although what we talked about is not directly related to the subject at hand, I will recount it anyway, if only to demonstrate the effect mysticism had on a certain class of people at the time. (It's an important point, I will return to it later.)

At any rate, my landlord told me on the staircase that he could see (for he wasn't blind, he still had a pair of good eyes) that we were such decent folk, my wife and I, we led such upright lives, the two of us, he hoped I would forgive him if he allowed himself the question: Did I believe in the unity of the Patriarchs? (He meant Abraham and the others.)

Now if I were to give him a melting, pious look at this point, I think the wine inside me would have started chuckling. *Now* he badgered me with this stuff? But I gave the old geezer his answer, as we shall see.

It should be noted that Father Lambert's tract on unbelief, which he wrote to counter the jurist Ingersoll's arguments, was at this time reread by many people, it enjoyed a veritable renascence, especially among the devout. Once I had to plough through it myself, in order to put a pompous fool in his place. (It happened near Melbourne, Australia, some time ago, but that's neither here nor there.) The point is I was prepared. If this nincompoop should start spouting his philosophy, I was ready to clobber him, too. With Father Lambert's own words, moreover. For he was the ultimate authority for these people. My landlord, in his pious zeal, grasped my hand and asked me the next question:

"Do you believe, sir, in higher intelligence?"

"What the hell is that?" I inquired.

"In intelligence like Vitruvius and Zoroaster," said the old man quite meekly, "who do think about us, after all."

"What do I care, man? I want to decide myself if that cabbage soup . . ."

"Oh dear, what cabbage soup?"

". . . that you send up for lunch is right for me. Or if the fireplace on the second floor is working." (About my wife I said nothing. . . . Life, life these people keep talking about. Others may be crazy about it, but I am unimpressed.) "No, sir," I shouted in the man's ear, "I do not believe in higher intelligence."

"You don't?" asked that old ignoramus on the staircase. "You mean you don't believe in cosmology, in a celestial order, in the purposefulness of the universe?" (That's what they all do: they trot out the fancy phrases about the stars and the heavens, instead of explaining the *reasons* behind all those things. As if a piece of carrot couldn't be used to prove this or that, depending on how you twisted it.)

"The movement of the stars is a thing of naught, then," he intoned. "Or the music of the spheres, the celestial harmonies? . . ." That's just what the old fool said, flinging out his skinny arms toward the janitor's booth.

"What if it is 'a thing of naught?'" I asked. "What if it is? Look here, holy man, maybe I am a fool too, but I am not alone. And I assure you that creation itself finds pleasure in ninnies like you, or else it wouldn't have inundated the world with them.

"Just listen to me. If something is cooking in your pot, what are you going to say about the hissing and bubbling? That these are some wonderfully harmonious noises? What is so harmonious, my dearest sir, about one creature devouring another? The only principle at work in the world is a parasitic one. This is predator's paradise, my gentle friend, predicated on extreme cruelty. Such a world doesn't attract me, it doesn't even interest me. How can it? How can there be harmony in a world that's governed by grandiose ideas and where the individual is ignored. Oh no, I am through with such a world, and through with you. Farewell, dear sir . . .

"And if the Swedenborgian fathers will not forgive me, tell them I shan't forgive them either.

"Just remember that it's the practical truths that are important, never the higher, abstract ones, never those. And to buttress my point, I shall have to refer to the words of Father Lambert himself. (I got into the swing of it by then and started quoting straight from the book.) 'Man's life is a tragedy; it is an awful subject'— this is his first thesis. 'Life is practical'—this is the second. 'It is neither poetry nor effeminate philosophy. The passions of human nature, civilized or barbarous, make stern alternatives necessary, and lugubrious cant will not change man's nature or the necessities that arise from it.' And with that I really must take my leave. Good-bye and good luck."

That's just how I held forth, in my early morning drunkenness, on the staircase of our shabby boarding house. I could have just as easily begun preaching in some park. "*Bravissimo*," an Italian tenant shouted from the first floor.

"How sweet you look when you're drunk," my wife said, laughing, and pressing me to tell her all about last night—where I was, what I did, did I have a good time? She asked for more and more details, though as it was, I couldn't stop talking.

I did detect a certain slyness in me, however, and remarkably enough, I felt good about it, better even than about being honest. That's how one ought to live, I said to myself; it would make things so much easier to bear.

What I did was to pretend I was even drunker than I actually was, for in such a state one tends to chatter away thoughtlessly. And that's what I did, though at the same time observing carefully the effect my words had on my tiny albeit curvaceous wife.

Curled up on the pink sofa in her blue pajamas, amid books and cigarette butts, she was indeed like a queer little ball, who'd also had a wild and exhausting night. Yes, like a ball she was, a blue tangle that's been roughed up by kittens.

Is that it? I asked myself. Is that all there is to her? The woman I am supposed to love? After the marvels of the previous night, that seemed inconceivable. Yet, at the same time, there was a heaviness around my heart, the realization perhaps that stray as far as I may, I would never be rid of this little woman. Miss Borton was right. The conclusion rang true, indeed so true that in the solemn silence of my fading drunkenness, in that curious morning glow (I had already opened the shades and the room was flooded with light), I could stand back and hear myself go on and on. As though I was no longer there.

I told her about my adventure with the two women but in the following manner:

"They were two millionairesses, whom I met while negotiating a deal with Kodor. I didn't bother to remember their names, I still don't know who they are, two scavenging vultures most probably, ready to swoop down . . . But they were beautiful vultures, like birds out of a dream, I swear (and I even raised my hand, as if taking an oath); one was a plump bird, the other as graceful as a violin . . . (The word made my wife burst out laughing. 'A poet, a real poet,' she squealed 'Birds, violins . . . how sweet.' They are so literal, these French.) Anyway, the two extraordinary birds went ahead and—this is God's honest truth—asked me to marry them . . .

"So watch out, sweatie," I warned her with a smile, "I am a real lady killer now."

Well, my wife almost rolled off the couch.

"You sweet, darling man," she enthused, hugging her hip.

"Oh, my side," she suddenly cried and her face contorted. (She did have a problem with her hip, nothing serious, some form of sciatica, I shouldn't wonder, but whenever she was in pain, it was my fault naturally.)

"It hurts," she reproached me, and even turned to the wall, to make sure I didn't see her face.

So I stopped talking, and though still unsteady on my feet, began to undress. But then I heard her again:

"How was it with those two?" And there was chuckling under the blanket. I took up my story again, and told her how flustered I was when a foot under the table started rubbing mine (another embellishment, as you can see) and when at the same time a hand—it could have been a nasty gremlin, I dare say—began to pull on my jacket.

"And you?" she asked, her eyes asquint.

"I made as though I had to tighten my shoelaces . . . Naturally."

"Ooh, that's so precious," she again squealed, "I love it, I love it." (Anything having to do with a secret romance got her going like this.) So I continued, telling her more about the two lovelies, about their black hair and black dress (Kodor I left out of the picture, said nothing about one of them being his lover), and kept weaving my yarn and arranging the ever more intoxicating details so that the central question remained:

"What was I to do with two in Heaven's name? I couldn't very well marry two women at once, could I?"

"Oh, dear, oh dear. But must you marry them right away?" she asked anxiously.

"That's what they wanted."

"What do you mean that's what they wanted? They actually wanted you to marry them?"

"They did, on my word. You still don't believe me? My word means nothing. . . ?"

Here I stopped for a minute.

"Didn't you say you were married already, that you *had* a wife?"

"Of course I did."

"And?"

"A lot they cared. In America such things don't much matter. (Oh yes, I made them out to be Americans.) They must have thought that even if I did have a wife, I'd leave her for them . . ."

Now I came out with it. And let's stop here for a minute, for at this point something happened; it got a little too quiet in the room. My wife raised herself on the couch, lit up a cigarette, inhaled deeply, and said:

"So you were again the man of the hour. Congratulations." And she snickered, lightly, mirthlessly. Then, in a dreamy, musing sort of way:

"Isn't it interesting? Just yesterday I was also asked by someone to marry him." But she said this quite casually, as if thinking out loud, though she did add, oddly:

"Will you let me go?"

Next day the first thing I wanted to do was search the house.

But let's for the time being stick to those crucial moments the day before. For we did pursue the matter. I tried to laugh it off at first.

"You must be joking," I said. "When did they ask?" (My legs, to be sure, were already trembling.)

"I told you, yesterday."

"Yesterday, really? But how, where? What *are* you talking about? All you do the whole day is lie in bed." My wife began to laugh.

"That's not even true. (It wasn't; she did wander off someplace the other day.) And besides, you don't have to leave the house for that."

"You don't, do you? I suppose it happened right here, in the flat.

She now laughed even more cheerfully.

"The things you keep thinking about," she said, though making sure not to look at me. "Why must it be here or some other place? Can't I get a letter?"

So she's been receiving letters. Hm. That I didn't think of.

"What sort of letter?"

"For Heaven's sake, a letter, a quite ordinary letter."

I didn't really believe it, certainly not right away, not the letter, though everything else . . . But what *was* everything else, what the hell was going on? If somebody could propose to a married woman . . . I tried to figure this out but couldn't; thoughts were churning about in my head but they didn't register; I was numb, empty, as if stunned by a blow. But then the storm began to rage inside me, and with such fury it made me shiver. I *must* talk about it . . . In due course, though, I am rushing ahead of myself again.

The first person who came to mind was the Italian chap. The business about the letter I dismissed, of course. This fellow, however, lived here in the building, he was handsome, a sculptor, and Italian, to boot. Maybe he was the one who sent her those violets.

Another Italian, then . . . Yet he was just a face, picked out at random from the turmoil reigning in my head, the same one who yelled bravo just before. But this sculptor fell off some platform the very next day and was taken to the hospital. So I waited for three days. And during that time my wife didn't leave the house, I made sure of that. And the Italian asked to see only one friend of his, who then left town the same day. And the sculptor himself died the fourth day. And my wife stayed in bed all that time, she never left our rooms.

So I had to search elsewhere. But where, how?

Would I let her go, she wanted to know. Just as I thought, in other words. The case of my old friend, the scalesman, must have scared her. She would have liked to leave but was afraid.

What was I to do with her now? I tried to imagine what it would be like to banish her from my thoughts. I told myself: Make believe she is dead, or that you never knew her. Try to get used to the void.

Or try to put up with a thorn in your flesh, it *can* be done. After all, in India people stick needles in their feet and go on living that way.

In other words, we, too, will go on as before, and when lover boy comes to call, you will go out for a smoke, how is that? And just don't think about it, right? But can you do that? Can you disregard the thing that your very circumstances compel you to think about? Ah, and life can be so sly, so cruel. Just then wherever I went I heard reminders. Did she cheat on him? Did he? It was all over: on buses, in newspapers—family dramas, jealous rages, crimes of passion, suicides. And there was the famous Bittery case, too, which had all of England in an uproar just then. A triple suicide: husband, wife and lover. It was the talk of the town.

I myself witnessed something similar right around then. And an ugly affair it was. I found out that an old friend, Gregory Sanders, was in town. Sanders was an excellent chap, serious, intelligent—I thought I'd look him up and have a little chat. Where he stayed it was always quiet and peaceful. A man like him needed peace and quiet, and so did I. He put up in an old hotel. But on my way to his room, after climbing four flights of stairs, a shot rang out, not more than ten paces away from me. Quick and simple. As if someone had just slammed a door. A small-caliber revolver it had to be.

A miserable little woman lay near the stairs, a mere child, really, a bundle of colored rags—a sorry little felt doll somebody just threw away. There was no blood anywhere, no sound—nothing. She yielded very quietly.

As I later found out, she tripped on the hallway carpet while trying to get away. But the man with the revolver caught up with her. And he seemed like such a fraud, such a buffoon. Again I couldn't help feeling that it was all a scene out of some trashy melodrama. He was disheveled, his eyeballs bulged, he wouldn't stop panting. It was like a picture show, really, so false in every way.

"She cheated on me," he whispered with a rattle in his throat, and then, he, too, collapsed. Bloody fool, I thought. Everybody is cheated, didn't the crazy bastard know that? And I kept on walking, haughtily, totally unconcerned. His woes seemed so ludicrous to me, and his act so abhorrent.

For what does it mean to cheat on someone? What is this silly word compared to that young woman lying there, silent and motionless, who only yesterday could do so much more besides cheating. She could laugh, she could remember—all of that had no significance any more, and she herself no more meaning? Only that one word, those few letters? We make our lives depend on it. We allow ourselves to be humiliated, to be dragged through mud. But why? What makes us do it? Why can't I understand this, because I can't, even if I cracked open my thick skull.

This incident made me lose my bearing again. I was in a daze, my head crammed with wild dreams for days afterward.

Just think: You go over to a woman and whisper in her ear: "You cheat . . . I killed you because you cheated on me." Maddening nonsense. How can death be a punishment for someone who is no longer aware of that punishment—because she is dead, of course. And at the same time, how can it be a source of satisfaction to the aggressor? It's all so ridiculous, *we* are ridiculous, down to our fingertips, our loftiest moral principles notwithstanding.

Such conversations I carried on with myself, even at night . . . But if I read on a movie poster or in the paper: the Deceived Husband, I felt I was being deprived of my manhood. Somebody ought to explain to me once how these things work. One day we see everything quite clearly, and the next our vision is blurred. Or maybe we never get a clear picture, it's all a deception from the beginning to end.

I keep wandering aimlessly in their midst and I learn nothing. What *is* behind all this? Maybe somebody comes up to my place, too, people around here may even know him, the chambermaids, for instance, they may laugh about it, laugh in my face even, and I smile back because I think they're being nice. And of course they discuss it amongst themselves, tell the grocer about it. They tell everybody except me; I am forever left in the dark. It's a conspiracy. They are tight-lipped and stone-hard. What, then, is the explanation for my ignorance? Is it sheer apathy on my part? Have I simply learned not to care? Yes, that's what happens, for a while, at any rate. Up to a point. But then the abyss opens up and I notice everything. After the fact, that is. . . .

What can I say? I suffered untold pain.

Other people's affairs, their complicated relationships, never used to interest me much, but now they did, I was all ears. That's all I paid attention to, in fact. Sometimes, while observing a lonely face, I'd say to myself, quite calmly: This chap's being deceived. Or here's another instance: A young worker says to his friend on the bus, "Slap her, why don't you?" And his eyes flash. "Let her have it but good," he advises darkly.

Is that really such a good idea, boys? I would have liked to say to them, and with all the warmth my heart could muster. Slap her because she doesn't love you, or not enough? Because she also loves somebody else? Act the bully, is that the idea?

The question that presented itself was roughly this: Is it so awful for a man to go under while living it up? To be debased by what he truly loves? And here I must cite the case of a friend of mine. This man loved going to night clubs and dance halls, he lived for them, you might say. He did have a steady income, a small annuity, actually, but to me the idea of spending it on such a diversion . . . And fool that I was, I even asked him if he didn't think it was all a waste, staking his future, everything he had on a single passion. . . . My friend was visibly amused.

"You mean it doesn't pay to live that way," he said cheerfully. And he was all fired up, ready to pounce. "But what's better, more edifying, according to you? Bickering with your little merchants while fleecing them? Or watching them fleece a hapless peasant, who in turn cheats his own mother? But pray tell, what are those things, those rare and lovely things that would not offend your squeamish good taste?

"To me that's what life is all about—the silken curtains, the colored lights . . . and the gold teeth in the dancer's mouths, and their bite which may be as deadly as a snake's. That's what I live for . . ." He was panting these words, singing them.

And what was behind all that fervor? We all know about such things: a fallen man who begins to applaud his own depravity, acting as though he wanted it, welcomed it. All that is clear enough: heading for a fall can be exhilarating, we know that, too. I do understand the feeling, I did even then. . . . But when we shift the scene, I am less understanding. She sits in front of the mirror and I see her smile. Or she is by the fire and casts a brief glance toward the door. And there are thoughts in her eyes, thoughts I will never ever find out. Who is she expecting in her heart, what memory just crossed her mind, what honeyed phrase . . .? Once I walked into her room unexpectedly. It was early in the afternoon and she didn't even know I was home. Her cheeks were on fire, her eyes glowed, but with a curious, wet glow, the kind you see in the eyes of young girls who poured too much rum in their tea. . . . But that *is* what you notice, invariably: that your wife is thinking about something else. Of unnatural pleasures, frankly. Can you ever come to terms with such a thing? Can you ever accept it? Well, maybe you should. Such things have their own conventions, after all. The wife's lover is recognized, given equal status in some Oriental societies. Why can't we apply the same rules and do as they do? But the very idea . . . oh, why does it strike me then as sheer madness. . . ?

So. She again had somebody. She always did, so why not now? Somebody who came through this very door.

And I again had the feeling I just had to clench my fist and— there, I got him. He had to be around here somewhere. I began to sense his closeness, as you do an animal's.

I was being absurd, I admit it now. But this thing was like a whirlpool, it sucked you in, it had nothing to do with reason. Sure, one may ask: how can a sane man get such ideas? When the woman spent all her time at home, in bed, and I, too, was in the house a lot, and even when not, could show up anytime. But what I did was turn the question around. Why did she lie in bed all the time? A young woman like her, in the best of health? What is more, I wasn't really home that much, that wasn't even true. And she was the one who kept sending me away. Why would she do that? Why would she tell me to spend as much time as I could in the fresh air, with Miss Borton yet—because she obviously knew I was with her when I went out. What did she do all afternoon on those days?

Should I just ask? Well, I did.

"Who was it then who asked you to marry him," I said. "You can't really blame me for wanting to know. And also: how can such a thing happen to a married woman? But what interests me most is what you answered. I do have to know that, If only to figure out *my* next move?"

This made her laugh in my face. And hearing this laugh, I felt as if she had placed her hand on my heart.

"Oh, aren't you being the old fool again?" she said. "You are the one who keeps telling me I daydream all the time, and like a child make up all sorts of silly things."

Was it all a crazy fantasy then?

She did laugh at me, as I say, with a look as bright and healing as sunshine, though with subtle cunning too, which the light of the sun is never without, I don't think. For all its blessings, I do believe it laughs at us.

With a heavy heart, then, I began to do some work. But in the end, I didn't go to Bruges after all, I just couldn't bring myself to do it. I did land a few odd jobs, appraising damages, settling accounts, things like that; at long last I was working again. And there was a stillness in me, an old, old stillness—I have no idea where it came from, what brought it on. Fact is I turned serene and somber. My heart was at peace, as if touched by a blessed breath of life. I would close my eyes and listen to the quiet. Then one night, quite unexpectedly, I asked myself:

Why call it a fantasy? I mean she did ask if I would let her go, didn't she? Had she ever said anything like that before? So the next day I confronted her again:

"Listen, what about that Dedin fellow, are you still in love with him? Come, be straight with me. What's the good of these riddles and dumbshows; you've got the gift of gab, why can't we talk about this thing openly for once?"

"We could if I felt like it." And already there was irritation in her voice.

And she was right. Was that how I hoped to find out more? By posing direct questions? No, no, she was perfectly right.

But what about Dedin, how did *I* stand with him just then? This thought forced itself upon me that night, and I couldn't shake the feeling that this time it was he who had followed her here, the way Ridolfi had before. And that he lived close by, maybe even in this very boarding house. As I say, I had this curious feeling . . .

"Watch him carefully now," he must have told her in Paris, "humor him, restrain him, so he doesn't get out of hand, like the last time. And I'll be there."

And hence her little acts of kindness, her lovable antics soon after we arrived. And it's why this old boarding house seemed such a cozy place . . . cozy and scary. Maybe he's here already, has even found himself a job. Which makes our lodging not so cozy, only scary.

But I'll find out, don't you worry, I thought to myself. I'll pin you down yet, my sweet. And there was some ruthless pleasure in all this, and furtive gloating, something of a hunter's thrill.

I began to turn up at odd hours, unexpectedly, like suspicious husbands have always done, since time immemorial. The first time I didn't even want to go into her room; I thought I would just look around in the parlor, and if I found nothing suspicious, I'd leave again. I wasn't going to sneak around the house, though I wound up doing just that. Sure enough, she heard me.

"Who's there?" she shouted from the other room. "It's just me, dear, I forgot something," and proceeded to pick up some small item I put out beforehand just for this purpose. I even looked in on her.

"There you are, my pet," I said through the door.

"Ah, you gave me such a scare," she answered, somewhat angry. "Why must you smoke so much?"

"Because. I just woke up. Must you nag me already?"

"You just got up and already you smoke."

"That's right. First thing I have to do is make my life bearable."

"What *are* you talking about?" I began, but then said nothing, just closed the door quietly.

But of course I returned like that many more times. I stopped on the staircase; the gramophone was playing inside and that was enough—I left. But there were times when I didn't find her home. "Did you go anywhere today?" "Yes, to the hairdresser." Quickly, then, to the hairdresser. "Did my wife leave her scarf here by any chance?" "Oh, that petite lady," smiled the hairdresser. Everybody who thought about her had to smile. One look from her and she turned their heads. If she wanted to, that is. And she did want to, she wanted everybody, even a bloody hairdresser. She looked at him, even at him, coyly, attentively, and with burning eyes.

So it was true about the hairdresser, true like everything else, although at that time neither I nor anyone else could prove it. I admit that for a whole week I had her watched by people from one of those agencies, in an attempt to find out where she went when she left the house. I am reluctant to talk about this, actually, for it makes me rather ashamed.

She is being careful, I thought, she must sense something. But the very next day I seemed to have forgotten all about this. And this was most remarkable, perhaps the greatest puzzle of my life at that time. I could still believe her, even if for a moment.

"Dearest," I said one rainy afternoon, for example. I remember it well. I was sitting in the parlor, reading something and musing about it, quite self-absorbed, when I suddenly became aware of her presence. She was right there in the room, keeping herself busy with some chore or other.

"Want something, my dear?" I said to her, but still as if in a dream. Her nearness felt so very nice. And I totally forgot that moment that I mustn't believe anything she says . . . But is that how we all are in the end? Is it any wonder, then, that we are forever deceived. For all I know that's our lot in life. I am inclined to believe it is.

One day, upon returning from the city, I again discovered she wasn't home. I walked into the other room, kept walking in and out, decided in fact to survey the place a little more carefully.

Why did we live in this boarding house? I asked myself. It was a dump—the rooms were terrible, the amenities mediocre. But she was happy enough staying there, couldn't there be something to that? She was the one who wanted to come here; she got the address from someone in Paris.

Couldn't there be a trapdoor or something around here? A secret passageway to another flat maybe?

I began moving the furniture, then opened the window and looked out.

Across the way I could see the rooftop of a smaller building and on it a row of pigeons; to the right of us there was a rather large square. I leaned all the way out, to get a better look.

Why did we always live near large squares? I wondered. And just then I remembered something: our maid in Paris, Äubchen Marie, who would often open and close the curtains in our living room. "What *are* you doing?" I once asked her. "Giving signals to my sweetheart. Letting him know if the coast is clear." And she laughed as she said this. I thought she was fooling, but why couldn't she have meant what she said? If there was somebody standing in the square below . . .

Maybe the square here serves the same purpose. Rubbish, I

thought. Still, I almost let out a cry at the discovery. What if they *were* in cahoots . . .

I even thought of that good-for-nothing landlord of ours. Who kept praising my life on the stairs—my own life, to me. Didn't he also laugh in my face?

For days I was trying to figure out a way to catch them. I *had* heard of a method on one of my ships once: something about sprinkling a mixture of flour and soot on the threshold, after which you are supposed to announce you are going away on a trip and early the following morning you show up unexpectedly . . . Why not do it?

For what if somebody *was* keeping a watch on the street, if they *were* passing signals and warning each other that I was on my way up? And by the time I'd walk through the door, everything would be back to normal, with my wife sitting on the couch reading. But with the flour and soot all over the floor and the carpet, it would be much harder to plead innocence.

I might as well give it a try.

Well, I must have presented quite a sight as I walked out of some grocery store the next day, clutching a bag of flour in my hand. I stopped in the middle of the street, utterly bewildered. How did I get here? What is this thing in my hand? What on earth am I doing? I had already told my wife I was going on a trip. In the evening I was supposed to stop in for my suitcase and at the same time perform this operation. But by then I lost interest, I was fed up with the whole business.

The anticipated complications alone got me all riled up. Just consider the number of possibilities a man embarking on such a course must take into account. What happens if, say, she herself goes out at night to get a book, or to make herself a cup of tea? He must then sprinkle the stuff not by the bedroom door but in the entrance way. But what if she should go out in the hall, there is a cabinet full of books there, too. So he must treat the area near the front door, throw the stuff on the doormat maybe. But what if the laundry boy comes for the wash in the morning. I would have to get back real early, before six . . .

Simple complications, all of them, but enough to drive one crazy.

I'd been roaming the city since early afternoon but couldn't decide a thing. And I wasn't home in time to make the necessary preparations. It was close to eleven o'clock, so I went up to see my friend Gregory Sanders. He was already asleep, I had to wake him, which was none too pleasant—the man was ailing and no longer young. I apologized for the intrusion and said I was in big trouble.

I simply had to talk to somebody, that's all there was to it.

And he had to help me, I said, I couldn't go through with it alone; I was afraid I was going mad—things have really gone that far. . . . I told him about the flour and what it was for—everything, in short.

Sanders wasn't angry, he just didn't know what to do with me.

"What can I tell you?" he asked me sadly. "Going away isn't a bad idea, though." He suggested I go to Scotland for a bit of rest.

"And leave my wife here?"

"Why not?"

"Now? And let her do as she pleases?"

"She does that anyway. Calm yourself, my friend," he said most solicitously. "Sit down. At least catch your breath here."

I had no desire to catch my breath. I was already sorry I'd come. He was no help.

But what does one expect from one's friend at a time like this? The impossible, I dare say. Still, I tried. Told him about the violets, at least. No response. Tried the cigarette business. That casual remark of hers that she must make her life bearable as soon as she wakes up.

"Well, what do you say?" I asked, my voice husky by now. "How can I make the woman's life more bearable than I already have? How can I be what I am not?"

But Sanders was a clever man, he didn't let me press him. And he didn't comfort me either. Or reassure me. Which also showed how smart he was. He just kept nodding his head:

"Yes, I see. But what are we to do?"

Or: "How true, but who said life was easy?" Such pearls of wisdom he fed me. It nearly drove me berserk.

I shouldn't brood, he said. Fine, I won't. There is thinking and there is brooding, he said, and one shouldn't confuse them, for they are two different things, opposites even. It stands to reason. With one you may get somewhere perhaps, but with the other, you're not likely to. It may even distort the true nature of things.

That too should be self-evident. For what does such a man, such a brooder do? He scrutinizes everything, to excess, chances are. Can such a man get a healthy perspective on things? Isn't it like wanting to examine the tiniest particles and atoms with a magnifying glass? "This world is not meant to be scrutinized that closely," concluded Gregory Sanders.

To myself I thought: What has all this got to do with me? And I was ready to leave. My friend meantime was reclining on a couch, surrounded by lemons which he must have used as medicine. Ah, a champion of natural cures, I thought with contempt. It was a priceless moment, I must say. Up until this moment I admired and respected the old man. But not any more. The scales fell from my eyes. The combination of his commonplace wisdom and all those lemons had a thoroughly disillusioning effect on me.

But then I realized he was broaching the subject of jealousy. And how cleverly he did it, to this day I can't figure out just how he ended up on that topic.

He called it a cramp, the soul's cramp, whose origin, too, was to be sought in this tendency to brood. But then, quite abruptly, he came to the point:

"Does faithfulness really exist?"

This finally made me perk up.

"What was that you said?" And at that moment he, too, seemed to warm to his subject.

"And if someone's not faithful, what then?"

"What do you mean what then?"

"That person can no longer be kind or sweet or good? It's not possible to love that person any more?"

"What do you mean 'kind and sweet'? I can't quite follow you. We're talking about opposite qualities. I don't understand the question. Can someone bad be good?"

"You are being ridiculous," Gregory Sanders said.

"And you are getting more interesting by the minute. One can be two things at the same time, you say?"

"Precisely," he said with some condescension. "Or haven't you ever seen such a woman? Or loved such a one? When she got married, did she stop being nice to you? Did she become so nasty and hateful to you that you could no longer look at her?"

"She remained nice enough."

"And perhaps to her husband as well. Why, of course. Except you weren't so particular then. Lovers usually aren't. They don't go around sprinkling flour on doorsteps." (All this made me uncommonly nervous, but I had to listen.) "No way were you particular then," Sanders repeated, with all the stubborn vehemence of his old age. And like a toothless soothsayer who could still roar, he raised himself in bed in his bitter rage. At first I didn't know what came over him. His very soul seemed to spill over. Where were his measly lemons now, or this very room? Whirling somewhere in space, I shouldn't wonder: disembodied, rarified. His words had an amazing power over me, and I again understood why I liked this old man.

"Or are you suggesting that such things don't exist?" he continued, breathlessly. "And a woman can't deceive her lover with her own husband, whom she might still love? It's useless trying to explain, though it's high time you understood. . . . We can love more than one, it's part of being human."

"As many as five?" I put in, but Gregory Sanders let that pass.

"You are greedy, that's what you are. You're after complete certainty. But is there such thing. . . ? Flour, you say, flour, for God's sake . . . I have nothing but contempt for you, my friend. Why aren't you jealous then of the cigarette she smokes, or of her past, or of the sun's rays that caress her skin and makes her shudder with pleasure, yes, with sheer pleasure, you might as well face it. Or do you suppose a woman lacks imagination. . . ? Well, she doesn't," he answered his own question. But he did this so despondently, with such an air of defeat, as if old ghosts were passing before his eyes, as if he were crushed by his own words.

And just then I understood everything. Suddenly it all fell into place. He was settling old scores himself, why of course. Such things do happen; one does often make amends to one's dead in this way. . . . So that's what this is all about, I thought with some sadness. He, too, is in the same boat.

And to prove it, he asked one more question: "Do you really think you can live your life without sin? In a white robe? Try reading the lives of the saints sometimes."

And then there was silence between us. At last.

After I'd recovered somewhat, I said to him: "The lecture is over, I take it." And then, with forced cheer: "This is all very instructive, but just what would you have me do?" For like a phantom, Ridolfi's stupid face appeared before me just then. "I should love her, lovers and all, is that it? Just ignore everything. . . ? Is that what you would want. Is it? Tell me."

"Yes, that's what my advice is to you."

"That I should just ignore it?"

"Yes."

"That *is* what I've been doing until now."

"You're doing it right now."

"That's right, isn't it?" And I was so mad, I could have killed him. "But the truth is I don't want to go on ignoring it any more."

"But you do, you do. (Well, that made me laugh.) Or if you don't want to, change your mind fast."

"And ignore it."

"Yes, ignore it. Anyway, one doesn't have to know everything. Man is not cut out for that kind of knowledge."

"What is he cut out for, then?" I asked, and realized I was shouting again. "Or are you suggesting that's all there is to us? But even if that's so, why do you approve, why acquiesce? Is that how low you have sunk? You don't even leave room for protest? (I was shaking with fury by now.) Or you no longer notice how odious you acquiescence really is, how humiliating this degree of under-standing can be? You don't care to see what's behind it, what misery? You'd rather look the other way?"

It was close to midnight. The people next door had already banged twice on the door, on account of the noise, and now they banged again. But I wasn't done yet. I began to pace the floor furiously:

"Don't you think she'd be the first to lose respect for me if I pretended to be blind?"

"All right then, do what you like," Sanders said gently. "I would just like to remind you that last time you were here you saw a man with a gun."

"Yes, yes; I think about him often enough."

"He was detestable, wasn't he?"

"He was. Yet, tonight it's quite different. Maybe you can tell me why I feel close to that man right now, why I keep telling myself that I'd like to be as far gone as he was . . ."

"You're crazy, Jacob."

"Yes, I am . . . But I learned a lot tonight; you've really enlightened me . . . I realized that no matter what I do, I've no other choice left but . . ."

"To kill?"

"To take my leave, actually. Because I've had enough. I will have no peace, no rest, until I can say: It's all over, finished. Everything, including life itself."

At that point I felt something in my eyes, tears, I think. The old man noticed: "You will give up then what you truly love?"

He then presented the following parable:

"Suppose you own a castle; it's your castle even if it's not in perfect shape. Say, the roof leaks, the plaster flakes, the whole place is in bad repair—would you stop calling it your own? How well I know these negligent owners . . . I am only sorry you are one of them. And you are—you are quarrelsome and senseless. You don't deserve the good in life; you don't know what to do with it. Oh, I know you people, I know all about you . . . The slightest flaw in the design and you are ready to set the whole structure on fire."

And he looked at me very very sadly, as if to say: It's too late. You are beyond help.

When I got home, my wife was fast asleep; she didn't stir when I walked in—at least not right away.

"What, you didn't go away?" she asked later, though, toward morning, when I turned on the light.

I couldn't really sleep. I kept seeing the happy blankness of Scotland . . . kept picturing the serene empty spaces, the deserted fields and mountains, and the locked-up restaurants with their overturned chairs resting against the bare tables. I imagined all of this quite precisely, over and over again, to the point of distraction, the way unhappy people do . . .

But back to why I was still there. A misunderstanding. She apparently thought I would leave right away.

"I changed my mind," I told her. "Besides, the old man—Gregory Sanders, that is—also told me not to leave just yet." That's all I said to her, then turned off the light. It was half past three.

Around five-thirty someone tapped very lightly on our front door, and then gave a few more taps.

"Who is it?" she asked and sat up in bed. Apparently she wasn't asleep either.

"Who the devil could it be?" I also asked, and reached for my robe.

"For heaven's sake, don't go out," she pleaded.

"Why not?" I couldn't figure out why she got so scared. She also jumped out of bed, I noticed. And she kept on telling me not to go out, she was afraid. It was so dark on that staircase, God only knew who might be lurking there—"Why it could be . . . anybody."

"Who cares? At worst, I'll belt him."

"No, no, don't," she kept begging, and clung to me with all her strength. (I never realized she was that strong.)

But I managed to free myself, and still clutching my robe in one hand, I grabbed the fire iron with the other and ran out. There was no one in the hallway. I raced down a flight of stairs, opened the hallway door—strangely enough, that wasn't locked either, no one was there. I pulled the cover off a table—no one was under it. I saw light seeping through one of the apartment doors, I turned the knob, and amazingly enough, that wasn't locked either. A man in a nightshirt stood in the middle of the room. I ran.

"What nerve," a woman's voice shouted after me.

"Next time lock your door," I shouted back.

I ran down another flight of stairs, and there on the bottom of the staircase stood that old scoundrel, our landlord, Mr. Horrabin Pit, smoking comfortably in the dark.

I put my hand on his shoulder.

"Did you knock on our door just now?"

"I did."

"And why did you knock so early in the morning?"

"I had to," he whined. "You took my key to the outside door and never returned it." And he went on about how it didn't do any good to knock on the caretaker's door, that good-for-nothing must have wandered off again somewhere, or died for all he knew, and he had to go to the Caledonian Market to do some shopping, it was Friday, didn't I realize, he was late as it was, those thugs at the market will make him pay double for everything . . .

He happened to be right. I did borrow his key.

"What a strange coincidence," I muttered to myself. That this should happen today, of all days, when my wife thought I was away. Odd, isn't it? That I should go on boxing shadows this way.

Needless to say, I didn't believe the business about the key, no sir. Who knows what strange confluence of events I may be witnessing, I thought, as I ascended those stairs. Otherwise why should she have gotten so scared.

She even discovered traces of the flour the next day, because some of it spilled in my pocket.

"What is this?" she cried. "It's ruining your clothes, darn it. What is all this smut and dust?"

"Dust, you say? Well . . . you guess." I was stalling, because I had no idea how to handle this. "It's . . . er . . . just some flour," I then said, quite flustered.

"What do you need flour for?"

"Why don't you guess?" I again said and thought: What now? Do I tell her everything? "Actually, it's a bit of cocaine," I averred, because it occured to me that that's what it looks like. I had seen enough of that stuff in the Levant.

"And what do you need cocaine for?"

"What do you mean what do I need it for? Good grief, I tried it. I need something too. To make my life more bearable."

"Is that so?"

"Ahem."

But a little later I relented: "All right, don't get scared; I have no intention of becoming an addict. I just want to kill myself." And then:

"It really is just flour. I wanted to sprinkle some on your doorstep, to see who climbs in here when I am away."

"You're crazy," she said. And you could tell she didn't believe me. For it goes without saying that the truth is always the hardest to believe, because it's always so fantastic, so incredible—the most florid imagination can't equal it.

Just the same, my revelation did produce the desired effect.

"What is the matter with you?" she asked and turned pale as she did.

"What should be the matter? Nothing at all. I am just not

feeling very well. My strength is failing me, that's all. I wonder how I'll go on working." In the meantime I was looking at myself in the mirror, for I had just started shaving, and my face was covered with foam. . . . God Almighty, I looked like somebody who hadn't slept for a hundred days—circles under my eyes, deep creases, a bewildered, animal look . . . It's high time I croaked.

"But really, what's bothering you?" she again asked.

"Bothering me? Nothing. Nothing at all, I tell you. I feel great, I adore you, as always, my life is all sweetness and sunshine."

She grew quiet.

And I could no longer bring myself to talk to her. Even though I would have liked to, I still would have like to. And to no one else, only to her. For hours on end I would have loved to talk to her. To sit down somewhere and just talk.

She, too, stood there, helplessly, like a poor old woman who didn't know where her children were. I noticed she had tears in her eyes. And she still had the clothesbrush in her hand, covered with white dust.

But it was no use. There was a lump in my throat, it kept growing, but it was all too late. She finds me unbearable, she said so herself, she used that very word. Her life with me had become unbearable. And I kept mulling over the phrase.

What is more, that iron poker was still there on the couch, waiting for me.

From then on it was simply more of the same; there was no stopping.

To begin with, I ran over the list of tenants in the building.

But it's hardly worth mentioning them. The boarding house itself took up two floors, with constantly changing boarders (we were the only long-time residents). Downstairs there was a glass shop, on the third floor, two families with teenage girls, plus a sickly law student. And in the backyard, a vacant studio.

With these I wasn't going to get anywhere, clearly. The glass shop downstairs held out no promise, either. It was run by a very officious, nervous owner and his old assistant, and the shop wasn't even doing well.

But then let's look elsewhere. Just how far one can get carried away may be seen by the following absurdity: There was an errand boy at the boarding house, a buttons of sorts, and I even put him on the list. Why did I? My own childhood experiences had something to do with it, I guess. I know myself how large and robust a kid of fourteen can be, how, in his reckless and clumsy passion, like an ox. I remembered the ladder—didn't I, in my own time, climb through the window of a strange apartment? She too was a lady of impeccable reputation, who lounged about all day in her flat. This was one reason why I suspected the kid. The other was that I knew, again from experience, that childless women can be very fond of young boys. My wife even said now and then: "Look, isn't he sweet?" I answered: "Yes, he is." The boy did have bright blue eyes, a ready smile, and would say things like "I am totally at your service, sir," and even exchange glances with my wife when he did . . . All right, we'll see.

I should mention, too, that he was the kind of kid whose eyes went everywhere. And I say this not only because I once saw him whistling and chuckling to himself in a doorway, but also because when he came up in the morning to deliver our laundry, he was ever so observant, and stood there gaping if he noticed something out of the ordinary—if I left something on the table, for instance, a novelty he hadn't seen before: say, my two-valved telescope, or some other strange instrument. He'd keep staring at it, reverently, like a savage at a modern city.

I felt like drawing out this curiosity of his, and produced all sorts of items from my trunk.

"What are you up to?" my wife inquired.

"I want to get rid of all this useless stuff. All it is is extra weight; I may be able to get something for them here. Miss Borton said she might sell it for us . . . if we are lucky." (But where was little Miss Borton by then?)

My wife, though, as soon as she heard her name, fell silent. And that suited me just fine. I didn't want her snooping in my affairs.

So I took out a miniature Chinese silkscreen, a lantern, a delicate oriental eyeglass case, the kind mandarins tuck away in the folds of their robe, a Dayak dagger called a "parang," and other trifles and knick-knacks one has the urge to pick up while traveling.

I was anxious to learn what the boy would have to say about all this stuff when he shows up in the morning with the fresh laundry.

Now it was late afternoon, he had no business coming up at this time of the day. But should my wife still want to see him, for, as she kept saying, "It's so nice to look at him" (sure, why not?)—in short, if the boy came up after all, then tomorrow morning I will notice it on him—he won't be all that surprised to see the wonderful toys. That was my train of thought, my strategy. And right afterwards I decided to go out. Decided to take a little walk.

"So long, my pet," I called to my wife. "I am going into town. Don't expect me before dinner. I have too many things to do."

And as soon as I stepped out on the street . . .

Why, it was most strange, unreal almost. Rarely have I experienced anything like it. First there was only stillness and an overcast sky. As if the whole world moved underwater, turning opaque and silent.

The colors are unearthly at such moments. The city suddenly turned a deep, exotic brown. But just as suddenly it got blinding white. A storm was upon us, unleashing all its fury; I was shaken up, tossed about, like an empty vessel.

The people on the pavement ran for cover, car-horns were bleating like sheep.

Oh no, I thought, this is how Harry Barbon, my chemistry teacher, died. And that, too, happened in the heart of London, for only here do you get such unexpected downpours. The shower was icy cold and abundant, I got splashed generously in the face, in the neck. But I didn't even try to dry myself—why not let my shirt soak through, why not be at the storm's mercy? Now if I also had a beard—and the thought made me rejoice—that too would be sopping wet . . .

That's how it started. I had to go on about it because rarely before had I felt such elation. . . . At any rate, I wound up in some out-of-the-way hole, a tiny room covered in red felt, which for this reason alone looked like a secluded spot in a brothel. . . . Well, in this empty little nook I drank a bottle of port.

There wasn't another soul in that tiny place, and ghostly silence reigned inside me as well; I was empty and dumb . . . Only after too much strain can one feel so vacant.

There was a painting on the wall—that's what I kept staring at. It showed a donkey carrying buckets of water, led by a man in a wide-brimmed straw hat. . . . I thought I heard the water sloshing in those buckets, and smelled the sweet fragrance of grapes ripening in the hills. A vast, blue expanse opened before my eyes, and I could swear I was singing. In Spanish yet, which was odd. But sang I did, a sunny Spanish song I picked up who knows where. Though the strangest thing was that I never could speak Spanish well, not way back then, anyway.

Next morning the delivery boy went wild over that dagger from Borneo. I could see; I was there, waiting, when he brought in the fresh clothes.

Well, let us then look into some other possibilities; her correspondence, for instance. Maybe that will provide us with some fresh clues. In this connection I must report the following:

In Paris I had bought her a neat little folder with some fine stationery, which for a long time remained untouched. But now, just now, marks began to appear on the blotter, which meant she had been writing letters. Let's pursue the matter then. Whom could she be writing to? Not her mother, that didn't seem plausible—she didn't care for her all that much. Not her relatives—they were all peasants living in or around Clermont—she wasn't close to them, either. Her old girl friends maybe? We shall see. In any case, I began my investigation.

I left the inkblot as it was, and in one of the better paint shops bought a preparation called Corbusta (it was probably nothing more than ammonium nitrate), and mixed it with the ink. When held over a flame, this stuff burns up faster than other substances, so anything written with it shows through on paper, even on a blotter. I tried it out beforehand and obtained a perfectly legible copy of a text.

So the idea wasn't bad, but I didn't get very far with it. All I could make out on the blotter was one insignificant word: *caractère*, and even that with great difficulty. What's more, the following day the ink was gone; my wife bought a fresh bottle. In other words, she knew by then, or at least suspected, that I had been watching her. But I wasn't going to give up that easily. If it's games you want, I muttered to myself, it's games you shall have. I will catch you in the end. And went on working.

Sure enough, things began to fall into place. It was November nineteenth—I still remember the date because the night before was one of the most excruciating nights of my life. I was all set to jump out of our third-story window; the depths below beckoned me with such force, I thought I'd have to tie myself to a chair. (It was a moment of utter weakness, a truly loathsome moment, I regret it deeply.) My wife was fast asleep at the time, so I was all alone when these magnetic, hypnotic forces began to assail me . . . (There are indeed such forces, I am convinced of that, we should talk about it, though not now.)

I am not saying it was that silly writing pad caused my frantic state, though it did have something to do with it. For on a brand new blotter I was able to make out with unmistakable clarity, even without the aid of the chemical, the following two words: "*Mon cher.*" In other words she wrote this to a man, there could be no doubt of that. This was my first significant discovery.

The second came when I happened to reach into some drawer and from the jumble of odds and ends which was to be found everywhere in our house, I fished out an identification card bearing her photo, authorizing her to pick up mail addressed to her and held at such and such post office in Paris. Now I have no idea why certain things—classified ads or mail held at the post offices—have such a disquieting effect on me. But for hours afterwards I was sick to my stomach. That's when I opened the window, for some fresh air, and experienced that mesmerizing spell, which I thought I would not be able to fight off.

And from that point on I often got dizzy or grew weak in the knee when I crossed bridges or leaned out of tall buildings. In other words this thing got to me where it really hurt, it undermined my very livelihood. For when a seaman starts having dizzy spells, he is finished.

I even wrote letters that night, letters to myself, discussing all sorts of non-existent business propositions. I didn't want to waste any more time. True, I had everything all prepared; from a printer I received business stationery with various letterheads (I had told them I was ready to order, but wanted to see samples first). One firm I still remember: *Litterton & Co. Brokers*. That's what I used for my first letter, in which I was requested to visit their offices at my earliest convenience to discuss one of Mr. Gregory Sanders's proposals. Then I typed another letter, and another, I kept churning them out—the only thing I was afraid of was that all that racket might wake her up. Every once in a while I tiptoed over to the bedroom door and listened.

What purpose this sudden flurry of correspondence served I can't really explain. It was nothing more than groping in the dark, I am afraid. I must have figured that here she was, writing letters, getting answers, receiving them at this very address, and I knew nothing at all about it. When did she get them, and how? There must be some secret understanding. But who with? No doubt, our rascally landlord, Mr. Horrabin Pit, had something to do with this, too. This line of reasoning must have led me to some shadowy conclusion. . . . The thing was that I didn't get any mail at the boarding house, I made arrangements to have it sent to the Brighton Hotel—when I had no permanent address, I always had my letters forwarded to a central location. Now I was hoping that since I would be getting letters here, too, I'll get to see some of hers. One day they might get the letters mixed up . . .

And the ploy worked, this one did. Life *is* extraordinary, isn't it? Sometimes the silliest ruses lead to surprising results . . .

Oh yes: I sent that ID card immediately to a friend of mine in Paris, a senior civil servant named Toffy-Ederle, and asked him to forward any mail still held at that post office. Actually, I was busy all night. In the morning I mailed the letter to Paris, express, and the following evening posted the first one, addressed to me, special delivery. I wanted to make sure it would arrive in the morning.

And later, when I knew I would be home in the afternoon, I posted one in the morning as well. I played around this way for a while. Actually, we'd be awakened early in the morning, because, as I said, I mailed most of the correspondence special delivery.

Sometimes I even mailed money to myself; I thought: why not try that too?

"You get so many letters these days," remarked my wife.

And I was again tempted to answer her: "Yes, I do; I've gone stark raving mad, you see."

Something did happen to me, that seemed fairly clear. To *me*, who'd always valued trust above all else. How on earth did I end up this way? Somebody had better explain it to me, and fast.

She is a sweet, gentle, lovely woman, Gregory Sanders would've probably said, had he known her. And he'd have added, I don't know what you want. She is an angel . . . What would you do, I wonder, if I proved to you that she *is* an angel—an angel besmirched by your sordid imagination ? Yes, what *would* you do? Blow your brains out maybe? The errand boy, you say. The mailman, you say. Good Lord, man, aren't you ashamed of yourself? That's what Gregory Sanders would have said, in all probability.

Let's try it, then, let's tell him everything. I couldn't be any worse off than I already was. But then out with everything, even if it kills me. Yes, the errand boy, too, *and* the mailman . . . And having listened to it all, and understood and appreciated it too, would he please tell me what I ought to do? Advise me for pity's sake on how to cure myself, how to restore faith in my heart? For surely, her writing "*Mon cher*" to some stranger, or having her mail held at a French post office will not do it.

I wanted to tell all this to her too, in a letter—I spent a whole night composing it. But when I looked at her in the morning, I tore it up, and said to myself: I can't. Not any more.

And that's where I left it.

There was nothing to be done; nothing. Two stones can't open up to each other, or two sticks of wood, or two whatevers that are no longer close.

In the meantime Toffy-Ederle answered my letter with a one-word telegram: "*Rien*," meaning there was nothing in that post office.

In that case we must push on. And push on I did.

One morning the mail was again delivered very early. This time my wife got very annoyed. Will they ever let her get some sleep, she fumed. Anyway, why didn't I let someone have power of attorney, or why not have my business correspondence sent to the Brighton, as I had done before.

"I had a fight with the people at the Brighton," I said rather sadly.

"Oh, you wind up fighting with everyone," she said. Frankly, I was getting tired of the whole thing myself. What's more, there was a new twist now: they didn't bother to bring up the mail, I had to go down to the office and get it myself. A further insult.

"There, you have two pieces of mail this morning," my landlord, Mr. Horrabin Pit, explained gently. "A registered letter and a money order."

I completely forgot about the money. I had sent myself twenty-five guineas the day before yesterday. Yes, that's precisely what I did.

But then, even madness must have its limits.

"Can't you have the mail sent up?" I asked the landlord darkly.

"It's a new mailman, you see, and you must identify yourself."

That was true, too, everything was; and the mailman was a swarthy, slimy character with sidewhiskers. . . . God, was I bristling, was I ever sick of my life? For just imagine: I had to go and get those absolutely meaningless letters which I had written myself, to myself—letters which didn't interest me in the least. And the money! It came out of my pocket, for God's sake. And for this they had to wake me from my pleasant stupor. Oh, I was so very bitter. If they had tossed my heart to the dogs just then, they would have surely spat it out in disgust. And to boot, the old man stopped me, he again stood in my way.

"Who created you, may I ask?" he asked in his insufferable, childlike manner, and went as far as caressing my coat sleeve. There I stood in that beat-up office, shivering, thinking to myself, I'll end up sick, I'll catch my death of cold. And sure enough, I sneezed. (I *was* very cold, all I had on was my robe and my socks.) My whole being railed at this indignity.

"Who created you, then?" he asked again, almost victoriously, as if he sensed he got me this time. The man had a voice like a schoolboy, which I really hate in people.

"Was it you?" he asked sarcastically, "you created yourself?" (His reasoning must have been: If I didn't believe in higher intelligence, I didn't believe in creation, either. But then how did I get to be so smart? Just like that, by myself? Hahaha.)

"Maybe there isn't even such a thing as creation," I answered without hesitation. "There just isn't. And I'll tell you why not."

"Oh, please do," the old fool gushed.

"Just look at the hair growing in your ear," I said to him, for I had a terrific desire to insult the old man. "Or in my ear, for that matter," I added, grudgingly. "Those hairs keep sprouting, right? With age they become thicker, denser, and while they proliferate, your brain atrophies. So much for your notion of creative evolution.

153

"I trust you have seen ropes made out of hemp . . . Don't get me wrong, I am not alluding to rope you hang yourself with."

"Of course not," he said with an obliging smile. "I know exactly what you mean, my dear captain."

"Well, then you know it's not a good idea to keep it out in the sun too long, because it rots. Creation, in short, devours its own products, just about everything it has wrought. Whatever it brings into being it also destroys. Whoever granted me life seeks also to wreck it." I was shouting by this time. But then I had always treated him as though he were deaf, that was part of my strategy.

"Or take the world of science . . . " I was going to pursue my little analogy, telling him how on the one hand there are all those useful and wonderful inventions heralding progress, and on the other there's dynamite . . . But I didn't pursue it, I had to stop . . . I felt a pleasant tingle in my veins . . . No, no, it was much more than that, it was rapture, I nearly swooned into his arms. I took another look at my letters, you see. They said there were two, but I was holding four letters in my hand, *four*, two of them for my wife, addressed, I could tell, by a male hand.

If Gregory Sanders's admonition could be applied here, then I'd have to say he had a point: it *is* possible to love what's mean. In fact, there is no greater pleasure in the world than wicked pleasure.

"Have you got a vacant room?" I asked the old man. And I won't deny it: I almost keeled over, my heart was pounding violently. Or was it simply fear?

"I just noticed I've got an important letter here. I want to read it first. Afterwards we can continue our Swedenborgian discussion."

And he did usher me into an unheated room filled with unused beds and chairs. I locked the door behind me and sat down to catch my breath. I was like a tiger, by God, that doesn't fall on its prey right away, but licks it first and groans with pleasure. I took another good look at the letters, and then another. Two of the four I had sent, they were all right. There was also a strange picture post card which must have got there by mistake. And then there was the real prize: a letter addressed to her. Strange. . . . How rash one can be when one is out to deceive. How careless, how bold . . . On a brand new blotter she leaves the word *mon cher*. And then she has her love letters delivered to our home. Such a woman I should not be able to catch redhanded? I am not crazy, my sweet. You *are* in league with that sanctimonious old scoundrel, and now I have proof.

The letter came from Paris and was written with a calligrapher's hand. On top it said: "No. 19." And then:

Dear Madame (much more than dear, no matter how petite you may be),

Just to round out my letter of last week: I am done with Epictitus and with Spinoza's *Tractate* on the relationship between law and state power, but my exam has been postponed a day. (Paris is glutted with philosophers.) As soon as I have some news for you, I shall write. Until then, or rather, until this neglected heart still beats, I am

Yours faithfully,
Maurice Tannenbaum

PS.: I meant to tell you: the slippers serve me splendidly. Not only are they lovely and faithful, the two birds on it sing to me every morning. (Consequently, my mornings are enchanted.)

A philosopher? I kept staring at the paper, dumbfounded. What was all that about exams and philosophies? If it wasn't a love letter, what was it?

I felt a bit let down, I won't deny it. Sure, it had the thing about a neglected heart and such, but still. The odd style, at once meticulous and sarcastic, the carefully formed letters—all of this made me quite anxious in the end. What's more, he numbered his letters. Was the young man a bookkeeper perchance? No, not a bookkeeper, a philosopher. I kept eyeing the letter suspiciously. Could she have started up with such young boys? Could he be the one who asked her to marry him? The one who sent him the violets from Paris? I could hardly believe it. And the business about the slippers—that was a puzzle, too. Was I to take it that when she was busy with embroidering in the Café St. Luc, right under Dedin's nose, she was doing it for someone else? Or was she embroidering slippers for two of her boyfriends at once?

* * *

Upstairs I calmed down, but only for an instant. Then, I put on my specs, threw some clothes on and got down to business once again.

What *about* those sweet little birds, damn it? They chirp away, do they? Why, that almost amounts to a confession of love, all that chirping in the morning.

And the relation between justice and power, what about that? Ah hell, do they really expect me to believe that all a good-for-nothing student wants to tell a beautiful young woman is how he did on some exam? He was writing allegorically, in code, why of course. What I'd have to do now is find out what the words mean. What, for instance, could the mysterious-sounding Spinoza signify for two amorous hearts?

So I gave her some money and told her to go out and do some shopping. She had been itching to go anyway. "Christmas is upon us," she kept telling me. (It wasn't, by the way.) And that London fashions were different. And besides, her friends had arrived from Paris, and they were all so smartly dressed. Fine. Let her buy herself whatever her little heart desires. A scarf, even a blouse, to make the shopping spree last longer.

And sure enough, she was all aflutter, got ready, had her makeup on, in no time.

"Wait a minute," I called after her, "while you are at it, buy yourself a raincoat, too. You've been meaning to, haven't you? My words had an astounding effect on her. She was so shocked, she didn't finish her cigarette.

"How generous you are," she said and hurried out the door.

I wasn't one bit generous. On the contrary. I waited a little, to make sure she wasn't coming back, and then got ready to do something I had always found quite abhorrent, which is going through other people's things.

But I had to. I was still hoping I'd find some fresh clue. A letter perhaps, a word even—any lead would do . . . A little house search, then.

It went against my grain, Lord knows, but . . . a seaman can never allow himself to be squeamish, and I am not, that's certain, I've done things in my time that were plenty weird, yet it surprises me still that I was willing to go through with it. And not only because it seemed so distasteful, I had another reason.

My wife was a very untidy person. I should have spoken of this sooner but couldn't. She was so very untidy, you see, I couldn't possibly do her habits justice. And now to penetrate all that clutter . . .

For instance, in one of her chest drawers, among her undergarments, I found apples; and as if that wasn't bad enough, some of them had been bitten into, and these spots turned a deep, unsightly red. And I came upon scraps of left-over cakes, also bearing her teeth marks . . . And pieces of ribbon, lace, tulle, yarn, all rolled into a tangled mass, and made even more solid by the odd pieces of sucking candy that adhered to it.

I won't deny it: my nerves got so jangled by all this, I could have easily set the place on fire.

But how utterly ridiculous one can be at a time like this. I had something major to worry about, but what made me furious were these trifles. The balls of matted yarn and silver foil, for let's not forget about the bits of silver foil—they were all over the house, too: in boxes and drawers, just stuffed in or rolled into balls. I couldn't fathom why she should want to save all that worthless silver paper. Was this, too, an expression of some childhood need? Because what I am talking about *is* ordinary silver foil wrapping paper.

And they turned up in the most unlikely places: in flower vases, in between valises in the foyer. . . . Would somebody please tell me why I had to marry such a woman?

And what about the cabinets? They were packed so tight, they almost tipped over when I tried opening them. Her drawers also got stuck when I tried to force them open, and they wouldn't close either, her bunched up fineries acted as a spring. Mixed together carelessly were all kinds of expensive fabrics: silks and velvets and moiré, and dainty suede handbags with scraps of crippled jewelry in them: gold brooches, broken bracelets. And a cavalcade of color everywhere: deep blues, lovely greens . . . And breadcrumbs in her purse, stockings in the sewing basket, and assorted change everywhere, Spanish and French coins, and stamps and streetcar tickets from a variety of countries, and discolored, sorry-looking bits of chocolate . . .

Was it from this . . . this chaotic mess that she rose so grandly when she went out at night? Yes, indeed. And how radiant she was in her white furs, her violet gowns. Her shoulders glistened, her face was aflush as she informed me casually, "I am off; is my skirt all right?" And after turning this way and that, she'd flutter out of the room.

(This happened not long ago. Some Frenchman had invited her, some new arrivals. And twice in a row. I didn't go with her, I wasn't in the mood. I just watched her as she left.)

Our marriage license I found in a cupboard, stuck to a bottle of cordial, so help me . . . But why go on. . . . ? It's a curse to be like me. There I was casting about for a word, a sign—a simple sentence would have sufficed—yet at the time of the Ridolfi business, I had everything I needed in my hand, and didn't do a blessed thing . . . I never did get over that. How could I be so indifferent? Or was it that I simply stopped caring?

Yes, that must be it. For indifference keeps you going, while passion pulls you down. Miss Borton had said this to me once and I realized now how right she was.

Nothing—not one letter or stray note—turned up, which might have provided me with a clue; she must have destroyed everything. I was ready to put things back in their place when I came upon two photographs, in one of her sewing baskets, stuck in an envelope. With some surprise I examined them. One showed a little girl, an attractive-looking child, and on the back of the picture, an inscription, in Spanish: *recuerdo* or, possibly, *collecion d'oro*, something like that.

The child, as I say, was quite appealing; her sad little face was framed by thick curls and her eyes radiated a dreamy sort of confidence.

"This must be her child," I said to myself right away, and stepped up to the window.

"Yes, her child," I repeated out loud. I couldn't even say that she resembled my wife all that much. And still. The hunch, the feeling was unmistakable. Quick and strong.

So strong in fact that I got all flustered. I confess I always had a soft spot for little girls.

But then I put it down and examined the other one again.

This was a picture of my wife in the company of high-spirited revelers, both men and women, with the men wearing high paper hats, looking a bit like bakers, a woman holding a live rooster, and all of them apparently having the time of their lives, laughing with abandon, as people do after a night of boisterous merrymaking.

And there was my wife in the middle, perched on some sort of stuffed swan, and not merely laughing but positively blazing with hilarity, with that special glow in her eyes, a glow I knew quite well. . . .

But then I put away the pictures, put them back in the box. I didn't really want to know that much about them, or about the possible connection between the two. There was an inscription on the back of the second picture, too, just one word: *La nuit*—another hint about its origin.

But we know all about such things. It's after a wild, champagne-filled night that one has such pictures taken in the Bois de Boulogne, as a souvenir.

I tried hard to put all of this out of my mind.

"What on earth are you doing?" my wife exclaimed when she walked in. "Why are you going through my books?"

"I'm looking for our papers, my sweet. Do you know where I found our marriage license?" I reminded her gently. "In a cupboard, stuck to a bottle."

This made her laugh.

"What do you need our papers for anyway?"

"For a job application. They want to see your travel papers, too. But you are so very untidy." And I looked into her eyes.

"I know," she replied contritely.

"You should really try to be a little more careful, and at least not mess up what I already tidied up. And while we're at it, why don't you try *doing* something for a change, anything at all, instead of lazing about with a cigarette in your hand . . .? Are you listening to me?"

"Yes."

"Saying yes won't do: look at me." And I turned her head toward me. (Her eyeballs were darting every which way.) "Look in my eyes. Like that. A woman brooding all the time . . . nothing good can come of that."

"I don't brood; I've nothing to brood about."

"You daydream then."

"Oh no I don't; not any more."

"One dream after another. First you sleep till all hours, till your head is in a fog, then you sink into another dream. You pick up a book and you start dreaming again. It may be a dismal day, the room is filled with cigarette smoke, the lights are dim—what can all this lead to?" I was still looking straight into her eyes.

But . . . inexplicably . . . I wanted to forgive her, too. After all that she'd put me through, I wanted to embrace her. To love her. It's true, I was feeling quite wretched, and I wanted desperately to be happy. I was glad she was here, glad that she helped me abandon my miserable profession. Seeing her was like seeing the morning after a drunken night, like getting a taste of real life after shadowy make believe . . .

"And how is the raincoat?"

"Oh, the raincoat . . ." And she brightened up. "It's nice. Just lovely. Thank you ever so much . . ."

On another occasion, however, I did go through her books, the ones I didn't get to the first time. And then I found something.

It was a book on human psychology written by a man named Condillac. On page 72 of this book I found a hand-written note: "When you get to this page, please be advised that you are the sweetest creature ever to walk on this earth. M.T." And he even added (lest she thought it was addressed to somebody else): "I am talking to you, *ma petite Madame*." I turned to the title page book and there saw the inscription: "Property of Maurice Tannenbaum." So that was that.

Actually I also came across a selection from Spinoza's works. It was a brand new book, quite handsome, I slipped it into my pocket. My wife was taking a bath just then; when she came out, I was sitting at the table, ready to eat. Pointing to the Condillac book I said:

"Let me take this with me, I'd like to study it." And to myself I thought: Maybe I'll find something in that, too.

My wife just stared at me.

"At least I'll have something to read on the train." She didn't know what to make of this. Of my sudden interest in psychology. But she left it at that, she didn't let on. Or perhaps she knew nothing about the confession concealed in the book, she may never have looked at it. Or at the Spinoza, either. That was such a small volume anyway, it wasn't even worth mentioning. I left for the city in a hurry. It was past two o'clock.

Shortly thereafter it came to pass that I cheated on my wife. I find it strange myself that I should dare use that word, that I should even express myself this way—*I*, who long ago forfeited the right to be considered a straight and upright Dutchman by my compatriots.

But man is such a preposterous creature anyway—preposterous by birth as well as by volition. And all the more so if he is helped along by events. The thing itself happened this way:

Gregory Sanders was no longer in town, Miss Borton didn't answer my letters (I'll have more to say about this, about the letters I mean, and the state of mind I was in when I wrote them). Fact is there was no one around, absolutely no one I could talk to. And to be in a constant state of anxiety, wrapped in endless self-doubt—why, I couldn't take that, either. For that, too, is like being in a fog: the more you tried to penetrate it, the denser it got. I had just about enough.

To hell with you, I declared. You are worthless, you are nothing. I said this to myself but while looking at her, hoping she'll get the message, or sense at least just how fed up I was.

We were sitting at the table, having lunch; next to my plate lay the Condillac book. Now I was willing to put up with a great deal, but engaging in small talk over lunch was the limit. What sort of woman was Madame Lagrange, she wanted to know for instance. What was my *feeling* about her? Such were the questions I was supposed to answer. (This woman, by the way, was a friend of hers who recently moved here from Paris. I met her once or twice before, I sort of knew her.)

What was I going to answer her? What did I care about this Madame Lagrange? When a woman, an extraordinary woman, a radiant beauty, was waiting for me just then. A woman who was a hundred times more captivating than both of them put together. I said to her rather abruptly:

"My goodness, it's two o'clock, I am late already." And with that I sprang up from the table and rushed out the door.

Where now? I said to myself once I was outside. I had an hour to kill. To the Brighton first. But once there, I got restless again.

What are you sitting here for? I mumbled to myself. When a woman—and what a woman—is waiting for you, and impatiently too, I imagine. Why waste your time here?

But it's about time I named this rare beauty, whose lovely eyes inspired such rapture in my heart. Let's just call her Mrs. Cobbet (I couldn't possibly reveal her real name); but she was none other than the lady who treated me so very sweetly at the Castle Nachoz, as well as in the back rooms of various other night spots. But why hem and haw? I am talking about Kodor's mistress, of course. In other words, with a single lapse I deceived both wife and friend.

At any rate, my liaison with the lady took the following course: First I didn't really feel like getting involved, for reasons I'd already discussed elsewhere. I had no qualms about it, mind you— a man who is given to entertaining young ladies in night clubs is beyond that, though it goes without saying that a man *is* in a different position when it comes to such things than an innocent young girl. I'd always hated the Biblical Joseph. Why did he have to be so skittish, like some frisky mare? But how *should* a man behave when two such lovely creatures begin caressing his heart? Should he reply, no, no, he'll have none of that? Should he act the saint and say sorry, I am not interested? That is no way for a man to behave.

And still. The we-had-fun-now-good-bye solution didn't please me, either. Yet, as it was, I was up to my neck in entanglements, should I let those two further complicate my life? One of them, Kodor's girl, even scared me somewhat, on account of her passionate nature. Then again, the other was the dreamy sort, and that also spelled trouble. Should I get mixed up with another romantic? No, I'd had enough.

At the same time, after what'd happened between us I had certain obligations. The morning after—and what a lovely morning it was, I was riding on a cloud—I went into the hotel florist shop (that one stays open all night), and sent each of them a beautiful bouquet, making sure it would be waiting for them by the time they got home. They were truly gorgeous, impartially selected identical bouquets of long-stemmed Riviera roses, all of them a rich, deep red, the kind that almost looks black. I owe them this much, I thought, but then: Adieu. And to Kodor's girl, in a moment of weakness, I even added the words "Sweet to the sweet," which, I realized the next day, was pretty stupid, as it's a phrase Shakespeare has someone say at a funeral. But what did it matter? (Actually, to the other one I wrote something better: "Flowers that pale in thy presence." With her I waxed biblical.) I wrote both messages on calling cards that said *Hotel Brighton, London* under my name—no other address. I figured it was better if they don't reply. But in case they do . . . why then, I am no longer there, I left, I can't be tracked down. Anything can happen to a guest in a hotel.

And for a while, there was no answer, which was fine with me. Let oblivion take over . . . But as long as I am thinking of these two right now, let me bid farewell to at least one of them, the one with the sweet smile, the timid one, whose eyes forever ranged over dreamland. I never saw her again, and never inquired, either, which, I admit, was not very nice. But I did think of her often. Even her name—Winny—I found captivating. Years and years later, on different continents, I still found myself mumbling her name. Why? Who knows? Maybe because I was always grateful to women who were good to me. And she was. We didn't spend much time together, but enough for me to have the feeling that she was a good woman. When I think of her now, her memory is like that of a fine wine: light, fleeting, but evoking very pleasant sensations. But let's leave the effusions for another time. The truth is one always likes to daydream about people one didn't get to know very well, and about affairs that were not destined to last.

The other lady, however—Kodor's black beauty—did answer, even if rather late. And she didn't seem to take offense at my inane message. A week later one of the bellboys presented me with a large lavender-colored note on a silver tray. All it said, in a script that seemed deliberately disguised, was:

"Now I am alone." (Also from *Hamlet*, no doubt.) And though it wasn't signed, it was easy to guess, from the quotation alone, that it came from her. The simple postscript read: "Tonight at seven." By George. I looked at the date: it was yesterday.

What could I say about this combination of caution and daring? About the disguised handwriting, which left no doubt as to what she meant: that at seven o'clock there'll be no one home, only she, she and I, that is, just the two of us, all alone.

Enough to make you dizzy.

I even took a whiff of the letter. It had a heavy scent. "Musk," I mumbled to myself. Musk for sure, it can be nothing else. (I even knew how that's done, how paper can be chemically treated—somebody once explained it to me.) Needless to say, the fragrance began working on me. And the paper, to complement the scent, was heavy and dark, and royal in size. I was quite taken by that, too.

Nevertheless, I resisted. One can be so heroic at times. I still kept saying to myself: Do I need all this? And besides, I still looked upon myself as a melancholy individual. So I wrote her another note, for some foolish reason still sticking to Shakespeare (perhaps to make up for that gauche first line), and this time consulting a book of Shakespearean quotations):

> We are such stuff
> As dreams are made on, and our little life
> Is rounded with a sleep.

After which I added that her letter had overwhelmed me, like the strangest dreams do, which make one roam about, dazed, ignited, like some distant, off-course planet. . . . In the same bombastic vein I asked her if it was ever possible to get to the bottom of such reactions, or of enchanting invitations such as hers. If I lived to be a hundred, and kept trying to guess all that time, I still couldn't perceive its true meaning . . . So much for the rapturous portion of the letter. Then, in a more matter-of-fact tone, I told her I was quite unhappy that I got her letter late, but I no longer resided at the Brighton (let her think I once did), though I still had my letters sent there (I muddied the water more than necessary). Thus, lest I again fall victim to such a mix-up, would she mind letting me know a few days in advance when she could receive me. And I hoped of course that I would have the pleasure of seeing her very soon. Hopefully there is enough pining in this, I thought, as I read it over. Now all it needs is a little postscript saying that right now I have to leave on business but that I will definitely be back. And if along with the letter I send her another bouquet (a smaller one this time), the matter is settled, put off, that is. For by the time I get back from my make-believe trip, it's no longer pressing or timely; I make a few more half-hearted gestures and the whole thing peters out.

Fact is I didn't add that postscript and didn't send a bouquet of flowers, either. And for a simple reason. The human soul, as is well known, is a dangerously double-edged instrument. It need not be believed, its laments can be disregarded. More often than not it does things for sport.

But why did this woman frighten me so? I kept saying no to myself, and kept insisting, heroically, that I didn't want her. And also, naturally, that I did. I decided not to say anything about a trip; it seemed unnecessary. Tomorrow I'll have a post card mailed to her from Paris, that should be enough. It will simply say I am in Paris. I'll write it here, send it to Toffy-Ederle air mail and ask him to post it from there. And with that the thing is settled.

Except that I kept putting this off, too, I just didn't get around to it. And a few days later I did receive another invitation, and this was indeed shocking—it seemed to justify my secret fears. She said: "We await you, noble Macbeth." Now why would she call me Macbeth, what was she trying to say? That I should kill Kodor maybe? I was so perplexed, I even thought of that.

I should add that all of this happened at a time when, out of all the curiosities of this world, my attention was drawn to the philosopher Spinoza. Or to be more precise, first to Shakespeare and then, thanks to my wife, to Spinoza.

Ah, those poor, disgraced masters, I thought, and almost felt like laughing. Never would I have imagined that my own crooked doings would shed light on my wife's affairs. Yet there it was: if Shakespeare had special meaning for me, Spinoza became highly significant for her.

But let's return to the scene at the Brighton. I was still sitting there, not knowing what to do next. This second invitation of hers was for three-fifteen; I could still send her a telegram, I suppose . . .

What the hell am I dilly-dallying here for? I said to myself quite suddenly. And stormed out of the hotel without so much as glancing back. Indeed, I was in such a rush, I dropped the Condillac book on the bus.

You have her post office ID and the letter about the slippers in your pocket, I berated myself, and still you have misgivings? What else, what *more* do you want? How long will you go on being a French floozy's Dutch dupe?

What I really want to note in connection with the incident, however, is this: The more troubled your conscience, the greater the promise of pleasure. How I ran that afternoon, my God. Turning up my collar, I was ready to assault the world. I had a few glasses of rosolio at the Brighton, and after getting off the bus, I stopped in at a little bar and poured down nine gins, straight. I was overpowered at once.

Now I am ready, I said to myself; come what may. I expected some stormy weather, but strangely enough, after all that booze there was only silence in my ear. My heart and my head were like two balloons, my feet felt leaden, when I rang the bell at Mrs. Cobbet's. It happened to be quiet inside her flat as well.

"These walls are very thin," she whispered right away. She had opened the door herself, which made me realize again that we were indeed completely alone. And she kept whispering, like Lady Macbeth on stage, imploring me not to raise my voice. I meant to ask why not, but the truth is I could barely utter a sound myself, I was so excited. My heart was pounding in my throat, the back of my neck felt damp. . . . Mrs. Cobbet was wearing a little black skirt, quite straight and so short it barely reached her knee. As though she were on her way to grammar school. This in itself was no mean sight to anyone interested in such things. And add to this that her hair, like a sweet little girl's, was smoothed back, but her lips, very unlike a little girl's, were flaming red . . . Only her lips, though, her complexion was otherwise rather-sallow.

But why go into so much detail? I am a hot-blooded man, and I can't always account for my actions. And perhaps she was, too, who knows? Suffice it to say that we shot up like two flames and fell upon each other with such fury we fairly shivered with excitement.

And at this point we were only kissing, right there in the hall. But how frantically we kissed, endlessly, I especially. I did that, too, like everything else, with utter dedication and resolve, wanting somehow to partake of her, to finish her off . . . What else is there to say? It happened.

A friend of mine once told me that after such passionate interludes he'd sit down in the kitchen with his woman and start peeling potatoes. I quite approved, but in a fancy sitting room you can't really do that. Ah, one can be so awkward. I stared at the wall for a while; I can still remember that magic moment when a slender, shadowy figure was pinning her hair up near me with delicate, ethereal fingers . . . And I wanted to tell her how lovely the wall covering was in the room.

And it was indeed, all shimmering and velvety smooth, but then the entire flat was very elegantly appointed, which made me feel all the more miserable. I was ashamed of myself for being so wild. God only knows why we get more embarrassed when our passions flare in hallways and anterooms . . . For that's what bothered me most, clearly. Though it was partially her fault. In that night club I had whispered in her ear, as I was leaving:

"I want a dozen kisses from you, don't forget." To which she replied, with a laugh:

"A dozen? Fine; you will get one a month."

And not only that, she remembered it now, which made her welcome so irresistible and so . . . bewildering in the end. For she said: "Here's what I owe you." Then, closing her eyes and grasping my head with both hands like an insistent drunkard, she counted off all twelve kisses . . . And then a thousand more. My lips stayed hot from these kisses, scorched even.

For needless to say, in the subdued light of this room she looked quite different than in the glare of the nightclub. Here she wasn't a slippery demi-mondaine but a serious pleasure-seeker, like myself. Perhaps that's the reason why she made such an impression on me. And if we add to this that beguiling whisper of hers . . . I had every reason to fear those big black eyes.

Soon afterwards I had a chance to observe how she lied to Kodor, for just then the telephone rang.

"Hello," she said brightly, melodiously. "It's all right, the captain is not coming tonight. (I was sitting right there, for God's sake.) He sent his regrets, in a letter," she explained, turning to me as she did. And she went on to tell him that if he didn't feel well, he should go straight to bed, she wasn't going to the theatre tonight—"I don't feel like it, I have a headache. But I'll run up to see you just the same. Later tonight, yes." And she hung up.

"What was this all about?" I said and smiled. As surprised as I was, I understood.

"Kodor knows you invited me up here?"

"Of course he knows. He knows everything."

"You don't say."

"Well, almost everything," she corrected herself with an impish wink. "Actually, he had been meaning to see you. There's some unfinished business he wanted to discuss with you."

"Business?"

Mrs. Cobbet didn't quite know what it was, but he did arrange for us to meet at his place. I thanked her for her courtesy.

"It's just that you happened to show up here first," she added, though by now she was blushing; even her neck reddened.

And all of this did square with what I was feeling, though it's hard to put it into words. I had the impression there are unfathomable mysteries here, the kind you always come up against when trying to penetrate the human heart. For what was one to make of her constant whispering, her saying that the walls were thin, that there was an echo in the flat? Or her warning me I shouldn't call her on the telephone (for she told me that, too, at the club already, adding she didn't find it pleasant to be receiving calls at home).

Why not? But I'd never ask such a thing. It's never a good idea to know everything; I've already talked about that. Or to find out what lies deep in people's hearts.

Let's just take one thing at a time. She gets ready to give me the twelve kisses she owes me but also calls Kodor over. Strange. And I thought: What lives these people are leading. He may even have her telephone tapped and keep her flat under surveillance. . . . That sly old fox could boast all he liked about women being unimportant him, even these trivial signs prove that they were indeed important. But what I really couldn't get over was the fact that this cunning man, the most cunning I had ever met, could be so easily deceived. Where did that leave me?

For if that's how things stood, vigilance got you nowhere, no amount of vigilance did any good. And what followed proved my hunch right. For the minute she managed to shake off Kodor, she flared up like a firebrand.

"Quick," she whispered, "let's just get away from here." And she was already turning off the lights, in a fever of excitement.

"Away, away from here," she kept repeating. "We'll go to the movies . . . Yes, that's where we'll go, that's perfect. We'll just sneak off and no one will be the wiser for it." She knew of a wonderful movie, she said, which was playing in a small, suburban cinema, she'd love to see it with me.

"Yes, with you," she repeated, her eyes flashing, "only with you." And in the taxi she said: "I can't be wasting the little time I have."

Once inside the theatre, ensconced in a secluded box, she was ready to start kissing. The film they were showing was unbearably drippy, full of love scenes, which I cannot abide. She, however, was enjoying it tremendously. (A clever woman like her, how could she go for that stuff?). "Ah, aren't they sweet?" she whispered, all aquiver—"aren't they, though?" And she snuggled up to me. And even bit me at one point.

"Oh, come on, love me a little," she implored with inexplicable ardor which, by then, had an edge of resentment. "Or at least say you love me. Can't you just say it?"

"You are a dear." I said.

"Say you love me."

"You are lovely." I said. How do you like that? I could not bring myself to saying that blasted word just then. Could she have sensed that? Possibly. (It pains me to think about it now.) And later could she have forgotten about it, or simply ignored it? Perhaps. Fact is, shortly after this little exchange, she got up and said she'd had enough, we should leave at once. And we did, right in the middle of the show.

Once out on the street, she told me I didn't have to walk her, she still had some business to attend to. (She reminded me of those restless chippies from my youth, fluttery little things, who ran hither and yon, unable to rake their thirst.)

"How would you like to drop in on Kodor?" she suddenly asked.

This was so unexpected, I didn't know what to say. What she meant was that I should go in her place, that way Kodor wouldn't have to stay alone. Would I do her this favor. Because, frankly speaking, she didn't much feel like going herself.

"You'd be relieving me, sort of," she added with a dubious smile. What she really meant was for me to keep Kodor busy while she ran around as she pleased.

I said: "Fine, I'll do it," though I thought the request rather peculiar. Nevertheless, not only did I promise to go, I even tried to put her mind at ease. She did look rather harried and anxious at this point.

"Hadn't we better call him first?" I suggested. "I'll do it right now. It would be a bit odd if I simply barged in at this hour. I hadn't earlier and now I suddenly do." She listened but not very intently.

"Oh you think so?" she asked, but I could tell her mind was elsewhere. "Yes, yes, of course, ring him up, by all means." And still pensive, she added, "Thank you so much . . . Well, good-bye, then."

And she smiled at me one more time. It was as though she suddenly remembered that evening at the Brighton: chin-chin and all that, when she raised her glass to me . . . that perfectly lovely evening. At any rate, her eyes lit up one more time, and she began walking toward the lights of the city, clearly in a hurry. I looked after her for a while, and wondered.

"That's what I am, a heartless, wicked man." Kodor roared, raising himself in his four-poster bed (he really was lying in bed). "Yes, I forged your name on the subscription form, I signed you up for a stock purchase. Because I figured here was my friend Jacob who didn't have a penny to his name, the poor devil, no job, no income . . . " He lit into me, just like that, as soon as I stepped into the room.

And he went on, calling me a pauper, a loser, a down-and-outer, cutting me down to size, in short, the way excessively benevolent people generally do.

"And that's why I did it," he continued. "That's why I cut you in on this lovely oil deal. Because you're hard up; because you don't know where your next meal is coming from."

I had to catch my breath; I went cold, just about.

What does this man want from me? This was my first thought. My life had taught me, you see, that with men like him you pay attention not to what they say, not even what they are trying to say, but to what they *want*—from you. They always want something.

It's also true that the possibilities of the deal made my head swim.

Because—let's face it—this was my ultimate dream. How many times I had thought despondently: Why doesn't he let me in on one of his deals? He could do it with ease. I went as far as making pointed remarks, dropping hints. But they never worked. Never. He didn't pick up on them, didn't even pay attention. He left me to my devices.

Nobody should think me greedy; I am not. I've worked enough in my life, while these sharks barely lifted a finger. But that I, too, should finally end up on easy street . . . Who would have thought it possible? And just now it should happen, now, after my little date with his lover.

Never you mind, I told myself; such is life.

Anyhow, that's why Kodor wanted to see me that day. And before long he had a shiny black filing case brought in, which contained proof of what he'd been talking about, namely that I, Captain Jacob Störr, was now a shareholder in an oil conglomerate—I was actually in on a dazzling speculation, part owner of a holding company, a consortium, and who knows what else. I held the signed and sealed certificate in my hand, though I still couldn't believe it.

How did I end up so lucky? Why did he do this, what were his motives? Had the world really changed?

But then it all became clear. It was as if the room were suddenly flooded with sunlight. You see, he began to talk to me like a father, confiding in me his most private thoughts, telling me *why* he needed my participation in this thing. Which was exactly what I was interested in, what a down-to-earth sea captain needed to hear. And here he was talking about it himself.

Yes, this *was* quite a different tune. Something I could believe, something I was used to. *This* was what my life revolved around, not noble sentiments. *Quid pro quo*, that's what it was all about.

He reminded me (as if I needed reminders) that he wasn't the kind of person who would do something for nothing.

"I am a crooked businessman," he explained. "I want to bleed you white, suck you dry—I am not at all a kind-hearted man.

"I want to make a profit," he went on, roaring by now, "on everything and everybody . . . on your blood, if need be; don't count on our friendship."

I nodded happily.

"If there is no profit in it for me, I am not interested; not interested in the least. You had better remember that."

He was letting me in on a little secret, he said. He intended to take those other partners for a ride, and for that very reason he needed somebody . . .

(Here came the decisive moment, the moment signaling my total capitulation. For if he wanted to cheat those poor saps, then this thing must be serious.) I could almost feel the four thousand pounds in my pocket. For that would have been my slice of the pie; that modest windfall was what we were really talking about.

He didn't want to cheat a lot, only a little. Or rather, he *was* thinking of a big swindle, he just let me in on the little one.

But let me get to the point. What he owned up to was this:

There were two deals here "cooking in the same pot," as he so elegantly put it. Only they—the gentlemen from the Brighton— didn't know this. The first was up front; I was going to make my bundle on the second. "After those suckers lose their pants," he explained quite openly, "*your* money will start rolling in."

"Sounds good," I said.

"Of course it sounds good, why shouldn't it, by God? Or should dullards make as much money as us clever ones?"

He was being quite playful, you see.

"What's important here, my friend, are the side transactions, the unofficial sales, and I am already in control of those. If you want to know everything, I got rid of the stuff already, the oil I mean, sold it to a friend of mine, it was that simple. . . . Why shouldn't I help out an old chum who also happens to be in trouble? It's no skin off my back, my profit is guaranteed. So he gives me some sort of promissory note, so what? *He* is even better off piling up his debt, he is about to file for bankruptcy anyway, the poor devil."

"What *are* you talking about?" I asked, utterly dumbfounded. But wait, there was more:

"Then what I did was buy back the oil. From him, from my friend; the company's oil, for myself. And why not? I could now get it for a song. My friend was hard up, he needed cash. So he bought it expensively for a note and sold it dirt cheap for cash. And that's all there was to it. Anyway, what did a bankrupt man need all that oil for? It's too fine a commodity for him . . .

"And that's the long and short of it," Kodor declared. "Except of course I am not going to let those lunkheads know. Let them believe, those distinguished nincompoops from the Brighton, that I already sold the oil—they're such idiots, they'll believe anything. Do you see now what I am getting at?"

"I guess so," I answered.

"That's because you are smart. In short: they'll get the promissory note and I'll get the lovely shipments of oil."

But how exactly should we work this thing? he went on. For him to figure in this transaction would not look good, that's fairly clear. Somebody might think it's all a fraud. And that's where I come in, because for this he needs a fine gentleman, a trusted insider (he stressed this word rather sardonically, I thought). Did I gather his meaning?

"Yes, yes," I replied.

"You've got brains, chum," Kodor said. True, he had a slight difference of opinion with the company just now, but he'll take care of that. "I'll lean on them a little harder," he said sarcastically. "There is one brazen chap among them who would like to upset my little apple cart."

"Upset it?"

"Yeah, ruin the whole deal."

"Ruin it? How?"

"He is a troublemaker, I tell you."

"But how can he ruin it?" I again asked and probably turned white as I did. Needless to say, a lot depended on whether or not the certificate I now held in my hand was worth anything.

"Who is the bastard?" I demanded. And from then on that's what Kodor called him, too. "Yes, a little bastard, a real pain in the ass, who got wind of something and is now raising all sorts of questions about our agreement."

"About the agreement?"

"Yeah, he is suing us already. But I am suing him back."

"Why, this can be none other than that rascally little doctor," I exclaimed. "The one with the squint."

"How did you know?" Kodor asked.

There was a moment of silence.

"What sharp eyes he has," he then said to no one in particular. "But really, how did you figure it out?"

"Oh well," I laughed, though my conflicting emotions just about knocked me over. After all, it's no mere trifle when a cunning man like he is willing to compliment you, and in matters of business, too. . . . So I notice things, eh? I have eyes too, it seems . . . I almost burst into song, I tell you.

"So what does the cheeky bastard want?" I again said, treating the man already like dirt. "I was there when the agreement was concluded; nobody then said anything about collateral."

For that's what he was suing for; the cheeky bastard was demanding collateral from Kodor. He did some snooping around and found out that the firm Kodor had sold the oil to in return for those notes was in deep trouble. It may have been in good shape at one time, he said, but no longer. For this very reason Kodor promised to give them a note at the time of the sale, that evening, in fact, when we met for supper at the Brighton. Indeed, their participation in the venture hinged on this.

What is more, he demanded a kickback from the sale price for himself, and not a modest one either—considerably more than what I was supposed to get. Now there was real insolence for you.

I maintained that he was entitled to nothing; every word he uttered was sheer impudence. Why did I maintain that? May my stern judges forgive me but sudden rapture is a strange thing. And money does make you blind, especially if you don't yet have it. I kept saying that although I didn't pay *too* much attention at that time (why should I have? the deal didn't interest me all that much, I was too busy entertaining the ladies, those refined and charming ladies), but it was plain to see that the thing was settled, just about wrapped up. That whole evening seemed like an occasion to celebrate. Those gentlemen said as much, each and every one of them agreed that everything was perfectly all right. I deliberately emphasized this last point, and told Kodor I was willing to repeat it in court if he so wished.

In other words I offered my services, without his asking for it. Which was odd; I was surprised he didn't laugh in my face.

"Eh, what do you know?" he said. "You know nothing." But he very quickly changed his mind. "If it comes to that, you may testify," he assented.

By then, however, I came to my senses, at long last, and almost burst out laughing.

I just about saw myself running into a wall, blindly, like a cow.

So that's what he wanted me for. The buying and selling had nothing to do with it. And here I was giving him pointers, telling this scoundrel what he ought to do, explaining to him how he should conduct his business . . .

It was quite a spectacle, I must say, and quite a follow-up. I was left with a jumble of painful, burning impressions, above all with the memory of Mrs. Cobbet's beautiful body, and with the thought: How did I end up there, at that woman's doorstep?

Ah, the human animal . . . what an ungrateful creature. Her flat, her letters, her inviting Kodor up just then, and all the other odd happpenstance that evening began spinning around in my head . . . until at one point everything stopped.

Is that the kind of woman she was? I thought rather sadly. I could still see her scurrying off after the movies, stepping very lively indeed. Because even then she was *so* busy. She still had pressing business to attend to.

Oh yes; if somebody had jumped on me from a fourth-floor window, I wouldn't have been more surprised. For that was the key to the puzzle, the solution to the great mystery, the explanation for all that passionate devotion—Kodor kept a little angel especially for his business associates, and what a shapely little angel, at that.

For who can say no with her around? Wasn't it she who sent me here, who asked me to entertain his friend? And didn't she have a similar mission at the Brighton? Wasn't she there to create the right mood, to win over wavering hearts for Kodor's schemes?

But then I had a good laugh over it all. Maybe it's better this way, I thought to myself. I can rest assured that I wasn't such a heartthrob after all.

Still, at moments like these, you do feel kind of dumped on. As if submerged in a tub of water, I couldn't bring myself to budge. For it didn't really make me feel good to know that Mrs. Cobbet was that kind of a woman—an ordinary procuress. (In some ports they call them soft grandmothers—aha, I even remembered that.)

But how can I back out of this shabby affair?

For one thing I must show I am above it all.

I first asked: "Couldn't these people lose their shirt?"

Kodor had fine antennae; he perked up immediately.

"Lose their what?" he asked jauntily. And proceeded to toy around with the phrase, as was his wont, testing the waters as it were. "Why shouldn't it be possible for them to lose their shirt? What an original question. Couldn't it also happen to me? Who'd spare *me* from a similar fate? If you bite into something hard, you've got to expect to crack your teeth. If you like big profits, you must be prepared to lose a lot. It goes with the territory."

I was still trying to make light of the matter.

"Look here, pal, don't take me for *such* a fool. Can't this thing lead to a nice case of perjury in the end?"

"Perjury?" he asked pensively.

"Why, sure. I mean, it's not as if I am able to prove anything. I didn't really pay any attention to you people, you know that yourself. I was busy entertaining the ladies. And eating. I can't be at all sure anything was settled that evening."

"You are right, you can't," Kodor said. "Then again, it depends . . . But you are right: you can't be sure," he repeated, rather absently. Then, in a manner that was quite exquisite, he moved his lips, ever so gently.

"But is it so terrible if something is not definite?" he suddenly asked. But like a real con artist: quickly, secretively. "No need to put too fine a point on it," he added amid inimitable smiles. But as I say, it was a brief nothing, a flicker. As if he—no, not even he but the wind—had momentarily lifted the veil off some deep dark secret.

But then he began to sound off again, blustering as usual:

"*Now* you think of this? Did I ever ask you for anything? Didn't you volunteer to testify? And tell me, have you found yourself a job already?"

Oh, how I would have loved to clobber him just then. But all I said was:

"You have some nerve, Kodor." And got up from my chair.

"Why? Weren't you quick to pooh-pooh that piece of paper. . . ? The marquis has no need of stocks," he declared sarcastically.

I turned to him now and even grabbed hold of his arm.

"Look here, I have no job and you know it. So what you are doing is dragging an unemployed man into your crooked schemes."

He didn't withdraw his arm, didn't even wince, though I squeezed it hard.

"Shut up, you hear?" he said instead. "What are you, a squeamish virgin? A knight in disguise? Why all this fuss? Just say I don't want it. As simple as that. I want no part of it." And with his free hand he reached for the telephone, which just then began to ring.

"Hello, Lotty dear. I have this Jacob fellow with me. Yes, he is here in the other room. (Why he had to say that I don't know.) No, no, I am no longer in bed." (What that was supposed to mean I couldn't figure out, either.) Then he began talking about me again. And what he said was roughly this:

"I had no idea he was such an ass. (I must say that upon hearing this, I began to feel a little better.) To tell you the truth, I don't know how to handle him. That's why I wanted you to be there too when I put him to work. (Those were his exact words: 'When I put him to work.') Your sweetness, your mere presence, is bound to have an effect on him, you *are* such an angel. (This was said quite sarcastically, to be sure.) He is quite taken by you, my dear, in case you didn't know. Yes, yes, of course I noticed it, with an oaf like him, how can you not notice? Our discussion? (His voice turned rude all of a sudden.) That's none of your business. (And now for the rousing finish:) You are a lady, and an angel to boot, just remember that. And what am I? A crank, that's what. An oddball, yes, an eccentric. You can chop wood on my back, my sweet, though not always. Sometimes I get real wild, you take my word for it." He guffawed at that and hung up the receiver.

You can chop wood on his back . . . is that so? I thought this as I stepped out the door. How very strange.

Though all it added up to was that I was right again. He may bluster and fret, but the truth was he was head over heels in love, the old phony.

I was on my way by then, though as agitated as I had been when I left my room earlier.

Then again, why get involved with other people's business? The only thing that gave me pause was that this female wasn't who I thought she was. For it she didn't even know what we were talking about, and in fact was eager to find out, believing as she did that I wasn't in the room . . . Or rather . . . but who the hell cared?

The devil could have them both, as far as I was concerned. Let them live happily, or whichever way they prefer . . .

Actually, I began to think about very different sorts of things. I felt I had to make a reckoning quickly; I could no longer afford to float in space.

So I stopped in at a nearby pub, ordered a pint of beer, and since I found a piece of chalk on the table (the people before me must have been playing cards), I made a note of what I wanted to do at this point.

First of all, I had seven hundred pounds in the bank, and since this was sure money, why not put it down? My other investments were more uncertain, and would probably have to be used to pay off my debts, so that part is negligible. Of course there is still my father's legacy, the Cincinatti Railroad stocks, which must be worth four hundred at least, even with the stock market being depressed and all. Let's enter that too; in case of need I should be able to count on it. But that was all: eleven hundred pounds was all I had to my name, and you can't perform miracles with that kind of money. I even emptied my billfold; I had close to fifty pounds on me. (I always liked to carry around at least that much when I was in town—with anything less I didn't feel secure somehow.) I may have another eighty at home . . . at most. But how long would it last me if I stay with this woman?

Eh, hang it all, I said and got up from the table. I don't want to end up in jail because of him, or turn crooked, for God's sake And I don't want to steal my friends' women either. I've had enough. I want my old, simple, straight and dumb life back. To live the way I had before, period.

I didn't even touch my beer. As if to show that that very minute I was returning to my spartan way of life.

And then one day I did manage to catch her redhanded. She went a little too far, you see, was beginning to live it up again, starting to go out more and more, which she did before, too, except now it became a regular, almost daily thing. Her battlecry became: "The Lagranges are here." Now who were these Lagranges? Real numskulls, both of them, and typical French provincial misers, to boot. What enabled them to live so damn well in this town I still don't know, and don't care to find out. The only thing that concerned me was that they were here, these asses. And ever since they arrived, there was no holding her back. I never quite saw her like this. I guess she really took a liking to this dismal city. "I am beginning to appreciate this strange town," she would explain to me in her own silly way.

But I said nothing. It so happened I landed a couple of modest commissions just then, from a naval club and a maritime insurance company. Both had to be completed fast, so I spent a lot of time at home, working, whereas she was always out. So the tables were turned; there were times she took off, quite blithely, way before noon.

But first she got all gussied up of course, like some fair-weather flier, and when her hat was in place, her umbrella stuck snugly under her arm, when she was all done up, in other words, and ready to be leered at by hungry males, she stood before me and stretched out her pink little palm, waiting for me to fill it.

And I did, dutifully.

"More," she said affably, lightheartedly. "That's not enough. Not nearly." She had expenses now, she had to buy all sorts of things. The social season had just begun. There were parties, gettogethers.

"Fine, I understand." And I didn't ask what sort of get-togethers she had in mind.

The truth was I began to turn away from life altogether, I came to hate it. I realized once more that the only thing that could keep me going was work. If I immersed myself in it totally.

Whereas she kept buying colored drinking cups and gold-plated teaspoons—what the hell for? I wondered. Perhaps so that she, too, could invite her friends over. And just then I began to think about the possibility of disappearing for good. That's right, I was pretty much resolved to do it. She was rotten to the core—I was more convinced of that now than I was of being alive.

Sometimes, you see, she came home with a hairdo that was different from the one she had when she left. And I am not talking about that perfect hairdresser look, which is easy to spot. Naturally, she didn't figure on my noticing the difference.

At any rate, in London it's customary to kiss and pet during intervals in dance halls—everyone knows that. People close their eyes over such things in this peculiarly hypocritical town. They would first give my wife a little whirl and then draw her behind some curtain . . .

Her books, as before, were strewn all over the apartment, but now they were all love stories—no more philosophical tracts for her. And the pages had lipstick stains—she must have moistened her fingers as she turned the pages. What's more, some of the passages were underlined (and that, too, with lipstick!), but these I didn't feel like going through any more. Neither was I—come to think of it—any longer interested in her friend, Mr. Tannenbaum, though I did receive some information abut him just then. It seems Mr. Tannenbaum was an eager young man, a dedicated student of philosophy with a promising future—this is what my friend Toffy-Ederle wrote about him from Paris. And also that he happened to be the son of the mover in whose warehouse we had stored our furniture before our departure. Now whether she befriended the mover's son during that short time while we were discussing the transaction or whether she knew him before—this I didn't ask. In her books the word *slender* was underlined six times, and it was always used to describe a man. Then, in another place (in a story about a stalwart cattleman, written by one Carl Jensen), the words: "his eyes were radiant" were underlined. I pushed aside her books, if only because I also came across the manuscript of a short story, written by a former friend of hers, Madame de-Cuy, a sixth-rate actress, and in this manuscript the following remarkable passage was marked with exclamation points: "I owe him nothing. I've earned his sacrifices—with some of my own." But this was only the beginning; there was more: "I will not be crippled by you; I will not extinguish, for your sake, that in me which *is* me. I won't let you do violence to my real nature, I will not stand for it. Please know once and for all that I am what I am; you may rant and you may rave, it will not change a thing."

So she is what she is. A clear-cut message, if there ever was one. All right, from now on I'll be myself too. And I'll chuck her and her precious nature so fast, she won't know what hit her.

"Who is your lover right now?" This was the only other thing I would have liked to ask her, not even in anger or bitterness but straight out, without fear or favor. Depravity *does* have something shockingly straightforward about it—has anyone ever thought of that? About how natural sin is, what elemental force it has? Like our dreams. And isn't there something innocent about it, too? If only because it has such a natural place in the human heart . . . Why, the way this woman looked when she came home at night . . .

As though she had descended from some higher sphere where she was enlivened by fresh air and song; as though she was returning from her French home—she exuded gaiety from every pore.

"You are still working?" she'd say to me and light up a cigarette. . . . Her face was flushed and in her eyes there were warm dreams. Yes, sin slumbered in her eyes, behind her half-closed lids, it glimmered like mischief in cats' eyes. I could almost sense those hypnotic, rapturous dreams.

One day, though, she did get somewhat scared. After some initial hesitation she remarked: "Your eyes . . . what's with your eyes?"

"What do you mean my eyes?"

"They are so . . . so motionless." And she laughed a bit as she said this. "Are you angry with me by any chance?"

I remember the exact moment. She had just got home, all frosty and ruddy-eared, she didn't even take her coat off, she just stood there in the living room, staring. It was late at night. I even remember her glossy black fur coat and the silence between us, and most of all my own imaginings: that in her ear, next to her tiny earring, music must still be playing, and echoes of whispers. . . . Next to that I must have made quite a drab and prosaic impression, with my five days' growth of beard, engrossed as I was in lists and figures . . . Though it's also possible she was suddenly ashamed herself.

Was I angry with her? she wanted to know.

I assured her I was not. And that was the truth. There was no anger left in me. I just got tired of her spending all that money. And told her so, soon afterwards, the very next morning in fact. I decided it was enough, I wasn't going to give her any more. She found it hard to change her ways? I found it even harder. I was not giving her another penny. Not for pubs and drink bars, anyway. Because we had to contend with that too now, with her not coming home even for lunch, which was pretty idiotic.

"Why don't you eat lunch here at the boarding house?" I asked her calmly. "It's paid for. I'd be a fool for picking up the bill in two places."

At this she smiled. But with what hauteur. Only a French woman could smile like that. And when this smile lasted a bit too long, and the curl of her lips and the shrug of her shoulder got to be too infuriating, I took hold of her ear, quite literally, and pulled it.

Nice and slow, the way you'd pull a mischievous kid's ear. After that I couldn't see myself telling her about the true state of my affairs. Anybody else, yes, but not her.

"If you go on like this, I'll be ruined. And I have no desire to be ruined." That's what I said. And one thing more: "Money doesn't grow in my pocket; and right now I have no job, either." Considering what just happened, I still managed to present my case succinctly, reasonably.

It was no use, of course. The ear pulling made her eyes gleam with fury. She was like an enraged cat ruffling its fur. But then she thought better of it.

"All right; it's just as well,"she said, rapidly, unthinkingly. "Besides, I couldn't care less about your business affairs."

"That's good to know," I answered. "When you won't be interested in my money either, I'll give you more."

Actually, this was a first; I had never before raised a hand against her, never. And I didn't deny her anything, either, not for a long, long time. Offhand, I can't remember a single instance.

"All right," she repeated, and this sounded like a threat. As though she could get money someplace else, and plenty of it.

And she started walking toward the door; her hand was already on the knob when she stopped and turned around. She looked as though she still had something to say, her face turned quite pale, her lips trembled. And then, suddenly, she began to rave.

She threw herself on the floor and kept tearing at herself; and when I tried to pick her up, she lunged at my eye. But I grabbed her hand in time.

"Easy, easy," I said; "better be careful, or I'll really let you have it."

"Get out!" she screamed, writhing in my hands. "Get out, you brute. You ought to be ashamed of yourself."

"What's that?" I shot back, and calmly put her down. "*I* should get out?" And smashed a flower pot against the mirror so hard it broke into a thousand pieces, the pot *and* the mirror. There was soil and rubble all over the floor.

"*I* ought to be ashamed of myself?" And the next second I overturned the bookstand with all her junk; one of her precious mugs missed her head by a few inches.

And I was ecstatic, I must say; I melted with pleasure, as if honey were flowing through my veins. The mere thought that I no longer had to keep quiet or bow in reverence before her fancy philosophy was simply delicious.

"You are what you are, eh?" I roared. "Well then, my pet, I'll also be what I am." Ashamed indeed. Should I be ashamed in front of a rotten little worm? And she *never* has to be ashamed?

Like a thunderbolt now, the chandelier came crashing down. I yanked that out, too. Dragged it down and smashed it.

At that moment, though, I pulled back. And I must say something about the sudden shift.

For in the end my wife did open her mouth. Not that she got scared, oh no; she remained uncommonly calm and serene. The destruction of her potted plants she withstood quite well. She lay on her ear amid the shards, calmly as can be, as though her only concern was to make herself as comfortable as possible in that position. Like a sweet little baby who watches quietly as the world around it comes tumbling down. But when it was her brand new disgusting red cups' turn to break, she did begin to stir, and even sat up.

"Have you gone completely mad?" she asked. "What's this playacting for? Or is this how you amuse yourself now?"

Well, this was the word that made me put down my spoon, as the peasants in our parts usually put it. And what I am going to say now is an attempt to describe what might be called delirium. I know I am compromising myself, but that's exactly what I want to do. What was it I said before? That I was in ecstasy, in seventh heaven. Yes, that's how I felt, no question about it. I was excessively happy, suspiciously pleased with myself.

My wife was right then, after all. For what *did* I want from her anyway? Nothing, nothing whatsoever. But then, why was I carrying on this way?

I realized the futility of it all. I felt as empty as a discarded sardine can; I was nowhere as dangerous as I appeared to be. And I had nothing further to say, it was all a charade, empty and false.

Yes, nothing but useless bluster, I felt it acutely. And that wasn't the worst of it. I also became aware of a certain amount of caution on my part, which was even more interesting—and loathsome. I realized that I threw *her* things at her with the greatest of pleasure, but was amazingly careful not to pick up my fine little traveling clock, for example, or *anything* of mine, really. Yes, let's just put that down too, for it's the truth . . . But that's man for you, all over.

He rants, he simpers . . . God, he's awful. That's why I never trusted human nature, or that of monkeys, either . . . because they enjoy themselves so shamelessly, so self-consciously. Even in moments of grand passion. Especially then. As soon as they notice their hands or feet and what they are doing with them.

But this whole business has another facet which should also be mentioned. When they are caught in the act, when their fakeries are exposed, then they turn serious. And that's when they become dangerous.

This is what happened to me, I think. I am playacting, my wife said. At that moment I felt something stirring in me, with a kind of bovine sluggishness, but threateningly, too. Because what she said was the truth. I don't dare imagine what might have happened if we'd carried on, for I felt my side quivering, and that's always an ominous sign with me. But just then there was a knock on the door . . . two knocks. Something must have happened to the bell.

My landlord stood before me.

Now try and imagine the scene: my wife was lying inside on her ear amid broken flower pots, and here was the old man trying to collect some neckties from me. I did promise last time that I'd give him a few, didn't I? He could use one now, he was on his way out to see friends.

What was I going to do? The truth was I did promise to give him neckties, two brand new ones, as a matter of fact. The old codger was smiling already, all set for a little intellectual stimulation. This is what he came out with:

"Ah, my dearest captain, guess what? I managed to solve the

puzzle of Jacob's ladder." And he began talking about the mystery of Jacob's dream, which under different circumstances would not even have been that uninteresting.

But I must relate how this unexpected pleasure came about.

It was quite simple, really. One day, when my problems appeared particularly intractable, I got this idea of paying the old man a visit. Why not talk to him a little? I thought. I'll try to win him over, get him to warm up to me—maybe I'll be able to squeeze something out of him. One little slip, that's all I needed. There wasn't a thing he could say which . . . At any rate, I was convinced it would work.

Except that in that cold, godawful room of his you couldn't really talk. And as the subject of Jacob's ladder couldn't fire me up sufficiently, I happened to mention to him, in a thoughtless moment, that he should come up to my place one afternoon when my wife wasn't home and then we could go over some of these mystical concepts. And to entice him further, I told him I'd give him two neckties.

And now he was here, though he quickly added it wasn't really the neckties he was interested in. But last time he didn't express himself properly, not by any means. Actually, there was nothing wrong with Jacob's ladder, for he always believed in these "literal visions," as he put it. What he couldn't believe in was that somebody should descend on Mount Horeb or wherever it was, to tell the Jews what they could and could not eat. "These things I tend to make light of," he declared rather solemnly. "I doubt them, in other words. But shouldn't one consider even this blasphemy? To doubt anything set down in the sacred book?" And he was seething with emotion already, warming to his subject right there on the landing, in front of the slightly opened door.

I had a little time to think.

"Look here, let me bring you those ties," I said, for openers. Then, suddenly:

"I can't do it now, how could I, my wife is not well."

"Oh dear," he cried, "she's not going to have a baby, is she?"

"No, she is not," I assured him, "she is out of sorts, that's all . . . She is definitely not having a baby."

"Shouldn't I still run and fetch a doctor?"

"For the love of God, don't run," I pleaded. But it wasn't so easy to get rid of him. He just stood there on the doorstep, letting me know how very surprised he would have been if she had indeed been ready to give birth. Very much surprised, really. Especially since there was nothing to suggest the "thing" might be imminent. But if a baby was indeed on its way—for argument's sake let's just say it was—what would be the nicest name for it? If it should be a boy, he might be named Abimelech, and if it was a girl, Nelly would be nice. It would go very well with my name, he'd already given this some thought . . . Well?

Thank goodness he left soon afterwards. I can't begin to tell you what a pleasant effect this sudden interlude had on me. That and the coolness of the staircase.

What is the matter with me? you ask yourself. I am alive, aren't I? And you suddenly remember that there *are* other things in the world. Besides, minutes after the blood rushes to your head, you can be so refreshed. It's a heavenly feeling, you seem rejuvenated.

Not so my wife, however.

"Are you in here?" I asked her, because the bathroom door was still locked. "Yes, I am," she said, but only after a while. For a moment I was ready to believe something happened to her. But no, she was fine.

Pulled herself together in a jiffy. Did nothing to the room but her face, her eyes, her dress she tidied up. Perfectly. You would never have guessed what'd happened by looking at her.

And of course, she ignored me completely. She pulled out a handkerchief from her wardrobe, sprayed cologne on it, spun around a few more times, and was already at the door.

"Where do you think you are going?" I shouted after her.

"Out; I have things to do." And she disappeared.

Like a wicked little apparition . . .

And it was only then I discovered that she left a brief note on the windowsill, atop a preserve jar which escaped the general destruction. All she wrote, in a careless scrawl, was: "Tonight I will sleep here in the parlor. I'll send for my things tomorrow."

Fine with me, I thought.

But there was still the clean-up, a distasteful chore if there ever was one. As when little dogs stick their heads into their own mess. It wasn't easy, but I had to do it, and not only on account of the boarding house people. The morning coffee spilled on the carpet, you see, and was topped by a layer of face powder; black soil and shards of pottery crunched underfoot . . . And such things I find pretty disgusting.

I also had to rehang the chandelier as best I could, look for new bulbs, etc., after which I, too, could take off. And I did without delay. I wasn't in a particularly happy mood, but not depressed, either. Not any more, that is. Resigned was more like it.

But what does one do when one feels so relieved, so free?

I hailed a cab but then changed my mind and rang up Mrs. Cobbet. Despite her warning I gave it a try.

"Is the lady of the house in?" I asked her maid. When she said yes, I gave her my name, or rather just told her that the captain would like to see her, could she receive me this afternoon?

My attempt failed, however. The maid returned with the message that Mrs. Cobbet was not receiving today. And that was it. She didn't say why not; neither did she suggest another time. The girl simply hung up.

Well, this I didn't expect, I could hardly believe it. She wouldn't see me? There must be some mistake. Why would she say a thing like that?

I had neglected her, it's true, but she herself didn't want to continue the relationship, she said as much when I last saw her. Could she have gotten that offended?

Let's see what's behind this, I said to myself, and hailed down another cab. . . .

Ah, that's just like me . . . but what can I do? Other people avoid hurts, I go after them. Could it be because I don't like unresolved, ambiguous situations? Refuse to hear what I am told?

Fact is I always had a hard time taking insults. Why would anybody want to hurt me, I always wonder. Suffice it to say, I went up to her apartment and sent in my calling card. And got what I asked for. She sent back my card, and had her maid inform me that she was very sorry, she wasn't feeling well. And again that was it.

My stomach began to turn . . . need I say more? I dragged myself down the stairs, my head filled with all sorts of weird thoughts. What was I to do now? Smash up her flat, too? All the flats in the world?

That feeling of nausea again . . . But such things do happen, one can get so very sick of oneself. A three-day-long hangover is nothing compared to how I felt just then.

But what *is* it with me, damn it. I even thought of Miss Borton. These females do put me in my place, don't they? One after another. But it *is* me, then, isn't it? It has to be.

And at such moments you do feel like turning on the whole world, you're mad at everybody and his brother, and yourself you'd like to give a good knock on the head. Or jump out of your skin, at the very least.

What's the best thing to do when this happens? Go to sleep. I thought of that, don't think I didn't. That I should just rent a room for the night in some hotel, take a few sleeping pills and go to bed.

Instead, for the second time in my life, I went to see a psychoanalyst. Actually, I had my eye on this chap for some time, he was a nice fellow at least. And I wasn't sorry for going to him, either, because for once I heard something other than Gregory Sanders's empty dictums. So I submitted the following preposterous questions to him:

"Why is it that I keep stumbling in the world, as if drunk, and can't seem to straighten my miserable little life. Whatever I do turns out badly. I don't really approve of anything I say or do. Do other people have this problem?"

The psychoanalyst laughed.

"I know I do," he said cheerfully. "But how could it be otherwise? The way this world of ours is set up, you can't really straighten out anything.

"*Obzwar*," he added, reflecting for a moment. "*Obzwar* . . . " (He *was* German, the poor chap, and was cracking nuts with his teeth, for as he'd informed me earlier, he was trying to give up smoking. Yes, give up that too . . . there was no other way. In the name of order you end up giving up everything, even that which you had a hard time getting used to.)

"Why don't you just get away?" he suddenly asked. "If somebody can do that, God bless 'em." (He was being quite solicitous, actually.) Did I have any idea how lucky I was? he went on. I was in a unique position. Being a shipmaster, a captain, I could turn my back on the whole bloody mess. Or must I keep doing the same old thing all my life? Whine after the same woman? If it doesn't work, so be it. No use beating a dead horse.

"To hell with them, I say." And he got so angry, he even lit up a cigarette. (But to me what mattered was he got angry on my account. That felt rather nice.)

"How many times do you want to experience the same disappointment?" he pressed on. "To realize this thing is not working? When will it finally sink in?"

He had me convinced there for a moment. Because the truth is that for as long as I can remember this has been uppermost in my mind—that I can never make myself believe anything. Like now for instance, this business with Mrs. Cobbet . . . my wondering whether she *really* meant to insult me. Ridiculous, isn't it? Or take my wife. How many more ways should she demonstrate to me that she doesn't love me. Hasn't she shown me enough already? And here I was trying to make up my mind if she loved me or not. As if again and again I had to fill up on the bitter doubts I'd been carrying within me since childhood; as if I could never truly understand what life was about.

At this point I had to confess to this man that I'd been planning to do exactly what he suggested; I'd been thinking about it for weeks. To leave and not even say good-bye. To conceal my name, pretend I had never existed, and prevent anyone from finding out if I was still alive. That's why I came here, actually; I wanted somebody to bear witness to my life before I left for good. I had no one, and that's just the way I would want it from now on.

"What do you think?" I asked. "Will I be able to pull it off?"

"It all depends on how determined you are," he answered calmly. "If I were you, I'd do it, even if it would cost me my life.

"To die, that takes real courage," the good doctor declared. "But before you do, you might regain your strength and run away. Get a reprieve, and live a while longer, somewhere . . . A wandering stranger. Wouldn't that be your real life? The real thing? To get one reprieve after another?"

At home I turned on the light with sudden decisiveness, fully prepared to find it empty. I thought she wouldn't wait until tomorrow and had already packed her things . . . But no.

Everything was the way I left it: the same miserable rubble, some of it, at any rate, though in it, blooming like fresh flowers:

colorful Christmas packages. Ah yes, she'd begun to do her Christmas shopping, had said more than once: "Christmas is soon upon us."

No change, in other words. Except the stillness, which was more profound than before, and outside as well: the stillness of dusk. For a few moments I turned off the light, and stood in the middle of the darkened room, gazing toward the window. Outside, low-flying doves settled on the roofs of neighboring houses; icy white, they fluttered for a bit before coming to rest around the weather-vanes and chimneys. Their white flight made me think of ancient dreams I could hardly recall. It felt as though I had seen those roofs before, in a different time, long before I was born . . .

I began to feel sorry for my wife, truly, for putting up with me as long as she had. With a beast like me; for that's what I am. What was it the psychoanalyst, that black-eyed, black-blooded fellow, said to me just before? (For he did make a few remarks I didn't yet concentrate on):

"Do you really think such women are for you . . . or me, for that matter? Just look at me. Wouldn't it be tempting the gods if I were to live together with someone?" He was right. I told myself the same thing, and more than once.

A piece of the broken mirror still lay on the floor; I picked it up and looked in it. I again had the same thought: he was right, they were all right. If only I wouldn't have to see this again . . . this hateful face. I threw down the glass.

"I drove her to her death," I said, stopping by the door. I listened for noises, for now I had the feeling she was no longer alive. This made feel so cold, I had to cover myself with one of her rags, my head most of all, for as everyone knows, you cover your head first when you are cold. But with a piece of female garment? I certainly hadn't done that before.

But even if something did happen to her, whose fault was it? I tried, you see, to size up the situation objectively. If I weren't here, wouldn't it be all the same to me if she was dead or alive?

Yes, yes, but I didn't want *this* . . . I didn't want her to die.

On top of it, the lights were burning so bright in the room you could doze off in their glare. And behind that glare loomed an emptiness, a baleful, threatening presence, which is familiar to anyone who has known anxiety, who has seen that ominous nodding in the background, like pitch-black flowers swaying in the wind . . .

I turned on all the lights, then turned them off again.

The poor wretch *must* come home, I told myself, and kept pacing in the dark. Though the darkness did seem to suit my mood, I still felt quite horrible.

One minute I said, "If she shows up now, everything'll be all right"; but the next moment it was: "I give her five more minutes and if she's not here, I'll strangle myself with this apron here."

She wasn't there. But if she were to show up . . . dear God, how strange that would have been. For all I know, I might have even thrown myself at her feet.

I kept thinking of the Chinese—I have no idea why. Another one of my compulsions, I shouldn't wonder. They work their fingers to the bone in America, in the Phillipines, or wherever, and like leeches, suck the earth and its people dry. . . . And after they've gotten all their acquisitions together (separate little suit-cases for their shirts, another one for their hats and shoes, and the right amount of gold coins under their shirts), they set sail for their beloved homeland. And on the ship they start playing cards.

On mine it sometimes got so, we didn't bother to slow down when they began throwing themselves overboard, one after another. Yet, how gracefully they jumped! Even their plunge was full of disdain. When their chirping and high-pitched screeching stopped, you could tell what was going to happen next: someone who had just discovered that nothing remained of what he slaved for all those years walked around the deck one more time, flipped through those longish playing cards of theirs, and then wham!— into the ocean. And we sailed on at full speed, we didn't even turn on the searchlights. For everyone knew that these people meant business—they snapped and clawed, like enraged animals, defend-ing themselves tooth and nail *against* their lives, after gambling it all away. Why don't we then? Why doesn't our kind? I gambled away not one but fifty lives.

I opened the window. I saw mud, felt tepid rain. Somebody tried to start up a car but couldn't. Misery everywhere. I quickly closed the window.

But there was no letup: I looked at her note again, and again. It said she'd come home. What else I did afterwards I couldn't really say, there's probably nothing *to* say. The fact is from five in the afternoon till two-thirty in the morning I kept pacing the rooms. They brought up my supper, I didn't even look at it.

I thought of calling the police. This was London, after all, a city she hardly knew, where every street has five names, where the policemen themselves warn people not to enter this or that neighborhood, not even in broad daylight, let alone at this time. It was a miserable, rainy night out.

Like mice, raindrops scrabbled on the window panes.

But . . . but why don't I come out with it? I couldn't get the thought out of my head that she fell into the hands of some Chinese thugs . . . or else why would I be reminded of them just now? At this agonizing juncture?

And again I listened, and seemed to hear voices, cries for help, through the wall . . . A room appeared before my eyes, a kerosene lamp on the table, about to be extinguished . . . Her nonchalance, her recklessness was boundless, beyond belief—I knew that all along. "I could get hold of any amount of money I wish," she told me in parting. Who knows what she is liable to do, to prove to me, and to herself, that this was true. I'd already decided to wake up the old man downstairs; I could not bear this any longer.

And then at two-thirty in the morning she walked in.

Now I don't know if other people are familiar with this feeling. You wait and wait for somebody. You picture in your mind a thousand times how it's all going to be. And when she appears, you don't want her. Not in the least, you'd rather die. Because you ask yourself: Is this the person I was waiting for, aching for, so very badly? The one I almost killed myself for?

It wasn't only that she looked totally insignificant, a little nothing, or that there was not a trace of today's misery on her— she was drunk, too. A woman, drunk! In a way my imaginings were not that far off. She went on a little spree, she informed me, and burst out laughing, and into song, too:

Et sans vigeur,
Et sans pudeur.

Oh yes, that's what she did, had herself a gay old time, what of it? And drank, too, *sans phrase*.

I said nothing.

Yes sir, she went on, tonight she had a ball. Met up with this wonderful group in the City, Parisians all of them, on an excursion, turns out they were related to friends of hers, or maybe only acquaintances, who remembers? Anyway, they treated her, bought her champagne . . . (Bought *my* wife champagne.)

"And portugaffe, too, if you want to know everything. I had it, for the first time in my life, and you know what: it's delicious. Though it did make me just a *little* tipsy . . ."

And as she still hadn't received an answer, she took out her dainty cigarette case, lit up, and then fished out a piece of candy from her pocket. And she couldn't resist singing to me again.

"*Don, oh Don,*" she began softly, "*where has all your sweetness gone?*" She also informed me that tonight she found out that cigarette smoke and chocolate mixed very well. "I learned this from a young man," she said, flinging her eyes on me, expectantly, brazenly. But her little maneuvers didn't get her very far; after a while she didn't know what to do. And I noticed that too, of course. So she just stood there in the middle of the room, under the light, on one foot, in her flimsy little coat, like a rotten little street urchin.

You are dirty, you are a disgrace, I thought to myself. And you are right, I have no desire to touch your precious untamed nature—I detest it.

But she, as I said, just stood there and began to suck on her candies, and looking for places to hide the silver wrapping paper. One she tried to stick in the table drawer, another in the cupboard.

This woman had no desire to leave this place, no desire whatsoever, she simply changed her mind and returned to her beloved fripperies. I knew it the moment she opened the door . . .

Oh, but how ashamed I was of these thoughts, and of my feelings especially, of the whole Chinese business. . . . To think that I fell for her every time, and she could still, even now, drive me to despair. And that I could grieve for her still, could actually grieve for her, even if it *was* for the last time.

"Wait a minute," she suddenly said, "didn't you notice my new hat?" So she bought herself a new hat, too. I didn't get it. *Today* she had to buy a hat, after what's happened? And what's more to the point: did she have to call my attention to it? Was it because she was so embarrassed, or so drunk? Or did she mean to be that provocative? (She *was* wearing a sorry-looking little hat.)

"And how much did that hat cost?" I asked. (These, by the way, were the first words she heard me say since she walked in.) "Where did you get the money to buy it?"

"I asked for it," she said.

"Is that so? And who gave it to you? Who's in the habit of giving you money?"

"Oh just somebody," she said, annoyed, and then hiccuped. "Oh, oh, how am I going to pay him back?" she added for good measure. It all began to sound quite interesting, quite amazing.

Is that what she came back for, a hat? To do a little more shopping?

"And how much was this hat?"

"Oh dear, I feel terrible about it. I can't even bring myself to say it." And she pursed her lips to demonstrate her inability. "Two," came the answer finally.

"Two pounds?" I asked quietly . . .

And that's when I decided to kill her. Right there, on the spot, that very minute, without a moment's grace. I'll just wait for her to turn her head. Now you shall die, I repeated to myself matter-of-factly, as if my mind wished to put its seal of approval on my emotions.

I watched her movements.

And at that moment everything fell apart, broke into little pieces before my eyes. My hands, my feet, my heart assumed lives of their own, nothing made sense any more. But it was my wife's breathing that had the most curious effect on me, I remember that quite vividly. The way her breasts rose and fell under her blouse. As if I had never before noticed how round they were. . . . But my heart, in the meantime, was ice cold, not one drop of affection remained for her, nothing. Only the memory of my sufferings and a cry for retribution.

You'll die—this was the only phrase reverberating in me.

And she still stood there under the light, and now began to

count her money meekly, ruefully . . . but also in an offhand sort of way, like crooks do, or streetwalkers, leaning against the table in some joint, before dawn.

"I do spend a lot, it's true," she said. "I hardly have any money left." And she laughed again.

(And what was that supposed to mean? It sounded almost like an apology.)

"But from now on I won't buy myself a thing, that hat was my last purchase." And with that she turned her starry-blue eyes on me. And there was a hint of pleading, entreaty even, in her smile.

What are we to do with this brazen hussy, those eyes of hers asked. At any rate, she knew pretty well what I was up to, I am convinced of that. And it was as though she, too, was seeking my advice: should she be sentenced to death?

That's it, I am not waiting any longer, I thought, and may even have made my move in that dark room. But then suddenly she spoke up:

"Where is my letter? One letter is missing."

"What letter?"

"Letter number nineteen."

"What nineteen, what are you talking about? You are in the habit of numbering your letters?"

"Yes."

"Yes? But why?"

She didn't do it, she said; somebody else did.

"And who is that somebody?" No answer.

"Who *is* that somebody else?" I again asked, and one more time everything went black. "You correspond with men now, do you?"

"What men?" she said, and laughed into my eyes.

"Look here, my dear Jacques, I can't tell you everything, you know that. I couldn't even if I wanted to . . . You don't, either.

For a while there was silence in the room.

But then she continued, telling me that if I had shown any interest in her affairs, I would know that she wanted to pass one more exam back home, and for that she had to beef up on psychology. And the young man who was writing her these letters was a very decent fellow who had promised her in Paris that he would help her over these last hurdles. . . . Did I think it was so easy for her to begin studying again . . .? *Now* did I understand why she could never explain everything?

It got quiet again. I didn't answer. All I felt was exhaustion; it came on suddenly, like everything else in those days. My heart grew tired, literally, I could feel it. And that I was at the end of my tether.

But at that moment it was also clear that she got the better of me.

"Oncle Douc Douc," she said, as though nothing had happened, "you listen to me: Give me that letter, do me that kindness, and everything will be all right. I am willing to make up."

"*You* are willing?"

"Yes. And I'll forgive you, too, how about it?" And with the amazing slyness and self-assurance of people who drank too much, she came up to me, quite close, offering up her neck as it were, and pressing her breast against my arm, as was her wont.

"Well, what do you say? And will you stop being mean to me? It doesn't become you, it really doesn't. I'll have you know that I came back because I felt sorry for you. Do you believe me at all?"

Well, *putain*, I should have said, what about letter nineteen, eh? Who is it you're corresponding with? And who did you drink with tonight? Won't you tell me for once who you drank with? Who it was bought you the champagne? Or that blasted hat? Or do you suppose you can just tell me how *much* it was and I'll take your word for it? Is that what you take me for—that big an idiot, that unmitigated a fool . . .? That's what I should have told her.

But I didn't . . .

Perhaps that is what these notes are for: to somehow compensate for the many things I failed to do in life. For I never said or did anything when and where they would have made sense. And there wasn't a thing I could do to change it.

Two things did become clear, however, as a result of this incident. One was that I would never be able to kill her, or even break that snub nose of hers—something I wanted to do so many times. But if I didn't do it now, I would never do it. It was no use alluding to the hot-tempered scalesman who served on one of my ships. It seems I always want to do something dreadful but am never up to it. Either I can't lose my head completely, or perhaps my emotions are not that overwhelming. But if that's the way it is, I'd better accept it and act accordingly.

The other realization was that something did change between us over the years. There was a time when the more we fought, the more I desired her afterwards. I'd go crazy, I'd burst with passion. But now it was different. All I said to her was:

"Go to sleep; we'll talk about it in the morning." And that was it.

From that day on I slept on the sofa in the other room, though otherwise I was quite friendly, affable even, a veritable joker, which proved more than anything else that I was improving. For instance, I'd call her *ma petite brute*, which wasn't all that witty but I loved it just the same—it seemed to suit her so well. Or these words: *ma petite bibi* and *bibiche*, which even made her laugh since it also described her hat, her little two-pound leather hat.

We even spent a cozy Christmas Eve together—the last one, as it turned out. I was in high spirits, and the presents were nice. Madame Lagrange got one too, for she was also invited. She was terribly worried about her sick child and showed up alone, her husband having gone to see the child in some winter health resort. But she had a nice enough time with us.

"Thank you for making me forget my troubles," she said to me early in the morning, before she left. "You are a kind and generous man." But even my wife was pleased with me.

"Tonight you were really sweet," she said ruefully when we were at last alone.

Maybe I *was* sweet, who the hell knows? I was in good form, that's for sure, for a while I felt quite carefree. I even said to myself: Here are these two idle females. What wouldn't I have given in my youth to have had a chance to spend a holiday dinner with them, enveloped in warmth, in fine fragances, with a fresh walnut roll beckoning from the table, and just listening to them chatter away. Who knows if I'll ever again be part of such an evening?

Ah, the things they were capable of, the wild mood changes . . . My wife we need not go into. But I couldn't figure out Madame Lagrange, either. Right now she was on fire. She was talking about spiritual essence, but with such intimacy, as if she'd spent the night with it. She shuddered as she blurted out her insights in the dark.

For in the meantime I turned off the light; rum was burning on the table . . .

Those bluish flames can have quite an effect on mystics, and she *was* a mystic, oh yes—a student of arcane philosophies that the world was full of just then.

"Consider the following paradox," she began. "If we have the capacity for love and compassion, and intelligent thought, too, which enables us to view the world critically, how can we say that these are not also present in that which summoned us into being?" Thus spoke Madame Lagrange, the silent one. (She was indeed taciturn ordinarily, but that night she talked a blue streak— maybe it had something to do with her sick child.)

"Could it be," she went on pleading her case, "that Essence does not possess the qualities we do?" And though at that time I couldn't care less about such things as Essence and Spirit, I felt like asking her if falsity and deception were also part of this Essence, as they were of human nature. But I didn't say anything. Let the poor woman believe that creation implies compassion, and that her child will soon get well.

At any rate, all this talk was as a hollow as a scooped-out gourd. Her incredible fervor—what good was it? And her great big eyes blazing with excitement—was there anything behind all that fire?

I didn't inquire. Instead, I cranked up the little silver gramophone, prepared some grog, made it nice and strong (let the two girls really come alive), and after turning down the lights, I again ignited the rum in the glazed decanter, and said:

"Ladies, it's dark again, and my heart belongs to the first taker . . . So if anyone feels like stealing a few kisses . . ."

And I even began to sing a little, some bawdy chanson, as I recall. Which elicited a few squeals.

"Can I give him a little kiss," exclaimed Madame Lagrange, "can I, Lizzy?"

For this she was pinched under the table.

"Ouch, not with your nail . . . But he is so sweet," Madame L. gushed. (*I*, sweet . . .?)

"Well, all right," said my wife. "But wait, I'll close my eyes first."

"Oh," countered Miss Flaming-Eyes, "you are a true friend after all." And she pointed to her temple; that's where I should kiss her.

So I kissed her on the ear . . .

And that's how it went that Christmas Eve.

The agent Gregory Sanders once told me (I say agent because that's what he was: he never rose higher in the world, though as far as I am concerned he was wiser than John Stuart Mill. Even if I never did agree with everything he said.) . . . At any rate, he once told me that one's woes cut deep into the heart, which then cries for more, the gash has to be filled with new grief. There are people, in other words, who are forever denied peace of mind.

I realized that this had been the story of my life. . . . But not any more, something happened: as if I were learning new ways to move, new melodies. "I'll stay around a while longer"—this was a new melody. As a result, I became less demanding, began to feel better about myself, decided, in fact, that I was in fine shape.

"What tiny ears you have, Madame," I told our friend, "and what big eyes . . . If it were the other way around, it wouldn't be nearly as nice, would it?"

"Tee-hee-hee," came the response. I could have said anything, the most monumental piece of idiocy, the response still would have been: "Tee-hee-hee."

But if that's the way it is, I guess it cannot be otherwise. One should be light and airy, indeed weightless, especially with someone one loves very very much. . . . There, I might even learn to be this way. If I should ever want to live with somebody again, that is . . .

Whatever ails one should also be concealed, along with everything else that is part of one's true self. If you don't burden them too much, their heart opens up. As long as you keep to yourself, they will say: What a pleasant man. And they'll be ever so pleased with you.

Let them be pleased, then, I thought, and stood up to get the presents. There they sat in the soft glow of the table lamp, warm and snug, clucking away like contented hens, totally relaxed and full. Their eyes were misty from the rum, and everything untoward seemed to vanish from their hearts. But how quickly they perked up now. Madame Lagrange got three lovely lace-trimmed handkerchiefs. My wife got lace, too, an even more exquisite kind.

And a fine woolen stole—soft and yellow. Oh, what sheen it had, what luster, as I held it up to the light and ruffled it before their eyes. It spilled out of the box, undulating like rich yellow liquid . . .

"Don't you love me anymore?" she asked me the next day, proving just how clever she was—coming up with a question like that after such a lovely evening.

"Of course I do," I answered, "why shouldn't I?" But that's all I said, nothing more—nothing that might have been more convincing. Naturally, it wasn't enough for her, how could it be? I who had loved her so much had nothing more to say? "You may have been the right woman for me," I remarked on another occasion, "but I am not right for you." And I laughed as I said it, and walked away, walked out of the room. In short, I was through, I had nothing further to say to her, and was never going to desire her or pine after her ever again. This is what I felt, and what I wished for—the strength to say no, the firmness of negation, something I thought I could never attain as long as I was with her.

As it was, she could no longer get to me—not with the circles under her eyes, nor with her distant brooding at dusk. The old fire went out, the grand passion gave way (that that's what it had been I knew of course, and knew, too, that it was the greatest force in the world, greather than anything else I could acquire).

Still, I preferred it this way. For wouldn't it be an utter disgrace if I were incapable of learning *anything*? You can't always follow your heart, I reasoned; you are bound to come to grief if you do. A tree, too, has its protective bark, I told myself the other day while walking in a park. And took a good look at a tree. Or consider this: there are dangerous waters somewhere, yet the devil in you keeps steering you there—should you let it? Again and again? Even if the place *did* hold a peculiar fascination for you. Whatever it was that made me be that way, I was done with it, I wanted out.

And seriously set about the task of making myself scarce, vanishing into thin air. These were my plans:

I had a very dear friend once, a sea captain named Gerard Bist. He was a good kid, a fantastic glutton, just like me, though he had to stop. The poor chap died, you see, completely and irreversibly—the victim of a freak of accident. The man who weathered many a storm slipped in his room—he wanted to crush a moth—and broke his neck. Fate does stage such comedies sometimes. What I decided now was to get all his papers from his mother, a very poor old woman whom I happened to like a great deal. (Now and then I even sent her a little something, and always looked her up when I passed that way.) She lived in Antwerp.

But of course—that's why I wanted to go there; or didn't I mention that before? If not, I'll do it now. I figured I won't have any problem getting the old lady to go along with my plan—there was no reason she shouldn't. And I could certainly make use of my friend's papers, somewhere—anywhere—in some other world perhaps that those around here never even dreamed of.

How nice that would be. I found the idea altogether pleasing. And it seemed so simple: From now on I'll be Gerard Bist. And since I liked the boy a lot, his name suited me fine.

My wife could stay right here where she was so happy. And we can keep the whole thing quiet. For a while—at least until I board a ship—I'll be sending her her allowance. I also decided that out there—since no one will know me and will not expect me to be the same person I was yesterday—I shall become a man of few words. Over here the babel of voices, especially my own (*and* the futile gestures, the meaningless struggles), became an impenetrable jumble. My only desire was not to utter another word as long as I lived.

I was truly ready; I had it out both with myself, and with the world, and my leavetaking, I thought, would be peaceful. For let's just recall what that psychoanalyst tried to make me understand: One must learn to die.

Let's suppose my time *has* come; why then, this will simply be a short excursion, which I will spend the best way I know how.

Putting it another way: whatever I had, I lost, and what I did retain was to be my bonus. I was no longer responsible for what happened, I was light, unencumbered. I had severed time and was glad. Why should I be concerned with such grandiose issues: Does she love me or doesn't she? From now on I'll worry about more trivial matters.

So I had my trunks fixed, picked up some travel items, as well as things I might need, or profitably use, out there: a couple of fine navigational instruments, for instance. . . . My passport was in order, I even obtained some foreign currency when, one day, in the lobby of the Brighton, I was handed a letter from Miss Borton. She wanted to see me, she wrote. Now that *was* a surprise.

Especially considering how that young lady treated me.

Three times I wrote to her—she didn't bother to respond. When I called her on the telephone, she was always out. I went to the music school where she took piano lessons and found she no longer played the piano. I hung about in front of her house—need I say more? I even called up her milliner. All this happened at the time I was grappling with the Tannenbaum letters and other phantoms. And when after all that she still didn't show, I gave up on her, I let her go. Now and then I thought of her, especially of the times when I crept past lit-up hotel windows; and when I did, I had to smile. Was I really such a meek little fellow back then? It's hard to imagine. I certainly wouldn't do it today, wouldn't for the life of me creep under any window.

At the same time I was sure she would show up one day; I had this feeling. I knew the young lady pretty well, you see.

And now she was here. What could she want from me?

She had to see me, she wrote, for reasons that were quite peculiar, and she underscored the word "peculiar." I had to laugh at that too. I was long past making distinctions between the peculiar and the ordinary. I was no longer so subtle in my ways.

First I wasn't even going to respond. This one time I won't, I thought. But just then I saw her coming towards me on the street.

She looked rather pale, and said in fact she had been working hard lately. "What at?" I inquired. She mentioned some crafts shop or other and said she was quite happy with the job—she'd had enough of doing nothing. In addition she was taking French lessons from Madame Lagrange.

"What's that? From Madame Lagrange, of all people?"

"That's right . . . somebody recommended her. Interesting, isn't it?" And she blushed a little. "Quite a coincidence, don't you agree?" She just heard that this lady and my wife were good friends actually. Was this true?

I said yes it was, and added, just to say something: "What sort of woman is this Madame Lagrange?"

"Oh nothing special," she replied somewhat contemptuously. But what did it matter if this impudent little judge of character thought Madame L. was nothing special? And what if she was? What did I care?

The point I am really trying to make is that seeing her did not impress me any more than did her letter. And our conversation was entirely without significance—we didn't *talk* about anything. I didn't even mention the letter; nor did I inquire about her "peculiar" reasons for wanting to see me. And as she didn't bring up the matter either, I decided it was just as well. Evidently she changed her mind. She walked with me for a while, then left. And that was it.

But the next day she again stood on the same street corner. This time I was a little put off. I ought to have mentioned that around that time I spent my afternoons in the library of a maritime club, working on a modest assignment. How on earth did she know I frequented this place? She must know, or else why would she come back? I simply had to find out.

"Was it Madame Lagrange who told you I had business here?" I asked.

"Uh-huh."

Now I was even more annoyed. How very well informed these women are. . . . But what she wanted to talk to me about was a letter I had written—except she didn't know how to begin.

"Anyway you like," I said. At this, she raised her head slightly.

To be perfectly honest, she began, she didn't know for a long time what to make of the letter or how to answer it. There was no denying that it had a curious effect on her.

"It *was* a strange letter, wasn't it, miss?"

I shouldn't misunderstand her, she went on. What I wrote . . . she found it quite unsettling. I did know, didn't I, what she was referring to—which particular letter.

Did I ever. I had a hearty laugh over this.

"Listen, my sweet, we are long past that stage." And quickly added: "You are late."

As simple as that. It happened to be the truth, too. What *was* in that darn letter, one may well ask. All sorts of things one doesn't like to recall. Anyway, you can't respond late to a cry for help. It's like somebody saying, I am dying, and then the next he is asked if he's all right. The chap has to laugh, if only because he's still there, still alive . . .

And this is what the young miss felt like discussing with me?

"My dear girl, it is like munching on a day-old roll," I said to her. I came up with regular little parables now, intending to demonstrate what is timely and what is not. For instance, how long did she think a thirsty man can wait for a drink? There comes a moment when he no longer needs it—did she ever think about that?

I offered further examples along these lines, though through it all I felt myself becoming more relaxed. My indignation, my rage—where were they now? Gone, the moment for them long past. Still, at times like these, you keep trying, you talk and talk, attempting to refuel your anger somehow, while the other person listens quietly and smiles. What could she be thinking of? Maybe you *are* wrong, all wrong.

At any rate, I did ask her to try and imagine what it was like for me to wait for an answer, for some sign—anything. A word, a message would have been enough. (What message? An initial or—I don't know—an applecore, as long as I knew it came from her.)

"But it just wasn't in you people to do that," I said, but again quite simply. "What possible explanation can be given for not answering letters like mine? After that what *can* one expect from you people?

"Or *did* you have a special reason?" It occurred to me just then that she may have had one.

"Finally," she said with a cheerful smile, "you finally thought of it." And her eyes flashed with anticipation. "You were not miserable because of me, yet it was me you turned to. What could I have answered? Besides, there were a thousand reasons why I didn't answer . . . though only one special reason."

"And that is?"

"I got engaged," she said demurely. And how demurely, like some little flower.

In fact, she looked so very sweet, I had to laugh.

"That's really something," I said. "You can imagine how heartily I congratulate you. Please accept my entirely good wishes. And who is the happy and altogether fortunate young man, the . . . heavenly suitor, who is he?"

She again lifted her head. "He is no heavenly suitor," she said darkly. And then with much more emotion: "My intended is a gentleman, what's more he is of noble birth. And to talk about him as you do is neither customary nor proper, I assure you."

"Oh really?" I laughed, "just don't tell him then." I could hardly wait for us to get to the nearest tree; once there I covered her pretty little face with kisses, while saying to myself: What will the Irish nobility have to say about this? It was a rotten thing to do, I admit, a vile and heartless thing—let me emphasize that for the benefit of those who like contrition. Yes, yes, I was being heartless, beastly . . . But even if I was, so what?

In the meantime the girl was crying . . . As for me, instead of being moved to pity, all I kept noticing was how nicely she cried. Let's face it: it was a pretty sight . . . Come to think of it, is there anything more splendid than a lovely young creature weeping? The tears just welling up, or trickling on end like quiet, steady raindrops? Frankly, even the way she blew her nose I found beautiful.

I just had to embrace her, to which she responded with a slap. We kept wrestling with each other under the protection of that wintry tree, with me still laughing. . . . These women do like to lash out at me, don't they? And they all go for my eye—my wife did, and now her. Funny, isn't it?

"You are crushing my hat. Ouch! Oh go to the devil, why don't you?" she hissed with fervid bitterness. "My father doesn't have the money to buy me a new hat every day, you know."

Her father? This made me look up. What about the air of preeminence and refinement? Or was that all make-believe? Probably. This strange girl let her fancy—and her feet—roam freely, I knew that pretty well.

"Do go to hell," she hissed again, all breathless.

"I'm on my way, don't worry," I assured her candidly. And then, in the same vein:

"You tell me: is this nice what you're doing? One little kiss you won't give me? A parting kiss? You're getting married and I'm going to hell. Just as you wished. You'll never see me again . . . at any rate, it's highly unlikely."

To be perfectly honest, I would have liked to tell her more about where I was going, what I was planning to do, but the moment was not at all propitious. Moreover, she wasn't paying attention. She was trying with all her might to free herself, she fought tooth and nail, as is the custom of her sex, and then folded her arm across her chest to prevent me from getting close to her mouth.

"No, no, you may do with me what you like, but I'd rather die first. Oh, I hate my life," she sobbed.

"Same here," I replied.

"But I hate everybody, without exception."

"My sentiments precisely," I shot back.

"I detest my parents, too," she raved, no doubt infuriated by my off-hand replies. And she was bent on drawing out even darker truths, it seemed.

"Oh and how my parents hate you," she challenged me anew. "Don't even try to defend yourself. They do, I mean it. Intensely."

But why? I would have like to ask. What have they got against *me*? Didn't everything happen the way their darling daughter wanted it? But as I say, things got so out of hand, she could no longer be talked to.

"Oh, if I only had a brother who could teach you a lesson . . . who could kill you . . ."

Oh sure. I would punch that precious brother in the nose so hard, he'd roll over in the snow three times . . . (There's a desperate man for you—whatever he can think of is an outrage.)

On the other hand, in between sobs, she blurted out: "You managed to ruin my life, I hope you realize that . . ." Now here was something even an obdurate, heartless man like me should have taken to heart. But I didn't. What did I do to ruin her life? Nothing, I calmly concluded.

"I loved you," she said, wiping her tears. "I didn't deserve to be treated this way . . . I loved you for nothing . . ."

I let her go at that point. It *was* all over, I thought. I heard the clasp on her pocketbook click.

"I loved you too," I told her gravely. "And if you don't believe me, that's all right, too. Good-bye, then."

"Stay a while," she said, a little gentler this time.

But I had no desire to stay.

"I am expected home for lunch. I have to go, dear . . . for now, anyway."

"What do you mean for now?" I let that go.

"You said you were going away; is it true? Are you going far? Can you tell me where you're going?"

The little damsel made me smile. She was itching to find out more, I could tell.

"Go ahead, ask away. Where am I going? To South America. For good? Yes, for good. I have no intention of ever coming back."

"And are you going alone?" she finally asked.

"Yes, yes, alone," I laughed.

"Then it's all right," she said ominously. Yes, ominously, but with relief, too. And she stayed as she was, she didn't move. Only a slight mist covered her eyes still.

But the truth is that this state of affairs wasn't really to my liking, either, as can be imagined. That's not what I wanted . . . to treat her so shabbily.

So I wrote to her, yes, *I* did this time. I wouldn't like to part this way, I said; it would pain me. Would she agree to see me one more time? She did, and when we met, we tried very hard, both of us: she was kind and submissive, as never before, and I . . . I was so anxious to please her, it almost killed me. But it was no use; attempts like these are bound to fail.

We didn't really know how to proceed.

But it's just as well. It's no good running after something that's already past. I was clumsy. Told her I'll always remember her, and who likes to hear that? And she, for her part, let me go, not very happily, to be sure, but she wasn't going to kill herself over me. And that's not a pleasant thing to realize, either.

For what does the human heart wish for at a time like this? The impossible, I dare say. Its very essence is such; it's in its nature to yearn and pine. It would have me knock down, like a storm, all doubt and fear; it would like me to be the wonderworker of old, so she could again rest her head on my shoulder and say, "This was a glorious afternoon." In fine, I should have told her, "I adore you, I worship you"—again these simple words, and everything would have been forgotten. The present as well as the past.

Instead, I started telling her about the Indians of South America, a foolish thing to do, and how well I knew it.

As absurd as if I'd started going cock-a-doodle-doo all of a sudden. She once told me she'd gladly live on a desert island with me. How nice it would have been to be able to say, "Why don't you follow me?" But what do I do if she takes me seriously? This girl might just have joined me, she was that type.

So what I began talking about was how strange that world was, where I was now going. It wasn't for everybody, I told her. (I was being cautious, no doubt: it may not be the place for her, only for me.) I had her believe that I always had my heart set on South America. (It's true, I often thought about the people living in that part of the world, as I had before about the Malayans and their frantic zest for life. But it was all rubbish of course. What is so special about that place? If you're homeless, you're homeless—you won't find your place anywhere; life is nothing but bitterness. And if you return home, you no longer *feel* at home: the feeling of strangeness stays with you.) Still, I maintain that I had indeed thought a great deal about that place, I did want to settle there.

"Just think of our lives and the lives of those Indians down there," I said to this poor, dear girl. And I regaled her, this angel, with my thoughts on voluptuous forgetfulness. Told her how glorious, luminous, naked life must still be to these people . . . How they are capable of sitting outside their walls all afternoon, in the shade, entrusting their souls to the play of light, to clouds, to things that glimmer and fade . . . While we kept wondering what, if anything, makes them smile all the time? Are their heads stuffed with that many dreams?

"Yet, this is how one ought to live," I declared. "For what do you have here, just look around. Hear the rumble? Feel the tension? The windows in this town sparkle, right? But people have to work very hard to keep those windows clean.

"And the trains?" I asked, pleading almost. "Ah, it's all duty and drudgery here, can't you see? People no longer know what enjoying life means . . ." There was more, but I'd rather not repeat *all* the rubbish I dished out to her.

But was it all rubbish, I now wonder. There had to be something to it, surely. But why, in God's name, was I explaining it to this girl, who wanted to hear me say something else, not this. Indeed, she walked away from me, and began to quicken her pace, the poor girl.

"We're not mountain-dwellers here, you know," she called back.

And: "All I really care about is my homeland." And she kept on running.

And I after her. I wanted to grab hold of her arm, stop her, tell her to please listen, for God's sake. Now how does one account for such behavior . . .? I am reminded of bright, bright sunshine. "Hey, where are you going?" some old crones shouted after me in a open meadow. I was a young boy wearing a velvet collar. "Careful, you'll fall," they cried. But I didn't listen. With complete self-assurance, and a haughty smile, I continued walking through the lush grass, with the crones following close behind. There was a drop not far ahead, you see; and sure enough, I soon found myself in a mill-stream—I walked right into it in my beautiful velvet collar.

It was the same now. I was like a sleep-walker. It does happen sometimes that you're simply unable to stop. As if you were adrift, only half alive. I was telling her about the marble quarriers' strong lungs, about the fine, rainbow dust in spinneries, and all along I had the feeling, it wasn't me talking, the words came out of my grandfather's gray beard. And one of the melancholy old willows seemed to fully agree. (We were at the edge of the park now, wandered inside, drifted out again.) It was only natural that I got more and more distracted, befuddled. I had the feeling my lips were askew, my tongue didn't move right—I wanted to say A and it came out B. For example, I wanted to instruct her in the pleasures of a nonchalant attitude and wound up divulging family secrets—was actually letting her in on intimate details.

Told her what a hellish thing it is, what infernal racket it makes, to have two people continue their endless grappling in you, in your soul—your mother and father: an always anxious, tensely ambitious clatterer, forever busying herself around the fireplace, and a lazy and sarcastic smirker . . . But fortunately, at such times something in you always calls a halt.

But it's no good, it's just no damn good, I thought, more despondent than ever. What does the lady want me to do, anyway? Amuse her, bring down the moon for her from the sky? The state I was in then, I couldn't lift a pebble.

"Watch out, fella," some loaders shouted from a nearby van.

"Watch out yourself," I shouted back from the vicinity of a shop window which in my daze I almost ran into.

"And I won't have anything to do with the new Russia, either," my little miss now declared.

"But I will," I shot back. To my basic tenets I was going to remain faithful, oh yes, unto death, if need be. That this was not living I would always maintain. "Just what do you think people here are after?" I asked. "More coal mines, more obligations? Besides, is that what the world needs—more things, more people?" These were the questions I put to this frightened little rabbit, to this child. It was also my last cry, my very last appeal to her heart. Did she hear me? I never did find out. For at that moment a beggar stood in my way; our unhappy race around Regents Park came to an end. I'd just delved into my pocket for some change, looked up, and saw my wife standing before me.

She smiled broadly, pretending to be quite happy about the chance encounter. "You great big captain, you," she said and poked me with her finger.

And she asked me to accompany her to a gentleman named De Mercier. He was having a small party . . . a few cups of punch, some fresh walnuts—a new shipment arrived from Southern France, from their village, in fact. Why couldn't I join her for once.

Did she notice the young miss? I have no idea. Perhaps she did. For though she was nearsighted, her eyes gleamed, suggesting somehow that she itching for a fight.

And for a moment the girl's burning eyes also flashed before me. She waited at the corner, and when she noticed my wife she looked at me.

And what her eyes told me was not: You great big captain; not at all. Poor, poor captain was more like it.

After walking but a few feet, I stopped and turned to her:

"Listen, do we really have to go to this place? How about spending a night on the town?"

It was a strange suggestion, I admit. But that woman still had such an effect on me, I couldn't resist.

"Not a bad idea," she quickly answered. "Let's go dancing," she added saucily.

What can I say about all this now? This was the voice, the voice I knew so well. There was no mistaking it, no need for explanations, certainly—she knew me and I knew her. In a word, it was like coming home after a long tiring journey. It was also odd meeting her like this, like meeting a stranger, quite different from seeing her at home. She was prettier. (Actually, I discovered this once before, in Paris, when I spotted her on the bustling Avenue de Tourville—I remember the exact moment.)

"Come along then," I said to her and took a good look at her, looked over my own wife.

And she looked spiffy, I must say: a smart pigskin handbag, neat little overshoes (it was still slushy out, even snowed a bit), a little fur here and there, and the crowning touch: a plum-colored scarf across her chest, which was truly beautiful, I almost felt like taking a dip in it, it was so blue, and so soft, she clearly enjoyed brushing her chin against it. And to top it off, she pranced down that sidewalk as if to say, "Look everyone: I am small but I am here."

And I thought: Why not go on a spree, one last time? At this point it won't make any difference.

And as she stepped into a telephone booth, to call up Madame Lagrange, I looked her over one more time: What a brash little thing she was. Utterly poised. And I thought of all the stuff this woman kept collecting in her closets . . . Who'd ever believe it?

"Hello," she said . . . "Just tell him I have a cold and I can't go. You won't believe it: I am off on an adventure." And she gave a titillating laugh. (I opened the door of the booth—I just had to find out what the laughter was all about.) "Well, can you guess who it is? A big hulking chap, broad-shouldered, tall . . . like one of those German opera singers.

"No, no, he has no beard," she added naughtily, "no beard at all, what *are* you talking about? Am I not an honorable woman. . . ? Well, still can't guess?"

The rest I couldn't hear; I thought of something else, so I closed the door.

"Come on, behave yourself," she said as she stepped out of the phone booth. "Where did he go . . . good grief, what *are* you doing?"

All I did was prance around the booth and play peekaboo, so she couldn't catch me. Then I let out a few loud whistles, like I did long ago, when summoning my birds, and slipped out of sight at the corner. She began walking alone, quite annoyed.

"Madam, will you allow me to walk with you?" I now said as I stepped up to her, lifting my hat. She looked angrily into my eyes.

"I don't mean to trouble you, Ma'm; my intentions are honorable, I assure you. I'd be a brief escort; brief and passing. Why wouldn't you agree? Nowadays people get acquainted in dance halls even."

"Well then, go to a dance hall. Good day, sir." She turned away, and then even took the trouble of crossing over to the other side of the street. As for me, my heart gave a leap—I really began to like this game.

"Madam," I accosted her again. "You are such an attractive creature, really, your smile alone tells me you are French . . . And your walk. Permit me to say that all of my life I've been an admirer of French women."

"Go to Paris, then. There you can admire them all you like." And she turned away again.

"But Madam, don't be so heartless. I'd do my utmost to make this short walk pleasant for you. All I ask is that you graciously permit me to accompany you. All the more as I shall soon drop out of sight. I intend to go very far, Madam, to the other end of the world, never to return . . . I am a sea captain, you see."

"Ah, you are a sea captain," she exclaimed. "Really? a genuine sea captain . . ." Whereupon I stepped up to her again, doffed my hat, and said:

"Captain Gerard Bist, at your service."

"In that case," she said casually, "you may walk with me for a bit. The question is, are you indeed a sea captain? For you don't look like one."

"I don't? Well . . ." And I proceeded to tell her that I had indeed lingered here a long time, too long—that's what must show on my appearance. "Being stuck on land doesn't do us any good, believe me—it's the nemesis of many a seafaring man. If you only knew, Madam, what I went through in this town . . ."

"Oh? What *did* you go through, tell me," she said. But like a little bird. "Tell me all about it, I am really interested."

"Could *you* talk about such things?"

"Could *I*?" But by now her eyes shone so brightly, so brazenly, I said to her:

"Madam, you must give me a kiss this instant, or I'll shoot myself."

"What??"

"I took the liberty of begging for a kiss, Ma'm."

"Of all the nerve . . . Get out of here before I call the police."

She may not be fooling, either, I thought. Just how reckless she could be in her games, I already knew.

"Do forgive me, Madam, please," I tried to make amends. "You misunderstood me; I am no skirt-chaser, I assure you. It's just that I am a little impetuous and I got carried away. Moreover, we seafaring men are a clumsy lot, do try to understand . . . I am really out of my element in these parts. And my heart, Madame, is so restless . . . And wounded, too."

"Wounded? Your heart is wounded? Ah, you poor man," declared my lawful wedded wife. "But aren't you married, sir?" And she suddenly looked me in the eye.

"Oh, why must you ask me that?"

"Because I can see on your face that you are—you must have a poor wife at home. Go back to her, if your heart is restless. Yes, that's my advice to you. And now, good-bye, captain."

"No, dear Madame, you will not get rid of me that easily, I'll . . . I'll stop at nothing . . . Do not send me away. You'd be missing such an opportunity . . . for at this moment my heart is filled with emotion, I could love you, Madam, with such great, desperate love. For as long as I've lived you have been my ideal, the woman of my dreams, truly. And now as I look at you, I realize . . ."

But I don't have to go on. As can be gathered, I told her things I never before uttered in my life—things that were nevertheless more important than anything I ever said. Still, until now, I had not been able to say them. And even now, only in this form, so it won't be embarrassing . . . From behind a mask, halfway in jest. A stranger could blurt it out, but not me.

"You're forgetting one thing, sir," she said, turning to me again.

"What's that?"

"I am a married woman, and I happen to love my husband."

"I see. You love your husband."

"Yes, why shouldn't I . . ."

"Love your husband?"

"Yes, yes; is it so surprising?"

"And you love him very much?" And then: "Life can be so strange . . . What sort of man can that husband of yours be? I can well imagine."

"I will tell you. He is kind and decent; and most of all, he is honest."

"Really?"

"Absolutely. I am sure you would like him, too. And how gentle he is! I couldn't begin to tell you."

"He's that gentle?"

"Attentiveness itself."

"That, too. My God, is he a man without fault?"

"No, I wouldn't say that. He is a little overanxious, that's his fault. And you can't live that way. One must live boldly, daringly," admonished my wife. "And yet, what is odd is that he is also very gullible."

"What do you mean gullible? Gullible in what way?"

"He tends to believe what he himself invents."

"He invents things, then, does he? A case of morbid imagination?"

"An overactive imagination," she corrected me.

"As I said before, some people can be awfully strange . . . Why, you are faithful to him?" I asked her unexpectedly. And it was as though the whole neighborhood looked up and listened, that's how quiet it got all of a sudden.

"What a laughable question," she said, without laughing, though. "The naiveté it implies is really charming. You are just like my husband. I mean that: you do resemble him. What do you men expect to hear when you ask such a question? A straight yes or no? Of course I am faithful. Every woman is faithful; or didn't you know that? In case you didn't, my dear captain, be advised right now."

"But that's wonderful," I said, and began gushing for a change. "A state of heavenly bliss . . . at least as far as you two are concerned. With both of you being so perfect . . . why, it's nothing short of a miracle—love and devotion walking hand in hand like twin sisters on some Elysian fields . . ."

I guess there is no need to point out that my sudden enthusiasm sprang from pain, though the bitterness underneath was fed by other sources as well. My mind wandered, and I was no longer walking next to her but somewhere else. It was like a sudden dream and this is what I saw:

I was near Kuilenburg, on my way home, walking towards my uncle's house. It was all quite vivid: the rainy street, the small, yellow house, I pulling my hat over my eye, and to the left of me a group of peasants. And I heard my father shouting after me: "Hey sonny boy, life's short; you wanna be your own man or always some dame's fool?"

The peasants, those complacent yokels, had a good laugh over this. That jeering laugh still rang in my ear, it still made me miserable. But now I also heard my wife say:

"Come along, you old monkey. Didn't you promise to take me someplace? Besides, my hands are getting cold." And with that she put an end to this strange confession. And stuck her hand into my pocket.

She now squealed with laughter, and when she got very scared she grabbed my ear, my nose. The people around us smiled.

I took her skating, you see. Not only did I tear along the ice like a madman, I even lifted her now and then, carried her in my arm.

After a certain age such feats are rather trying, of course. She didn't weigh much, but to run with her like that on the slick ice . . . The truth is I was puffing like an old steam engine, and there were moments I felt I was going to burst from the strain.

"What if I just dropped you now?" I said. I didn't, of course, and managed to perform all my tricks, and as flawlessly as in the old days. I just turned a little somber afterwards. I felt death itself lurking behind my back—not even behind but inside, in my veins.

"You never ever made me feel special," she pouted when we walked into the restaurant's warming room. "You never did."

"Make you feel special?"

"Oh and you need that, you need it so much," she said, and her words were like a last sigh, a prayer for her youth.

"Cheer up, you're still young." But she'd have none of that, she wanted to be sad.

"What's more," I added, "I am not that old, either. We can go on strutting a while longer, for a few more years."

Then I looked out at the gathering dusk. . . . Is it true? Do I really have a little time left?

It happened to be a lovely sunset; the horizon was a deep red, and below, near the ice, a bluish shimmer, cold and frothy. It all felt so peaceful, so beautifully quiet.

"A painful flowering," I thought with a wry smile.

We said very little. She drank hot punch (I ordered it to compensate her for having lured her away from De Mercier's party), and standing over her I quietly smoked a cigar. Oh yes, at one point I said to her:

"I could have died for you, I loved you so much."

"And that's past?"

"Yes, it is."

"Too bad."

"It is. Or maybe not. One shouldn't live life that passionately anyway . . . But why not start a new life," I proposed, still smiling. "Would you want to?"

"Yes, I would," she answered and began to cry.

But things again turned out differently, naturally. Not that I began to love her less . . . There's just no way you can figure out— or map out—life. I'd have to begin by mentioning that I began to shiver already in that restaurant. It wasn't heated properly, like the rest of London. (Why that should be I'll never know—they certainly have enough coal.) That night my throat began to bother me, I was running a fever.

In short, I got sick: pneumonia, pleurisy, the works. And this indolent creature, this lazybones of a woman did not so much as change her clothes after that. I well remember the sunsets, the descending darkness all around, the reddish glow of the table lamp and, most of all, the way she kept dozing off next to me. She struggled, her head tilted to the side, but she did fall asleep in the end. I would gaze at her for a long time. And I remember, too, the dreary mornings, when I kept staring at the big white patch on the window: the curtain—and how nice it was afterwards to have her come over. Actually, I had the feeling she had lockjaw or something, because she had a hard time getting her words out. I didn't talk much either, I didn't have to.

Isn't it nice to be in their hands? Or was it just her hands that were so special? The illness itself was awful and at the same time sheer bliss—being consumed by fever is in any case an exalted experience. (A man's life is like a house on fire—it flares up, it blazes fearsomely, and then it suddenly comes crashing down.) Oh, but what an experience . . . With every nerve ending you feel death approaching; you go on flying, tumbling for a while, as though on a roller-coaster, then you're ready to slip through, and that moment changes your perception of things. For example, I can hardly recall the doctor. But I do clearly remember her hands, always her hands. For that's what I kept looking at, and at her eyes. At times they darkened, deepened, while her hands expressed such terrors. When I saw that, I sat up in bed.

"Why do you have to feel so sorry for me?" I asked her more than once; "I am happy right now." Which was true. It *was* remarkable that this was her, that she could be this way. Was it another self? Or could somebody change so drastically?

I now had the feeling she loved me and wanted me to live.

"I'll be good, you'll see," she told me one night, and it was like a desperate plea. I still remember her beseeching voice. But I couldn't answer her, I wasn't up to it just then. Besides, I wanted my eyes to speak for me.

Then there were long walks, though we rarely talked even then. For when you think about it, what *is* happiness? A slow convalescence, probably. A shaft of light cutting through heavy fog. A bit of clarity after chaos. With all her might she tried to save my life, after which she wilted a little—at least this was my impression. For one day when I went out for a walk alone, I found her in a rather strange state. She kept stretching and smiled at me sleepily. I didn't know what to make of her behavior. There was sweetness in her eyes, and secret, unplumbed bliss.

"What's the matter?"

"You want me to tell you? I just had some booze." (That's right, that's the word she used.) "Honest-to-goodness booze," she giggled, "and now I am good and drunk."

"And what did you drink?

"Rum."

"No!"

"Yes."

"But so early in the morning?"

"Yes, so early," he said, slurring her words. "Just don't scold me," she pleaded, "don't scold me, please." And then, leaning closer: "You know how much I had? Six glasses."

"In that case I *am* angry. You know who does that? Common coachmen."

"It was so good, though," she said with a quizzical smile. "But what's happened to me . . .? You see . . . I am so very sleepy." And her head dropped on her chest.

I put her to bed and covered her up; she was asleep in no time. Needless to say, it was all very strange. Outside the rooftops shimmered, churchbells rang—it was high noon.

Apart from this little incident, however, stillness surrounded me, profound, comforting stillness. Let me write about this, too. It's after fierce storms usually that the quiet, like a kind of deafness, settles in your ear.

But come to think of it, I did have music around, and plenty of it. The gramophone was on a lot. I had a nice, shiny gramophone and that's what was playing in the other room.

Now and then my wife sang. She sings rather pleasantly, I thought, and continued working.

This wouldn't be half so bad, I mused sometimes; if I could work at home from now on. You raise your head and know exactly what she's doing—mending underwear, or reading, or just staring at the the stringy-bearded rain through the window pain. . . . It wasn't regular singing, more like audible musing, random vocalizing, fluttering, and then sudden silence.

Now she was humming behind my back. I again found some work; a maritime insurance company asked me to check out some average adjustments (claims related to sea damage, that is, the pay for which was pretty decent). I picked up the new files every day at company headquarters, but didn't spend much time there. I turned right back and continued working at home on the dining room table.

Once, when she walked into the room, I simply took her hand and said, "I love you . . ."

What more can I say about this? How is one to define happiness when no one really knows what it is. A state of obliviousness, most likely, an absent-minded state. I can be very absent-minded, actually. Once I finished off a pound of quince jelly all by myself, simply because it was there on the table in front of me. When I left the house, I would stop on street corners and keep brandishing and swishing my stick in the air.

Like a young dandy.

Incidentally, that's when I came to the conclusion that emotions do spring from the heart, they truly do. And to my landlord I had this to say:

"Tell me, is it possible that it's all one big delusion?" And as if he knew exactly what I had meant, he replied promptly:

"Yes, it is." And he looked as dignified as a statue at dawn. Then, somewhat more amiably:

"The only reason we are endowed with intelligence is to be able to see this—to notice that nothing makes any sense. Not what you do nor what you think. Still, the world stands," he averred triumphantly. "And that is a sign of God's special grace, isn't it? Not only does it stand, mind you, it absolutely flourishes. In all its stupidity. England especially." I didn't quite know what he was getting at. He must have have meant English politics, I suppose.

The boozing I still don't understand, I muttered to myself.

You understand nothing, came the answer.

Fine, fine, you don't have to be so severe. I guess I am not such a good judge of character, after all. But is that a failing necessarily? Many people are like that. Besides, she *lets* you misunderstand her, that's the kind of person she is.

No, that's not the kind she is, replied the wheels below.

Yes, she is, I am sure of it now.

You have to get to know her. Like a fine instrument. That was the kind of comment Gregory Sanders would have made; I almost thought I heard his voice.

It seems I carried on an all-night debate with him, wavering back and forth, to the clatter of the moving train. I was on my way to Bruges, you see.

It was a restless journey. Again I was in a kind of fever. I could think of nothing but the past. And it was a shameful series of recollections, I must say.

How was I to look upon myself after all that? After what I'd done to her, *with* her?

I thought of the nicotine business, too, which was the most shameful of all my doings.

You see, you see? Gregory Sanders would have said.

My wife an angelic being? True? False? Nothing doing, I wasn't going to delude myself again. And I knew I was never going to make her take an oath, either, regarding her past, her darkest secrets . . . For who can tell what lies in the human heart, in its very depth? Only the sluggish crawlers of the ocean floor have something of that murkiness.

But let us not forget my old battlecry: I was ready again, for the umpteenth time, to face the same stormy weather. I gave the matter some thought, was clear-headed enough to do so, sober enough to size up the situation. I can't even say I glossed over anything.

But the very idea that she may have wanted to do away with me was plain nonsense, painful nonsense. Didn't she stay up nights for weeks just recently, while I was sick? It was inconceivable, utterly bewildering that not so long ago I was able to imagine such a thing, namely that she had intended to mix nicotine in my tea.

Am I really that callous, that unfeeling?

All the way to Bruges I kept tormenting myself. I *must* be callous, uncaring, oh yes. Just consider: She has a child and I know about it. I find a picture of this child, decide it's hers, in all probability, then calmly put away the picture and don't give it another thought—I simply shake it off.

And that's not all. (For this part of the story one might perhaps understand.) But then what do I demand of this woman? I expect her to be cheerful all the time, to be all smiles, even when her heart is not in it, when it's aching somewhere else. I want her to look happy, to cater to my every whim . . .

And all this never even occurred to me. Though once it did, it drove me wild—I kept pacing up and down in that hotel room.

Maybe that's why she is so unpredictable, I thought. She is scared of me. God only knows what a brute she thinks I am, one who'd be beside himself if he found this out about her. That's it: she is leery of me, she shrinks back from me, which is only natural—this *is* her deepest, darkest secret, one she wouldn't dare confess to anyone.

It explains the stealing, too, it suddenly occurred to me. And I must say that by now I admired her endurance. . . .

But wasn't I like some diligent researcher always willing to reexamine the evidence, always ready to start afresh? For now everything must be seen in a different light: her hat (which didn't

220

cost two guineas of course), the purse-snatching, the clandestine correspondence, as well as all the rest: the duplicity, the secretiveness, the lying down, the running about, the bouts of depression— it was all on account on her having that child. Was it any wonder that she grew to hate me? Why, she didn't even have money for the girl. . . . And to complete the picture: two rather distant thoughts, her drinking and the story of the child converged in my mind just as I pressed the bell on the door of Mr. De Vries's villa one morning, in one of Bruges's more fashionable suburbs. The rum-drinking, then, was also on account of the child, I decided finally. And perked up as I did. The rays of the early spring sun also had a bracing effect.

I learned one thing that morning: if you are in a good mood, you get what you're after; I hadn't scored such a triumph in a long time. Not only did I get a position, I was given permission to take my wife along, on my first voyage, too. . . . I didn't count on that at all; the idea of asking occurred to me right there. Why not try it? I thought; it might just work. And it did, by God. The luck of the Dutch, I guess.

As soon as I walked into the office I smelled something funny. What's this? Melons? No, it's linseed oil, I quickly decided, and mentioned it straightaway to Mr. De Vries. And a good thing I did.

"Yes, it *is* linseed oil," the silver-haired Mr. De Vries said with a rueful smile, gently inclining his head forward. "That's exactly what it is. Might you know something about oils, sir?"

Did I ever.

He found out that not only did I know about oil, I also spoke my native tongue beautifully, with neither a French intonation nor with sophomoric pretentiousness, though he did admit that my round letters at first made him think I might be Flemish in origin.

"Flemish? Me?" I said indignantly.

He also learned that I was partial to pea soup, and to the poet William Bilderdijk, and that a better dish than larded cabbage I could not imagine.

"But only if it's well seasoned," the old man said, raising his finger gently. I was all right in his book.

It became quite clear to me that I was talking to one of those lonely, melancholy compatriots who worries more about the homeland than those who stayed home.

"What's to become of that tiny country of ours?" he intoned, "what with her colonies and all . . ."

There were pictures of ships on the wall, fine ships all of them—and all his. A bluish light filtered through the window of the hot house outside—he evidently had a first-class nursery, too. But it was the pea soup that did it; the word itself was magical. It was as if a huge girl snatched him up and set him down on a meadow of yore, amid knolls and hillocks, which had one common name: Youth.

He went on and on about our homeland. And I confess I almost began to cry myself. I rarely thought about my vagrant life, my homelessness, in those days. What good would it have done? But now I was moved. And maybe that is why everything worked out. My heart was tender, full of emotion, I was like a man dreaming. And my dream that hazy morning was ever so odd. Tentative. Maybe the world is not so cruel after all, I mused. Maybe I misjudged my life all along . . .

At any rate, I really liked that old man.

Perhaps the world *is* more considerate to an easygoing man. Sadness brings punishment, cheerfulness is rewarded—that much I knew. Blessing and affliction come in pairs. After we had reached an agreement, at the very last minute in fact, I brought up the business about my wife. This proved to be too much for Mr. De Vries, however, because he said:

"What are you, newlyweds?" When he learned that we weren't, he continued rather bitterly, "Do you enjoy being with her that much, then?" To which I calmly replied, "Yes." Only because the question was so curiously phrased.

This was a mistake, of course; I mean, to say such a thing to a divorced man was not only stupid but inconsiderate. (Mr. De Vries *was* divorced; what's more he was a confirmed woman-hater. I made it my business to find that out before coming here. It never hurts to be well informed.) But as Mr. De Vries was a profoundly unhappy man, he took note not of my gaffe but of his own shortcomings, in the manner of unhappy people everywhere. He looked into my eyes and said ever so sadly:

"I am glad to hear you say that. I have so much more trust in people who are blessed with good fortune." And he kept clicking his scissors over his desk, apologetically as it were.

At any rate the man rewarded me in advance. I cannot begin to describe my feeling of triumph as I walked out of that room.

Who would dare say now that I didn't have the capacity for joy. I was just called a lucky man—*I* lucky. Wasn't it a good thing that I stayed put and didn't go running off into the wilderness? I wondered what Kodor woud have said if he knew what I accomplished in an hour what he couldn't finagle with all his tricks.

What finagle? As long as we're on the subject, I might mention that I saw his letters—two in number, letters of introduction, supposedly, that he'd sent here. A few casual lines they were, a cool and lightsome recommendation that didn't amount to much. He didn't knock himself out, in other words. The letters were instructive, though—revealing of people who, after you pinned all your hopes on them, prove they have no intention whatever of taking your troubles seriously.

Still, your typical loser bows down before them, for no good reason, only because they *are* fortune's minions. The poor wretch is quick to humble himself; nothing is being done for him but there he is bowing and scraping, perhaps in the hope that he'll get a little something out of it—a little bit of the glitter and the wealth. But he gets absolutely nothing—and that's what people ought to finally realize, the unlucky, bitter ones, that is.

It's no good bowing your head. Not only is humility distasteful—it's utterly useless. And though it's never been my strong point, I'll probably succumb to it too one day. . . .

But no more of that . . . I handed Kodor's letters back to Mr. De Vries.

And now the thing was to get home as quickly as possible. My God, I had so much to tell her. What shall I talk about first? The weather? The crazy and marvelous spring? (The weather was indeed crazy. Rain, brilliant sunshine, then light snow—one was tempted to believe the rest of one's life will be as improbable.)

A slight chill was still likely to touch your face, but the crisp air had fragrance, texture; you could say to yourself: this is spring. Or rather, not yet, but you knew it already left its secret feeding ground.

She and I will be sailing toward Java—incredible, isn't it? Who would have imagined it even a month ago? And I have eight weeks until we sail—I could do so much in that time. I'll write to the photographer. That's the first thing. To find out about the child. I could locate her address.

And then? I have to think this over carefully. I can't just bring her home one day. It could be disastrous—nice but disastrous. Fine, there was no need to rush it, I had time.

When I arrived at Charing Cross Station, my wife wasn't in town to greet me. Things went so well in Bruges, I got back two days before the date she and I agreed upon.

What happened was that while I was away, she, too, left town. Why should she stay home all alone? she had argued. Madame Lagrange was about to visit her sick child, and with her she'd be at the seashore at least. It wouldn't cost much, either.

"What, her again?" I had told her then. "The Lagrange woman?"

Whereupon she walked away.

"You never take anything seriously," she shot back angrily. We had a little fight about this, actually. It tickled me to know I could torment her now with impunity.

"Madame Lagrange . . . what a silly goose." And I began to whistle a tune. "They don't come any sillier. Her face is a blank . . . make that fifty blanks." And as she didn't respond, I continued:

"Wasn't she a midwife at one time?"

"What the hell do you mean by that?" she snapped and sat down, deeply offended. And for a while she just sat by the window, crestfallen.

And I kept on humming, and calmly began packing my suitcase. When I was all set to leave, and with my coat flung over my shoulder seemed to be waiting only for the final train whistle, I walked over to her:

"Have a very pleasant stay on that island resort," I said with a broad smile. "Enjoy yourself, have a wonderful time. And remember me to that . . ."

I wanted to say something real coarse, but she looked me straight into the eye, like a little tiger. And even sank her nail into my flesh.

But she also kissed me good-bye.

On the train coming home, however, the sinister feeling that something may have happened to her gave me no peace. I forgot to tell her not to smoke in bed. (Just then somebody near us got burnt this way.)

I did call the boarding house while still at the station, and was told she was out of town. . . . So she did leave after all. I was relieved.

But listening to an instinct, I didn't give my name, didn't say who it was wanted to talk to her. Why should I have? I was going to go after her anyway. That very night, if there was a train.

"What's new?" she'd be sure to ask.

To which I'd respond casually: "Nothing."

"What do you mean nothing?" she'd say.

"I lost half my money playing cards."

"Oh yes?" she'd answer, walk over to the window and sit down, offended again. There'd be complete silence, not a word would be spoken. Then, during supper, I might say:

"Madame, wouldn't you like to come with us? We'll be sailing toward Batavia." I would address these words to Madame Lagrange of course, and to my wife I'd say:

"You'd better go home and pack *ma petite*, we'll be leaving any time now."

"Leave? What are you blabbering about?" And then: "Stop it, Jacques, or I'll throw something at you." Whereupon I would reach into my pocket, take out a picture of my ship, the Ardjuno, and ask her gently:

"So? You like my little boat?"

One thing is certain: rarely in my life was I as calm and hopeful as that afternoon when I hung up the receiver at the railroad station. But let me quickly recap that brief period, and describe how I felt just then.

For one thing, I was quiet, at rest. Of course I felt that way before, in my youth, but that was a dark sort of restfulness. Now I was light and airy.

"You see, now it's you who's calm and kind," my wife had said to me at one point, way before my trip to Bruges. I had to laugh then but said nothing. I no longer expected my feelings to be understood. I cast off my burdens, and what was mine to know I accepted with equanimity.

I now endorsed my fate, I approved of whatever it still had in store for me. It was as if I no longer had to think but simply yield to my own momentum—it was really like being lifted and carried along by a swelling wave.

But then I had to stop short, I was thrown out of kilter, jolted out of my complacency. A word about this: about that afternoon still, when I returned to London from my Belgian escapade.

From the station I went straight to the Brighton to see if I had any mail. Sure enough, I did. A letter asking me to see the general manager of the Blue Rivers Shipping Co. What do you know . . . Sometimes there's nothing for months, and then all at once, a flood. For, interestingly enough, there was also a very sweet letter from Miss Borton. She wanted to know if I felt like going to a masked ball. The theme alone was enticing: "Nights at Lahore." She'll be there, she wrote, with her fiancé, who would very much like to meet me since she's told him all about me, and this would be a wonderful opportunity—one couldn't ask for a better one.

And in the entire letter, not a hint of recrimination or resentment for what happened last time. On the contrary, she stressed how she couldn't see herself saying good-bye to me for good, how she hoped we'd find a way to see each other again without ill feelings and so on.

Then some lighter, more frivolous words. (That I was ill she didn't even mention. Hm. Or didn't she know?) She thought of the following costume: long feathers, low-heel shoes (or better yet, slippers), a wrap flung boldy over the shoulder, and pale yellow, silky knickers. She'd come to the ball as Nurjehan, an Oriental beauty. (Why not be immodest for once?). And she suggested that I appear as the Flying Dutchman, with a blue cap, or, if I wanted to be modern, why not as Jack the Ripper?

As I say, it was a perfectly charming letter; she, too, acquiesced in her fate, I thought. And that pleased me . . .

Oh yes, she also mentioned that Madame Poulence, who was giving the ball, was one of Madame Lagrange's patrons, another devotee of sorts, a curious creature who ran a society for the study of Eastern religions. I looked at the invitation—the ball was to be tonight.

Now then, should I go or shouldn't I? With my wife away, should I go gallivanting off to a ball? It *would* seem a bit odd. At the same time, I owed this much to the little miss. Especially after what'd happened, for her fiance's sake, at least, and since she was decent enough to take the initiative. There was no convenient train connection, anyway; I would reach the coast late at night. . . . But why not get to the point? The truth was I wanted to have a bit of a fling. Something was egging me on. Which was kind of strange when you think about it.

At any rate, I decided to go. To the ball, that is. Tonight I'll go there, I thought, and in the morning I'll join my wife. I'll take an early morning train and that's that.

But where do I get hold of a costume? Amazingly enough, the problem was soon solved, it all worked out like a charm. Just as I was leaving the hotel (I thought I'd first go home, whip up something, get some shut-eye while I am at it), I saw this huge black man standing in the service entrance, holding what looked like a harpoon in his hand; like a veritable Neptune he was. And his figure was not unlike mine.

That's providence for you, I laughed. They were just delivering ice to the hotel; he was the iceman. He said he couldn't leave just then, but promised he'd be back with his getup at nine o'clock sharp, he'll even have it cleaned for me, his wife'll take care of it, not to worry.

"And the hook, too?"

"Sure, that's the best part." So we struck a bargain. He was going to drop the package off at the desk and pick up what's coming to him.

I was all set.

Having decided it didn't pay to go home any more, I checked into a room on the fourth floor. I was tired, I wanted to get some rest, though before falling asleep I meditated a bit.

"Philosophers!" The word jolted me out of my sleep. And how amazed I was. That word: how much meaning it had for me just a few months ago! I couldn't stop laughing now for I thought of how grand I will look as an iceman. And I did, I looked captivating, devastating. For just think: I even got hold of a fake red beard from a local barber. I very much wanted to look like the real thing.

And oddly enough, I did.

Three

WHILE STILL IN THE HOTEL LOBBY, I BUMPED INTO A DOOR, and where I come from that's considered a bad omen. But fortunately nothing happened, I was fine.

In fact I began to feel a bit warm under my skin, as when you've just had a full, satisfying meal.

But what followed *was* a remarkable experience. You leave behind the dirt and grime of London and find yourself first in lovely woodlands; then you enter the vaulted doorway of a stately mansion, flooded with light, and in the light you see a most curious procession of doll-like human creatures. Saracen kings carrying ripe lemons, Oriental acrobats in red and black, an Eastern wiseman, as well as Negroes, Arabs, Chinamen—a curious bunch, in short, all agape. You get so excited your heart, too, begins to kick and bounce. And why? Partly because you realize how foolish, impish this world is, and also because you like the scene, enormously. I looked at myself in a mirror and burst out laughing. My apron, the iceman's apron, was splendid, I must say. And the hook, too! And my beard, let's not forget my beard.

It suddenly occurred to me that this is how I'll go to my wife in the morning. What would my sweetheart say? I wondered. Would she get scared? Would she laugh?

And then, I discovered an old friend, Nicholas Hoshkin, leaning against a marble column. A dear man he was and an excellent sea captain.

"Nick," I cried and poked him with my hook. "Nicholas, old chap." And I stared right into his eyes. (He was also wearing some sort of Indian getup.) "Don't tell me you can't recognize me like this? Don't you know who I am?"

"Of course I do, you old growler," he answered. "It seems only yesterday that we were in school together. But just give me a second, I am after someone . . ." And he winked at me.

"Still the old rascal, aren't you," I laughed.

"Run along, I'll catch up with you. But now I must wait for my ladylove . . . In a moment I shall know true bliss," he enthused, and began walking toward the music.

A band was playing in the middle of the room and all around people were swaying and whirling, bending toward each other and toward the empty space, it seemed to me; now and then fire-kings and fauns in shimmering turquoise and slender water nymphs would step out of this mad swirl, and like I did before, look at themselves in the mirror, adjust their costume, and even scratch a little.

Oh, what was there not to like here? Dear God, I thought; could the joy of make-believe be this pervasive? In my country, in the homes of rich folk, this is the expression you see on the paintings of long-dead ancestors. Like giant beetles they were, interrogating each and every guest: How do I look in this dress? Yet, they've been dead for ages. That's how these people struck me now; they churned up fantasies, they took pleasure in toying with them.

Now and then Nicholas Hoshkin turned up and whispered: "Not yet, she hasn't appeared yet . . . Until she does, I'll cruise some more."

Only then did it occur to me that I was also waiting for someone, and she was nowhere to be seen, either. I walked around the room several times, even looked into the small chambers off to the side, but there was no trace of Miss Borton.

Just as well, I thought; this place is interesting enough without her, and not just the people, either. In one of those small rooms, for example, a separate little world opened before me, a curious little world. Aside from mystical drawings of a king named Petasois, there were all kinds of enigmatic exhortations and mottos on the wall, by such people as Saint Benedict the Bridge Builder, Bonaventura, Prudentius Clemens, Johanna Southcott. I noted down a few of these, though I didn't quite understand them. To this day I don't know who the "The People of Benjamin" are supposed to be. But that's who the inscriptions were addressed to; and they also kept mentioning "The New Jerusalem." Among the admonitions I found this, for instance:

"He who defies joy defies God." (We know that every five hundred years or so this idea makes the rounds, but to no avail.) Diametrically opposed to this notion was a little prophecy from a book of esoterica by Philo of Alexander:

"The fire was out before they arrived." (An illustration went with this one, showing a fiery red figure, a late arrival, obviously, before whom the glowing embers had just stopped glowing. And all around there was winter, a hopelessly bleak, dusky landscape.)

And there were other curiosities, other theosophic fancies as well. For example, I got acquainted with two little old men; like a pair of buzzing twins they were, dressed up as senators. And there was talk of honey in the comb, and of people with a weakness for honey, and of a naughty fellow parading as a conquistador, who kept disappearing with some actress in one of the upstairs rooms, or studios, as they were called here.

· "The kind of studio, my dear sir—someone informed me— which is ideally suited for loveplay." Very well, I thought; as long as we're here, we'll have a look. I couldn't help feeling of course that I got myself mixed up with a mighty strange group of people, a crazy, eccentric bunch. I bet they must all be dying to have honey straight from the comb; God only knows what brought them together. Not just these mystical disciplines, that was fairly obvious, not simply Bonaventura.

I note this because my suspicions were confirmed by what was to follow.

"Who is *that* queer-looking character?" I exclaimed around midnight, somewhat alarmed, and stared at one of the new arrivals. A whole group of butchers walked in just then, equipped with meatsaws and knives, led by a burly master butcher. They were all French and seemed to have a head start on the merry-making—quite uninhibited they were, especially their leader, a particularly jovial young man. I could tell immediately he wasn't a member of this set, though a number of people knew him.

"Hey, no slip-ups now, do you hear?" they shouted. And: "Look, here's the brigadier general." "Ah, the billy-goat, well hello." and other such niceties.

But he paid them no heed, he just laughed as he passed them. He was a handsome man and he laughed rather attractively; he had nice teeth. And such drive, he seemed ready to take on the world.

"I am looking for new kicks," he declared unabashedly, and before long he pounced on the Queen of the Night. (She was some kind of a doctor, this enchantress; her real name was Dox, Nox, something like that.) The butchers were hard on his heels, but like savages, their untrimmed sidewhiskers all aflutter.

But who *was* that bloke? Where did I know him from?

What he said to that heavenly creature I had no way of knowing. Most probably that he adored her, for the lady laughed and even waved her fan at him, mock-menacingly. While he, disregarding her gestures, simply nodded and moved on.

"Well? Well?" the others quickly inquired.

"It's not her," he said, on his way to his next victim. Now it was he who smiled broadly. (This new lady looked positively Roman, like a fugitive from Pompey she was, though extraordinary just the same.)

"I wouldn't mind taking a bite out of *her*," he declared with no less relish than before. But then, quite abruptly, he stopped.

"Who is this one?" he asked sternly.

I should have mentioned that the music had stopped some time ago, refreshments were being served, the buzz of conversation could be heard all around. If you closed your eyes, you could imagine yourself in some Parisian park, with the birds chirping away. But now the buzzing died down . . .

A servant girl entered the room. Actually she was no ordinary servant, but the personal maid of Madame Poulence, the lady of the house, her protégé, it was rumored, an orphan girl living in very difficult circumstances. But she was a bright little thing—not even in King Petasios's garden could such a flower be found. I don't know if others have ever noticed it, but there are human beings who seem to epitomize youth; the gleam in their eyes, the smile on their lips, every buoyant move they make seems to proclaim: I am young, I am a delight. And it's as if they keep asking you: Is *anything* else worth paying attention to?

Well, that's the kind of creature this chambermaid was. A little freckled, but that made her even more exciting. (In youthful beauty such as hers, even a flaw can be a source of radiance. For perfection we admire; tiny imperfections we love with a passion.) Her hair was flaming red, and such women know that green, deep sea-green, goes well with those flames. She was wearing a green dress and on it a tiny, tiny lace apron—next to such simplicity, the above-mentioned nymph-like woman, vastly, scientifically beautiful, did not have a chance. In her tiny hands she carried a trayful of cold drinks, and even that lent her face a silvery glow—looking at her, you felt both hot and cold.

When she walked past Mrs. Bagpiper, a millionairess, she cast her eyes down, but when stood before the Queen of the Night, she raised them again, and the words slipped out of her mouth like tiny birds.

"A drink, Madame?" she chirped. The lady took the proferred glass and said: "My, you're charming." Others smiled and whispered "thank you" or a simple "oh," but they were all obviously taken by her beauty. A man with stooped shoulders who apparently was fond of philosophy had this to say to the person standing next to me:

"How is it that the Creator places such enticements, such wonders, on externals? Life's essence lies on the surface—would I have believed that when I was schooled in logic?"

"Right you are," nodded a plump, sad-looking woman, "and goodness lurks in the depths"—though her intonation suggested she could easily go on about this.

What impertinence, I thought, that someone should want this miracle all for himself. And closing my eyes, I thought about my own sorry lot. Nicholas Hoshkin was standing not too far from me, and I knew that the same thing was eating him; actually, he looked quite drunk, his eyeballs were ready to pop out.

"Ask her for some lemon squash, why don't you?" the butchers were urging their leader in the meantime, though he—mark that in his favor—didn't make a move. He just stood there with a timid look in his eyes—he, too, was overwhelmed by this vision of a girl.

"Dedin is crazy," I heard his friends grumble. "He's been hypnotized." "Since when is he such a ninny?" blurted out one of the men close to me, but so loud, I thought he was talking to me.

First I looked at this man, then at the chief butcher . . . It *was* him. Paul de Grévy. Known to his close friends as Dedin.

But why didn't I recognize him right away? I haven't the foggiest. Because of his sidewhiskers? Not bloody likely.

Perhaps I *didn't* remember him all that well; maybe I never did take a good look at him . . .

Anyway, there he was. And after that I couldn't think of anything, silence descended, the wheels stopped turning.

Actually, there was something, a faint ringing in my ear, a strange and distant call, which lasted but for a few seconds.

"So he is here, too," I mumbled to myself. I should have known. And I tried very hard to keep my balance. . . . Slowly, very slowly I left the room.

I hung about for a while outside.

It was chilly in the garden, and I didn't have my coat on—no wonder I was shivering. Early spring: a cold and bleak season, when nothing stirs, and there is no sign leading you to believe that someone, somewhere is watching over you. The night was massive, immovable, indifferent. And above the trees, the slow swirling of mist and light: London's nocturnal wreath.

How pleasant this city is, I now said to an unseen party, though what I was really saying to him was: Just what am I supposed to do now? The man I was addressing was in all likelihood the old Dutchman, my shipowner. In that moment I felt so much affection for him—overflowing affection, unjustified affection. Or maybe what I liked was not him so much as doddering old age, and death . . . Oh I was so flustered, so troubled; blustering fool that I was.

Otherwise I was empty of feeling. Yet, like someone on the look-out, I was watching, listening . . . The night was dark, starless; now and then I looked up. It seemed I was yielding to some outside power, I let it do with me what it wished.

"Francesco," someone shouted across the garden. Before long I caught up with the fellow.

"Is there a studio anywhere in that house?" I asked him, in

Italian. He was pleased by my question, he even touched my arm. Actually, he came out for a smoke. He was a youngish man.

We proceeded through the bowels of the mansion, through corridors and a huge kitchen, toward the mysteries of the "studio." It was I who wanted to take that route; I had no desire to go back to that noisy reception hall. Along the way we got some strange looks; the cooks and kitchen maids were lolling about, yawning—it was that late.

"Good evening," I greeted them as we passed their posts.

"Good morning," they replied with English precision; I felt their sardonic smiles on my back. I must have looked a sight: a man in outlandish costume amidst all the pots and pans.

I kept seeing my Dutchman's eyes before me. I have seen white ones, dark ones, his eyes seemed to be saying; and some of them were quite interesting. But I've had enough. And what is it *you* are after, dear sir? Oh, nothing, I replied. Just keeping busy, I suppose.

I stood outside the door for while. Applause could be heard, but I couldn't go in—a performance was in progress.

"What's going on in there?" I asked the boy.

He didn't really know. "Some sort of dance recital."

"Dance recital? When there's a big party downstairs?"

"Yes, yes, this is something else, a school of some sort." Which struck me as rather strange. Mightn't it be a sink of corruption, a den of vice? This was my first thought. But the answer was much simpler, as I later found out. The mistress of the house had a sister, an impoverished society queen, a pathetic has-been, who held lectures here on art, capitalizing on Madame Poulence's considerable social connections. But how was one to know this while one stood before a closed door and heard applause, whispers. . . ? I wouldn't have been all that surprised if there were naked girls dancing inside.

But there were no naked girls. The same group was dancing as did in the salon downstairs. (I forgot to mention before that they were there too; in colorful head-dresses and with little bells on their ankles, they performed some kind of pious Oriental dance—in keeping with the tenets propagated in this house.)

On the whole, I saw nothing out of the ordinary, either upstairs or downstairs. However, I did find what I was looking for, what I came here for, in the first place. . . . Sitting in the first row in that studio was my wife.

Correction: not in the first row but even closer to the stage, in one of the chairs placed sideways under the proscenium. She had a powdered wig on and held a lorgnette in her hand. Naturally, she looked kind of strange this way, at first I didn't want to believe it was her. Could it all be a dream? I wondered. (Indeed, there are moments even today when I am not at all sure if it wasn't.) Yet, it was her all right. She began to wet her lips and then I was quite sure. I inched my way closer, slowly, along the wall, and soon I could see for myself how fast pupils could dilate.

For at one point she did notice me, raised her lorgnette, and that's when her eyes began to grow under the glass, expressing sudden horror, no doubt, at seeing me. She must have thought: God, he looks just like my husband. And her heart must have skipped a beat, surely. But then she got over it, it seems.

(Only now as I write this do I begin to wonder about what actually happened. For instance, why didn't she come down to the large hall, why did she stay in the studio? She had a premonition—yes, that's what it was, I am sure of it now—that look gave it all away.)

Later, though, she probably decided: No, that can't be my husband. In other words she didn't recognize me after all, that became fairly obvious, too, if only because she began to wet her lips again. All of which seemed again like a bad dream. For just at that moment the lights dimmed, the next attraction was about to begin; I slipped out through a side door. I had enough of the show, enough of that house.

Once more I hung about in the garden for a while, and again thought I heard those distant calls.

I ought to have my blood thinned, I decided once I was on the street; that's what does it to me . . . too much blood. And just then, swift, soothing images passed before my eyes: a sunny deck, gentle splashing, pitter-patter, happy boredom, real peace . . . and old sailors pressing cupping glasses on each other's backs under the burning sun, in the shade. I was still young then.

"Twenty cuppings every spring and all's well," said the old

timers, the ones with brass rings in their ears. And who's to say they weren't right? They seemed hearty enough. And wasn't it also smart of them to punch holes in their ears? Human nature is inscrutable, after all.

But even now I didn't feel any different. I didn't do much thinking either, hardly any, and even that only in faint images, the way animals are supposed to think. I let myself rest for a change—rest and drift . . . my soul too.

True, I thought about that certain scalesman, but I brushed him aside, as I did Gregory Sanders and that oracular psychoanalyst—all of them, in short, the whole lot. Who the hell needed them? They made me sick; their wise counsel—now amiable, now stern—turned my stomach . . .

Idiots! They all wanted to explain my own life to me. Well, right now I could give them a pointer or two; they'd be pretty surprised, those fine gentlemen, it would sure as hell put a stop to their jabber.

I had an overwhelming desire to demonstrate to them how very stupid they were, forcing their passions and prejudices down another man's throat—and brain.

On and on I went, from nothing to nothing. But sometimes even that can be refreshing. I roamed the city for hours, entangled in futile debates.

I thought I'd stop, but no, there was more, and more roaming, too; actually the fresh air felt nice. I thought I'd walk a little more, then head for the Brighton and get some sleep before doing anything else. Mustn't forget about our health, right? Besides, I wasn't in London yet, I was still in Bruges. At any rate, I started walking in the direction of the hotel, which wasn't too smart, either. Who the hell can find his way around in a town this size? To boot, there was a shift in the weather, fog shrouded the streets again. I found myself near a large square; I turned around.

A car had been following me for some time; I'd noticed it but tried to ignore it.

"Cab, sir?" the driver said gently, courteously, as if certain I wanted a ride. He drove slowly, staying close behind. His headlights cut through the fog and picked me out as I turned the corner; I still remember those two shafts of refracted light. But his little game got to be annoying; it lasted too long.

What does this fellow want? I wondered, and stopped on the sidewalk. He must have gotten tired of it just then because he, too, stopped, alongside of me.

"Cab, sir?" he again asked, and as he did, I noticed his beady little eyes. Peering inside, I also noticed a gun in his hand, and that gleamed, too, the little handgun actually sparkled.

That's all I needed . . . But whatever he was up to, I knew I wasn't going to let him off lightly.

"What is it you wish, sir," I asked politely (if only because I saw he was an older man). "What can I do for you?"

Whereupon he made the mistake of getting out of the car.

A mistake, I say, because if he remained inside, what could I do? Faced with a loaded gun, I would've done as he said. But like this I had a chance, and I knew it.

"Some money, sir," he said, friendly like, with a touch of sadness in his eyes. Must be a novice, the poor devil. Some of them act tough but are scared stiff. A novice, for sure. But in such hands a gun can go off that much faster; I had better watch my every move.

"Hands up," he said rather quaintly.

"How much?" I asked.

"All you got." He meant business, apparently.

Now then, I've been around, I have seen plenty—dark and rundown seaports, and dives where there is so much rough stuff, so much white-faced terror, a knife, as they say, stops in mid-air. But I liked these places. Once, in Bremenhafen I had to jump in the water when a couple of nice boys gave me chase just after I'd gone ashore. But why enumerate? In Palermo one night, under an ancient bridge, I struck a fellow so hard, I heard his bones crack. And I never did find out what happened to him after that, and didn't much care, either; I simply continued on my way. In other words I hadn't had much trouble of this kind until now, I always scraped by. But this time it was different. I *knew* it was serious— my legs began to shake.

God damn it, I got old. This thought crossed my mind as he relieved me of my watch, my wallet—the bastard even took my fountain pen. Then he leaned over real close, almost brushing my cheek, and reached into my shirt—on my instructions, it's true; I told him myself not to waste time fumbling about. (I usually have a pocket sewn on the inside of my shirt, and when I have a great deal of money on me, that's where I put it. And now I took just about everything I had with me, in case I needed it in Bruges—you can never tell.)

So I told him that that's where it all was. Which meant I had nothing left. The thought made my insides shiver. Damn this crazy world, *now* this had to happen? I hadn't a penny to my name, I was strapped. What was I to do, run around and try to *raise* money? Who would give me any?

And already I felt the blood rush to my head, and thought I'd crush his blasted revolver with my bare hand.

There was a large open space behind me and a roadway in front; we stood at the edge of a park (somewhere in Kensington, as I found out the next day), in the gray of early morning, a time when streetlamps don't give much light but the sun is still too pale. Yet, I took in so much during these moments, I saw entire processions through the haze—workers returning from the night shift, errand boys making early deliveries, a woman running after someone, a cyclist passing right by, though heaven forbid that one of them should look at me. Could it be that none of them saw me? Maybe it was just as well. At times it's better if they torment you with their indifference. It takes your mind off your real misery.

So I began conversing with the man, and what a laugh that was. But to stand there helplessly like a moron with your hands in the air was also pretty awful. Or did I simply want to distract him?

"Where are you from?" I asked.

And amazingly enough, he told me: "Shetterland."

"And what did you do before this?" (An unusually stupid question.)

"Shut up," he answered. Quite rightly. Though he also got me angry.

"Hey, what do you think you're doing? Don't take my scarf, it's cold. Can't you see how flimsy my coat is?"

But he wanted that too, he even took my cigars, and flung my iceman's pick on the grass, quite far . . . And that about wrapped it up.

He began backing up slowly, towards the car, watching my eyes as he did.

But that was a fatal mistake.

For I was looking not at his eyes but at the gun, to see if it quivered in his hand. And it did, by Jove. After he took his first step it tilted a little; he was aware of it himself and tried to straighten it out immediately. But he did it too neatly, too self-consciously, and that's when I knew I had him, that was the moment I was waiting for—in a second I was upon him. On his head, to be more precise.

It's a unique kind of leap—French sailors call it "Old Francis"; I tried it out many times in the old days, and to my surprise it worked beautifully now, too. The trick is to fall on the other guy with the full weight of your body, as if you came crashing down from an upstairs window, in a split second, almost without bending your knees, using foot muscles only.

Now imagine, if you will: I weigh over two hundred pounds. And if at the same time you also let out a shriek, which I happen to be very good at . . . The poor bloke got so frightened, so terror-stricken, he pulled the trigger.

But it didn't do him any good; I sideswiped his hand in time. The rest is no longer interesting, only sad.

With my chin I pinned his head back, and struck him just once—that's my way. And then I heard that cracking sound again, oh yes. I must have snapped his spine—he died in front of my eyes. And what makes me feel sad even now is that then I felt nothing.

All I could think of was: I am not that old, after all. And: Haven't done that in a while. Then I bent over and noticed the familiar red ribbon: blood trickling from the corner of his mouth.

After all this I robbed the old man or rather repossessed my own belongings, then calmly walked on.

I still didn't see anyone on that side of the street. I continued walking at a slow, leisurely pace, with the same relaxed air as before. Even more dreamily, as I recall, because my limbs felt incredibly light. Only after intense pleasures does one feel this way. I even found my handy hook, and that too the same way: without haste or bother. Still, I would've rather not have anyone else find it; I certainly didn't want the police to be in on this. At this point I wished to avoid even the appearance of a fast getaway.

So if anything, I was proceeding slower than I should have. And stopped after about fifty feet. There he still lay, dead, and though the sun was up by now, you couldn't see much of him, only that his head hung over the curb and his car looked very forlorn.

I continued walking and turned into sidestreets, cut through parks, took detours, the way you are supposed to after an incident like this. I also tore off my beard, of course. . . . There are many buildings in London whose gates are not locked for the night, so I walked into one of these courtyards and stuffed the beard in a drain pipe, along with the old man's handkerchief, which I had also taken from him, quite by accident, I assure you. And oh yes, my heavy ring, too, which I had worn on my pinky for twenty years—that I tossed away out of anger, because it proved to be such a perfect weapon.

For I didn't really want to kill that old man. Not me, not that. To actually kill someone? What for?

"So, did you live it up last night?" the house manager of the Brighton asked. "Had one too many maybe? And by the way, what do you say to the bloody Irish?" (He was just reading the morning paper; there was trouble again in Ireland.) "But what did you do with your beard?" he continued and laughed as he pushed up his spectacles to get a better look.

I said nothing.

He went on just the same, confessing that he was rather surprised at me last night. For a serious-looking man like myself to put on a crazy costume like that—he hoped I didn't mind him saying it, but it *was* a bit out of character. And then to go as far as sticking a beard on my chin. . . .

Next, we began to argue about the Irish question. But then, oddly enough, I started telling him a story—*why* I did is only now becoming clear to me . . .

I had a little nephew who one night sat up in his bed and began to weep over the fate of a complete stranger—a poor old man who was hit by a train, his head cut off by the clattering wheels. The little boy wailed and sobbed, inconsolably.

It turned out he was ill with fever. But the story happened to be true. He heard his parents read it out loud from the newspaper the night before.

It seems such things can happen at a later age, too. You are wracked with pain but don't care to notice it. So I began to tell him about the Manadoans, and sure enough, in no time I was feeling miserable.

"Are you familiar with the history of the Manadoans?" I inquired of this insensitive man. "They are the descendants of the one-time conquerors, the Portuguese, and though they are Christian and have even retained their old family names, they've become dark-skinned. Since in that climate one has to change, you can't remain what you were and survive. . . . Have you ever heard anything so silly? They've become a curly-haired people, just like the natives, except they are quite sad.

"You may well ask, why so, why are they sad? The answer is they feel they don't belong there. But do you understand what I am getting at?" I asked him suddenly. "Can you appreciate the absurdity, the tragedy, of their situation?"

The manager stared at me.

"I do; I can. But what are you so angry about?" Which made me that much angrier.

"Don't you see?" I cried. "These people, when they first went there, were strangers, conquerors, occupiers; they tried to oppress and drive out those who did belong. They persecuted the natives because they were colored. But now they are colored, too, and therefore despised." On and on I went, bitterly, furiously, about the tragedy of those distant peoples; I nearly broke into tears. But did *he* have any idea what this entailed, this endless cycle of hate and affront, this eternal abuse of the human heart?

"Ah, life . . . what a deceiver," I said, striking a new chord. Which made even the manager blush a little. "Just think of the indignities we are made to endure—why it's an outrage, an abomination. And when it comes to personal hurts . . ." I wanted to elaborate but stopped myself.

A vision, clear and unmistakable, appeared before my eyes. It was Paul de Grévy, my wife's lover . . .

So what is so unusual about that? I asked myself. For God's sake, why make such a big to do over a worthless slut?

Having come out with that, however, I wavered, I lost heart, I dissolved.

But now it was the manager who warmed up to the subject.

"Over there they look down on blacks, while here people go to the Riviera to get a tan," he said, laughing. "It's a mad world, you're right." And then, to add more fuel to the fire, he began to tell me that once he saw a movie about how they capture polar bears. "They do it with nets, catch 'em like fish . . ."

But who felt like paying attention?

"What, what is that?"

"Why it's the same story all over again. They are taken from a place where they belong to a place where they don't. They like the ice and the cold, and then they're shipped to California. They like their freedom and they lock them in a cage. Such is life," he said, smiling, and calmed down a little. Actually, he regained his composure by repeating that stupid phrase: Such is life.

"But what an emotional man you are," he remarked sarcastically. "I had no idea. Are you all right? Maybe you're running a fever. Or you did have one too many." And then he said one more thing which I still keep wondering about.

"Don't tell me you're now the frog-king of Tilsit?" I really thought he was off his rocker. To this day I don't understand the question. I even asked around: *was* there ever such a legend in Tilsit, about a frog-king? No one seems to know.

Could it have been fever? Very possible. After all, I *had* gone without sleep for three or four nights before.

And felt groggy for days afterwards. It's true, I kept taking sleeping pills—that may have added to my giddiness, as well as the very strong pain killers, which I regularly carry with me when I travel.

But the night of the killing I did sleep well, untroubled by dreams, until around one-thirty in the morning, when I woke with a start. The evening paper said that a cabbie had been killed and robbed, and the assailant must have fled the scene in a hurry because he left his pistol behind with one bullet missing. No more than that. Oh, and that the search for the perpetrator was on.

Well, the perpetrator was sitting in his fourth-floor room at the Brighton, scraping bits of mastic off his face, taking a bath, giving himself a close shave . . . He even had something to eat, then took out his most comfortable shirt, his traveling clothes and went out for a stroll. It was drizzling outside.

I thought I'd just walk around a while, the fresh air might do me good. And the rain, too. I wasn't feeling ill or anything, only weak; I just wasn't my usual robust self.

Next morning I had a sudden idea: why not call up my little miss. And as luck would have it, she answered the phone herself.

"This time I'd really like to see you," I told her curtly, "at your place, if possible, I want very much to talk to you."

"It'll be my pleasure," she first said, then added she'd rather come down to see me, it would be nicer that way.

"The pleasure will be mine," I replied. "At the Brighton, then."

"No, not there."

"Where then, in the park again?"

"I wouldn't mind. If it still rains I'll put on my raincoat." And she named a busy spot near a market.

"Fine," I said, "I'll be waiting for you." And hung up.

In the meantime I continued walking in the rain. Now you'll get what's coming to you, I fumed. For it was fairly clear that all of this was her doing. She was the one who kept arranging and manipulating everything. . . . She knew damn well Dedin was in town, that my wife didn't leave town—Madame Lagrange kept her well informed. And now she dished it all out, made me see what I got myself into for not choosing her. The little snake. That's why that letter of hers inviting me to the ball was so sweet. Fine, but just you wait and see.

Now I'll let her have it; she'll hear a thing or two from me.

Who does she think she is, I will say. How did she have the nerve to go so far as to poke her nose in other people's most private affairs, and so shamelessly, so cruelly, too. A young lady like her, from a good family, supposedly. So what if she disliked my wife? I wasn't interested in her reasons, whatever they may be.

My wife was a depraved woman, yes, a loose woman, and she'll get what she deserves, but even she was more decent than her— she'd never stoop this low. . . . Yes, this was what I will tell her, I'll use these very words, and will stress how much *more* decent my wife was, especially in view of what had happened.

I rehearsed all of this a few times, though there were a few details that didn't jibe, I mean the whole scenario. If she is so well informed, how come she didn't know that I was sick, for instance, or that I went away. She surely didn't know, or else why would she have invited me to the ball? If she knew I wasn't here. As I said, none of this occurred to me, though a couple of dark suspicions did. Perhaps she kept an eye on my wife, spied on her already in Paris, and here in London most certainly. Or else why would she have taken lessons from the Lagranges? And how could she have found out that Dedin was here, that I was made such a fool of . . .

Wasn't this the reason, then, why she was so angry, why she advised me to kill him? This, at least, was nice of her, her sympathy, I mean . . . But for a young girl to go this far . . .

But here she was, in person. And then everything fell into place.

"It's been a long time," she said. Just like that. Her voice was calm, the look in her eyes crystal clear.

No, I was wrong, I said to myself. She could not be that underhanded.

"But why didn't you come to the ball?"

"Oh the ball . . ." she blushed, as if still regretting she couldn't make it. Why, did *I* go, did I really?

"Of course I did, didn't you ask me to? How is it that you first invite me and then don't even bother to explain why you stayed away?"

Oh there were so many reasons, she began. Family complications, her fiancé's cold, and who knows what else. And since I didn't respond to her letter, either . . . anyway, she did find out eventually that I wasn't home but had gone to Belgium . . .

"That's quite correct, you are certainly well informed." At that point I thought I might as well tell her everything—that I got back earlier than expected, and went straight to the party without even going home first.

"Why should I have?" I explained. "My wife wasn't home anyway. We agreed she'd come home the next day; because she left town, too, accompanied Madame Legrange to the coast to see her son. But don't you know about that?" This last question made the little miss blush, finally.

I'll give you a run for your money, don't you worry, I thought.

"Too bad you didn't come, though," I continued, "it was quite, quite interesting. The costumes were terrific, first class, each and every one."

"What were you dressed as?"

I told her all about my iceman costume, and she seemed to like the idea very much.

"How brilliant," she beamed. And then, with a hint of intimacy and tenderness: "I really am sorry I didn't see you." (We spoke French on that crowded street corner.)

"And there were many interesting costumes, you say?" she asked wistfully.

"Were there ever? And the company! Fascinating people, all of them. A butcher, even . . . But he's not the one I should start with. Listen to this:

"I walk into a room and who should I bump into but my wife. I had no idea she was back, and she didn't know that I was, neither of us knew, isn't that something? And you should have seen her; she looked positively regal in a silvery wig, a blue velvet dress, a lorgnette in her hand . . . She was an eyeful, I tell you. Of course I didn't go over to her; I wanted to see how she acts when I am not there . . . But why are you so quiet?"

"Because I do not like her. I told you that before."

"But why ever not? I don't understand . . . Come now, I don't even believe you. Why shouldn't you like her when she's so sweet? Well, isn't she? Sweet, I mean? You *used* to like her."

"Yes, but that was then."

"When?"

"In Paris." So I continued my account of the ball.

"We had a grand time, we truly did."

"And what about Madame Lagrange?"

"Oh her. She's not even home, I already told you. But there were all sorts of interesting people, impeccable gentlefolk, too, titled nobility, from France. And wouldn't you know it? The whole crowd swarmed around my wife."

"Really?" she asked and again blushed. But I took no notice of that.

"There was a falconer, for instance, with a falcon on his arm, and other unlikely characters. But the most interesting of all was still that butcher . . . yes, the butcher, an extraordinarily entertaining fellow, mischievous, good-looking . . . you know the type: nervy but graceful. Paul de Grévy is his name and he is a croupier by profession who also works as a procurer in gambling clubs. His distinguished name and family background comes in handy in that job. But why are you making faces?"

"Oh nothing. Was *he* there?"

"Yes, yes, that's just what I'm telling you. Nothing surprising in that. You know him by any chance? Among his friends he is known as Dedin."

"I know, I know. A disagreeable fellow. He is one of the instructors at Madame Lagrange's language school."

"Language school? Is that what that woman runs? She's really got it made, then. And how long has he been there?"

"A few months, I guess."

"A few months, you say? Strange that nobody told me about this, not even Dedin himself, though he's such a good friend of mine."

"A friend of yours??"

Naturally, I wasn't going to leave it at that.

"But this is very interesting," I continued, almost cheerfully. "That you should know him. How about telling me something about him?" I put the question to her so lightly, my words seemed to take wings. "He's a splendid fellow, isn't he?" The young woman stared at me.

"You don't think so? Well, he is. Ever see his hands? They are quite delicate. I don't know much about these things, but that's what they say. And his lips . . . real puckery, made for kissing. Like a ripped heart they are, don't you agree?" My young miss was quite ill at ease by now.

"You are joking, surely."

"Why should I be joking? I just spent a terrific evening with him."

"With that horrid man?"

"Is that what you think he is? Horrid?" I took her arm and went on:

"What do you really know about him? Or about my wife, for that matter? (She remained quiet.) That she humiliated me and cheapened herself time and again, a hundred times, a thousand times? Do you know that? No need to be embarrassed, I know it, too. And do you have any idea how I feel about it inside? Disgusted. Rotten. But what is it you people want? To forever hang my head in shame? Well, I won't. Though this is something that will never penetrate your little heads. I am honest now, you see, you can be pleased with me.

"You always complained I wasn't. But now you have to put up with my honesty. Did I ever love you? Yes, I did. And her? Her I despised. From the very first, when I saw her cross her leg and nonchalantly light a cigarette. And still. I knew it was going to be this way, I knew everything, but it was worth it. I got as far as realizing this, which is a long way, as you can see . . . It was hell but still worth it . . . It isn't *my* fault that this glorious world is also a living hell. And now tell me what's on your mind—let me burn up with shame for once."

I was almost hissing by now.

"But don't you see how silly you are being? I *have* come a long way. For don't you know how easily I can crush a man—crush him like a fly? But then why can't I do it to them? What makes them so invulnerable? That woman . . . she is all desire, that's all she has ever been. And me, I see a new face lurking in every corner; and all I want is to wrap my fingers around their neck, oh yes, I want that more than I want my own salvation . . . You are a grown girl, you tell me why I have no power over them. Why is this like a spell, why am I mesmerized by them?"

I never thought the kid was this strong. She took it all, unflinchingly, she stood her ground like a tree in a storm. She didn't protest in the manner of bashful maidens, though *she* was let in on . . . well, ticklish business. Through it all she looked me straight in the eye. We were standing next to a park bench, getting drenched, because in the meantime there was a sudden downpour and nasty gusts of wind. In the end she did open her mouth, to tell me that she could never lie to me.

What I had told her, though it hurt, also made her feel much better, if only because she felt it was the truth. I might not believe her but she knew this about me all along, or at least had sensed it. And until this feeling started fading away, she'd keep on loving me. But after that she'll be relieved and give thanks to the Almighty God . . . And all this was said without tears, sternly almost.

Even if there was a lot of whimsy and foolishness in what she did and said, she went on, and there *was*, she'd be the first to admit it, there were also true feelings—feelings she was not likely to get over; indeed, she couldn't even if she wanted to, they had such a hold on her—she never thought such a thing could ever happen to her. And now she was ready to say good-bye, she was offering her hand . . .

She also asked me to please calm down because, truth to tell, she was terribly afraid she, too, was at fault somehow. There was such sadness in my eyes, such profound sadness, it made her think I might try to do something . . . oh, perish the thought . . . And then petulantly, almost like a child, she added that she didn't think my wife was worth all that suffering. If I really wanted to know the truth, she thought she was a heartless woman.

"You mean to say she doesn't love me?" I asked.

"Yes."

"But that's where you are wrong. Even if she told you that herself, it's still not true."

Miss Borton blushed to the roots of her hair.

"She told me no such thing. What she did was ask me to love you." And she blushed again, deeply, and this time there were tears in her eyes.

"As far as that gentleman is concerned," she declared, "whatever is said of him is none of my concern. What I had told her in Paris was simply this: 'I want to be an honest girl, Lizzy . . .' In other words, I told her I loved you, but that I would soon disappear for good. Why would I want to disappear? she wanted to know. And her saying this made me so happy, I embraced her. 'You are so generous,' I said to her. (I was such a child then.)

"But she didn't want me to embrace her. 'Stop it, you silly,' she said, but with a hard edge in her voice. 'I am not all that generous.' (And she laughed a bit too strenuously.) 'You got it all wrong, girl; I am not generous at all. What I am,' she said, 'is a bad woman.' And that's when I woke up finally."

That night I had a beautiful dream. But before going into that, let me talk about some other matters, above all about that interminable night. I was sitting on my bed for a time, in a thoughtless daze, when something seemed to stir next to me. I looked up and my glance fell on my old diary.

Well, well, what have we here? I reached for it and began to peruse it. Let us just see what thoughts I had at the other end of an endless reach of time.

This is what it said on the first page: "Be sure to remember that he [Dedin, that is] made a note to himself. Do not forget."

That was when he urged us, my wife and me, to go to London. Oh yes, it was he who persuaded us to come. And didn't I have the feeling right away there was something fishy about his suggestion? Didn't I immediately think of *him* when I found those violets?

You do perceive these things, with your senses, your soul. I made no mistake. They knew already then they were going to come over—first Madame Lagrange, then Dedin. But then what *did* he jot down in his notebook that time? I mean if everything worked out so perfectly, and I, like a complete fool, agreed to move here?

"A perfect dupe" is what he must have written down. They treated me like a dumb animal, in other words. And you don't do that to a human being, no matter how inferior I may have appeared in their eyes. It was cruel and indecent of them—no *way* did I deserve to be treated like an animal. . . .

"I'll follow you, don't worry," he must have told his lover, precisely as I'd imagined it more than once. And he told her to calm me down, to humor me, to treat me with kid gloves . . . it won't be long. Who knows where, in what far-off danger zone I'll be by the time he comes? Because he recommended that, too, that blasted rescue service—remember? It was no joke, either. Maybe he'll drop dead by then—that may have occured to them too. But it's all right; it's all been duly noted.

But then again, I went along with everything, in defiance of my deepest instincts. And this is what's so inexplicable, so stupefying. Can anyone be this submissive? Like a vision now, Madame Lagrange stood before me, that flaming-eyed slut, that nirvana-craving fraud, the woman I spent Christmas eve with this year.

"Isn't my wife an absolute darling?" I asked her once in a fit of tenderness. And she just stared at me with her burning, vacant eyes. As if she was surprised; as if such stubborn devotion really stunned her.

Only now do I understand that smile of hers. And realize how very hard I tried, until the very end . . . And as for my reward for all my patience . . .

Oh, but no matter, I wrote everything down in my little note-book—*I* did this time, so as not to forget. For as a rule, one does forget. There is an ebb and flow in one's heart, and come next morning, everything changes. But this was the night to clarify things. And carefully note the date. Until three o'clock in the morning I did nothing but record facts.

First of all, the names of all the theosophists: my landlord (an ideal person from their point of view) was evidently chosen well in advance; and then there was Madame Lagrange and Madame Poulence—wasn't this a single tightly-knit group? The realization hit me so suddenly, I nearly cried out. Especially since I also remembered Mr. Tannenbaum, whom I hadn't thought about much any more. I am not at all sure why, but I had great disdain for that man.

He, too, was a philosopher, wasn't he?

But I was also driven by another impulse. I obviously wanted proof, for future reference; I was hoping that the tangle of facts and details, so incomprehensible at first, would fall into place, make a precise pattern, a reliable construct, like a clockwork. Which then would start ticking.

On a separate page, I put down the words of my one-time scalesman—words addressed to his judges at his trial: "I am right in more ways than I can say. May God have mercy on my soul. And on yours, too, Your Honors."

I made these entries and went to bed. But I kept waking up, even after taking two sleeping pills. Around four a.m. I was still up, so I took another pill.

Late next morning I heard knocking on the door. My room looked cheerful, sunny, but also unfamiliar—at first I didn't know where I was.

But then everything came back: the cab driver, the attack, everything.

Must be the police, I thought. But it wasn't, only an urgent message from Mr. De Vries, asking me to go at once to the docks at Cuxhaven—there were things to take care of: my ship was already at the dockyard undergoing repairs. I didn't even finish reading the note. Why bother?

I wasn't going anywhere any more . . .

Only then did I think of the beautiful dream I had, though to recall it now would be kind of difficult.

It was so slight, next to nothing, yet indescribably sweet, like a glimpse of heaven. Someone bent down close to me, in the dark, and held a lamp to my face. She also drew aside the curtains, like an attentive, good-natured maid, and then asked:

"Why are you always in the dark?" And that was it.

I thought I knew exactly what she meant, and wanted to answer her quickly, but she disappeared, slipped away, like water through your fingers. Her smile, though, was real, the gleam in her eye reassuring, like the light of the moon when it suddenly appears at the edge of the sky on a restless night, with a flickering, sleepy smile. . . .

How gladly I would have pondered this little vision, and contemplated womanly virtues, which I believed this dream came to announce, lest I forget it still exists. . . . But I fell asleep, and as happens after such an experience, my sleep was long and deep. When I awoke—it was like rising from the dead—I saw darkness outside.

Actually it was fog, but so dense it shone. I sat up in bed.

Now the fog seemed to take on a reddish hue, as though fueled by flames.

Another storm is brewing, I surmised, and gave a shudder. And then kept staring out the window, as though I had never in my life seen such a sight. But then I jumped out of bed. After having slept for nearly eighteen hours.

I washed up in cold water, quickly got into some clothes and hurried downstairs.

Once I hit the stairs I felt better, relieved. Here everything sparkled, the lights were so much friendlier—God only knows why hotel rooms are so dingy and flat. Oh, and after my first sip of port . . .

The English are right; port *is* the best medicine around.

For as soon as I felt its warmth spreading inside me, tears came to my eyes, as though I were putting the crowning touch on this mysterious rebirth of mine. Life itself felt so wonderful, I was almost ashamed of myself. I mean there it all was: the lights, the warmth, the drink, my growing appetite . . . And other things: the soft carpet, the buzzing in the lobby, the clinking and clattering at the tables. I was like a man who just came down from a frozen mountain top. My face burned and these light noises echoed in my ear.

Oh and the tiny trills of laughter. And the darting waiters. And the stillness. And the new arrivals stepping on the soft carpet, with wreaths of fresh snow sticking to their coats . . . all this was sheer enchantment for me. As though I had never awakened from my drug-induced sleep.

But should I be ashamed of writing all this down? Embarrassed that I, *I* of all people could actually be happy about something? No no, I have no intention of glossing over, or belittling, what I felt. It was real. And no wonder: when something shakes you to the very core of your being, you stand completely exposed, naked, your soul does. All petty annoyances and aggravations are swept away, as in a fierce storm, and the joy of existence, unsuspected, wondrous, peeks through like the morning sun. You keep marvelling at being alive. Wasn't this what I felt when my ship was on fire? Then, too, and at the worst possible moment, I drank a glass of lemonade. And my skin tingled with pleasure, as if prickled by the rays of the sun.

I freely admit that my tears began to flow and fell on my food in front of me. And if the manager of the Brighton hadn't sat down next to me, I would have really started bawling. Not only because of what I'd just realized . . . though the mere fact that I was still sitting there under those brilliant lights did move me. Except in real life nothing is *all* nice: the manager began jabbering away, much to my annoyance.

"Sailors," he said, "what a dreadful lot." (It was his peculiar way of making me feel good, I suppose.) Once he went rowing with two of these loutish characters (they *are* loutish, most of them, didn't I agree?), and he had to keep telling them: "*Aber nicht spassen Sie, meine Herren, nicht Spassen Sie, meine Herren.* (That dimwit was also a foreigner, an Austrian—London is full of strangers.) Could I guess what they were up to? he went on. They started rocking the boat and, laughing uproariously, were ready to rock me right into the ocean.

"In a way you are just like them," the manager went on complimenting me. "You are also a wild one . . . Why, there's the bottle again in front of you. You drank all night, and now you are at it again . . . Why drink so much? This morning, or last night rather, it hurt me to look at you. (He also chuckled, as if he could just guess what that look concealed.) No but really, you do look a mess."

"What's that to you?" I said. "There's nothing wrong with my looks."

"Come now . . . You are being eaten alive by women. There's nothing underneath your skin any more. Except a little fat maybe."

"You don't say," I laughed.

"You are all chewed up, my friend," he said with a smile and rose from his chair.

"No I am not," I replied with great dignity.

"Yes, you are; you are all chewed up." He must have liked that word.

Luckily, he was called away, and I could again lose myself in reverie, and lose myself I did. I kept looking at the snow-covered window panes and listened to the wind sing. For now there was indeed a storm outside, snow flurries mixed with rain—on the windows thick snowflakes gave way to raindrops. And cold drafts of air rushed in and out, making the curtains move. But it suddenly broke off—not the storm but the quiet around me . . . As I was sitting there peacefully eating my dinner, still immersed in thought, in reverie, the sound of laughter, light, sweet, familiar laughter struck my ear.

"Wouldn't you know it? Eating red meats again. A true savage, so help me."

And at that moment I knew what to make of the dream I had the night before.

I can be very brief about what happened next.

First of all, I drank an awful lot, though that's not the point.

It was Mrs. Cobbet who stood before me, telling me to leave my dinner and go with her quickly—Kodor was waiting outside . . . I could get whatever I wanted at his house, much better stuff than what I had here . . . Just like that, as if nothing had ever happened between us.

Kodor came to the Brighton, she went on, to order a few cases of his favorite wine and some choice cigars, and the manager told him I was here, wouldn't he like to see me. Of course he would: go and get me old Jacob, he said. And ever so sadly, too. Because he still cared for me a lot, even if I *had* given them the cold shoulder of late. He talked about me more than once and said he wanted very much to see me. Besides, he's been quite depressed lately, was no longer his old self. Couldn't I do it for her, spend the evening with them, as a special favor? It would make Kodor very happy.

"And me too," she added bashfully.

All this time I kept staring at her as if she were an apparition.

How very odd that she should show up just now, I thought. But she was real all right, in a mauve fur jacket, with diamonds in her ear. Her nails were perfectly polished, as were her teeth, her eyes—the woman looked perfect in every way, she sparkled like a gold watch . . . And add to this those sinful little fires in her eyes . . . As I bent over to kiss her hand, she laughed. But I did it, I kissed it, and she let me, she didn't move or duck, but put up regally with this bit of chivalry, standing there tall and slender like a Christmas tree. Though such things are not even customary in England.

"Oh, Mrs. Cobbet," I told her, enraptured. And then: "Is this true? Am I really seeing you again?" And other such phrases . . . I plumb forgot to be angry with her.

In other words, it was the same story all over again. Yet, for me to fly into raptures over meeting *any*one, or in any case to act like such a jellyfish, was . . . was unheard of. And the truth is I never did act this way before. To back down, to take flight—these were moves I had not been familiar with before. Faced with a challenge, I usually pause and then meet it head on. But not this time. This time I balked, I shrank back, there's just no other way to put it or explain it. There was such a burning desire in me to live again, such an uncontrollable and passionate yearning, I thought come hell or high water, I shall not lie dormant, shall not sleep again, nor return to that awful, dingy hotel room, but go out, walk around, talk, do *something*, for God's sake, to keep me from going mad.

But then maybe I should take the morning train to Cuxhaven. Actually the thought occurred to me as soon as I laid my eyes on this luminous creature, while staring at the glittering rings in her ears, at her flushed face, at her smouldering eyes . . . How these creatures love to live. As though they just got started, and then started anew every minute, again and again . . .

But what about me? Was I no longer interested? Didn't I want any of it any more? It's easy to say, of course: that's it, I've had enough. But when you yourself make the first move . . . What was it that charming maid told me the night before? "Why are you always in the dark?"

Kodor was writing out telegrams in the lobby with a gold pen, and ordered Mrs. Cobbet to pick out the wine.

"Have them put some in the car," he commanded. "We can take it with us; I feel like drinking." Mrs. Cobbet did as he said but then remembered to ask:

"Do you think you ought to?"

"Yes," Kodor replied, pragmatically and unequivocally, and continued writing. "Nothing can hurt me, I am made of heavy metal," he added, amusing himself, as usual, with homegrown witticism. I noticed right away how rudely he treated Mrs. Cobbet, and at the same time how very friendly he seemed toward me.

"Ah, it's so strange to see you," he said. "Lotty talked about you so often . . ."

So that's how it was: She said it was Kodor who kept talking about me, and he said she did . . .

I must say, though, he looked sharp. No sign of depression that I could see; if anything he looked stockier, more substantial. And more solemn, too, more formal, as though he'd just walked out of a barber shop. Nothing slovenly about him, his pockets weren't bulging as in the old days. He wore black—brand new black, at that; a fine hat, fine gloves, and all of it understated. There was only one bit of shiny yellow flashing through his fingers: the gold handle of his cane.

So he became a gentleman, finally, how do you like that? A genuine millionaire. Quite a change from the quirky con-man I once knew.

But didn't the man go bankrupt? Those shady oil deals . . . didn't they do him in? I tried to sniff out the cause of the change. But it wasn't anything like that. What his face reflected was something else, a kind of placid indifference, the same expression I must have had after my own vicissitudes. Even his gentleness was different. Strained.

"Ah, my dear friend," he said. (He never used that word before: not "friend" and not "ah.") "How *are* you, Jacob? (He never used to say that, either. He was never interested enough.) But why are you staying here? Why in a hotel? Got divorced perhaps?"

He still had his sharp eyes, the old scoundrel.

"Yes, I did," I answered quietly, and was surprised myself how easily the word slipped out.

"Quite right, quite right," Kodor said, stealing a glance at me from behind his spectacles. "Nothing wrong with getting a divorce. *If* you can go through with it." And he calmly went on scribbling.

But then we started out; the bottles of wine were put in the car, and we were off.

But let me interject two things here. First, I couldn't figure out what smelled of topsoil in that car, yes topsoil, or was it a dank cellar smell? Actually, freshly dug soil has that smell, or sod that's just been turned over. I had the terrible feeling that this time I really went off the deep end. How could I smell soil in the car? But then I *had* one hallucination already the night before, so it all made sense: I *was* going crackers.

There I was, smothered by the smell, yet I couldn't even say anything to them, lest they, too, lose their head. Those few minutes were sheer agony, I considered jumping out of the car.

Oh, but why does one cling to one's memories? Why hold on to them with all one's might? It's so futile, so utterly senseless. All it produces is pain and more pain. The past I can never change—according to Thomas Aquinas (whom I am reading just now), not even God himself can. If somebody never loved you, what's the use of reasoning or pleading? Move heaven and earth, dislodge the moon with your bare hands, still you will not change it. Yet, you keep straining, you rehash everything, wondering if it really happened that way, praying for a miracle, hoping that the mass of contradiction and pain—this hard and bitter lump—will somehow budge, give way, though it so happens, this pain is also impalpable, untraceable.

Where *is* my past anyway? What remains of it? What mark,

what sign is there to show: this is how it was . . .? The waves subsided long ago.

But even if they have, can one ever acquiesce in this? Accept the inevitable, the unalterable; behold it, helpless, stupefied?

Oh, I loved her, of that there can be no doubt, loved her deeply, madly even . . . Yet, look where it's got me . . .

I broke out in a cold sweat by now. What was I really thinking about? What did the smell of freshly dug soil come to announce? I refused to believe it, I resisted it with all my being—it's the reason why I wanted to jump out of the moving car. Why, it's Lizzy's grave; I am anticipating Lizzy's grave!

The horrifying realization hit me and I thought I could take it no longer, could not cope with this anxiety.

And then Kodor chanced to remark: "Open the window, Lotty, will you? It's so stuffy in here. Smells like a cellar.

"Because she never asks them to wash the bottles," he turned to me. And to his mistress he said: "They must have brought it straight from the wine cellar."

As far as the effect his words had on me . . . only a drowning man could appreciate that. When he is pulled out of the water . . .

This is one of the items I wanted to cover. The other was over something else.

When Kodor ordered his chauffeur to drive home, I thought nothing of it. I was sure we were going to his house—he had his office there, I knew the area; I'd been there often enough. My surprise was all the greater when the car came to a halt on an unfamiliar street.

But then I remembered: this is where Mrs. Cobbet lived. I got out and started walking toward the door, thoughtless as always.

Luckily, I caught myself in time and turned around. The driver was unloading the wine from the backseat, while Kodor stood next to him and lit a cigar. It was raining again. He let me lead the way—to test me perhaps? Behind the glow of the cigar I could see his tranquil though watchful eyes.

There you have it, I thought; a simple nonchalant move can be quiet enough. He has the right idea. Why didn't I do that with that delivery boy back at the boarding house?

Because if I knew my way around here . . . I'd better watch my step.

Could he be pulling the same sort of trick on me? Not telling me anything and just bringing me here?

But there was no follow-up. I drank a lot, too much, in fact. And handled Kodor rather curtly. Told him for instance that I was in Bruges, got a position, was put in charge of a vessel, and what's more, received permission to take someone with me. It was to be my wife, but that has changed now of course, since I got a divorce in the meantime. And all this in a matter of fact voice, just to see if he was going to make any snide remarks. And when, instead, he started telling me how happy he was to know that the good word he put in for me helped, I cut him off:

"It had no effect whatever. You had nothing to do with it. But never mind."

This silenced him finally. He grew very small, in my eyes at least—it was like looking at him through a pair of binoculars.

But he gave it another try: "Listen, Jacob, I know very well that an unimportant person like myself cannot . . ."

"Spare me the false modesty," I snapped. "You are not unimportant and you know it. The truth is you didn't knock yourself out. But let's just forget it."

In short, I stopped being Mister Nice. That crooked ladies man and his shabby tricks really got to me by now. I would have given my right arm to find out that he did come in for a fall, that he really did lose his shirt on that oil deal—that is what I wanted confirmed above all, it was my heart's most fervent desire. I took a long, hard look at him this time, and believe me, I didn't like what I saw. A rodent, I said to myself, that's what he is.

But enough about him. Mrs. Cobbet I treated much more gently, like an angel, or a beloved sister. Why this solicitude? Because I saw that for all her sparkle she was a very sad woman—*she* was the sad one, not her friend. I mentioned already how rough he was on her; well, I tried to be that much more courteous. I noticed something else, too, which never fails to have an effect on me: how very grateful she was for every scrap of attention. Is that how that woman really is? I wondered. That servile? The thought depressed me, because I had treated her wretchedly myself in the past.

But besides all that, you can't go on too long with only hatred in your heart. I had to start feeling tender toward *somebody*.

"How nice you are to me tonight," she whispered in an un-guarded moment, and even touched my arm. And her eyes, like a shady garden, had a warm, quiet glow.

"Do be careful, though; don't antagonize him." And she gave me an imploring look. Why did she say that? Oh yes, because I stepped on one of Kodor's "extraordinary" cigars.

"Pick it up," he said to Mrs. Cobbet when it fell on the floor.

"No, she will not," I said and crushed it with my foot.

Kodor took it lightly, or at least acted as though he did. "Serves me right for being a skinflint. It's only the best Mexican cigar money can buy. But fifteen bob will get me another, right?"

There was silence in the room. No one answered him . . .

And then we began to sing. I must say I enjoyed drinking that night more than ever. I kept saying to myself: nothing can top this. It's exactly what I needed: to drown my life in booze. And wouldn't you know it? Everything began to look rosy, and even more so when Mrs. Cobbet sat down to the piano.

"Why don't you sing something?" Kodor asked. Mrs. Cobbet suddenly looked up. "I am sure Jacob would like to hear you, too." And to me, by way of explanation:

"She has a lovely voice. I ought to know, I am paying for her lessons. But she never wants to sing for me."

The glass began to shake in Mrs. Cobbet's hand, and she spilled some wine on her dress. She got nervous, it seems. And then something happend that I didn't quite understand.

"How am I to sing?" she complained indignantly. "You always come up when . . . eh, they'll grumble again that I am not letting them sleep."

"Now, now," Kodor said. "When it comes to me they are not so touchy, you know that. Anyway, they are not home. You were right here, weren't you, when they said they were going to the movies tonight."

As I said, I didn't know what they were talking about, and didn't much care. Anyhow, Mrs. Cobbet relented finally and burst into song, accompanying herself on the piano. The music resounded in the room, it swelled and flowed, I was awash in sentiment.

"Cloud, dark cloud, why hang over me?" she sang. "My heart aches only for yooou" was next. Then this: "The night is full of secrets, dear / But whispering leaves make them clear." Silly hit tunes they were, as can be seen. But with what conviction she sang them, what passion! She practically melted into a world of cheap fantasy, she was transfigured.

But truth to tell, I got caught up in it, too, I couldn't resist the urge to sing myself. And Kodor was beside himself with joy at seeing me like this.

"See now, you can still have a good time with us." And then added: "I feel honored."

But who cared about *him*? I was like a heady explorer making his way through unchartered territory; I felt powerful, expansive. Besides, I know nothing more pleasurable than drinking and then breaking into song. The whole world seemed to be mine, I felt at one with the vast outdoors. It's true, what I sang were rousing sailor songs. One of them was about the shin-shin-girls, which begins like this: "You shin-shin girl, Tokyo's pearl," and ends with a loud cry of "Shin-shin-shah!" The other was the more familiar: "When the last penny's out," but I sang that lustily, too, I belted it out . . .

Mrs. Cobbet, in the meantime, was beaming with pleasure, why I don't know. A trained singer I am not. And those songs! Inane little ditties, all of them, not sentimental even, which she might have expected after her sappy tunes. Maybe she's admiring my strong lungs, I thought. That I have, no question about it. My performance made the windows rattle. That and the storm outside. It's true: the wind howled and lashed the windows while I was carrying on inside. And when I stopped, the racket ceased, too, or so it seemed. And Mrs. Cobbet must have thought she was already on the high seas—her smile was beatific.

We made the mistake, you see, of gabbing away foolishly right in front of Kodor. At first, it was only things like: how pleasant all this is, how happy we are to be here and so forth. To which Kodor automatically answered, Yes, yes, he was awfully glad I was so pleased. But he was really out of it. He just sat there in an arm chair with his eyes closed, as if dozing quietly. I knew he wasn't but still . . . I sat down next to her on the piano bench, and leaned closer, as if getting ready to turn the page but making sure her gorgeous black hair touched my ear. And indeed, I felt her snuggling up to me, nestling her flushed little face close against mine. Now who could resist such advances? Looking down, giving my shoes a thorough inspection, and addressing the floor, all I said was: "How very sweet." And immediately thereafter:

"I am sailing towards India. Will you come with me?"

But all this right under Kodor's nose, as if he were no longer around.

But he was. And he proved it soon enough. We heard noises outside, the door slammed.

"I guess they are back," Kodor mumbled and gave a big yawn.

"Back? But who?" Now I had to ask. How many times was he going to mention it?

"What do you mean who?" Kodor said. "Why, the neighbors, of course. Actually, they are not neighbors—this is a single apartment. Except I had it made into two when I rented it for her."

But even this he said as if he'd just been awakened and didn't feel like talking yet.

"I want her to live in a place she can be watched," he continued, somewhat louder. "I want to know about every move she makes."

At first I didn't understand. All I saw was that Mrs. Cobbet turned crimson, and in her embarrassment was picking lint off her dress.

"At least you admitted it now," she said and tried to smile. It didn't work, though, for instead she turned very somber. And stood up.

"Why shouldn't I admit it?" Kodor countered. "Should she be here all alone? And worry about keeping house and all that? I had a relative of mine move in, who does it for money—my money. Supports his wife and kids on it. Spint is the name, if you really want to know."

"You don't say," I said, incredulous still. "And you really do know about her every move."

"Of course I do, it goes without saying—where she goes, who comes up here, everything. These people know precisely what their benefactor is interested in . . . I bet you think I have no business doing this. But I'll have you know that this is just the way I want it."

I looked around. Mrs. Cobbet stood with her back to me, packing something away, Kodor's fancy cigars, I shouldn't wonder, lest they again fly out of their case. This was a bad sign, though—the sign of total submission. The gilded, finely-crafted wall clock pointed to three, which was a bad sign, too. What the hell was I doing here, anyway? I was quite perturbed, yet couldn't make a move. Was it simple curiosity? To see this thing through? To find out what the old man was up to?

"Wait a minute," Kodor reminded himself. "You mean to tell me you were never here before . . . Ah yes, how could you be, you are such an *Ehrenmann* (that's precisely the word he used), a real *cavalière*. If you were here, you would have been sure to tell me. 'I went up to see your lover last night, old chum,' you would have said . . .

"Yes sir, that's what you are, a splendid cavalière, you demonstrated that the last time. Oh yeah, before I forget: I won that suit, you know, I was vindicated . . .

"Leave us, will you?" he barked at Mrs. Cobbet now. "I want to talk business with our gentleman caller. And make me a cup of coffee; I have a headache." Mrs. Cobbet silently left the room.

"Well, bugger," I said to him promptly, "let's hear what you have to say. But I bet you want *me* to talk, right? You thought *I* was going to start spilling the beans now. You'd just love to make me drunk, wouldn't you? You must think you're the only one with brains under your hat, while our heads are filled with . . . what? noodles? (In my rage I didn't know what to tell him first.) And what if I do love your mistress, what then? No one else can love her, only you?"

Ah, but all this felt so good . . . my eyes fairly twitched with pleasure, I was foaming at the mouth from the rush of words that wanted to stream out. What's more, I would have loved to—I don't know—prance about and pick up that miserable old man and force him to dance with me. And pat his bald spot maybe . . .

"Well scoundrel?" I said to him again, "you got plenty scared this time, didn't you? *You*, who always told me that the weak ought to fall by the wayside. Still feel like taking me on, hunh?" And I guffawed right in his face . . .

Dear God. No matter how you slice it, there's cruelty in all of us. And the more ashamed we are of something, the more it comes out. It wasn't very pleasant to think of what I did just before: how I went on and on, making me believe he was fast asleep. I nearly came out with it, nearly told him that *I* was her lover, too. Of course I could have even embroidered on it a little, spiked it with a touch of remorse, moved him with a bit of calculated anguish, pull on his heartstrings with: "Ah before we knew it, we went ahead and did it . . ."

"What a clown you are," I said to him in any case, "what a jackass. What can you do to me? What if I do love her and she loves me? What if that's the case? What if I take her away tomorrow or the day after, if I take her aboard my ship? What will you do then, scratch your head?"

"Take her away? Just like that?" he said quietly. Before this he hardly spoke up, but now he began mumbling again, as if confiding secrets to me, rapidly, voicelessly almost.

"No need to scream," he whispered. "She doesn't have to hear every dumb phrase, she's pretty dumb as it is. You can always have your way with her . . . she'll go for anybody."

"That doesn't scare me," I said. "Don't you try to discourage me. Or do you think people like you can go on shortchanging me forever, and I will say nothing, just laugh it off? Do you *really* think I will never grab at anything, that my greatest pleasure is to see *you* happy? You misjudged me, my friend; I am just as ruthless as you people, or will be, at any rate. This time you've met your match. If you want one thing, I'll surely want another. And exactly *what* I want you'll find out soon enough." And with that I rose from my chair.

"Are you through?" Kodor said. "Do you want a dowry, too? How about the clothes off my back?" And he actually began to unbutton his coat. "Here, take my dentures, too." And he removed his dentures from his mouth.

I could have laughed even at that, but I happened to look at him just then. (Before I didn't.) And what I saw was not very pretty. He wasn't just ashen, he really looked as if he was about to croak. That's what loose living does to you, I said to myself once, after seeing a dead man with puffy cheeks and rings under his eyes. The poor fellow wasn't even that ravaged, but the look was unmistakable. That's how it was now. Kodor's mouth twitched, his eyes were moist, as if he could no longer cry with real tears. And on top of it: no teeth. He looked like his own grandfather.

"Out, out!" he screeched at Mrs. Cobbet when she opened the

door. "I am still talking." He then lay down on the sofa in shirt-sleeves and continued mumbling to himself.

And I, for some strange reason, began to think, or rather was struck by the awful suspicion, that Miss Borton might have given me away after all; in her excitement or fear she may have told Madame Lagrange that I was in London. If she said only that much, it was enough. A great deal hinged on that . . .

Oh what an utter fool I was. I should have thought of it before, what with her being such a jittery little thing.

The whole thing was like a flash in the dark, but enough to make me want to leave at once. For by now I knew exactly what I should do, where I should go—the one place in the world where I should be now.

That I fully recovered my senses I need not emphasize. I was cold and hard, like the pipe in my pocket.

"What is it now?" I said to Kodor and stared at him for a while.

He was slow to answer: "I am dying of cancer . . . But what will become of that woman?"

Now he was neither sarcastic nor highhanded. He was sick, visibly, desperately sick. A broken old man.

"Just don't tell her," he warned with his finger. "She may be dumb, an untamed animal . . . still, she loves me."

When I got home I saw a car in front of the house, about to leave. It was around five in the morning. I heard the car door slam—I can still picture the gently falling snowflakes illuminated by the headlights. Suspecting the worst, I pulled down my hat over my eyes as I passed the car, which was just pulling out.

"Bon voyage," someone from the house shouted, and I immediately recognized the voice.

"Who were they?" I asked, stepping up to the well-wisher. And because he was very much taken aback, I also took hold of his arm.

"Who were these people?" I inquired again, and began leading him toward the nearby square which was still enveloped in darkness. Needless to say, the man was Mr. Horrabin Pit, my earlybird landlord, who upon seeing me got so frightened, he almost passed out, even letting his cigar drop.

Would I please stop torturing him, he pleaded; how was he

supposed to know who these people were? Whereupon I pushed him just a little.

"Was my wife in the car?"

He began to whine annoyingly, as if he had a nasty earache.

"Well, was she?" The old geezer was tougher than I thought. So I said:

"Listen to me and listen good: I am going to knock your brains out right here, where no one will see it. Nobody will know how it happened. *Was* it my wife sitting in that car?"

He looked at me like a madman.

"Why of course it was," he said all choked up.

"And you call yourself a decent man . . . Protecting people like that? Why, you mean little bastard . . ." And I almost let him have it.

"But this is terrible." And he went on moaning that he was the most miserable of men, and all confused, too, his tongue was stuck, his nerves shot . . . Wasn't it I who told him before I left that my wife was going to spend some time at a seaside resort? Didn't I ask him for a reduction in rent while we were away? He had no idea what was going on, and why I was treating him *so* very unfairly?

"Let's not waste any time. Who else was sitting in the car?"

"Good gracious," he exclaimed, "the world *must* be crazy." Didn't I inform him that that French lady who was here last Christmas would pick her up?

This time *I* almost had a fit.

"There was no man in the car?"

"How should I know? There may have been . . . a gentleman, that lady's husband."

I calmed down somewhat. In moments like this it's always better to stay calm. Besides, why badger him about who else was sitting there—I knew it only too well.

I looked around the square and saw several cabs. One of them responded to my whistle. So far so good.

"Here's a cab. Don't you make a move if you know what's good for you . . . Where are we going?"

"Charing Cross Station," he said, utterly defeated.

"That's better."

"To the Dover boat-train," I shouted to the driver. "But hurry, we don't want to miss our train."

I hustled him into the car, too, for who knows what reason. To pry a little more out of him? I couldn't deal with him as it was.

He told me to take him to the nearest church, where he'll swear that he saw "that certain gentleman" only twice in his life, he didn't know him well at all, he never lived in his boarding house—actually, this was the third time, he once saw him in the doorway. Because he, Horrabin Pit, sees and hears everything, I ought to know that by now, and in case I didn't, I should just take his word for it . . . And he remembers everything, too, nothing ever escapes him. And now I should just stop the car and he'll swear on anything I care to hand him.

I had no intention of taking him to any church, but I was able to ascertain that I was right: Miss Borton did apparently tell them something—that she saw me in London or met me on the street. Because my wife left me a letter in his office with word that it be sent to the Brighton in the morning. And no one besides Miss Borton knew I was staying there. Furthermore, they had been packing all night long, all three of them, taking "numerous items" with them, and departing with quite a few pieces of luggage, which—I can take his word for this—surprised him to no end, since they were only supposed to go on a brief vacation.

I didn't need to find out more. Even if he was in on the getaway. Which he probably wasn't. He was more of a simpleton than I thought. Why pester him any further. I let him go.

But not before I made him pay for the cab. This time he mustered up his courage.

"I will press charges against you," he shouted after me rather officiously. "For deprivation of personal liberty and other offenses."

But who heard him? I was off and running. No one can imagine how fast my two feet can take me in a real emergency. True, people helped me out at the ticket office and elsewhere. Besides, men over two hundred pounds are generally given the right of way, that's been my experience.

"To Dover! To Dover!" I shouted with a sudden sense of abandon and exhilaration. People kept pointing and waving, somebody nodded his head. And I did finally manage to board the train. The engine was already in motion.

"In God's name," I said as I got to the corridor and stood there erect, like a matinee idol.

I had to catch my breath first, my heart was beating mighty fast. Then I walked through the train, and after some snooping around, I opened the curtained door of a first-class compartment. With my house key dangling on my finger I said:

"Good morning, folks." And as they didn't return my greeting, I added:

"Have you taken to wearing a lorgnette, my dear?"

She was holding the same lorgnette that I saw at the ball. Quite handsome, too, with a gold frame. She picked it up hurriedly now, to see if it really was me she saw. And I could again watch those eyes grow.

But Paul de Grévy looked quite handsome, too, in a Japanese silk vest, a fine shirt, brown traveling suit . . . quite dashing, actually. Now, after some quick thinking, he was about to jump up, but I knocked him down in short order. Not even with my hand; I kicked him in the shin, which broke, I think, because he fell back in his seat as if he was suddenly sawn in half. And he pursed his sweet little lips with pain.

"Not a word out of you," I said. My heart slowed down a bit by now.

And when he did stir again, I grazed him on the nose, just enough to make it bleed.

At this point I decided to take a closer look at lover boy. Is he really such a pitiful weakling? I would have dearly loved to complete the hangman's job, to put out his eyes at least, and then throw him off the train, right before his lover's eyes. But why rush it? Let's turn our attention to her now.

She sat in her seat, motionless, not uttering a sound, apparently waiting for the next blow which would be aimed at her. And her nemesis—I—rather than quickly deciding what I ought to do, turned to her and said:

"Traveling quite comfortably, aren't you? In first class . . . On my money. What nerve! Let's have those stocks."

This was unexpected, even for me. Until that moment I swear I didn't even think of it. I did have some Cincinatti Railway shares left to me by my father, which I had removed from the bank recently, just before I left for Bruges, to be precise, intending to take them with me, though in the end I didn't. Now it suddenly occurred to me that they must have stolen it. And it looked as if they really did.

It's not even the value that bothered me. But that I should pay for their pleasure trip . . .

"What stocks?" my wife asked as stonily as if she were already dead.

"You just hold on, my sweet," I said, because I noticed that she began to eye the emergency brake. And Dedin stirred, too, holding a bloody handkerchief to his mouth. His foot must have hurt, too.

"Let's do this with as little fuss as possible," I warned, and raised my finger, the one with the key on it. "I thought out very carefully what I am about to do. I have my reasons."

And then I looked into her eyes. Until now we tried to avoid that. Besides, I had the feeling she couldn't see very well. Her eyes had a glazed, blank look. She herself was pale, but the white of her eyes was actually more red than white. And she stared at me as hesitantly and vacantly as blind people do.

But the moment I caught her eyes, something did seem to stir inside her. It did finally dawn on her that it was me standing there. She got up, and from that point on she was as docile as a child. With the result that everything after that went quite smoothly and pleasantly, just as I ordered it.

The train, in the meantime, clattered on.

Silently, she took down her suitcase, fished out her keys, and before long I had the shares in my hand. Still, it must have been terribly embarrassing to take them out and hand them over, to admit with that gesture that in this, too, she grossly and shamelessly abused my trust. So even in her present daze, she said:

"Here are the stocks . . . Please don't be angry with me." And she quickly turned around, away from me, away, so she wouldn't have to look at me, not ever again.

But for me this was enough. That for once in her life she was overcome with shame; that I lived to see the day. I really had nothing more to say.

Anyway, she looked kind of plump, kind of chubby . . . disappointingly so. Must have put on quite a few pounds. Or was this the old delusion? How many times it happened before. . . ? Whenever she filled my imagination for too long, I didn't want her any more. And that's how it was now.

For a moment I had this absurd notion that maybe this person isn't even my wife. Oh yes, I went that far.

"The fire was out when they arrived," read one of the posters at the ball. That's what I am reminded of as I write these lines. That I am a man accursed from birth . . . Oh, I must be, or else how am I to explain that satisfaction invariably eludes me. It must be my fate to be forever thirsting and never finding relief.

Did she deceive me? Yes? No? What difference does it make? Let us suppose she didn't, she just loved that rotter more than she loved me. But how petty all this was—a French woman who loves another man. How many thousands of times has that happened before? Oh, God . . .

But then I took out my pen and on the stub of one of the shares I had her write this:

"With the help of my lover I stole these shares from you. But you repossessed them on such and such date, on the Dover Express."

"I need this for the divorce proceedings," I said to her. "No alimony for you, my dear."

At that point she broke down and began to cry, intensely but quietly. I watched the tears roll down her face. Obviously it couldn't have been very pleasant for her to put her name to such a deposition.

I myself in the meantime stretched out quite comfortably in the firmly padded seat and took another good look at Monsieur De Grévy.

He leaned back, his eyes closed, like a suffering Onegin. His foot must have still bothered him.

And I kept thinking: Is that it, is that all there is to him? Good God. And I must say I felt terribly ashamed of myself, ashamed of my anxieties, ashamed of my whole life. Even at the ball he cut a better figure.

And this is the man I should now finish off? This worm, this nothing? I won't do it, by God . . . Let the wretch live. I got up from my seat.

"Good-bye, Lizzy," I said. "We won't see each other again. And this gentleman here had better marry you, I am warning him . . . because that still matters to me. I will not stand for my former wife becoming a whore. (I said this straight out.) But I have no desire to support the two of you after what's happened. Whatever money I have I need for myself."

"Did you hear me, Monsieur De Grévy?" I yelled over to the corner.

Monsieur De Grévy obediently nodded his head. And I accepted this nod, as satisfaction for a lifetime.

"For if that doesn't come to pass, dear sir, you will be in for a very rude awakening." And with these words I stepped back toward the door.

My wife still stood there, motionless, staring at me, intently, as if I were some exotic waxwork. Though her eyes were still bleary. And filled with tears.

And as I considered the matter satisfactorily settled, and had nothing further to say, I left the compartment. And heard not a murmur from inside.

Well done, I said to myself as I stepped off the train. This thing turned out just right. For who wants to be like that scalesman? Who wants to be his wife's hangman?

(Here was the evidence: you never leave off brooding and rationalizing—you keep at it until you pop off. Then you stop.)

Nothing hurt any more. Or I should say, one word still did: the word Lizzy. When I uttered it—this funny bauble of a name—one more time. I shouldn't have.

Nevertheless, I kept whistling.

It happened to be a beautiful morning, quite springlike again, with brisk winds and brilliant, penetrating sunshine.

"I am free," I said. "At last . . . I belong to no one; I cast off my burdens." And what a pleasant feeling that was. Indeed, I felt as vast, as solitary, as the open sky.

While most other people (I would have liked to tell Gregory Sanders) were hopelessly bound to one another—the victims of a foul obsession.

And the thought that but a few days ago I was still indescribably happy with her—why, that thought melted away like fog, turned into a vague, unknowable dream . . . But why be happy, anyway? For all we know, happiness could be our stubbornest obsession.

I no longer yearned for it; all I wished for now was peace of mind. I very much hoped I would attain it, that it would be mine, soon. It felt good to gaze after that disappearing train.

Did it come? Were my hopes fulfilled. . . ? Let's rest a little. I will talk about it in the next chapters.

Four

ACTUALLY, I HAVE VERY LITTLE MORE TO SAY.
I worked for a while for the firm of Mischang and Nadoldy, especially for Mr. Martin Nadoldy, supplying him with chemicals: paraffin and such, plying many a sea route in the process; I also struck a couple of good deals with a Hungarian named Carolli . . . But why go into such details?

Suffice it to say that I was again able to put away a little something, though I was still not pleased with myself. I couldn't rest, I was after big money, I threw myself into my work like a fiend. Actually, I never could stand idleness of mind. Andy perhaps for this very reason the old routine, the trivial chores associated with minor transactions could no longer satisfy me. Neither could the sea. Which didn't surprise me, of course.

After all, one does change over the years, especially if one spends a long enough time on land. I was no longer the seafaring man of old, that's certain; but being a sailor is so improbable a condition anyway, it could never be understood by anyone who's never tried it. Just to give one example: A man like that hasn't got anything he can call his own; fact is he hardly knows what the word ownership means, not in the sense it's used around here, at any rate. If he is asked, "Is this yours?" and he answers straight from the heart, he should say: "What do I know?" For whatever he does have is his only temporarily. It's swept away by the first wave, pinched by his best buddy, or snatched from him by the devil in a smoky dive. But after it's gone, he appears again with the most curious of smiles, saying he'd like to serve again, start from scratch, that is, and again finish last.

Oh, the hours I spent trying to figure him out!

What makes such men go on, anyway? To be stuck for months on end on an old windjammer, say, with nothing to look forward to but hard work, atrocious food, and no family, no women, until you end up snarling at your buddy like dogs—what's there to like in all that? Or take those never-ending storms . . . But who can see into men's hearts? What do they really like—that unquenchable thirst, the scurvy they can never get over, the bouts of depression, the boredom?

I was getting restless, the ground under me scorched my feet, and besides, I couldn't keep up the pace over here, though at times all you do on land is tread water.

Or is it possible that I wasn't such a great sailor even in the old days? I guess it is possible. But never mind, I said to myself. Let's do something else, let's start from the beginning.

My health wasn't what it used to be, let's not forget that, either. the old wear and tear, you know. The wind forever blowing outside made me uncommonly edgy, and what's worse, it cut through me like ice, especially in the early morning hours. What ended up happening was that my joints began to hurt.

Before long I did indeed give up the sea, as soon as something else came along, that is. And I did it without much regret. Enough, I said; because I do like quick decisions. At one time I did expect a great deal from the sea, total peace of mind, enormous calm, God knows what else—everything the human heart could desire, I suppose. But I was in for a rude awakening. So I got fed up, I'd had enough—let's move on, I said.

But before turning my back on the sea, let me recount my farewell to it, too—I want to note it for myself. As luck would have it, I ended up sailing past the Greek isles one last time, not too far from the cliffs where the poetess Sappho was supposed to have thrown herself into the sea. And here, following an old custom, I sounded the ship's horn—three short signals and one long one. And I repeated it a few more times. For you see, in the old days, there lived around here a poor lighthouse keeper, whom I had known for a long time, when he was somewhat better off. Now I was curious if he was still here. And he was, by God.

"Oh that Jacob, that Jacob," he cried, waving his flag on a bluff. Later he informed me that his wife gave birth and that he needed some aspirin.

So I sent him a few packets. And figuring this had to have been our last meeting, I bid him farewell in my letter and sent a small gift along with it, for the baby. For that was my very last voyage. By then I knew where I was going to live, what I was going to do—I knew everything, in short. For at long last I began consorting with *my* kind of people, the right kind: schemers, cut-throats. Whatever these guys grabbed hold of was sure to crack.

By chance I got acquainted with a clever rubber dealer named Bobeniak and then with one Aurelius G. Anastasin—but let's forget the details. Suffice it to say that I was able to scrape together a small fortune. First, a very small one, here, and then a larger one in South America. How very simply one can state this, yet it was rather strange. As when the wind changes direction, my good fortune took me quite by surprise, and held on with such force, it was almost too much. Such things *can* be scary. Let me illustrate. I spent some time in New York; I had been collecting money right and left, the green stuff was just pouring in, I was up to my ears in it, my very soul seemed to be made of money; and then one morning I was awakened with the news that a department store sent me a refund—they accidentally overcharged me for their merchandise. And I hadn't the slightest idea how they managed to find out where I stayed, who I was . . .

In a word, I was showered with blessings—deals, connections, one after another; a shipment of coal led to freight cars, that, in turn, to the transport business and so on. At last I could work again, and keep at it until I was ready to drop. I hated Sundays, in fact, when things came to a standstill and there was a yawning emptiness in my office. I really had trouble finding things to do on those days, I could hardly wait for the week to begin, for the machinery to start clattering and rumbling again—I preferred not to think about things, I just didn't want to any more.

And then I grew tired all of a sudden . . .

Ah, those unforgetable lovely apple trees which, sparsely planted but stately, led me through various gardens, all the way to the mountain top, to the spot, that is, where Miss C. H. Inez lived. (In this near-tropical region fairly good apples were grown, though not nearly as sweet as ours.) It was Sunday again, the blissful calm of late afternoon, with a hint of the coming dusk. The trees here were like the golden apple trees of fables, with perfectly rounded crowns and pale gold, full-bodied fruit. It was in the shadows of these trees that I decided to bid South America farewell; to wind up my affairs and return to my home in the North . . . preferably to lovely French soil. . . . At least this was my plan. From the hilltop, where I was standing, I could see the ocean.

And when I laid eyes on that endless expanse, the scene of all my futile exertions, it became even clearer to me that I had to come to rest; it was time. Life itself was winding down, the fire, the fury, was out. For good.

Why ride around in this place, I thought; why go on joyrides? (It was a custom in this town to trot about for a while before dusk, to gallop under the trees of the promenade in a light two-wheeler drawn by a small, black, thick-maned horse. Little lanterns were hung on these horses' oversized heads which, illuminated thus, looked like those of magic steeds . . . as imagined by chambermaids, of course. In the end I was even tempted to buy me one of these domesticated pegasuses, especially as there was little else in town by way of diversion.)

"Why *don't* you buy one of these ponies?" asked Miss C. H. Inez, the sister of one of my business associates, himself a very influential and distinguished gentleman. Hearing her question, the young men around her began to smile mysteriously, detecting signs of secret pleasures in our exchange. One of them even touched my elbow, his eyes burning with passion. In a word, my taking out Miss Inez for a ride became a distinct possibility. And what this means in these parts everyone knows . . . the obligations it entails, I mean. Stern elder brothers watching over their sisters' honor and all that. What's more, in view of our business connections . . .

No, no, I thought; I don't want them any more. Not the sultry black ones, nor the angelic fair ones, who are all soul, whose meals consist of nothing but green leaves. Who with their penetrating eyes can espy the very pit of your miserable soul. She happened to be one of those. In brief, I was no longer interested in such things.

It's not even that she was homely, but one couldn't really talk to her properly—I couldn't, at any rate. No one can be expected to be proficient in all languages—Spanish did me in, I will admit. And though she adored chatting in German, and tried ever so hard to prove she spoke that language (why shouldn't she? her mama was German), she didn't really speak it. "*So mankes*," she'd say all the time. When she couldn't think of anything else to say, she'd come out with "*so mankes*." What was I going to do with her? Besides which she had this martyr-like disposition.

No, no, I thought to myself, I am better off returning to the continent of my origin.

So I told my business associates that I was sailing back to Europe to look after some of my bigger projects. At the same time I put a man named Perjamin in charge of my office, and a very decent young man he was, almost like a son to me at that time. . . . He made out all right, I dare say, but so did I, having reserved for myself a sizable annuity.

With this agreement in my pocket, as well as with a fortune said to be respectable, I set out, like Sindbad the sailor. Having bid my friends a proper farewell, and after an absence of exactly eight years and four months, I was on my way back to the Old World.

And this, briefly, is the story of how I ended up a rich man. If time allows, I may yet return to the subject.

London was my first destination. And I thought, as long as I was there, why not look around one more time—it was, after all, the place where I had gone through so much a decade earlier. I could not bring myself to visit my own flat, but I did want to look up the one-time Miss Borton.

"Oh, it it you?" she cried when, after some waiting around, we stood face to face. For I showed up at their house one cloudy afternoon completely unannounced. They lived in a nice little cottage, of course, with a garden . . . I thought I'll surprise them.

"Is it really you?" she repeated, with a shocked clap of her hands. "How you have changed, Captain . . ."

Not as much as you, I would have liked to say. To be perfectly honest, I didn't dare take a good look at her.

Nature can be mighty strange.

I mean: is it possible for a grown woman to keep on growing after she gets married? Is there such a thing? I had the distinct impression, you see, that this lady became gigantic, and very very flabby. What is more, she was wearing a loose-fitting, flouncy sort of a dress, all white, too—she looked like some Niobe, so help me. In short, you could tell she was constantly nursing, and that—may God forgive me for saying it—she's had no other ambition for years.

And what could I say about the husband? He addressed me in the following heartfelt manner:

"Welcome, welcome, Captain. Please note, sir, that in this abode you are revered." And he turned his clear, girlish-blue eyes on me. Like two great crystal-clear lakes in America—that's how they sparkled.

Coming here, in other words, was a fool thing to do. Damn it. And I already saw myself, or rather, my happier self, pulling my hat down over my eyes, and taking on the wind, the night, melting into darkness on an out-of-the-way London street corner . . . What I am really saying is that you must never go back.

But then we started talking, about this and that, human happiness for one thing, an inevitable subject on such occasions. The gist of the discussion I no longer remember, only that while we were talking, their dog kept barking, and they were hushing it in French. With the dog they spoke only French. And of course my wife, too, came up in the conversation. Mrs. Eders-Hill could not help mentioning her, gently, subtly—still, it wasn't very nice of her, that's my feeling about it to this day. Did I really divorce her, she wanted to known. Yes, I did. They brought in tea.

"Don't you like butter?" this same woman asked, my one-time lovely, my own little Miss Borton, my angel. Don't I like butter, she says.

"Why of course I like it. And will go on liking it till the day I die."

"And sweet rolls? What about sweet rolls?"

"That too. Unto death. Though I *am* loath to spread one on the other. And will be, I think, to the end of my days."

Oh what a decent, upright couple. They said things like:

"We are two very happy people, Captain." Or:

"We lead very sensible lives." And they asked me if I really believed them. And about their children they said: Didn't I want to go upstairs to look at their little brood. True, there was a slight problem with the kids just now.

"They are not sick, I hope," I said.

"Oh no, God forbid, how can you even say such a thing? They were a wee bit naughty, the little darlings, that's all. Like a bunch of frolicking mice they were." And just for such situations, they had a technique that worked like a charm. Was I interested in hearing what it was?"

"Why sure," I cried.

"Here it goes then," Mr. Eders-Hill said.

"Don't spoil it now," his wife warned.

Well, for one thing, he began, they didn't use a whip on the child, like backward schoolmasters all over England. They thought of something else . . . did I want to know what that was? Yes, yes, I did. In that case they would tell me. If the child misbehaved, they dressed him up in his Sunday best, and in those clothes, of course, they couldn't run around and kick up a fuss. . . . And at this point they looked at each other, significantly, like two animal tamers.

And if that didn't do the trick, they just stuck them into bed. That was the best technique of all.

"Why this child is sick," they'd say and pretend he had fever or the cramps. And the kid would be besides himself because there was nothing wrong with him. But there is, they'd insist, there must be, or else he wouldn't be such a mischievous little devil, would he now? And he got a cold compress on his tummy, a spoonful of castor oil maybe, something like that. This is what was going on right now. Well, what did I think of their method? Fascinating, just fascinating. I even slapped my head a little, for emphasis.

"I like your approach very much. Madame is absolutely right. When dealing with children, it's no good to dilly-dally . . . to shilly-shally." Such things I told them.

And that's how we spent the afternoon, full of affability and hight spirits.

But why all this sarcasm? Really. They were robust kids, actually, as I later found out, because in the end I did penetrate the very warmest part of the family nest—I had to, they insisted on dragging me upstairs. They lay in their tiny beds like little lions, grim and fierce; there were at least five of them, all boys, I think. One of them remarked quite angrily: "Let me at least have some chocolate." Whereupon the parents looked at me with pride.

But there is no sense mocking them, as I say. They were so very sturdy, the whole bunch, like a vitamin ad, on my word. It even occurred to me: couldn't they actually burst from all that health.

I was ready to get the hell out. But before I did, I took one last look at something. Even the devil glances back before leaving a house.

In their small parlor there was this beautiful portrait of a young lady with a celestial gaze. It was my little Miss Borton in her green silks, her little breasts like a prohibition, her mind sharp and hard. And her two hands sweet like a pair of lovebirds. Only the flight of stairs was missing, on which she could ascend to some higher realm, and my picture of her, as she once was, would have been complete.

But where does all that go, where does it disappear? *Do* they fall apart, these creatures? Melt away the moment they are fulfilled?

And I almost felt happy for not choosing to stay that other time, long long ago.

But before I forget: I saw one more thing as I was leaving the children's room. The door to the master bedroom was wide open, so I was able to cast a glance toward the sacredness of the conjugal beds. Nice size beds they were, too, damn it . . . though that wasn't all. Over them hung images of religious martyrdom, and this I couldn't understand at all. Did they feel like indulging in marital pleasures under those things? I wouldn't, that's for sure. In point of fact, the mere thought gave me the shivers.

After these unpleasant experiences, I decided I had better not look up Kodor. I was content with information received about him.

Let's see now. He didn't succumb to that illness after all, though at the time he did seem to be at death's door. But one day, miraculously enough, and to the astonishment of his physicians, he recovered. (It wasn't even that remarkable when you consider that his whole life consisted of miracles.) Yet the medical experts did say it was cancer, and were proven right of course when it came to the operation. . . . They opened him up, saw it was a hopeless case, and didn't even touch him, just sewed him back up. Then it happened that on a spring morning he asked for beer. And from then on he drank two pints of beer a day.

Could this have really been the cause of his recovery? He certainly claimed it was. Then again, I heard elsewhere that this was not an unknown phenomenon—there are such unpredictable tumors. When exposed, they miraculously dissolve, from the air, it would appear.

But this is neither here nor there, important thing was that he was well again, felt fit as a fiddle, what is more, he was richer than ever. For that man kept climbing higher and higher, all the way up to the starry sky, as the manager of the Brighton, that dullard, put it.

He was there all right, still at his post, unyieldingly present. A whole world moved underground in the meantime, excellent men among them, another Brighton manager, for example, and Gregory Sanders, whom I liked so much. Time didn't seem to leave its mark on this chap, though; he hung about as before, near draughty doorways and elevators, plump-bellied but ageless. Even the look in his eyes was the same: contemptuous, vacant—a camel's look.

"You see, that's life for you," he said. "For some of us it's all the way up, for others, the opposite. There is no rhyme or reason behind it. Mrs. Cobbet, for instance, hit rock bottom. Yes, she really did," he nodded, amidst meaningful smiles.

She went to America and got lost there, melted into some sinful night, he shouldn't wonder. He spoke rather oddly of this, sarcastically, but with some alarm, too. Evidently the poor sap believed there was nothing but carnal pleasure over on the other side, and night itself was like a vampire, sucking out your bodily fluids.

"Drats," he suddenly cried, "what sort of a man are you? I've never seen anything like it. You leave without a word, nothing about where we ought to send your letters . . . Come to think of it, you have one." And off he ran, to get it from the strong box.

Oh, and when he saw that I didn't even open it, didn't really look at it very closely! One quick glance was enough; I threw it in my briefcase, next to my other papers.

"Well, I never! You are an amazing man, Captain. Aren't you

curious at all? I've been saving this letter for you for four years and now you don't even look at it."

"Listen, if you held on to it for so long, it can't be that urgent."

"I guess you are right. I'm beginning to see how you operate. It's the way to amass a fortune."

"Why don't you try it sometime," I said with a laugh.

The fact of the matter was that when I left I did not leave a forwarding address. Only one or two people knew where I was going, the rest didn't bother with me after that. In short, I cut all ties, eliminated even the possibility of further contact.

And now I should read this letter? When I knew the second I saw it that it was my wife's letter?

It was quite obvious, for though the address on the envelope was typed, it bore a Barcelona postmark. And since I had no one in Spain (and since I heard from various sources that that's where she went and settled somewhere near Madrid), I could be quite sure the letter came from her.

She always talked about Barcelona and said how much she liked that city.

But I wasn't going to read another letter from her. I knew well enough, of course, that she would write, but there was no reason for me to write back, there was no unfinished business between us. Let us just say I ceased to exist and anything having to do with us ceased, too. As if death itself tore us asunder, utterly and irreversibly.

And that's why I tossed it in my briefcase, without any hesitation. I'll burn it upstairs, I thought—it couldn't be sent back, there was no return address on it. I noticed that, too, right away. But to tear it up before this bloke's eyes? No, no, he'd love that too much.

He was much too interested in my affairs as it was.

"Well, did you get married over there?"

"What do you mean get married? I *am* married, my friend."

"Married? How is that?"

"Nohow; never mind."

And then, finally, he got offended. He puffed a little and got up.

People do keep track of your affairs, it seems. He knew I got divorced. What is more, wherever I went people were after her; almost automatically, and just about everywhere, they would have me produce *her*, though many of them didn't know who she was and I certainly never talked about her.

As strange as it sounds, that is exactly what happened. And as soon as I set foot in Europe.

And it went on, too. I had hardly arrived in Paris, and it was her again I had to deal with. One day my attorney rang me up and told me there was some money deposited in my name at one of the banks, credited to me, it seems, in connection with some shipping transaction. "Shipping transaction?" I asked. He had no idea what it could be.

I didn't, either; I had no recollection of ever being involved in any such transaction. And though the next day I got a note from the bank saying I had money there earning interest, I was none the wiser for it. But the fact is I always liked to have a clear picture of all my business affairs, and I don't allow even unimportant matters to slide.

I remember the incident quite well; it was early in the morning, about a month after my arrival in Paris; I was still living in a hotel then. Sitting on my bed, I kept staring at the letter with the feeling that again something has surfaced from the past. But what, what could it be? I never had anything to do with a public auction, not in Paris, at any rate, though that, too, was mentioned in the letter.

Naturally, one never thinks of the simplest solution.

"Why don't you give a call to the firm that we referred to in our letter? You have the paper in front of you, just read off the name." This is what an insolent officer told me when I telephoned the bank. (The French can be quite arrogant, especially with foreigners.) And you can imagine my surprise when I called up the firm and a voice said this to me, these very precise words:

"Hello, Tannenbaum here; who is this and how can I help you?"

I almost fell off my bed.

"You don't say," I said. "The young Monsieur Tannenbaum, in person, really?"

It's when you are embarrassed that you ask such dumb questions. But he replied with the same flawless composure as before.

"Who else would I be? What a question. I can only be me, in my own person. What can I do for you, sir?"

A philospher, why of course. After these words there could be no doubt.

But how did he get here; how did he just walk into my brain? I never did want him there. If, by chance, I ever did think of him, I began whistling. Him I never paid any attention to. And now, all of a sudden, he was here. What for, I wondered.

But as long as we were in this thing, let's see what happens. I tried to present my little problem to him, and interestingly enough, I didn't have to explain much, he knew right away what I was getting at. As it turned out, the young man remembered us very well.

"Ah, that petite woman," he cried cheerfully, "the one who first went to London, and from there to Spain, right?"

On and on he went, but the gist of the matter was this: to cover the storage charge, he was forced to auction off my belongings, the furniture we had stored with them before we moved to London.

"It was quite simple, sir," he explained: "the storage fee was not paid, there was no one to notify, so the proceeds from the auction were used to settle the account . . ." Or rather, the remaining modest balance was deposited in a bank, and I can collect that money now—that's what the letter was referring to.

"To Madame's *odds and ends*," the young man averred, who in the intervening years had apparently become fully engaged in the shipping business. But what interested me now was that word, that phrase. Not only because he was so high-handed about the affair, degrading my one-time property to odds and ends, but because he automatically assumed that they were my wife's odds and ends. This made me sit up and take notice.

"And you had the heart to auction off your lover's things?" I asked quietly, still in my most affable manner. This startled him somewhat, naturally, and his voice took on an altogether different tone.

"What was that you said, sir?"

"Look here," I said, "let's just stop pretending, I am getting a little tired of this. You were my former wife's lover, that much we all know. Still, you could not bring yourself to hold on a little longer to her few sticks of furniture, the pitiful 'odds and ends,' as you so chivalrously put it.

"Don't act innocent with me," I continued peremptorily, "I am fully informed. I know you were a philosopher, I knew you two exchanged letters. Just stop prattling. The slippers, the birdies—I know all about them, too. My wife confessed everything in the end."

"Wha . . . what?" he flared up. And I felt he was about to tear into the receiver.

But then he burst out laughing.

"How interesting . . . Really. Would you mind telling me exactly what your wife confessed?"

I said nothing. He kept guffawing.

"Too bad I didn't hear that confession . . . There must be some confusion here, my dear sir, a case of mistaken identity, I am afraid. Fact is I would have *loved* to seduce your wife but couldn't . . . She didn't let me . . .

"Are you still there?" he yelled after a short pause.

"Go on," I said impassively.

"Will you refresh her memory, then, if it has indeed become that feeble, and write to her in Spain that she has me confused with another man; she did not deceive you with me—I am someone else. I am the one who was in love with her, who was mad about her, and whom she kept leading by the nose. For she was a nervy little woman, you can tell her I said so, tell her I used that very word . . . That's my message to her. Am I glad I have nothing more to do with your wife . . . I would have wrung her neck if I had the chance—why shouldn't I have auctioned off her furniture?

"I tutored her, for free; should I also watch her furniture for her?

"And if you find all this offensive, *sir*," he concluded, "I shall have to meet your challenge—I am entirely at your command. Good day, sir." And with that elaborate flourish he hung up.

Should I have actually gone out and fought a duel with the man? Over someone who's gotten so far away from both of us? He didn't have his way with her, the poor chap. . . . One of the few who didn't. And for that I should bash in his head or he mine?

Yet all of this was besides the point. The real question was what to do with all that free time.

While I was still in South America, my plan for a long time was to have my friend Gregory Sanders move in with me in Paris. We would live quietly, like two devoted brothers, I thought. It was an agreeable plan, for I really liked the old man. Perhaps he was the only one about whom I can say this without uncertainty. . . . But life is so very strange: I realized this only after we parted ways, when I no longer saw him. Though the realization may have been due to something else as well: it was then that the old man's bad luck began to multiply.

What a life that was . . . Yet it was he who consoled me in his letters. There he was utterly alone in his old age; his son squandered much of his fortune and then ran off with some woman. And he himself was quite ill to boot. So I thought, why not bring him over to Paris—we'll have a chance to chat, he and I. This, at any rate, was my plan. And the following thoughts and recollections tumbled through my mind:

He once sent this letter to me in South America: "City of Hastings, July. Today a wasp flew into my room and headed straight for the electric fan you sent me earlier this summer. It got caught in the blade which then whirled it about, depositing it near my hand, on a book I happened to be reading. I took a real good look because something about the insect interested me. It was still alive, it was moving its feelers, it wanted to sting me still.

"But there was no resentment in the insect, none whatever. It did not berate itself or curse its fate, saying: why did I have to fly in through this window? It seemed the tiny creature did not distinguish between necessary and chance happenings . . . Thus, it did not torment itself with the futile conclusion that this or that happened through a fault of its own. For whatever did happen had to happen. In short, this creature judged even accidental occurrences to be inevitable . . . And this is what we must learn from it, because, apparently, this *is* how our world is run. We must somehow find our way back to this truth: we must learn to be more humble, my friend, learn to bow our head even deeper, lower it for good. It would do you, and me, a great deal of good to heed this lesson."

His words had such a profound effect on me, they assuaged my feelings of guilt and self-reproach to such extent, that it was at that moment I decided I was going to have him brought to me. And I won't deny it: I was rather pleased with myself for choosing, instead of some far more grandiose plan, this simple one. I was happy to know that I came this far: I knew now what I needed and what I was really after.

He wrote me yet another significant letter, right before his death, and for that I am even more thankful. This is what the letter said:

"What's so singular in all this is that no creature until now has come to the realization that I inhabit it . . . No one ever felt my life (the life of one Gregory Sanders, that is) to be his. The world has been around a long long time, yet never before has this happened. Then, at one point in the middle of the last century, it suddenly did. I was shocked into an awareness that not only am I here but *I am he*, no one else is. For this, you see, is the heart of the matter, this feeling of separateness and isolation. No one ever mistook himself for me, and never did I make such a mistake myself, although we are all alike in so many ways. In this one thing, however, we are not and never were—not in the beginning, not in the end. In this we were always utterly, fatally alone . . . and shall remain so forever. And that, my friend, is nature's great consolation. It's what Oriental societies immerse themselves in, and consider more desirable than the light of the sun. It's what they've been proclaiming and explaining for thousands of years. The insight is simple: Energy doesn't dissipate, life-forms keep recurring, except for that intimate feeling I have about me, the feeling that I am me—that is a unique, one-time thing. Only now can I appreciate the reverence in which they hold this insight. I know I couldn't come up with anything more profound myself."

There was one more thing: he asked not to berate his son, it would do no good; he himself no longer had an opinion about the boy, nor about anything else; people, things—it was all the same to him now. He'd suspended all judgment.

This letter of his, as I say, had a decisive influence on me during the years of silence. The main portion, too, but that postscript in particular. For what a relief it is to be free of a cherished conviction, especially if, at the same time, one would like to hold on to it to the bitter end. In time it can become an unbearable burden. For what *is* one to do with one's conviction. . . ? Finally I did tell him about my plan; I heard he was beginning to get better, and I, too, was getting ready for my return trip. But then, a few days later, on October fifth, he suddenly died.

It'as as if my own ill-fated life story were making the selfsame point—that from now on I must live alone. Why, he himself told me as much in his letter: "This is your fate, it seems," he wrote. "Learn to live alone then." And he even added: "Totally, unrelievedly alone."

But what hurts me still is that I spent so little time with him while he was alive—him of all people I neglected. You spend your life troubling yourself with all kinds of riff-raff, and when it comes to the deserving few, you've run out of time. But perhaps that's the way it should be . . . It, too, is part of the overall scheme.

I just had to learn how to lead an idle life, that's all. But where was I going to find the thing that would fill out my days? That's when I started writing these notes, but they are a bother, too . . . Words are a burden, and for that reason alone I can't express myself decently. In short, it isn't easy not having to earn a living or worry about the future . . . especially when you no longer have a future to look forward to. . . . An antiquarian offered me a set of fine old telescopes and suggested that I gaze at the stars; another wanted to sell me a litter of Angora cats, assuring me that they were very quiet pets, virtually voiceless—ideal as companions. Both men had to be gotten rid of, though the star-gazer made me remember something. I always liked chemistry, had even studied it at one time; what is more, I began my second career down south with a small chemical firm. So in place of the telescopes I set up a well-equipped laboratory in my new home, in one of the small upstairs rooms. I had seen something like this once near Naples, in the house of some aristocrat, except I furnished mine much more cleverly, to suit my very own need. And before long I was in there, working.

It seemed right . . . perfect, in fact. Yes, being occupied *is* wonderful; and being like a student is even more splendid. To drift through time with not a care in the world; to be wrapped up in the tiniest tasks . . . But how very strange: it was as if it had only been yesterday that I put down my spoon at the table—as soon as lunch was over, I used to rush back to my room, to do nothing; I said I had to study but instead sneaked a smoke and just whiled away the time. And now it seemed as if I'd always done just that, as if I had idled away my whole life this way. It was surely gone—much of it, anyway.

No matter, I thought to myself, I'll pick up where I left off. That I was born to become a scholar I no longer doubted, it became more self-evident than ever. To be sure, I always knew it, but a wicked little fiend invariably distracted me: first there were all those dreams, then the harsh reality. But now, at last, it was different; studying gave me real pleasure, and everything connected with it: the solitary early-morning hours, that hard but rewarding, self-reliant solitude, when you know beforehand what work lies ahead, and when the time comes, that is precisely what you concentrate on, dismissing everything else. . . . In short, things began to look up, but then I was stricken again. It was the same illness that gave me so much trouble down in South America: a chronic respiratory condition, the miserable legacy of my last sea voyage. I had a bad case of it this time, it wore me down completely—there were times I coughed the whole night through. So the same thing happened again, the same wicked devil stepped in: you'd better chuck the whole thing. I really had to; fumes and such were bad for my lungs. But what my esteemed doctors wanted was not to my liking, either. I caught my sickness on the sea; should I now go to the Riviera? Anyway, I don't like to be out on a promenade early in the morning, clutching a walking stick.

But then one of the younger physicians had an excellent idea. Why didn't I visit the country now and then? I was my own man, after all, with all that free time on my hands. I could go anywhere, stay if I so desired or return and go someplace else; I could seek out the very best places. The man was absolutely right. Why shouldn't I roam the world a little? It would do me so much good: new surroundings for my disposition, a change of air for my lungs. And that's just what happened. I woke up one morning and realized I was breathing free again. The little doctor was proven right, what do you know . . . But sometimes the assistant does outshine the professor, such things do happen.

As far as my spirits were concerned, I felt renewed. All the more as I'd never before had the luxury of traveling about without set plans or schedules. I had always been in a hurry, always full of anxieties; and whatever I did want to see, I had to squeeze in quickly. Not this time, though. I had nothing particular in mind. Whatever came my way I looked at, what didn't, I left without regret. And I dare say this was like being buffeted and bathed by the spring wind.

When I arrived in a new place I didn't hit the streets, as before, or the market where there is always such a racket. I went up to my room to rest a bit, that's how I started now, or ensconsed myself in tiny out-of-the-way inns, hiding behind dark glass partitions or plants, preferring places high up from where I could take in the whole town. And sit motionless, like a statue. And what caught my attention at such times? Mere nothings, most probably. The wind or the rain; a trayful of cheese cake put in a window to cool; a man who may be the mayor; a bunch of girls . . . All these goings-on never did seem as strange as now. As if I had just tumbled down from a distant star. And couldn't stop laughing.

What's more, it seemed like an innocuous, neutral kind of laugh, neither sarcastic nor supercilious, God only knows exactly what kind—soulless perhaps. But this, too, felt so good; for the first time in my life I had a real rest. And let's add one more thing: I traveled without luggage. The first time I saw anything like this was in Sweden. I met up with an American millionaire who—and this is God's honest truth—arrived there hatless with only an attaché case in his hand. I couldn't get over it, and decided then and there that if I ever became rich I'd do what he did. Just think, how very comfortable it is to step off the train like that, not having to worry about anything. If I am cold, or if I need some-thing, I just buy it as I go along. And when I have no more use for it, I simply leave it in the hotel—let the chambermaids rejoice.

Let me add just one more thought: happiness is the highest expression of self-love, its greatest fulfillment, yet it can't be conceived of without obliviousness, without abandon. Actually, this is one of the reasons why I quoted at such length from Gregory Sanders's letter just before—because he, too, comments on this, on what it means to let go, to be free of ourselves. Well, that is exactly how I lived then. It was almost as if I wasn't on this earth any more. I was truly happy.

Only once in a great while did dreams, born of selfishness, appear before my eyes, and even then, quite faintly, hesitantly, in the following form, for instance:

I roam the French countryside until I spot a young maiden . . . Ah, how clever an invention it is in the ancient Jacob story to have him catch sight of that girl quite suddenly, near a well, and learn that they are distantly related. That's what I would need, I say to myself, someone who would not need any explanation about myself, who would know all there was to know. She'd know *me*, God only knows how or from where, from which secret recess of forgotten time.

There was this sign in the café window—I still remember the two names: Los Vivienos and Carricada, Spanish musical clowns, and underneath it in big letters: DODOFÉ. But all of that was long gone, the café was empty, only a few glass lamps flickered inside—it's true it was almost three o'clock in the morning, yet very much nighttime, totally dark, and stormy, too.

Actually it was a beautiful winter storm, the kind in which oversized snowflakes swirl hypnotically about, like so many cherubs, in the great blackness.

All the murdered children, I thought . . . Who the hell knows what was going through my mind?

I had just gotten off the train and thought I'd sit out the night in this café. I have always liked such places with their papier-mâché roses on the wall and the mirror. A nice fire was still crackling in the stove, so I sat down nearby. Behind me there was a wall-hanging, also made of paper, with painted swans swimming in some lake.

It was quiet in the place, quiet all around, with only a single waiter on duty, and even he was pretty sleepy, though after a while he perked up. When I ordered a bottle of champagne and some brandy to go with it, that's when.

But the room itself seemed to stir in response to my voice, I somehow sensed attentiveness in the air. Actually, it started earlier. From the beginning I had the distinct impression somebody was standing behind that wall-hanging, possible more than one person, and they were all listening. And—what do you know—I was right.

I took a closer look and saw there was a little hole near the edge of that drapery, and in that hole I could discern the gleam of a human eye.

Well, well, I thought to myself, something's going to happen here, after all. There is no denying that until now I'd been criss-crossing France, this wicked land, as though it were some garden paradise. And I couldn't be more light-hearted and carefree doing it. In spite of the stories one kept hearing. A foreign professor disappeared without a trace. (So what? He probably didn't weigh two hundred-fifty pounds.) An Egyptian lady was slain on the train. (Poor dear; what a cheerless death.) . . . I could go on.

This time, though, I was a bit startled. To see that eye in the hole *was* rather disconcerting. And I happened to have quite a lot of money in my pocket.

So, the next few minutes were sheer agony, as if the passing seconds were moving across my taut nerves in the manner of tightrope-walkers. But then all that passed, dissolved into something amazing.

A young man emerged from someplace, an incredibly young man, all dressed up in silks. He was so white, his tunic so sheer and sleek, I hardly dared to look . . . This man was Dodofé.

A regular little chap otherwise, with modest sidewhiskers and bright rosy cheeks. All in all, a modest chap, truly—he very politely nodded towards me, even bowed when he saw the champagne. Then he stretched, walked around for a bit, looked outside at the snowfall, acting like a man who had been sleeping in some corner and just awakened. Finally, he asked where Lizzy was—asked the waiter, that is, not me.

"Lizzy," he cried cheerfully.

At that point I put down my glass.

It all seemed like a vision. A man wrapped in silk, the paper flowers and all . . . and that weird storm outside . . .

Is this where she ended up? I asked myself. Is it possible??

Yet, how can I ever describe the effect a single word can have on the human heart. Lizzy, he said.

Once, long ago, I also said Lizzy. It wasn't even that long ago; it *seems* like yesterday. In all that time, though, the name never once passed my lips.

Must be a rare name. I never once heard it since then.

Oh God, *did* she end up in this place?

I never would have believed it . . . though I could imagine her doing plenty of strange things. But the mere thought that this is why she went to Spain, to do this, and that same road should lead her back here . . .

Then again, that's what she wanted to be: an actress . . . always.

At any rate, I had this absurd feeling that she was right here with me in this room. It was more than a feeling, it was certain knowledge. I was caught up in a mad whirlgig by now . . . She *was* there, I would have staked my life on it. And quite close, too, no more than a few paces away.

Why of course she was here, she even saw me just before, why sure . . . The one staring at me, that was her . . . that's why she's afraid to show herself.

"The bill please," I called to the waiter. But then . . . then all the blood rushed to my heart.

I'll wait for her, I suddenly decided.

Why not? What's the sense of running away? Maybe this is what's been foreordained for us: that we shall each roam the world, on our own, until one day in such and such location, in this very dive, we shall accidentally meet. But then why should I run away? Why couldn't we meet and talk for a while?

Why couldn't I just see her for an instant. . . ?

As I was saying, I couldn't adequately describe the pressure I felt in my heart. Nor the terrible and melancholy longing, which then found all sorts of expression, revolting expression, too, let's be totally honest about it.

An early morning fling was what I was really after, and with the person I had once loved so much. It was an intriguing and utterly shameless feeling. But you see, it was lightness I wanted, pleasure without consequences, without soul; I wanted to pretend I had never seen her before. And that is why my heart was racing so . . .

But then it passed. This Lizzy person turned up; it seems she had been sleeping, too—another sleepyhead. She was a heavy, sluggish, disheveled-looking woman with matted hair. Presently, she threw a black robe over her husband's shoulder—these folks from the south must shiver in this snowy weather . . . And by then, what I took to be a vision melted away.

But I remained seated for a while longer; I was tired.

Just then soldier boys streamed into the café, soldiers on morning duty. Not even young officers but ordinary conscripts. And what seemed amazing was that they overran the place, like mice, in a matter of minutes. I had no idea where they were coming from.

By then I was really getting ready to leave. In a wink of an eye, in a flash, I decided so much . . . I will relate only the essentials.

I must never ever see her again; I mustn't even think of the possibility of meeting her. I had resolved this before, but now I felt stronger about it, more adamant. Or rather . . . but this is precisely what I have trouble expressing.

It's true I had made up my mind long ago not to see her again; yet the hope in me could never be extinguished that this would only be temporary, and that one day we would talk again. If not here, then in another life. I had a gentle feeling about this, a feeling that promised great calm, ultimate calm.

So when this strange plump woman entered, this other Lizzy, I got so depressed, I said to myself:

Why don't you look her up? So you travel a day to get there and another to return—half hour is all you would need.

And hence the new vow. Because this momentary weakness, this faltering, was frightful. And this is the thing I couldn't possibly explain. But why try even? My sufferings are mine alone; whatever I learn from them are lessons only for me. The justice inherent in suffering can be known only by he who *must* know, who's experienced it. I may protest again and again that I shall be stronger, but words remain words, and I've had enough of them.

Only this much I knew: neither here nor in the hereafter; never again.

Remember those morning soldier boys, I instructed myself. And only I could say what lay at the bottom of that instruction.

And thus my adventures came to an end. I forced myself to go on traveling a while longer, but the old thrill was gone. Before long I returned to Paris for good.

Let me backtrack a little now, for I just realized I had completely forgotten about something. While still in London it occurred to me that as long as I was there I might as well have another look at the place where my life took such a radical turn—the house where they had that ball. Let's just see how it looks in broad daylight, I said. And who knows: under some pretext or other I might even be able to make my way into the salon. Well, it worked. I found Madame Poulence in the telephone book—the address was still the same . . .

Only thing was I got there too early. I have this habit, you see, of getting up at the crack of dawn and as a result I misjudge things—

eight or nine o'clock for me is not nearly as early as it is for many other people. But I realized of course that it's bad manners to ring somebody's bell at that early hour.

But no matter . . . Let me just retrace my steps. I had other plans that morning, actually; I wanted to see other things as well. As long as I came this far, I decided, why not follow the same route—the one I took going home after the ball?

And this, too, turned out better than I expected. The sun began to shine gloriously, and I, too, was urged on by some fortuitous instinct. Of course at times like these one is also guided by certain associations and inferences, like where did I walk past a theatre, where exactly did a sidestreet join a thoroughfare, on which side did I spot the dome of St. Paul's, and so on. It so happened I remembered all the details—remembered them so precisely, in fact, so sharply, I was quite surprised myself. For apart from minor slip-ups, I found everything I was looking for: the pillared gateway where I tore off my beard, that tiny street where I slipped and almost broke my foot—except the square where ill fate had me confront that cabdriver, that I couldn't find, not for the life of me. It seems to have vanished, or been swallowed up by this huge city. Or was the square built up? Is it possible? I tried in vain to explain to people that there was a church somewhere nearby—I clearly remembered the flickering lights in the windows, and faint organ music floating through the mist (at the time I was even surprised at that: a mass with music at this hour? or was somebody practicing?). At any rate, I was walking up and down now for hours, the midday bells had already been rung, but nothing. The square seemed to have disappeared off the face of the earth.

I felt badly about this. And although it wasn't feelings of melancholy or grief or anything like that made me come here, I did in the course of time develop a kind of attachment to that old man. Not only did I feel sorry for him, his sad fate rather interested me—the odd happenstance, for example, that brought us together. . . . Why did he have to die? My rage at that time sprang from quite a different source, yet I went ahead and broke his neck—wasn't that a monstrous deed? To make him the victim and myself the instrument of that rage?

In spite of all that, however, I was neither agitated nor sad, really; I contemplated these scenes of past turmoil rather indifferently. Though not when finally *the* door opened before me, and I walked through the same Gothic archway once again. By then my stomach had risen all the way to my heart.

For this *was* different, you see. It was the place where my life had suddenly turned around . . . For ever since then—let's come out with it finally—I am not really alive any more . . . Oh, I go through the motions, I eat, I run around, still I am not at all convinced I am alive. Could *anybody* be that fatally important to a serious and mature person? Least of all a two-legged caterwauler in a skirt. . . ? These are the sort of questions I used to amuse myself with. For needless to say, I refused to believe it could actually be so, except when I walked through that pseudo-Gothic entranceway.

Though the extraordinary impact of that moment could also have another explanation. Some of our memories we put to rest. We do not recall them, we never wish to evoke them, they seem to run their own course in the heart. The yesterday of such memories is not the real yesterday but the last time we contemplated them. I myself have never thought about this house; the cabdriver was often on my mind, but never the house. The fateful, tragic events of my life I keep quiet about. Their memories reside within me, lodged there like a bullet, sentenced to utter silence.

You were sitting right here in this garden, I said to myself. And it did seem like yesterday that I was here; that garden seemed so close. I was only going home to change or something . . .

I hadn't bothered to go back to the ballroom downstairs, I just didn't have the strength. When I came down from the studio I said to myself: Enough.

Actually, there was nothing special about that studio—it was an informal acting school, that is all, a preparatory course for film-acting, something like that—big cities are full of them. As I later learned, Mme. Poulence set it up for her older sister who was sick or something. A retired ballerina she was, that's it . . . She not only gave dancing lessons but taught you how to move gracefully, and oh yes, how to court, how to love . . .

There were expensive cars parked in front of the house, young men in top hats darted to and fro in the hallway . . . From under their half-closed lids their eyes glistened coldly, like water. These privileged gentlemen are so cool, they never let you know they noticed you.

Oh, I know how magical, how delicious it could be to neck with some Persephone in a darkened studio, while a play is in progress, with the young lady herself still panting, still affected by those classical passions. Idle gentlemen in every age are given to such diversions. But to think that the one I once loved could come *here*, could find pleasure in *this* . . .

This was merely one side of the coin, though; the other side was this:

At times like these the notion of near and far plays tricks on your nerves. For all this seemed to have happened only yesterday, yet where was that yesterday. . . ? In the unreachable distance, as far removed as the dead. Impenetrable fog, cries, gestures, confusion separated us . . . And what lay behind all that were clearly those sleepless nights when I endlessly tossed and turned in bed, or those afternoons, when I walked down the agave-lined promenade with the already mentioned young lady, whose tress was as beautiful as her demeanor, and tipped my hat to the gentlemen passing by in their light runabouts. How very strange human life can be! How fleeting, how insubstantial. Perhaps it's best expressed by a mere sigh. Who would ever believe, for instance, that I even wore a beard in South America? That I kept lovers there— this or that mysterious Italian or other foreign lady? It's these things that are truly far away.

And still, although so much had come between us, so much time, she herself lived in me unchanged. Wrapped in a kind of enchanted, crystallized silence, she remained next to my heart, in another room as it were, which you just had to enter and there she was, immersed in silence, reading one of her odd books. That this was really so I only now realized; all these years I was unaware of it, or what is perhaps more likely: unwilling to recall it. But now how I would have loved to walk into the Brighton, sit at my usual corner table, lean against the wall, and from there go home and spread out my notes and lists under the table lamp's warm glow.

This, then, is the reason I had to relate the events of that day.

For her nearness that afternoon *was* portentous. In this town, I realized, I was in her hands. Hadn't she once snatched me from death's clutches? Of course she did. The same image kept going through my mind—something I hadn't thought of in all this time: I am sick and pretending to be asleep . . . yes, pretending because I want her to get some rest, too. But just the same, she leans over and looks at me—her face is all flushed, her eyes filled with anxiety.

In other words she still loved me—that is what I wanted to prove to myself of course, and as ardently as I could. At this point I had to stop on the street. I was overcome with bliss, a sweet, sweet feeling; a radiance seemed to envelop my heart.

All because of that momentary hope that she did love me after all.

But wasn't this terrible! That the mere thought could still cheer me up?

Oh the little chatterbox . . . I kept muttering, trying to brush it all away.

To no avail, for as I said, I would have given anything to be able to go home as in the old days. That *is* where I wanted to go, nowhere else. Back to those despised rooftops, where at dawn white pigeons take to the sky.

And now that early morning encounter with a strange Lizzy in a wretched café . . . But that's when I realized I had to lock the door to that other room . . . for good.

I can hardly remember the color of her eyes, try as hard as I might. I said blue before but that may not be so. They were jade-colored, I believe, which grew deeper and darkened into blue as her emotions grew more intense, or as the weather turned gloomy.

Furthermore: Was she sweet-natured or dull? Pretty or homely? Nowadays when I see her face it's usually heavy with sleep, her hair is messed up . . . And she looks lovely.

And that about does it, too; that's the extent of my early-morning woolgathering; I indulge myself a little. This much luxury I must allow myself. For if you are the kind of person who won't take morphine or cocaine, what will you do for an addiction? What *will* I end up with if, having abandoned all hopes of a future, I also renounce my past? What should I be contemplating at the breakfast table—the pipetta I happen to be holding in my hand?

Besides, I realized something during my early-morning rumina-
tions, namely that you cannot ever get to the bottom of things. I
may turn them inside out, still I will never truly comprehend
them. Life cannot be lived through, it seems, not totally, not fully;
we merely skim the surface, dip into foam.

For if this were not so, how do I account for the doubts I
sometimes have as to whether things I desperately try to pin down
had ever actually occurred? I confess I am not entirely certain they
did. They are always ready to vanish, melt into air; memory
releases them so easily . . . But then, how *does* it all work? Is our
soul like air or water that the tempests inside can disappear
without a trace?

But looking at it another way: if I *was* able to comprehend
everything that happened, how do I then explain the fact that I
can rehash it even today and discover new elements every time . . .
and that the memories sometimes seem sweet and sometimes
bitter . . . Eh, I won't pursue it further—it leads nowhere, to
endless brooding at most. It's enough if I occasionally take the
trouble to be with her, the early-morning darkness is just the right
time for it. I wrap myself in my blanket and wait for a glimmer of
light, in me and outside. It just makes me feel good—though the
feeling would surely get the better of me if I were not my own
master. But I am. It is like a spiritual exercise: half hour of
daydreaming is permitted, after which I jump up and start the day.
For let's face it: the best antidote to this sort of addiction is still
unceasing activity. And while we are on the subject of activities, let
me briefly recount my more recent Parisian exploits. Let us begin
with the most important: I entered the university.

Not as a regular student, of course, only as an auditor. How did
this happen? Why did I decide to do it? Well, by myself I wasn't
getting anywhere with the chemistry, so I hired a tutor. But then
he left, got a job abroad somewhere. And since he had already
brought me to the university a few times, to demonstrate things in
the laboratory (he was an assistant in the Chemistry Department),
when he left I didn't bother to hire another tutor but registered
myself.

And that was it.

With that simple act I overcame all the anxiety that was inspired in me by the halls of science ever since I was a child—an

anxiety exacerbated by my advancing years. I no longer belong there, I kept telling myself . . . Except now I saw that nobody gave a damn about me, so I got an even greater urge to go through with it, was all fired up about being a student.

And I did indeed work a great deal, from morning to night, no student could work harder. Had my nose in my books all the time. To be sure, there were things here and there that annoyed me, but I got over them quickly enough. To name just one: I found the young people of today quite strange, I didn't know what to make of them.

We were different, weren't we? one feels like saying. Like hell we were; we were the same. Man remains the same in all ages, his clothes are about the only things that change—today they're somewhat shorter. And his manner is a little more forward. Maybe.

The students came in droves; they surged into the lecture halls, not with any enthusiasm even, but in great, indifferent masses, like a river, like a Mississippi. They slammed their notebooks on their desks and whistled between their teeth. What they meant to express by this was that they were tough and unyielding. Unyielding in what? I wondered. Just then I was reading Leopardi's prose works every night. Now Leopardi, I thought, was a very smart man, a great mind, and sometimes it occurred to me: what would he say about all this? He would say nothing, in all probability. In that case I don't have to say anything, either.

I even thought: Maybe this is the Communist generation.

But no, that wasn't it. Because I happened to overhear exchanges such as this:

"Do you think I am interested in a collective society?"

"Do you think *I* am?"

"Hahaha," somebody else put in; in other words there was one more person not interested in a collective society. In what, then, were they so fierce and unyielding?

In being young, you miserable old man, I scolded myself. And continued working.

There was one young woman who angered me even more, for a while anyway. She happened to be the person who was picked by my tutor to supervise my lab work.

She was a nice enough woman, I had no objections; she was

decently dressed, her ears, her nose, her feet were all right—but why was she so incredibly boring? These people are actually qualified to be boring, I thought. She wore clumsy, thick-soled shoes, her hair was brushed back, though such things were perhaps the consequence of being in the sciences. But that she should not have a kind word for an older gentleman who was so lonely and such a hard worker . . .

"That's pretty good," she'd say to me in her offhand manner. I expected more. It's childish, I know, but I did.

"That's good; that's not so good." That is as far as she was willing to go in expressing appreciation for my greatest endeavors.

Yet, I even tried my luck with her at first. Would tell her, for example: "It's overcast today." To which she answered: "Yes." When I said: "It's not, any more," she said: "No."

Just you wait, I said to myself. You'll change your tune yet. I know my own eyes. They can stare such a splendid young lady down until she gets so flustered, *she'll* be talking about the weather. And that's precisely what happened . . . But more about that later.

I continued working, with ever-growing interest, and that was the important thing. Anyway, nothing is quite as interesting as chemistry.

Anyone who hasn't tried it cannot appreciate the aesthetic pleasure that comes from making a discovery in this branch of science. Or what a thrill it is to simply observe certain transformations. Let's say I have a gas, a blue gas; I fidget with it for a while and before long it's so hard I can hit it with a hammer, in other words a gaseous substance has turned solid—isn't that a pleasure to behold? Actually, I envisaged a dandy little laboratory where the experiments would be centered around a few exceptionally malleable substances. Carbamides especially tickled my fancy; they are not only acid- and water-proof, they are never brittle—exactly the kind of substances modern industry needs. I've been hearing about them for some time.

But enough of chemistry. Every evening I read: "high-class" books, this time; not systematically, of course, but whatever the bookseller happened to recommend. That "serious" literature is not really for me is amply illustrated by my brief appraisals of these books. Needless to say, I didn't enjoy them very much. Let's see:

"Edgar Lee Masters: His tombstones are fine, the rest: forget it.
Ulysses: A real hodge-podge.
Romain Rolland: Nauseating mishmash.
Werfel (his Belgian book): Nausea again, and mishmash, too
... " And more of the same ...

But let's forget about this, literature is not my forté. It may be ridiculously naive of me to say it, but what did give me pleasure was Dickens, especially one of his books. The Christmas I spent with him I shall remember as long as I live. Outside it was raining steadily, and all day long I did nothing but munch on bread and read. And I couldn't stop, either, but read way into the night, until thoroughly intoxicated. In other words, I responded to the book the way I did to things in the most ardent period of my youth. I got up only to stare at the rain outside ... I also smoked my pipe endlessly.

This, for a change, was literature. Let me just add that the book was *David Copperfield*.

I bring all this up because my above-mentioned, unschooled comments I did convey to that scholarly young miss at the university. To my patroness. Let's call her Madmoiselle Brebant-Jouy. We've gone far, you see, our relationship improved markedly, beyond expectations. It happened in the following manner:

Very simply, actually. I treated her exactly as she treated me. If she made a comment about my work, I began to scratch my head and stuck out my tongue, not much, just a little, as though I didn't have a good night's sleep. And I never said things like: "I am much obliged, Mademoiselle, I quite understand." In short, I didn't eagerly agree with her, or laugh politely, or look smilingly into her eyes, according to the custom of bygone, backward ages. Was it sour faces, wry looks she was after? I obliged, gladly, and behaved the way a thoroughly blasé, modern gentleman is expected—nay, requested—to behave.

And this achieved the desired effect, I must say—this and my steady gaze, which reflected neither curiosity nor indifference. It reflected—nothing; simply a glance resting on its cbject. Now imagine if you will: an experienced pair of eyes like mine persistently fixed on her flushed face or cool breasts . . . Something *is* expressed by such a look, the question is what? My little mademoiselle would have to be quite a hero not to be just a little bit intrigued by it. Every two weeks we had these *assemblées*, at which lecturers explained the latest experimental techniques, as well as other relevant material. Well, I gave her my special look even then. Not very conspicuously, but still . . . Then I stopped and abruptly looked away, as though I had already forgotten she was there.

On one of these occasions I discovered that now *she* was doing it. And getting to be very good at it. She wasn't looking at me, it's true, but at my pencil, but so intently even her eyes quivered. As if searching for an answer to a most nagging question: Won't she *ever* get married? She was also panting a little.

What's more, her face turned red as soon as she discovered that I was looking at her.

That's all right, I thought, that's just the way I want it. And it was.

Shortly after this she did open her mouth. Wonder of wonders: she deigned to address me.

"It's hot in here," she said to me. But still in her superior, offhand manner.

She just happened to be analyzing some color compounds, and pressed her full bosoms against a stand that was used to hold some of the heavier instruments, though it happened to be empty now. From the pressure these breasts were pushed up and thrust out. That they were quite nice I will not deny. The sun happened to shine on her hair just then, and seemed it set it ablaze. That her hair was lovely, too, I will not deny, either.

She was blonde, like the Swedes. (Except that she came from a Croatian family on her mother's side, as I later found out.) What is more, she was slender, especially around her waist.

In spite of that I didn't feel like responding with some helpful inanity; I didn't jump up to open the window, either. Instead of this old piece of idiocy I chose the new kind, which is to disagree, disagree at all cost, damn it, to show you have a mind of your own. So I said to her:

"It's not that hot." Even though it was.

"Pardon?" she said at first. Then she thought of something better.

"Why of course . . . You were a sea captain, you got used to the heat."

I was again quite pleased. It's true, even sea captains can be hot if the weather is such, but she did say the magic word. . . . What exactly did she mean by it, though?

Well, what did you? I looked into her eyes. For one thing she knew who I was. That's something. And what else? That we can now start a charming little conversation. But I showed no inclination to do that right now. Instead, I fixed my expressionless eyes on her, and with the mysterious tenacity of animals I said to her, smilingly:

"Quite true, quite true . . . "

And so the thing continued. A few days later I had some reading matter with me, and she did me the honor of looking at the title. I had just picked it up in the shop—it was a book by John Bunyan who is a classic only in England. But as the bookseller impressed it on me that no educated person can pass over this work, I bought it. I thought that perhaps I could become religious—that might lead to something. My lady friend, as I said, picked it up, leafed through it, then put it down.

"Is this a religious book?" she asked breezily.

"Yes," I answered; "The only reason I am reading it is because the author is a friend of mine." How do you like that? Of a man who's been dead for three hundred years I said he was my friend. But who cared? She didn't know who Bunyan was anyway. And if she did, let her be perplexed by what a man of mystery I was. Yet all that is not enough, I realized. We need a little more—but what? A little heroism, confound it, which has the same effect on the female soul today as it did in the time of Lancelot and those other jousting knights. It will peel the papier-mâché façade off these grim little scientists' faces, and we'll all discover that they are pussycats at heart, sappy schoolgirls, even my little Mademoiselle. This is roughly what happened. The lab assistant wasn't around and she needed oxygen badly, or else her whole experiment would have gone to waste.

So I picked up a metal oxygen tank (it must have weighed around a hundred pounds, I dare say), cradled it in my arms as you would an infant, and gently set it down in front of her. Let her feast her eyes on it. She started blinking a little, was already touched by this display, I think. But we still had problems. That tall metal stand (the one that was empty before) was in the way again, the oxygen pipe didn't quite reach, so the whole thing had to be moved. Now the stand weighed about 200 pounds, I would say.

I waited a while—let her first struggle with it. Only when she was cursing away under her breath (this, too, is part of the tough girl image, I suppose) did I take hold of that heavy piece of metal and with one swift move swung it aside. This she could no longer pass over in silence.

"You are that strong?"

"Eh, it's nothing," I replied, but so contemptuously, so haughtily, the Princess of Guise would have been impressed.

A few days later—what do you know—the two of us went to a concert together. She told me she had an extra ticket for sale. We know all about such extra tickets. I thought to myself: I am such a boor, I know next to nothing about music, though at one time I did decide: I'll be a connoisseur of this, too. But why shouldn't she be explaining certain things to me? I found out, you see, that she just loved explaining, it was a passion with her. Though I also realized that I was right—she *was* simply a wide-eyed, eager kid.

She was telling me all about music—why this piece is so beautiful, why that is even prettier, etc. . . . Because from that point on, you see, we went to all kinds of concerts together; at least two of my evenings every week were spoken for—I couldn't really complain about my social life. Even less so because she usually brought her sister along, an even younger, slighter creature, but with a shock of hair ever so resplendent. What is more, she had eyes that were so gullible, and at the same time so brazen and provocative, she would have been ready, as a revolutionary, to prove *all* her points. I dare say that even a graying gentleman like myself could not help but respond with quiet gladness to those burning eyes. Oh, and when they started arguing on the way home . . . Because they did, every time. I deliberately slowed down, to make the pleasure last. Needless to say, this meant more to me than all the musical surprises in the world.

"When I get married," said the little one to me on one occasion, "I want to be one with my husband in *every respect.*"

You sweet little thing; I love you, I said to myself. But showed nothing.

Because you've got to handle these creatures very gently, cleverly, like you would a stray puppy, avoiding abrupt moves, so as not to frighten them away. So I said nothing, or maybe this much, and even that very solemnly:

"Oh yes, miss, you are absolutely right."

"You see, monsieur agrees with me," she said right away to her sister. (She couldn't remember my name, or didn't want to. We even talked about this. "I can't for the life of me remember your name," she said to me on one occasion when we were alone. "But you won't be cross with me for that, will you?" And she was quick to console herself: "What's in a name, anyway? All it does is prejudice you. What difference does it make what you are called? Main thing is whether a person is kind and generous . . . isn't that so, monsieur?"

I assured her that it was most definitely so, and that I do happen to be kind and generous. Whereupon she commented that I need not mention that, she discovered it already.

But how did you, my dear girl? How did you discover that so quickly?

I should leave that to her, she said; she was a pretty good judge of character . . . But let me go back to describing their discussion of marriage.)

"Why should an independent girl like me get married, if not for psychic fulfillment?" she asked her sister. "Mere sensuality does not interest me."

I was even happier to hear that. And what else could I have said to her but this again:

"Oh yes, miss, you are absolutely right."

"See that? Monsieur here also has the correct idea on the subject?"

"Because he happens to agree with you?" the older sister laughed.

"Not only because of that, but in general, because he happens to be on the right track." I was beginning to be proud of myself.

On just what issue did I agree with her? On everything, I think.

In all honesty, I didn't pay much attention to the discussion itself, only to the details . . . to the tone of their voices. I was a little like a gold panner who is oblivious to mother nature and is interested only in scooping out the precious stuff from the river. The little one's voice tinkled right in my heart—no chime could produce that sound. What did I care about those hifalutin sentiments about marriage when I had this . . . Now it was the older one's turn:

"You are such a little ass when it comes to understanding pivotal institutions." (I figured expressions such as "pivotal institutions" were as much a part of the spirit of the age as "little ass.")

She also said that marriage as a permanent institution was a thing of the past.

"Can't you see that? Are you blind?" That's just what she asked her. Of the little one. If she was blind. When she had such bright, beautiful eyes.

"Anyway," she continued, "where will you find people today who could stand living with each other for, say, forty years . . . Forty years!" this sweet creature exclaimed, the older one did (by now I found her sweet, too). But the younger sister quickly retorted:

"Go ahead, make yourself look ridiculous in front of monsieur." This one was defending devotion with all her little might, maintaining there *was* such a thing under the sun, devotion unto the grave, unswerving devotion.

"Yes, I do believe in being faithful," she said, "and in having one great love." Poor me. In spite of my own bitter experience in this area, I was touched to no end by what she said. That's man for you—an odd creature, I tell you; there is no end to his peculiarities. And how quick she was to defend me:

"That's right; monsieur here is a very objective monsieur. I happen to like him a lot and think we might be able to win him over to the cause." She said this as soon as we settled down. (For one night, after the concert, I did get them to stop in at a café with me. I'd been meaning to suggest it for some time but until now did not dare to actually come out with it.)

To what cause were they trying to win me over? I kept asking them, but got no answer. In fact, they left me out of their conversation altogether.

"Yes, all that sounds very nice," declared the older sister, "but there are things you don't know."

"What don't I know?"

"That our cause requires not just impartiality but passion, too."

"And I am not passionate enough?" I cried, overwhelmed with pleasure; but they paid me no mind.

"Because you don't know men yet: how careless and indolent they can be."

"*I* am careless?" I asked her, imploringly, but also radiantly. Because by now the argument was over me, my very own person; in my presence they were discussing me and ignoring me completely. Yet, all this made me feel wonderful, as if I was being tickled or something.

"Come on now, miss, that's not a nice thing to say. Am I not a hard-working student; don't I knock myself out? And don't I go out of my way to earn your approval?"

"It's not a question of hard work," said the older one ... "Would you have killed Barthou, for example?"

"That's right," chimed in the other. "Or Trepov, or Uncle Drenteln, for that matter?"

"Kill, did you say? Ladies, please ... I don't even know who Uncle Drenteln is. What *are* you talking about? Is this some sort of a joke?"

"Not at all. We meant every word we said, every single word." They were both at it now, as militant as ever.

"Please answer our question, monsieur. Openly, truthfully."

"Yes, don't try to skirt the issue."

"But for God's sake, ladies, what have I to do with Croatian politics?" (I suddenly remembered that these men may be enemies of Croatian independence.)

"This is not merely a Croatian question," one of them said. "And we'd be surprised if you were not interested—very surprised, for it would reveal a great deal about you.

"Oh yes, a very great deal ... But didn't I tell you? This gentleman has no convictions."

"Monsieur, I am afraid we are worlds apart," the older one declared. But luckily, the waiter showed up just then.

* * *

So in this political matter I fell flat on my face, and just for that I became cautious and ordered only grog for everybody. But the girls also wanted some egg nog, so I ordered that, too. I was in a quandry, actually, as to which one of the lovelies I should love. But in a way, the thing was decided already. I picked the little one, if only because she kept calling me monsieur (wheres the other one didn't call me anything). And this was enough of an honor, I dare say; I loved my new title. If she didn't say anything all night besides monsieur, monsieur, I would still have been overjoyed.

But how was I going to handle Croatian foreign policy?

"We are members of the C.G.T., you know," declared the younger sister, a little more gently by now, licking the spoon with which she had been stirring her egg nog. (In the meantime the other one went to make a phone call, to tell their folks not to wait up for them.) "But don't mention this in front of Madeleine," she added. "She wouldn't like it."

Member of the C.G.T. . . . how mysterious, I thought, and almost began to laugh.

"What about you? What are you?" she asked.

"What do you mean what am I? I am nothing. Just a crazy Dutchman, my dear girl."

"Don't 'my dear girl' me."

"I won't. But you *are* a dear, and you are still a girl."

"Perhaps. But not yours."

"All right, not mine. If you insist on being so heartless. But let me just remind you that you are not entirely right. For as long as I can look at you, you *are* a tiny bit mine. You had better get used to the notion, mademoiselle."

"In that case I'd much rather put on a veil," she said. "If I am to be subjected to such bullying."

"Bullying?" I laughed. "Will you deprive us even of this small pleasure? Don't put on a veil," I pleaded, "please don't. I'll be more modest, I promise—modest and sad."

"Don't be sad."

"All right, I won't."

"But how is it that you have never joined . . . that you've not been accepted . . ." She suddenly remembered what we had been' talking about before; naturally, she would not be sidetracked. "How is it possible?" she said, quite exasperated. "You've never given any thought to political convictions; never to the party of your choice?"

"No, but I will now," I said rather guiltily. "I will try to make up for my negligence; you will see how very hard I shall try. And do you know why?" And here I looked deeply into her eyes. "Because . . . I adore you . . ."

"Don't say 'adore'"

"All right, I won't."

"Because it's such a hackneyed word . . . such a dubious, thoughtless bit of gallantry."

"It's not thoughtless, I swear . . . And I'll prove it to you. By doing whatever you ask me to. You will call the shots; I will obey. And make you see it was much more than thoughtless, idle talk."

At this she did turn serious, finally. And said that in that case, I should be willing to give away my fortune; for they had heard how much money I had, and what a beautiful house I maintained. "But what's the good of all that?" she asked, turning her radiant eyes on me. "Why own all those treasures? When there is so much poverty in the world? Why don't you use your fortune to support a worthy political cause? Or share it with the needy—there are plenty of those around . . ."

But was it also true, she continued, that I was very strong, as strong as an athlete? It was, I said. (And blushed probably.)

"That's quite important, you know. Don't let it ever bother you. Physical strength can be very useful to us at times." And she looked into my eyes rather significantly.

It was Monsieur Peti who told them all this, she went on. (He was the man who had tutored me and then left for America.) But she was sorry to say that this Monsieur Peti was not an honorable man. He led Madeleine on, and that's why her poor sister was so sad all the time . . . I did understand what she was getting at, didn't I . . . ? He promised her he'd marry her, yes. But all this was a secret, of course, and heaven forbid that I should let on in front of her that I knew about it . . .

The poor dears. Only now did I understand her awkward, hesitant moves, or why she would sometimes toss her head back and stare out the window, into the vacant air, toward America, I shouldn't wonder. Oh the poor, poor dears . . .

But then we drank champagne, and from that they lit up like so many little lightbulbs. And they gazed at me with their sheepish eyes . . . happily almost, though uneasily, too. I had to reassure them, inspire their confidence, lest they take fright again.

So I started thinking . . . I really opened up and *talked* about things. Things like . . . like music, for instance. I praised music, classical *and* contemporary; told them how much I loved it. Whereas the truth of the matter is that I realized, at these concerts more clearly than ever before, how much music bored me—much of it, at any rate. It could be I am way off on this, but I'll put down my thought anyway. I consider the direction art is heading in to be hopeless—a blind alley. Because it is overblown in its means; the apparatus simply got to be too big . . . though it's no use complaining, of course. It's well known that nothing is more tempting for a composer, nothing can lead him more astray, than this technical overabundance. Yet, with more modest means art becomes warmer, more intimate . . . That's all I really wanted to say. A few voices, a light accompaniment, the way it was when the lute was in fashion, or small orchestras, chamber groups—who needs more? Yet, today we have homophony, polyphony, what have you—a thousand different tonalities, combinations, and for hours on end, until you are dead tired just listening to it.

What about the masterpieces created with these riches? someone might ask. Yes, the masterpieces; nobody who's admired them can simply disavow them. Yet, truth to tell, they, too, tire me out, their brilliance does . . .

What is more, there are all sorts of adagios in this new type of music, which abuse the right to be effusive, and I don't like that, either . . . that insubstantial quality, about which I never know just what it wishes to evoke in me—my first love, grief, what . . . I am expressing myself in very rough, general terms, I know, but I am essentially on the right track, I think. For the more definite and recognizable an emotion, the better; on the other hand, the more formless and indistinct it is musically, the more disquieting it becomes. But enough theorizing; needless to say, I didn't share my doubts with *them*—why should I have? If I did, our evenings would be finished, I couldn't go to any more concerts with them. Why deprive me of these lovely children's company?

I won't do it, no sir. Soon they had this to say to me:

"Please, don't neglect to look into Madame Kollontay's books, we beg of you. A man of such refined sensibility as yourself must get to know her."

Tears came to my eyes, I tell you. For these two darlings went as far as joining their hands together, in a gesture of prayer. . . . They were tipsy, the little darlings, and were exuding the spirit of youth. Which may be muddled or sickly green, yet for me it remains most beautifully evergreen, and as such must be admired.

"I hope you know, monsieur, that we really like you," said my sweetheart, the young one. "We like you a lot, dear, kind monsieur. And that's nothing to trifle with."

Should I now have frightened them with my scientific theories, with my views on life and death or this heartache called love? Wouldn't that have been an outrage? So I lied instead. Somebody has to take it upon himself to lie. As a rule it's the older person who does . . . And he is right, the poor devil.

On the street I delivered myself of the following admonition: "You naughty, naughty girls. Going home this late?" And I laughed heartily. Night was gone; the new day rose from the teeming darkness like a shimmering emerald. I took the two girls' arms, because they were rather weak on their feet. And continued thus:

"You could be my daughters, the two of you. In the morning you'd be off to school; but before that, you would say: 'Give us some money.'

"But I wouldn't give you any, I'd pretend I didn't want to. You'd have to stretch out your little hands. And I'd laugh to myself and think: What do I need sweets for . . . at my age? But they love it, these naughty, good-for-nothing children."

I avoided looking at them, though, because I simply got too emotional.

"And now it turns out that I love the two of you," I said more to myself than to them. "Yes, yes, that's just how it is, why deny it? I love you both, really."

The two little sisters looked at each other.

"I adore you. And what this will lead to I don't know." I even explained this a little further. Told them I didn't want to tempt fate, or make myself ridiculous, I explained all that. But then, suddenly, I said this:

"Just look at that dawn, isn't it beautiful? As if it just wanted to take off and fly away . . . Yet, it never does."

But what *is* one to make of all this? Who will explain it to me? How can I, or anyone, believe that all this beauty is here only to make man miserable?

And I *do* want something out of life, how do you like that? I said this defiantly, to an unseen opponent. As there has always been a wild streak in me, I could hardly hold myself at bay now, and was pacing my rooms all night long, furiously, hatefully.

Should I maybe help fate alone and lower my head, too, so it could strike me down even easier?

I will marry her, by God, come what may. Provided she'll have me, of course. She just may, you never know. She did tell me how much they both loved me. And that this was no trifling matter.

But *how* could it be, for God's sake, especially for a man such as myself? Where will he end up, what will he ever accomplish, if he just manages to get by, timidly, and at the same time squeamishly, too. . . ?

Hang it all, shouldn't I rather live a little? If it doesn't work out, I can always do something about it.

That was one day. On the very next, I thought all this was sheer nonsense. Unworkable, unfeasible. Fatally flawed. And as always at such times, I kept examining myself in the looking glass.

"The fox is the same, only the pate is grayer," my father liked to say. And now me; that's where I am at. For this thing creeps up on you, oh yes. It wasn't even my hair that was gray but my lips, under my eyes . . . those pale shadows here and there. And this simply *had* to be noticed by anyone so affected.

Except it was no use. I could offer myself any explanation I wished, there is no remedy for bedazzlement. It came over me even more forcefully in my sleep. In one of my dreams (only Father Barham's legends or Tenniel's drawings had such a profound effect on me), I implored a giant named Fion Cumhall to let me live a little longer. For he did vanquish me, alas, and what had never happened before: his foot was on my throat.

But I tried to reason with him: "What good will it do you to kill me?" And what was also a first: I begged him to spare me because I was still young, my time hadn't yet come.

It's quite true; in this dream I was merely eighteen years old. And pale and skinny.

I will marry her—that's where I was just before. Or I'll marry the other, the older one, I suddenly thought. It will be lovely. I'll be able to see her at least. I'll arrange it so that she will have lunch with us every Sunday. For never to see her again . . . no, I couldn't take that.

The little one was called Louise, and she was ever so slight, my Louise was. She had big, serious eyes, but no breasts, no curves, only a brooding hardness. And it was precisely this hardness I was in love with . . . Or is the mere thought that something like this can still happen to me downright ridiculous? I didn't ask. Anyway, in front of whom should I have been embarrassed at this point? Everytime I was with her I had the feeling that this world—creation!—was a worthy piece of work after all. Not art or music or things invented by man, but she.

Oh, and when she got sick . . .

What emptiness, what yawning boredom at those concerts. The older one was sitting right next to me, but even that didn't help. In fact I thought: how can I marry her if she keeps yawning that way?

And when she finally showed up after weeks of absence—how strange that was, too. I spotted her right away, as soon as she entered, though there were lots of people in the hall, a full house, quite a crush, actually. But it was almost as though the hall itself rose a little and became brighter—I had this distinct impression. In short, I had not been this heady since my youth.

Let me just point out that Madeleine was only three years older than her kid sister, yet she would have been willing to marry me, I could already tell. Were there any indications? There always are. For example, she began to fix my tea, too, of late . . . Actually, this may not mean all that much; at the university it's customary to do that for a fellow student. But the way she took care of me now, gently, subtly, asking me if I was tired, if it wouldn't be better to go home, and so on . . . And what was most revealing: the way she accepted my flowers. For now I brought her flowers almost every day, a few stems or even a small bouquet, and as I was usually there early, I simply put it on her desk without saying a word. And she didn't comment on it, either. In this silence lay the true meaning of the moment. As she picked up the flowers, put them in water, nursed them, nestled them . . . every movement she made expressed the significance of the act. And the flowers, placed in a clean glass, stayed on her desk, right next to her laboratory reports, until evening.

In a word, the message was clear, there was no mistaking it.

But if she was willing, then perhaps the little one was, too, dear God . . . Why wouldn't she be? Three years is not that much of a difference.

But then one day I got very scared. It happened the very night she came to a concert again. She was standing under a huge chandelier, surrounded by people, and naturally looked rather wan, but brightened up as soon as she glanced over my way. She immediately left the group . . . and oh the gleam in her eyes . . .

"Oh, my sweet monsieur," she said radiantly, "I am so glad to see you." And in front of everybody pressed my hand to her heart.

"But we will remain friends, won't we?" she whispered. For just then Madeleine arrived.

And that was the word. It turned me melancholy in an instant. For what could she mean asking me if we'll stay friends? She didn't leave me hanging too long:

"I talked about you with Madeleine," she whispered to me during the concert, and in her silly way she added: "We both know what a respectable, eligible monsieur you are."

In other words, I should go ahead and marry Madeleine; this had been decided for me.

Oh, those damn flowers. What have I done again?

I should add that this concert, too, was overlong, and incredibly boring besides—maddening, I dare say. They performed the ravings of a famous gusher named Mahler for two and a half hours straight; my soul just about shriveled up, my nerves, on the other hand, began to rear like horses.

And no wonder. I was really beginning to get ill from music, especially such music. For just think: at least five hundred different tones could be heard, there was even a huge organ and choruses up in the balcony . . . The composer must have said to himself: Why not? Let them ring out, let them blast away, damn it. And blast away they did. The horns by themselves, the double basses by themselves, then altogether, all five thousand of them, until even the ceiling seemed to be swaying back and forth.

Now at least I won't have to put up with this bloody racket, I thought. I've had enough—of this as well as all my other twisted and murky affairs. I am through playing hide-and-seek, I've had it.

And just then—what timing!—they said they wanted to stop in someplace for a drink.

"I'd love to have a capucino," said the older sister.

"I'd love some egg nog," put in the little one. Sweetly, demurely. And smacked her lips just a little. But then she remembered:

"Oh Lordie, what am I doing? I have just gotten out of bed." It occurred to her, it seems, that this was the right moment for her to take off and leave the two of us alone.

"The very idea," she said, somewhat annoyed, as though she were blaming us for trying to lead her into temptation. For of course, in her heart she was rather conflicted about that egg nog. Still, she was ready to sacrifice herself, the poor darling . . .

"Don't worry about me," she said sullenly. "I can go home by myself." And sure enough, she began to walk without so much as glancing back.

Just as well, I thought to myself. At least I'll be able to get everything off my chest. It's better this way.

So without delay I began to present my views on music.

And not in oblique parables, either, but quite openly, and I must say with such surprising ferocity, as if I wanted to devastate her with those views.

I began by saying I didn't like that music . . . didn't like it one bit. Though I may have had reasons up to now to conceal this from her, the time had come to end the silence—we'd both be better off if we told each other the truth.

"Wat a minute . . . You mean to tell me there was nothing you liked about it?" She stared at me, mildly astounded as she said this.

"Absolutely nothing," I said emphatically. (Of course I was exaggerating; needless to say there *were* things I liked. But that's what happens when repressed anger suddenly erupts.)

"I didn't like it at all, miss. I think these works are dull—dull as a stick of carrot."

My skin tingled with pleasure as I said this; I felt exhilarated for having come out with it at long last.

What I found astonishing, though, was the calm, the tolerance with which she greeted all this. She wasn't that surprised—she did close her eyes for a moment, it's true, but did it as one who knows full well she will pass over this and turn to the next page, as it were—unpleasant truths are often acknowledged this way by people of science.

That's just the way it is, she must have thought to herself.

And this high-minded serenity drove me absolutely up the wall. Or maybe the sad truth is that I *am* a savage at heart. Why did I have to treat her so cruelly? Or was there no affection in me, no kindness toward her? I can't even say that because there was . . . But if so, why did it give me such murderous pleasure to tell her off? As if I were pounding her head with a weeding hoe; as if I tossed a heavy sack off my heart and flung it in her face. Except that these so-called people of culture are phony even under their skin; they have no idea what art (let alone life) is really all about, and never know what to consider good or beautiful. Sophistry is the essence of their being; the question they invariably ask themselves is: How would a distinguished mind react to this? And then they gauge their own enthusiasm accordingly. . . . Then again, what's wrong with all that? Why shouldn't there be falsity in the world?

"Don't think, miss, I am all that ignorant," I said to her and looked slyly into her eyes. "Even if I do express myself clumsily . . . In my youth I gave these questions a great deal of thought."

Now I was quite worldly again, fair-minded, charming. I didn't want her to think she was dealing with some beast, some coarse *Naturbursch* who didn't know what the hell he was talking about.

"I'll have you know, miss, that at one time I played the oboe, in addition to the violin; it's not an easy combination, but with us Dutch music lovers, it is almost a tradition."

And then I told her just about everything: that oratorios were a crashing bore, with their interminable dactylic verses and arrid parlando passages—everything, in short, that preyed on my mind.

"They're just no good, these 'great' works, believe me," I said to her. "For one thing, they are far too long. And they are full of unsurprising technical displays, which are a strain on the ear after a while. For what *is* art, really . . . have you thought about that one? It's all play; froth and whimsy . . . How can we enjoy anything that doesn't exhilarate the senses, that doesn't somehow affect our spontaneity? The trouble with you people is that you confuse duty with pleasure. You want to learn, you want to educate yourself, and *think* you are enjoying yourself. You are a hard worker, miss, and are convinced you are in raptures. You feign an unquenchable thirst for culture even to yourself, and say: This is no joke, this is Bach! Consequently, even those dactyls must be splendid . . ."

She again closed her eyes, and again ever so patiently.

"And the shorter works?" she asked impassively.

"How do I know, for heaven's sake?" I was doing an admirable job restraining myself but was filled with spite just the same. "I am not crazy about them, either. Why, let's just look at this little song: 'There are things ever so small and still precious. Take pearls, take roses: they're small, yet are worth so much.' Now is this a song, I ask you? It is a philistine commonplace. The composer may very cleverly stress that a pearl, though insignificantly small, is 'sooooo very precious,' yet what's the point?* Is this what women should sing while ironing? Is this what will cheer them up while tending the baby? It nearly drove me crazy when I heard the audience going wild over this song at one of the concerts, clapping until their hands were sore."

"You were, too."

"What do you mean I was, too?"

"Oh yes," she said and tossed her head back defiantly. "You were applauding too, and how . . . And afterwards, on the street, you even remarked—I remember it clearly—how clever and simple that theme was."

"Could be," I said at first. For why blanch over things? What she said was true. She put me in my place, I won't deny it.

---

*For the sake of accuracy I offer hereby the full, original text of the song—I've looked it up since then. It was written by Paul Heyse, music by Hugo Wolf:

> Auch kleine Dinge können uns entzücken,
> Auch kleine Dinge können teur sein.
> Bedenkt wie gern wir uns mit Perlen schmücken.
> Sie werden schwer bezahlt und sind nur klein.
> Bedenkt, wie klein ist die Olivenfrucht
> Und wird um ihre Güte doch gesucht
> Denkt an die Rose nur, wie klein sie ist
> Und duftet doch so lieglich, wie ihr wisst.

(They left out green peas—that's tiny, too. Captn. J.S.)

"It could very well be," I repeated. "It happens. One says so many things during a lifetime . . ."

"Even things that go against your convictions?"

"In my despair, even that."

"What do you mean in your despair?"

"I mean out of humility."

"Out of humility? But why?"

"Do you think I know? One humbles himself, Mademoiselle Madeleine; not only me, lots of people do; many an artistic success is born this way, I assure you. You sit there in that great hall and say to yourself: These people clapping so enthusiastically cannot all be idiots. There must be something wrong with me. And maybe there *is* something lovely about the pearl being so tiny and all . . . And then you start clapping, too, as hard as you can. Because the last thing you want, miss, is to look like a fool."

"All of that I can understand. But why the enthusiasm? Why pretend to be enthralled, and then even account for the rapture? Don't you see you've overdone it? That you've been . . . playacting almost?"

"*Even that* happens sometimes, mademoiselle," I said. And slowed down because, frankly, I didn't know what else to say.

"Yes, even that. There are times when one is compelled to do all sorts of strange things."

"What do you mean compelled? You *are* being strange. Am I to take it, then, that you do not always tell the truth."

"Not always. And that's a definite not always. But how could I, miss? Life doesn't allow you to . . . You will discover it, too, and will remember my words. But you will still believe me, won't you, that right now I am being honest?"

"I guess so. But how do I know when *now* is?"

"I will let your heart be the judge of that."

"Oh but my heart has deceived me more than once," she said, throwing her head back again. (Just like at the university when, lost in thought, she smoothed back her blonde hair.) "It seems I've experienced another disappointment," she said with a smile, and signalled to the waiter to bring the check.

"I thought I would marry you," she suddenly said.

"Come again, miss?"

"Didn't you notice that I . . . I welcomed your attentions? I thought I would bind my life to yours, for a time, anyway, as long as you find me pleasing. I had the feeling, you see, that I've finally found a likable, decent man."

"Is that what you thought, miss?"

"Oh, even my little sister encouraged me; she said this time I had nothing to fear. She'll be so disappointed, the poor girl . . . But it's all the same now," she added as her eyes misted over.

By then, however, I could say whatever I liked.

Still, I wanted to know why such a trifle should make her lose her trust in me.

Even if it is a trifle, she said, it alienated her from me. She was very sorry but she felt alienated.

"For to go on acting out a role, and for such a long time, too . . . We never expected you to bring such a sacrifice."

"Wait a minute," I said; "let's not be hasty about this. You are still young, Madeleine, you haven't had much experience. Life is no joyride, you know; it can teach you a thing or two . . ."

"I know," she interrupted. "It teaches you to cheat, to be ruth-less, right? Depending on your preference. You choose it and life teaches you."

"Hold it, will you?" I said again. "You are a very smart woman, Madeleine, but you don't know everything. You have no idea what a man has to go through, how many times he must fall and hurt himself before he realizes that with the naked truth he won't get anywhere . . . he'll never be content."

"Content? Why should he be content? If it means humiliating himself?" And she blushed all over. "Anyway, I have only con-tempt for such theories. Theories which hold that we cannot exist without lies, that lies are better for us than the truth. Yes, I despise them . . . They emanate from the rubbish heap and that's where they belong."

What did I answer her? Nothing, most probably. And not only because I couldn't, because she was so right—purity is always right—but because my own youth stood before me that instant; I saw the same proud bearing, the same uncompromising sternness. I, too, had contempt for such theories then.

And with the passage of time all that is forgotten? Perhaps I myself blushed at that moment.

In short, up to that point I hadn't taken mademoiselle too
seriously. I was too busy smiling at her childlike silliness, not
realizing that I was also laughing at her cherished beliefs. That I
didn't feel like smiling any more became pretty obvious, I guess.

For after all, how low can a man sink?

As far as Madeleine was concerned, she stuck to her guns, and
with good reason, I thought. "Wait five minutes," I used to say in
my younger years to people who very zealously advocated a certain
position, only to defend the opposing viewpoint with equal enthusiasm moments later. In other words, they had no problem aban-
doning their position. I never liked that sort of thing, found it
pretty contemptible, in fact. Your original convictions do deserve
some allegiance.

As do your experiences . . . In short, I did try to plead my own
case, arguing that I was young once, too, and not that long ago,
either, or at least it didn't seem that long ago. What is more, I also
had ideals; except that ideals were one thing and experience quite
another. Of course this was something I also refused to accept—
from anyone.

"But then one day I did; and you will, too, I assure you. And
when you do, think of me. A proud young lady like you will bang
her head against the wall many more times before realizing what
this jamboree is all about . . ." I coughed up a few more of these
commonplaces, in short. Except that now she wasn't going to let
me off the hook.

I shouldn't take it ill of her, she said very seriously, but she first
began to have doubts about me when I told her that John Bunyan
was my friend.

This wasn't a pleasant thing to hear, needless to say, if only
because it happened to be true.

"Look here, dear," I said, somewhat angrier this time, "I can't
very well explain everything to you—after all, you are still both
children. It would be churlish of me, and anyway, I don't know you
that well. Should I have told you that I was an unbeliever who
wanted to believe, and picked up Bunyan for that reason? Should I
have burdened you with all my doubts and torments?"

"Yes," she answered without hesitation. "You could have
trusted me. And even if you didn't, there was no reason to say such

things. I mean: wasn't this an attempt to make me look ridiculous? I wouldn't do this to anyone, monsieur—least of all to someone I respected."

"You are quite right." And to myself I thought: I might as well tell her off . . . it hardly matters now.

"You were crazy about the music, right?" she taunted.

"How else was I going to worm my way into a kid's heart?" I countered. "Two kids' hearts, as a matter of fact." Oh, I got into the swing of it all right, the dark street resounded with my eloquence. (We were walking up and down winding passageways near the Vielle de Temple.) In other words, I fully recovered my wits, found my voice, hit upon the right arguments; and after that things went smoothly enough. I never did like to express myself too delicately. I called them annoying little ninnies, and asked her if she had any advice on how to deal with such creatures.

"I grant you, I am not worthy of their friendship," I went on. I won't ever see them again, and that's all right, too. . . . But what could I do about it? One can put up with an awful lot, that is one of the things life taught me. "Just the same, you will allow me a few parting words, won't you."

"Go right ahead," she said coolly.

"I loved you, too, but your younger sister I loved even more. (Her behavior annoyed me to no end, so I came out with it.) And do you know how I love her? Like one loves a daughter, yet not quite the same way. Miserably, in other words, perversely; with the knowledge that this is corruption itself, like everything else I was destined to go through in life. What should he do who is too old for his emotions—tear out his heart? What should *I* do, miss? You are a wise one, you're as wise as they come—you tell me."

She gave me a shocked look. And then said something to the effect that I was still fairly young, something like that, though it really doesn't matter whether or not she actually said it. Fact is she then went on to say this:

"That's all right. You were being honest at least. I'll talk to my sister, whom I love, too, of course . . . For whom I'd give my life and blood," she added, painfully, passionately. And with that she left me, most probably because tears appeared in her eyes.

* * *

322

Let's just go on, I said to myself. Actually, something happened right around then. I sat up in bed one night and asked myself: You really don't want your misery any more, do you?

No, I don't, I answered. But then I said: Yes, I do.

For that's the way man is. He goes on killing himself, tormenting himself, to silence in him the very thing that would fade away anyhow; and when it does, when it finally dies away, he looks around in great surprise: Is it possible? Could it be that he is no longer interested in his own life; in what he lived for until now: his grief, his deep-set anger? And before he knows it, he is desperately reaching out for it, like a miser trying to retrieve invested capital.

But as we know, such attempts are bound to fail. You can't dispose of your past . . . especially when you don't really want to . . . For nothing terrifies you more than to end up with nothing.

So I worked even harder than one ought to at such times. Being alone was becoming harder to take; I had no one by now save my servant boy, of whom I grew so tired, I began to treat him most cruelly. . . . Oh but let's skip the nasty details.

After what happened I left the university, of course. Actually, I managed to transfer to nearby Alfort, where at a school of veterinary medicine, chemistry was taught quite decently. I am in attendance at the school to this day. I commute from Paris four times a week and am quite satisfied with the establishment—all the more as I happened to make a couple of discoveries, one right after another, before even settling in. One had to do with a new electronic process, the other was this (I'll be brief, not to worry):

Actually, I was busying myself with something entirely different then—titration, I believe, but the result was quite surprising. The mixing of two liquids gave me the idea for a splendid new cooling process—it came to me so fast, I could hardly believe it myself. I mean, it was hard to conceive of such a sudden illumination.

The thing was so simple it spoke for itself. As soon as I combined the two liquids, everything congealed around them, they even cracked the water bowl in which I did the mixing. What was most important, though, was that the two frozen liquids could easily be separated; they were adaptable, in other words . . . And a discovery like that always opens up new vistas.

The truth is whenever I am involved in something like this, I am slow to get started—locomotive was what one of my former wife's friends called me, and that was an apt description, because I do huff and puff a lot at first, but then I take off. And there's no stopping me then, until I am all through . . .

So I buckled down and read all the books and journals I could get my hands on. For a whole week I didn't sleep, didn't even take my clothes off. But when the excitement got to be too much for me, I lay down and stayed that way. This was my old system—it never failed. Whenever I got too tense, I'd just chuck everything and start staring at the ceiling.

It was the same now. For three whole days I lay in bed in a kind of stupor, feeling pretty unhappy. What do I need all this for? I thought. To make more money. . . ? Ah, vanity . . . what a strange thing it is. One gives the very best of himself, casts it in front of others, and the only reason for doing it, it seems, is to solicit praise. And you do it for nothing, isn't that a laugh? For a casual nod of the head. (This, then, is what holds the world together— vanity. People have been saying it for a long time, and now I've come to agree with them.) Is that what I am after, that nod? And if not, why all this drudgery, when what I really want is peace and quiet . . . what I have right now, this very moment, and find so pleasant . . . since I don't even have to stick my hand out of the bed.

And still. In the end I got back into action. One night I struggled to my feet and with my still stiff and bandaged hand I began to draw diagrams. I quickly sketched out plans for two systems, I even filled in some of the details, so as to have it all on paper. This way I wouldn't have to let draughtsman in on my idea, for they would be sure to spread it around. I even thought about the manufacturers I would approach and get estimates from—for that's how you usually proceed: order each part of the planned machine from a different manufacturer, and when they're all ready, assemble a prototype . . . Well, I had the whole thing mapped out and even began thinking about the actual production, when I suddenly faltered, my spirits flagged, and I was overcome with shame.

For the heavens responded to my ambitious notions with a peal of laughter. *I* was needed to come up with a new solution? *I* had to play the inventor? Weren't there enough chemists in the world?

And *they* never thought of this possibility?

What can I say? I grew to hate chemistry and everything connected with it, including my own diligence. In short, I had only contempt for all this busywork of mine.

But what else could I possibly be after?

I heard nothing from the other side, you see, nothing from the two girls, that is, although I had been working on my project over a month and a half now, and Madeleine gave me her word, promised me when we parted at the university, that she'd apprise me of their decision as soon as possible. Though her sister was still recuperating, and therefore she didn't want to excite her unduly, she said she'd have a talk with her just as soon as her little sister got better . . . She promised this twice, using these very words.

So I waited another two weeks. But as it proved to be a fruitless extension, I came to the conclusion that the younger sister also condemned those poor, untrustworthy people who in moments of weakness or embarrassment were capable of lying through their teeth.

Except it didn't help to think that, nothing helped. Over the years I may have become adept at giving up on things, but I also grew older, and when that happens, your strength and resistance diminishes also, alas.

So what I decided one fine spring Sunday, early in the morning, was that I would look them up—that very day, it *was* Sunday after all, and they did mention it more than once that they spent Sunday mornings at home—the older one usually rested, the other wrote letters. I knew all that. And knew also that they were living with their aunt, but quite independently, meaning they could receive visitors any time they wished.

I thought to myself: Maybe I still had a chance. Why should one give up prematurely and retreat unnecessarily, permanently? I have time. I will tell them that when it comes to matters of social conscience I will defer to them without fail. I never did pay much attention to those momentous issues, I don't have a feel for them—they can make all the important decisions . . . Now could I have come up with a more honorable offer? Oh, and something for the little one: Should she fall in love with someone, I will get out of her way. That's what I'll promise them, I decided, and swear to it if need be.

There was nothing else . . . but could anyone do more than that?

As for the rest, we must submit to our fate.

And with that I left the house—it was early still, and as I said before, a beautiful spring day.

I must begin this chapter by saying that basically I live as I always had, there has been no real change in this regard. I do have a nice, pleasant house now, and I realize that is nothing to sneeze at— there aren't too many people who can say they live in pleasant surroundings. I even have a greenhouse now . . . I've always wanted one but for the longest time didn't do anything about it, God only knows why. But now I had one installed. And that's about it. Apart from the fine cigars I now smoke, that *is* the one bit of extravagance I've allowed myself, nothing more. And that is as it should be. Modesty had always been my strong suit—I've grown accustomed to the simple life, and never yearned for more. And don't now, either; that's the reason I will not buy an automobile. What do I need it for? I am not in such a hurry. Do I need another strange face, a chauffeur? My man is enough for me to handle.

Besides—and this may sound ridiculous—I love to ride on buses, even if the ride's bumpy. There I see people at least, and there's even a slight chance I may meet someone—an old friend perhaps, a captain from the old days. Oh, how happy that would make me, how eagerly I'd embrace them. I would take them straightaway to some joint, and wouldn't get off their back for at least two weeks. . . . In a word, I am alone much of the time anyway (weeks go by without my talking to a human being)— should I now bury myself even deeper, and huddle and brood in the back seat of the car, in the shade, in the dark? Must I be more miserable now than before, just because I became wealthy?

I have related all this by way of explaining why I kept riding the buses that day, too. Because I did: I criss-crossed the city several times. I was restless, it seems; I couldn't settle down.

I also walked a lot, it's true; now and then I got off the bus for some fresh air—in the Bois de Vincennes, for instance, or around the Étoile, where I think I even bought two bunches of violets. I thought: it's no big thing either to give or receive these. As a matter of fact, from the *way* they'll react to it I could figure out what to do next. If they accept it reluctantly, without much enthusiasm, I just leave.

I mulled over this a few times during my walk. Actually, I picked up speed now and then, shifted to a fast jog, then slowed down again to marvel at the city a bit. It was, as I said, a beautiful morning, a beaming, sparkling morning in the middle of April.

There were passing clouds, to be sure, but they quickly yielded to airy brightness. Such weather always has quite an effect on me, like a fast-paced drama almost. It even rained momentarily, but afterwards the sun began to shine so fiercely, it burned, as in the heat of summer. Oh it was blinding, this flood of light, with all the tiny flashes refracted in it, as if some naughty kid was annoying the world with a mirror. After a while your eyes began to hurt, and when you stopped at a doorway and looked in, all you saw was darkness.

And the stream of people—why that, too, was a flood. But they were so fresh, so spanking clean, as if they were emerging from underground bathhouses, and honoring this bright and festive morning with their bright and airy walk—the world itself seemed all lightness, without weight . . . Now we could sound the trumpets, I thought. And the color black disappeared. Or rather, now it was here, now it was gone . . . it's hard to explain. I saw a woman, for example, riding a horse on a remote bridle path in the Bois de Vincennes—it was dreamlike almost, you didn't want to believe she was real, she only half existed, she seemed to melt into a sudden atmospheric disturbance. Never have I observed such a phenomenon so intently. She was trotting along, patting the horse's neck pensively; dressed in black, she was surrounded by a kind of radiance, a halo . . . And that is just what I mean to point out: at moments like this the flashes of light seem to dance around the blackness, there is a swirling, boiling brilliance, and while the figure itself fades away, the contours seem enhanced, transfigured . . .

She ambled along, and I, too, kept on walking, in a daze. For I did calm down in the end, and grew languid from the many sensations of that morning. What was I going to tell the girls?

Chances are, nothing. I was deflected from my purpose, my plans dissolved.

And I felt good about that, relieved. And though it was almost noon by now, I was neither excited nor restless. I wasn't sad, either, even though a great deal hinged on the outcome of this morning's interview, as can be imagined. If nothing else, it was going to decide whether or not I'll stay here at all . . . in this sweet and wonderful city which I love so much. For this *was* my home; I realized only now how much I loved it. And what a strange feeling that was, too; I never experienced it before. For if I look back, I realize I never really felt at home anywhere—it may have been nice to arrive in a new place, but to stay? And here was a city at last where I did want to stay. I was surprised myself. Impressed. I even began to whistle quietly.

In my pocket was an admission slip to an evening lecture course in political theory. I enrolled in the course two weeks ago, but didn't bother to go—I've always hated theories. I also had the score of Handel's "Messiah" with me, giftwrapped for Mademoiselle Madeleine, meant to be a surprise. . . . What will Mademoiselle Madeleine say, I wondered, when she finds out that I had made a thorough study of this music? Will she be pleased or merely nod her head? I was still whistling.

During these reveries I strayed far from the center of the city, so I got on a bus again with my little bunches of violets.

After all that enchantment, though, the inside of the bus seemed cold, unfriendly. It was also empty, I was the only passenger, and I never like that. So I walked to the rear platform and for a while watched the world go by.

I also wondered what I would say to my son (if I had one), in parting, before letting him go off on his own. Perhaps I would simply describe to him how I spent this morning—he may not even need more. At any rate, advice I could not offer him.

I would talk about fleeting things, vanishings, that would be enough. For that's all the world is: playful shifts, glimmers . . . It's futile to look behind them for something more definite: systematic intelligence, a higher purpose, for there is nothing there. . . . Just as a burst of light flashes by, our own life flares up and goes out. And the world becomes a different place. What, then, would I say to my son?

I would tell him not to let his soul grow too heavy here, for if he did he is bound to be disappointed, like all the others who believe they'll remain here forever. But if he does understand the world the way God intended it: as unceasing motion; if he learns to appreciate this truth and will not do his utmost to resist it, the way I did at one time, then he will turn into a creature that will please Him . . . This is the first thing. The second is that having known both joy and grief he should not insist on yet another day, and say he needs a little more cheer, just once more the same old thing: to see the sunrise, to eat fresh bread. . . . In other words, he should not grasp at life with greedy ardor but should accept with equanimity what life has in store for him. After having tended the eternal flames, the flickers of gladness, in his heart, he has no business staying here. Whoever lives with a light heart should depart the same way.

I noticed my eyes filled with tears as I thought this through. And I was no longer certain I would visit the two young ladies—I did not wish to go there, either, alas.

For what could I tell them? Or to someone as splendid as that Amazon rider in the park this morning? Should I tell them all this? Bore them with my other experiences perhaps? One seeks solace from them, but it seems nothing scares one more than finding that solace . . .

My one desire at this moment was to go home, and without having to see even my servant's face, immerse myself in some interminable night and continue writing these notes. Because I had the feeling that these notes were the voice of my conscience, the source of my peace; any gladness left in my heart now resides in them. The only possible atonement for me is this: to render an account of my erring ways.

These lonely hours are my only counsel, and also my consolation, and the one proof that I was once here . . . I tried out life, it didn't work—what can I do? But this last thing I am not giving up. I begin to understand now what prompts some people to write. For how else can one undo the curse that is life than by recreating, reshaping, reexamining it? Like an accursed god one pounds away in complete solitude, and in one's wrath creates a new world. Out of revenge sometimes . . . or so it seems to me.

So I decided to turn back, shut myself up in my room, amidst my papers, and get ready to . . . go over my bank statements? (I really should do that.) Work some more on my diagrams? (Maybe.) But when night falls I would again get down to a more serious kind of reckoning; would try to see myself and all that has passed more clearly. For one thing I would give my boy the night off and make the tea myself—I'd smoke for a while, and leave the rest to time.

And just then, from the bus, I spotted my one-time wife—at an intersection, on the corner, the bus itself stopped for a moment. And it *was* her, nobody should talk me out of that—every cell in my body knew it, every drop of my blood affirmed it . . . Yes, it was, it had to be.

She walked along rather nonchalantly, absently even, toward the light—in a black wrap with a closed collar. I talked about the color black before and the white sparks—well, it was the same all over again: she, too, was insubstantial, a whipped-up lightness, not even a physical presence, only spirit—because she seemed so young, impossibly, incomprehensibly young, as if nothing had happened to her all this time, as if time could not touch her.

And that was it.

For who could ever describe the rest—the things that go through one's mind at a moment like that?

Suffice it to say that I even dropped my bunch of violets; it fell on the pavement. Because, as I said, I was standing on the rear platform, all the way on the edge.

And now I have to refer to a rather ordinary occurrence: You are walking up a staircase and suddenly see yourself coming towards you, that is, your reflection in a mirror, and you are stunned . . . Well, that's what this was like in a way. For it wasn't she who was walking there, but I myself, I swear—some integral part of me. It was almost as if my two eyes went out for a walk and I saw them coming towards me now. I can't tell the two of us apart any more, I get mixed up even in my imaginings . . .

At the same time she frightened me so—my mouth got parched, my throat burned, and her pull proved to be so strong, *I* myself almost fell down before her, not just my violets.

And this is again something to which I have given a great deal of thought.

Could I have received a lovelier gift from life? I described in detail just before what a tremendous impression all the things I saw that day made on me—the lights, the colors, the swelling and receding world, the tiniest flutter . . . There *are* times when you become so eager, so alert, it's almost as if you were expecting a miracle to take place. But there it was; could I have imagined a greater one. . . ? My cup ran over, that is what I really felt that day; that I reached the limit, the end of both the good and the bad allotted to me in this life. And still . . . this apparition made my blood run cold. To be in the same city with her. . . ? It was no use, I was still bent on fleeing. And this is what seems so incomprehensible to me now, this fear, the fear of staying after what had happened.

The moment I got home I said to my man: "Let's pack." I was going abroad for a longish stay, I informed him, and was leaving the house in his care, for the time being, that is, because I didn't yet know what my long-term plans would be . . . But I'd let him know. For now, I wanted him to help me pack.

But then I changed my mind.

What did I need him for? I can pack myself. So I let him go out for the night as I originally planned. I knew then that I was much better off staying alone.

"But where is that letter now? How will I ever find it?" I stood helplessly in the middle of the room, having just drawn the blinds and turned on the lights. Two of my cabinets were cram-full of papers, among them lots of overdue stuff, no doubt. I neglected even my routine bookkeeping of late. There were all sorts of things in those cabinets: cancelled checks, receipts, legal notices— so much clutter, in other words, except the one thing I was so desperately looking for.

That disappeared without a trace. I was looking for my wife's letter, of course.

The letter which, it will be recalled, I received from the manager of the Brighton, before coming here, and which I tossed into my briefcase, unopened.

But where did I put it afterwards; where could I have mislaid it? For I again dropped it someplace. Yet, I do remember holding it in my hand not long ago; I certainly remember seeing it somewhere.

So I began to empty the cabinets again, because by now I decided that no matter what was in that letter, I would definitely open it. I had to know what her last words were to me.

Yes, because that would decide my own actions.

For how was one to know? I could learn something from it even now, even after all that had happened—life's surprises are boundless. I might even find out that . . . I might even be surprised by the contents of that letter. So why retreat before the battle?

My hands were shaking uncontrollably, and in ransacking those cabinets I made an even bigger mess.

But what if . . . what if it contained nothing but hate? A parting shot, a single word, one I could never ever live down?

And maybe that's why I dreaded it so. And even burned it not too long ago. Because I did burn an awful lot of things a couple of weeks ago, after having drunk a little too much. I can't say I was actually drunk, it was simply too cold in the house. I came home very late that night. It was cold, and almost daybreak; I could see the morning twilight, but my boy forgot to feed the stove. What about all that paper? I thought. What the hell, who needs all that junk? In less than a half hour it was nice and warm in the room. I had plenty of wood, of course, but threw lots of other things in the fire as well, including pictures.

I kept only a single photograph of her, taken long before we met. She was quite young then, a student in a teacher's college. I had the picture framed and it's been on my desk ever since.

But everything else I mercilessly destroyed.

And what utter bliss it was to see it burn! Could I have thrown that in, too?

But who could make me do it? In front of whom was I so ashamed? I finally asked myself. Is there anybody here? A single human soul? Look around. And even if there was, is it someone whose laughter scared you that much? I conversed with myself in this manner for a while. Then I rummaged through my other closets.

But the letter did not turn up anywhere. After a while, however, I got another idea. And reached straightaway for the telephone directory.

One more word, though, before going on. I did find something which made me glad.

In South America this is what I wrote once on a sheet of paper:

"Just think: The Chinese would consent to stare at a flower for a lifetime, without getting tired of it. And if someone were to ask them: what is there to see in a flower, they would gently laugh."

And right afterward there was this:

"M.-Heights, by the lakes, May 2nd. Stop struggling. And think of your life in this light: you wanted pudding and got chocolate instead. But chocolate isn't bad, either; so do take what's coming to you: instead of gay Julie the pensive Cathleen, in place of heart-warming repose disquieting ardor; either genuine novelties or raucous frauds, drums and not sheperd's pipes, Italian basil rather than a French rose . . . But if you're not happy with these, don't be surprised—all of them put together may not please you, for all you know. It's true enough Julie may not be the only pretty girl, or a sheperd's pipe the only instrument, but what if that's what you're hankering after . . . True, she may give you lots of trouble (they all do in the end, everything does that goes under the heading of earthly love, which we all yearn for and pursue)—yes, yes, all of that is quite true, but don't for a moment forget that this is what your heart desired all along, it is what you reach out for from your private hell, it's your gauge, your guide. . . . Whose fault is it if you took the wrong turn and proceeded in the wrong direction? You wanted to turn right and ended up turning left—but how do you expect to be happy, then, you luckless man?"

After reading this admonition, I felt much better about making the next telephone call—even though the person I was calling I always found thoroughly disagreeable. I am talking about the mystical Madame Lagrange.

I guessed correctly: they were in the telephone book. Which meant they were back in Paris, too.

I was even lucky in that she picked up the phone. I began the conversation quite smoothly, deftly even; my voice was calm, somewhat high-handed actually, only my hands kept shaking still. All afternoon they were trembling, unstoppably.

She even recognized my voice, I didn't have to say who I was.

"Is that you, Captain?" she cried, and quite pleasantly too. Indeed, I was moved by her good memory, her loyalty.

"How did you end up in our neck of the woods? We thought you disappeared somewhere in the fabulous East Indies . . . For we heard that's where you went." (She said this without a hint of sarcasm or malice, quite straightforwardly, really.) "We thought you gave up on us poor Parisians. Are you here on a visit?"

I told her I was, but that I had arrived some time ago. And of course I thanked her for her kind words. But she blithely chirped on.

Did I remember that wonderful Christmas Eve we spent together in London once?

Did I remember? "My memory is everlasting, Madame," I said with a smile. "You can try me. Wake me up in two hundred years and I will be able to tell you what we drank that night." She laughed rather sweetly.

"Two hundred years?" she said, more somber now. "Where will we all be by then, Captain? You should see my hair—it's all white. What about yours?" And she again laughed a little. And went on to say that she will remember that particular Christmas as long as she lives. Oh, and how very sweet *she* was then, the poor dear . . . And she began to rave about her, as was her wont.

"In her youth she was such an extraordinary, radiant creature . . . God's precious little gift."

"You really think so, Madame?" And to myself I said: You see, you see, other people liked her, too. I wasn't crazy for being mad about her . . .

Did I still remember her? she sadly inquired. Did I remember the poor dear?

The question irritated me.

"Madame, if I can remember what drinks we had who knows when . . . But why do you keep saying 'poor?' It's the second time you've done it; I don't understand."

Madame Lagrange didn't answer.

"Or are you trying to make me feel better? I am not in need of such consideration, I assure you." Why is she to be called poor? Because she left me? She obviously thought it was the right thing to do.

"Or perhaps because she may have suffered hardship in Spain, lived from hand to mouth. . . ? Dear me . . . But she got over it, and that's what's important. She doesn't look the worse for wear. You say in her youth she looked oh so special—she's the same now, surprisingly young looking, that is . . . amazingly so.

"I happened to see her on the street just today.

"But why are you so quiet," I now asked, rather anxiously, in fact very nervously. (Why was she being so damn mysterious? Why not answer my questions?) "Did she get married by any chance?" I inquired, and my heart did skip a beat, to be sure.

"But who are you talking about?" she finally asked.

"Who am I talking about?" I grandly declaimed. "My dear Madame, not about water nymphs, I assure you. First you ask me if I remember her, and now this. Believe me, I remember her very well and I *am* talking about her. What is more, I'd like to know her address—that is the reason I called you today, as a matter of fact . . . if you don't mind."

She was again silent for a while.

"And where did you see her today, Captain?"

I told her where. What could I do—she's that kind of a person, always was. Nosy. Officious. I saw her on such and such corner, I said, not too far from the Opera; I even named the intersection.

"And you are sure it was her?"

"Yes, I am. But why do you ask, Madame? I adore you and all that but why do you keep asking these questions? Are you needling me? You *can* safely assume that I know her.

"Or you didn't even know she was here?" I just thought of that and was overjoyed to hear her say that she did not.

"You see, you see," I cried. "Then this is a great surprise for you. But that's wonderful. I tell you what: We'll track her down this very night and pay her a visit—what do you say?" And for all my excitement I began to laugh. I thought of how strange I must seem to her. Yes, just as she struck me rather strange, I must appear odd to her, too, with my fits of sudden zeal—wasn't she the one who used to call me mister steam engine, and precisely for this reason? I *am* ready to take on the world when the spirit moves me.

So I gave her a full account of the episode—how beautiful the world appeared to me today, what with the extraordinary atmospheric conditions, the radiance, the luminosity, and how she happened to fit right in. I went as far as describing her clothes to her, down to the last detail, just so that she should realize there was no mistake. . . . She was quite happy about this, actually. (I did describe her from head to toe, although, needless to say, I saw her but for an instant, the bus barely slowed down.)

"So, what do you say to all this, my dear Madame?"

"Yes, it had to be her," she replied. "Wearing the very coat I had sent to her from Paris. Oh the poor darling," she exclaimed; "how out of fashion she must have looked." And I could sense tears in her voice; her joy overwhelmed her, it seems, and she began to cry.

"Her coat had a high, stand-up collar, right?" she enthused, "and she wore it *à la Crétoise*, right? And it was a smooth fabric, trimmed with fur? And tiny flowers on her chapeau . . . Oh, I am crying, you see? I sent her that chapeau shortly before her death."

"What are you saying, Madame?"

"You mean you didn't know?" And she began to gush again. "You didn't know she died, that sweet, darling woman died?

"You see how very lucky you are. What a radiant little guest you had today, and, while you had her, what a brilliant little mate . . .

"And what a sweet, sweet soul she is now, appearing before you like that. She wanted to show herself, that's certain . . . Perhaps to protect you from something . . . For she did love you so."

That's what Madame said, those were her words. That she did love me, she had always loved me, and spoke of me until the very end.

The rest of what she said passed right by me.

Though she kept on telling me that this was not at all an uncommon phenomenon, and went on about when these events are most likely to occur, what exactly brings them to the surface . . .

"But you see how skeptical people are," she insisted. "Even though it occurs many many times, and there is plenty of evidence for it, still, people won't believe it, not for all the world . . . It may happen to them, still they refuse to believe it."

All of which boiled down to one thing: she was no longer of this world . . . or however that's put more politely. The truth is I still find the whole thing incomprehensible, unutterable.

Madame Lagrange, on the other hand, found it astonishing that I did not have this experience before, at the time it happened, or that she had never before given me a sign. It had been six years almost . . . She died of pneumonia in a Barcelona hospital.

Yes, it was all true. For that night I did find that Spanish letter. It was written by a strange hand and that's all it said, nothing more—that she died. Apparently, before the end she asked some-body to notify me.

But even this was so uncanny, the business with the letter. It was again getting on toward morning, and I was about to stop searching—I was tired, as can be imagined. Then, I happened to reach into some drawer, and there it was on top of a stack of papers, in front of my nose . . . I must have opened that drawer a hundred times.

So I didn't burn it that morning, after all. And a good thing I didn't: I could still be happy about that. But it's neither here nor there; if anything, that's another story . . . I should really wind up this one.

I'll be fifty-three years old in the fall; I am no youngster, in other words. And even though I have that letter in my hand, I still can't believe it's really so. I do believe, however—and no one should tell me otherwise, for I have every confidence—that one day, one bright, sunny day, she will appear somewhere, on a deserted street, on some distant corner, no longer that young perhaps, but tripping along sweetly, familiarly. And the sun will shine right through her black cape.

It will happen, I know; I am willing to stake my very soul on it. Or else, why go on living? That is all I am waiting for right now, and will go on waiting, for as long as I live—I can promise that. To whom do I make this promise? That I don't know.

All Pan books are available at your local bookshop or newsagent, or can be ordered direct from the publisher. Indicate the number of copies required and fill in the form below.

Send to: **CS Department, Pan Books Ltd., P.O. Box 40,
Basingstoke, Hants.   RG21 2YT.**

or phone: 0256 469551 (Ansaphone), quoting title, author
and Credit Card number.

Please enclose a remittance* to the value of the cover price plus: 60p for the first book plus 30p per copy for each additional book ordered to a maximum charge of £2.40 to cover postage and packing.

*Payment may be made in sterling by UK personal cheque, postal order, sterling draft or international money order, made payable to Pan Books Ltd.

Alternatively by Barclaycard/Access:

Card No.

Signature:

Applicable only in the UK and Republic of Ireland.

While every effort is made to keep prices low, it is sometimes necessary to increase prices at short notice. Pan Books reserve the right to show on covers and charge new retail prices which may differ from those advertised in the text or elsewhere.

NAME AND ADDRESS IN BLOCK LETTERS PLEASE:

....

Name—————————————————————————————

Address—————————————————————————————

3/87